The *Other* Bridget

Once upon a time (briefly) Rachael Johns was an English teacher, then her dreams of becoming a novelist came true. Now she spends her days writing romance and women's fiction in the Swan Valley, Western Australia. Her book *The Patterson Girls* won the ABIA Award in 2016 for General Fiction and she has won the prestigious Romance Writers of Australia RUBY Award twice. When she's not writing, you'll find Rachael reading, hanging with her adorable sheepadoodle, listening to audiobooks while cleaning up after her three teenage boys, or running the Rachael Johns' Online Book Club on Facebook.

rachaeljohns.com

RACHAEL JOHNS

The *Other* Bridget

MICHAEL JOSEPH
an imprint of
PENGUIN BOOKS

MICHAEL JOSEPH

UK | USA | Canada | Ireland | Australia
India | New Zealand | South Africa | China

Michael Joseph is part of the Penguin Random House group of companies
whose addresses can be found at global.penguinrandomhouse.com.

Penguin
Random House
Australia

First published by Michael Joseph, 2024

Cover images by Ksenica/iStock by Getty Images; Ellegant/Shutterstock;
BarksJapan/Alamy and Cienpies Design/Alamy
Cover design and illustrations by Nikki Townsend Design
© Penguin Random House Australia Pty Ltd
Author photograph by Jess Gately
Typeset in Adobe Garamond Pro by Midland Typesetters, Australia

Printed and bound in Australia by Griffin Press, an accredited
ISO AS/NZS 14001 Environmental Management Systems printer

 A catalogue record for this
book is available from the
NATIONAL LIBRARY OF AUSTRALIA   National Library of Australia

ISBN 978 1 76134 171 7

penguin.com.au

*We at Penguin Random House Australia acknowledge that Aboriginal and Torres Strait Islander
peoples are the Traditional Custodians and the first storytellers of the lands on which we live and
work. We honour Aboriginal and Torres Strait Islander peoples' continuous connection to Country,
waters, skies and communities. We celebrate Aboriginal and Torres Strait Islander stories, traditions
and living cultures; and we pay our respects to Elders past and present.*

*For my cousin, Lizzy Dent – I can't believe
we both grew up to be novelists!
And for librarians everywhere – thank you
for spreading the love.*

The person, be it gentleman or lady, who has not pleasure in a good novel, must be intolerably stupid.
Jane Austen

1

Alone Again

There's only one thing that could make me agree to dress up like a playboy bunny and parade around half-naked in front of my colleagues and library patrons on a Wednesday night. Yep, you guessed it: a boy, or, rather, a man.

Tonight's the night I'm going to introduce my new boyfriend to my friends, and, despite the outfit, I can hardly wait.

I'm in the staff bathroom putting the final touches on my costume – adjusting the rabbit ears atop my head – when my phone pings with a text. My heart thuds even before I read it. If that's Kieran saying he can't make it, I'm going to kill him. He's the one who convinced me to dress as my namesake in the first place. We've only been seeing each other for a few weeks, but when I casually mentioned our adults-only Library Lovers Night, he not only said he'd come but suggested we dress up as a tart and vicar, a la Bridget Jones.

To say I'd taken some convincing would be an understatement. Quite aside from the whole baring much of my body thing, I usually try not to draw attention to the fact I'm the *other* Bridget Jones. Hold the jokes, please. I've heard them all.

The good news is the message isn't from Kieran.

The bad news is it's from someone much, much worse.

You total bitch! I know what you've been up to with my husband. If you ever touch him again, I will hunt you down, skin you alive and feed your innards to my Rottweiler.

'Oh my God!' I shriek, slapping my hand over my mouth. The face looking back at me in the mirror goes pale. Five seconds ago, I'd been quite pleased with my appearance – I'd tousled my shoulder-length, caramel-blonde hair and accentuated my boring green eyes and lips with bolder make-up than I usually wear – but now I think I look like a clown. A foolish one at that.

'What is it?' Fred asks as she emerges from a cubicle, dressed in a shiny faux-leather, skin-hugging full bodysuit and a dark wig with a long braid down one shoulder. She's dressed as Katniss, her favourite kick-arse literary heroine.

Unable to bring myself to voice the words, I thrust my phone in her face.

'The prick!' Her eyes widen. 'He's married?'

I shrug in shock. 'His wife certainly thinks so.'

According to her text, she'd found our explicit messages in his phone. Why is it always the woman's fault? *I* didn't know he was married but *he* obviously did. With any luck she's feeding *his* innards to their Rottweiler this very second.

'Oh, Bee.' Fred's been my best friend since university and we've been through numerous highs and lows together. Although she isn't one for much touchy-feeliness, she pulls me into a hug. 'I'm so sorry. I know you really liked this one.'

Fred's right. Although I hadn't been dating Kieran long, I'd 'caught feelings', as she would say. I knew from five minutes of chatting to him on the app that I wanted to meet him, and after hundreds of awkward first dates, ours was anything but. We had so much to say to each other – we liked all the same movies and shared many favourite books. We even had the same tastes in food, both of us agreeing that pineapple and olives should never be seen on pizza. It had felt like maybe, just maybe, this one had take-home-to-meet-the-parents potential. In the short time we've been together, we've seen each other every other night and messaged constantly in between.

Where the hell was his wife when all this was happening?

'I guess he's not coming, then,' Fred says, giving me a sympathetic smile as I pull out of her embrace.

'Should I reply?' I ask, feeling an urge to apologise, to tell this stranger that I'm not the kind of woman who sleeps with married men. Not knowingly anyway.

'Fuck no! Block his number and move the hell on.' Fred turns to the mirror and scrutinises her appearance, making sure none of her black crew cut is showing. Wig or not, she looks stunning as usual. At least a head taller than me, Fred is model tall and model thin. She has the kind of body I longed for as a teenager, only it comes naturally to her, and her face doesn't look gaunt the way mine used to either.

The bathroom door opens and Mary Poppins, aka Persephone, one of the other librarians, pops her head in. I'm surprised she didn't come as Elphaba or Morgan le Fay, as she's Pagan and a practising witch. Then again, Mary Poppins is also a witch, I guess.

'Hurry up. We're about to open the doors and get this party started.'

Fred looks anxiously to me – 'Yeah, we'll be out in a moment' – and waves Persephone away.

'I'm going home,' I say, ripping the bunny ears off my head, ready to change back into my pink boxy T-shirt and denim skirt. You didn't think I walked through the streets in black bathers and fishnets, did you?

Although this is a work event, none of us is being paid over-time and my colleagues are all here, so I'm not *needed*. We might be celebrating Library Lovers Day rather than Valentines Day, but Janine, Persephone and Xavier's partners will be here and even the guy Fred hooked up with last night has agreed to come. It'll be couples, the oldies from Janine's book club and me.

Once again, dateless on Valentines Day.

'Like hell you are, girlfriend,' Fred says, tweaking my fluffy bunny tail as she tugs me towards the door. 'We're not wasting this fabulous outfit! And no way am I letting you spend the night alone after receiving that crappy text.'

Alone. Did she have to use such a loaded word?

'I won't be alone. I'll be with John Brown and Stephanie Plum.' No matter how much I wish Janet Evanovich's famous fictional heroine would just pick a guy – preferably Morelli – and end the series, I can't stop reading. Her books are like crack and if anyone can take my mind off my latest relationship failure, it's my favour-ite bounty hunter.

Fred rolls her eyes. 'Pets and fictional people don't count.' Then she squeezes my hand and hits me with that sympathetic expression again. 'I know you're upset, sweets, and you have every right to be, but married Kieran isn't worth your tears.'

'I'm not crying!' Maybe I will later, but right now I'm simply angry and humiliated. What is wrong with me that I keep attract-ing men who have weird fetishes, believe dick pics are pick-up lines or are already taken? 'Besides, it's not fair to leave JB alone all night when I've been out all day.'

Fred raises a perfectly preened black eyebrow. 'He'll be fine. You went home after work, walked him, fed him and gave him a treat, remember?'

In this moment, I'm regretting the fact that I share almost every detail of my life with her.

'Come on, just stay for one booktail, then if you still want to go home and mourn the worthless jerk, I won't stand in your way. I'll even come with you.'

Fred has a talent for getting her own way in any situation, and I'm too emotionally shocked to put up a fight. Besides, Rory does make amazing cocktails.

'Okay, fine. But please don't tell anyone what's happened.'

Fred mimes fastening a zip across her lips, then picks up her plastic bow and arrow and we head out to face the music, me wishing I had something to pull over my skimpy costume.

Fremantle Library is one of my favourite places in the world. Just before I started working here, it moved from its old location on the corner of Newman and William Streets to the Walyalup Civic Centre, a state-of-the-art building with meeting rooms, galleries, public rest rooms and a customer service centre on the street level, the library underneath. As I descend the stairs or escalator, I always feel that I'm venturing into a whole new world where nothing matters but books and sharing my love of them.

Tonight, this place of my heart is decked out with pink, black and silver streamers and balloons, and hundreds of paper hearts that Xavier, assistant library manager and all-round great guy, made with the Story Time kids this morning. We spent the afternoon decorating and I'd been proud of our handiwork, but now all these gorgeous trimmings feel like a slap in my face.

My colleagues are standing around the drinks table, alongside which is another table boasting a massive grazing board and tiny heart-shaped chocolates wrapped in pink foil.

Xavier, dressed in tight, faded jeans, a red flannelette shirt pushed up to his elbows, black cowboy boots and a black cowboy hat, all but hiding his short-cropped, dirty-blond hair, wolf-whistles as we join them. 'Bee, you look smoking!'

I blush, always awkward with compliments because I never really believe them. 'Thanks.'

'You've got great pins on you,' his partner, Rory, adds with a wink, his diamond earring glinting beneath the artificial light.

'That she does.' Dave, husband of our library manager, Janine, is taking a little too much interest in my near-bare legs.

Janine – dressed as Daisy Jones in white knee-high boots, leather mini skirt, bohemian top, yellow fake-fur coat and chunky pink, square sunglasses – swats his arm. 'Oy. Don't be an old pervert.'

'Ah, don't be jealous, luv,' Dave says, planting a noisy kiss on her cheek. With his shaggy, salt-and-pepper hair, he looks like an ancient rocker, and I wonder which band member he's supposed to be. 'You know I only have eyes for you.'

Oh, to still be that smitten after more than forty years of marriage.

I look back to Xavier and Rory. 'You guys look amazing too. Jack and Ennis?'

They nod proudly and smile adorably at each other. Or at least it would be adorable if I wasn't currently dateless and bitter.

'Nice one,' I say. Most people have no idea that the movie *Brokeback Mountain* was based on a short story by Annie Proulx, but I think the boys were just looking for an excuse to buy fancy cowboy boots and, frankly, I don't blame them.

'I think we all look great.' This is from Persephone's husband Nick, who's dressed as a very dashing chimney sweep, his thick black hair and equally thick bushy eyebrows the perfect match for Bert's.

We all blink in surprise – usually he's a man of few words who only speaks when spoken to – but I'm guessing the beer he's already nursing has helped lure him out of his shell.

Janine claps her hands. 'Let's get a group selfie before we let in the hordes.'

We all squish in together and then Nick – because he has the longest arms – snaps a quick pic.

Janine pulls me aside as Persephone heads up the escalator to let in our guests. 'You okay, chicken? Is it Kieran? Don't tell me he's running late.'

I blink, a lump rushing to my throat. With my mum way up north in the Pilbara, Janine has become like my surrogate city mum, and as with my own mum, I can't hide anything from her. 'He's not coming, but I don't want to talk about it. I'm fine.'

'How about we get you a drink?' she asks, squeezing my arm. I can tell she doesn't believe me – the absence of the new boyfriend I'd told them all about speaks volumes – but I'm glad she doesn't push.

'Yes, please.' The sooner I have my one beverage, the sooner Fred will let me leave.

We head over to join the queue that has quickly formed behind the drinks table where Rory and Xavier are whipping up the kinds of cocktails – or mocktails, if alcohol's not your thing – that you'd usually only find in upmarket bars. I wait in line behind Wally and Wendy, two Cats in Hats, another Mary Poppins, several Harry Potters and Pippi Longstocking.

'Bee, this is Ethan,' Fred says, breaking into the queue and gesturing at a stocky guy in a bottle-green jumpsuit beside her. 'Ethan, meet Bee, my colleague and BFF.'

'Nice to meet you,' I say, trying not to feel hostile that her guy turned up. Bet he's not married either. 'So who are you dressed as?'

'Maverick from *Top Gun.*' He grins, touching a finger to the dark sunnies perched atop his sandy-coloured hair.

I raise an eyebrow at Fred – although *Top Gun* was inspired by a newspaper article and later made into a book, I'm guessing Ethan only knows the movie, and this is supposed to be a book costume party. My friend just shrugs.

'What can I tempt you with, Bee, dearest?' Xavier gestures to the menu as we reach the front of the queue. 'Anne Shirley's Raspberry Cordial? A Tequila Mockingbird? Or a Margarita Atwood?'

I'm a huge Green Gables fan, so I go with the first. 'Mmm . . . this is good,' I say after taking a sip.

He leans forward and whispers, 'Wait till you taste Rory's Pitcher of Dorian Gray. He's going to make them later when we've kicked everyone else out.'

With any luck, I'll be long gone by then.

'Hey, Bee. Ethan and I are heading home. Want a lift?'

'What?' I yell down to Fred from where I'm dancing with Janine and Persephone on the function room table. Thankfully, it's made of very solid wood.

'She said she's leaving,' Persephone yells back, taking a sip of her Atone-mint Julep, inspired by Ian McEwan's beloved novel.

'What? Why?' After a very successful bookish trivia night and a fashion parade of costumes, we'd finally shut the doors on our patrons. Aside from staff and partners, Janine's senior book club members were last to leave and I saw the lone male member, Edgar, stuff his library bag with chocolates before giving me a once-over on his way out. 'The party's just kicking off and it's still early.'

At least I think it is. I lost track of time after I moved on from spiked raspberry cordial to Atwoods, which have turned out to be very effective medicine for embarrassed/broken hearts.

'Let her go. She's going home to be with her boyfriend,' Janine says, gyrating her hips and waving her arms above her head to Miley Cyrus, which Xavier has just cranked up on the speakers.

When not in costume, Janine looks like a conservative sixty-something librarian. Aside from her signature bright-red lipstick, she usually wears linen dresses, sensible shoes and keeps her hair trim in a short, grey bob, but she's anything but prim and proper.

'He's not my boyfriend,' Fred yells. 'I just need to get out of this costume before I combust.' It's a miracle she lasted this long – the library might have good air-conditioning, but it is the height of summer.

Whoever said librarians were dull must have pulled from a parallel universe, because in this one they party hard. Below us, sitting on plastic chairs, are poor Nick and Dave. Nick is an accounts manager for Bunnings and has exactly the personality you'd expect. It's a mystery how he and Persephone ever connected. She's charismatic and spiritual and he only believes in things that science can prove. Dave's a retired maths teacher, so it's no wonder the two of them get along well. Both men look as if they want to go home now too, but I don't like their chances.

'Party pooper,' I shout at Fred.

She gives me a firm look. 'Do you want a lift or not?'

Despite the tequila pumping through my veins, I have a moment of sanity where I think of my dog and decide it's probably time I leave too. And although I live only a short walk away, it's late enough that the streets of Fremantle could well be harbouring all sorts of undesirables.

But Janine grabs my hand before I can climb down. 'Where do you think you're going?'

'I—'

'Dave and I will drive you home.'

I look to Dave, who dips his gold sequinned cap in compliance, and shrug. To hell with it. JB is probably sleeping by now anyway, and dancing off my woes sure beats sitting at home, glumly ruminating on my doomed love life and the fact I'll probably be alone forever. According to the historical romance novels I love to read, twenty-seven is already considered an old maid. And come September, I'll be twenty-eight.

'Okay, I'm staying,' I shriek, then blow Fred a kiss goodnight. 'Don't do anything I wouldn't do!'

As Fred takes Ethan's hand to lead him out, she says, 'Don't forget it's a school night. We all have work tomorrow.'

But we're all too full of alcohol to be worried about the future.

2

Russian Roulette

Finally all danced out, we migrate to the nearby children's section of the library, where Janine, Persephone and I sink into beanbags, while the men sit awkwardly on tiny plastic chairs. This part of the library is always the most welcoming, with its little reading nooks and primary-coloured furniture. There's also more space to stretch out than between the shelves in the other areas.

'Any sightings of your new neighbour yet?' Persephone asks as she removes an errant copy of *Where is the Green Sheep?* from beneath her.

'None whatsoever.' I live in a semi-detached turn-of-the-century townhouse and my neighbour, a kindly octogenarian who often chatted to me over the fence, died late last year. Next door had remained empty until two weeks ago when a moving truck arrived and a tall man wearing a cap and sunglasses appeared to move in. 'If I didn't get a glimpse of him that first day, I'd think he was a ghost. I'm guessing he works nights and sleeps during the day.'

'Maybe he's a serial killer,' Rory offers. 'I hear they work at night.'

I laugh. 'Don't worry, Fred and I have already thought of that.' Along with fantasy, gory crime is Fred's favourite genre and, while romance might be my go-to, you don't read two hundred books a year without cultivating a rampant imagination.

'Or a drug dealer,' Nick adds. 'I reckon they must work nights too.'

When we tire of theorising what my mysterious neighbour does for a living, Dave says, 'So, Bee, Janine tells me you have a new young fella.'

Janine glares at him and shakes her head, but he doesn't get the message.

'Thought he might be here tonight.'

'Turns out he's married,' I say, my alcohol-and-dancing-induced good mood fading fast.

Their faces all echo the shock I'd felt upon first reading Kelly's text.

'And you didn't know?' Dave asks, frowning slightly.

'Of course, she didn't know,' Persephone snaps, reaching across to pat my leg. 'I'm so sorry. What a bastard.'

'I just want to forget I ever met him and get on with my life.'

'Hear, hear.' Xavier and Rory raise their glasses in a toast, and we all drink again. I don't know what's in the Pitcher of Dorian Gray but it's quite possibly the best beverage I've ever had.

'Does that mean you're going back on Tiiinder?' Janine slurs.

The mere thought makes my stomach lurch. I'd deleted Tinder, Bumble and Hinge when Kieran told me he wanted us to be exclusive – *ha* – and the thought of putting myself online again leaves me cold. 'I think I might take a dating break for a while.'

'I'm a tad jealous of your generation, you know,' Janine continues as if she didn't even register my reply. 'In my day, you married the neighbour or your high school sweetheart, but for you young things, the world's your oyster.'

I raise an eyebrow. Hadn't she heard the horror stories Fred and I told of life on the apps? It might seem like there are more fish in the sea, but the majority are duds you'd throw back without even considering eating. Even Fred, who isn't looking for anything serious, has enough tales to fill a novel (or two) – good thing, considering she's currently writing one.

But me? I want something real with someone who wants more from me than what I can offer between the sheets. I want the kind of love Janine has with Dave, Xavier with Rory, my parents with each other, or even the weird opposites-attract thing Persephone and Nick have going on. Is that too much to ask? Sometimes I wonder if I'm cursed because of my name. The original Bridget had such terrible luck with men, maybe in giving me her name, Mum also inflicted on me her misfortune.

'Hey! What's wrong with marrying your high school sweetheart?' Dave asks.

'Nothing,' I assure him. If only I hadn't grown up in the middle of nowhere and had to go away to board at a bitchy, all-girls private school, maybe I'd have met Mr Right years ago. I glance at Persephone. 'How did you and Nick meet?'

She lets out a girlish giggle. 'I literally fell on him at the races.'

'What?' Xavier and Janine ask in unison. It appears I'm not the only one who hasn't heard this tale.

She nods, her smile growing as her gaze slides to her husband. 'A friend dragged me along to the Perth Cup because she was dating one of the jockeys, and I was wearing these ridiculous heels. I stumbled as I was walking by a row of seats and fell right into his lap. I was mortified, but he was so sweet and wanted to make sure I was okay, so I gave him my number.'

'And you called her?' I'm gobsmacked.

Nick shakes his head.

'Of course not.' Persephone laughs. 'But two weeks later, I was in Bunnings looking for some paint to refresh my crystal shelves and I ran into him again. I asked if he'd lost my number and he admitted he was too shy to call. I kissed him right there in the paint aisle and then told him we were going out that night. The rest is history.'

'That's some story,' I say, then turn to Rory and Xavier. I don't know why I'm torturing myself with other people's happy-ever-afters but I can't help myself. 'What about you two? What's your meet-cute?'

'We met on a Swan River boat cruise,' Xavier begins. 'I was on a buck's night and Rory was one of the waiters behind the bar. It was love at first sight.'

Rory snorts. 'Maybe for him. I thought he and his friends were a bunch of wankers.'

'I liked him so much, I bought a ticket and took my mum and my sister on the same cruise the following week.'

'His family were delightful and without his drunken friends around making lurid comments, we were able to have a chat. We agreed to meet for coffee—'

'But it turned into something else.' As Xavier winks at Rory, I have an epiphany.

None of them met their significant other in the artificial manner of online dating, and neither do my favourite romance novel heroes and heroines. True love is *always* organic.

'That's it!' I say, sitting up straight, spilling the dregs of my drink onto my bare legs. 'That's where I'm going wrong!'

'What do you mean, chicken?' Janine asks.

'I'm not downloading any dating apps ever again. Love happens when you're least expecting it. You guys are the proof of that. I need to stop trying so hard. I need to go about my everyday life and trust that Fate will work her magic for me too.'

Maybe it's the alcohol, but suddenly I feel energised. The hope that Kieran's wife's message crushed at the beginning of the night has been revived.

'Besides,' I add, 'it's all too easy for people on apps to pretend to be someone or some*thing* they're not.'

Kieran isn't the only guy who's deceived me. I've met men lying about their age, their career, their fetishes. And they were the better prospects. Even Tim, the most serious relationship I've ever had, lied about wanting kids on his profile, leading me on for five months before coming clean. The apps are okay for people like Fred – people who are happy with hooking up, not looking for commitment – but how can you ever really know anyone you meet this way?

Persephone frowns. 'That's all very well, and no offence meant, but you don't really go anywhere besides the library and the beach, and the only men you meet here are children or *way* too old.'

I briefly think of Edgar from Janine's book club. *No, thanks!* Ten years older than me would be my absolute max.

I'm also slightly affronted that a married, 45-year-old woman with two kids is insinuating I don't have a life but . . . perhaps she's right. Between work, my beloved dog, my friends and the Russian roulette of online dating, I haven't had the time or inclination to take up a hobby or join anything.

'Okay, well, that will change too,' I decide. 'I'm going to start taking *myself* on dates to different places. Maybe I'll do an evening class or join a gym. It's not too late for a new year's resolution, is it?'

My colleagues laugh.

'Never too late,' Rory says, stifling a yawn. 'But I think I'm gonna have to call it a night.'

'Good idea.' Now my life is sorted, I'm eager to get to bed, so I can wake up tomorrow and kick-start my plan. I down the last of my Dorian Gray and shoot to my feet way too fast.

'Whoa. You all right?' Dave asks, reaching out to steady me.

'Yeah, sorry,' I say, realising I've lost track of the number of drinks I've had. 'I'll be fine after a big glass of water and a couple of Panadol. Are you guys still okay to take me home?'

'Of course,' Janine says. 'Help me up, Dave. I think my leg's gone numb.'

Persephone gestures around us at the half-empty cups, plates, screwed-up serviettes, streamers falling from the ceiling, tables, chairs and many books no longer where they should be. The library looks like a hurricane has torn through. 'Shall we clear up this mess in the morning?'

'Yes!' we all agree far too quickly.

Xavier offers to lock up, and Dave leads Janine and me out into the car park and assists us into his ancient Commodore.

'Thanks,' I slur as he pulls up in front of my place a few minutes later.

I stumble out and up the short path to my front door, my feet aching from dancing and my head now throbbing as well. As I fumble in my bag for my key, I turn to see Dave and Janine watching to make sure I get safely inside.

'I'm okay,' I shout, holding my keys up in the air like a trophy. Janine waves hysterically as Dave pulls away.

It takes a few attempts, the key scratching on either side of the keyhole, before I finally shove it into the lock. *Eureka!* But my glee is short-lived – the key is jammed.

I try to yank it out again but it's royally stuck.

My heart rate picks up as I wonder what's going on. It worked perfectly fine earlier today.

Just when I'm starting to think I might have to sleep out here, my door flies open and I fall into the house, right into the very hard, very bare chest of a . . . a *man*?

'What are you doing in my house?' I demand, the alcohol making me braver than I probably should be. What kind of idiot confronts an intruder like this? I think of all the romantic suspense novels I've ever read and shudder. He could be a murderer or a rapist in waiting. I should be running in the other direction, calling the police on my mobile, but then I hear a muffled bark.

'Where's John Brown?' I try to look past the man. 'What have you done with my dog?!'

'*Your* house?' The very built burglar/murderer/rapist looks most unimpressed.

'Uh-huh.' I nod, feeling less confident of this fact.

Although it's almost pitch-black inside, the light from the nearest streetlamp allows me to see a glimpse inside, and this place is nothing like mine. Whereas my house is what you might call cluttered, with overflowing bookshelves, mismatched lamps, colourful rugs and throw pillows, this one looks like an Ikea showroom where nobody actually lives.

Oh my God. I feel a sudden tightness in my chest. Is this my new mysterious neighbour?

His reddish-blond hair is ruffled, he boasts at least a three-day shadow on his chiselled jaw, and the only item of clothing he's wearing are black running shorts that sit low on his hips. *Very* low.

My mouth goes dry and my near-naked body erupts with goosebumps.

Shit. Does the bark sound distant because it's not inside, but next door?

I take a step back to assess the front of the duplex properly and my head spins. I should never have had that last drink. Whereas my front courtyard boasts several pot plants and my prized collection of colourful garden gnomes, this one is bare, except for the most boring doormat I've ever seen.

It doesn't even say WELCOME.

Oh, sugar. I gulp and look back up into my neighbour's scowling eyes. I think they're emerald green but would have to see them in daylight to be sure. 'I'm so sorry,' I gush, thrusting my hand out towards him. This is not the first impression I was hoping to make.

Although he looks reluctant to take it, his grip is firm.

'I'm Bee, your neighbour, and I . . . I've had a few drinks.' A few? Ha! 'And I must have had a moment of confusion. I hope I didn't wake you.'

'You did.' He glances down and I realise I'm still gripping his hand tightly. *Whoops.*

'And now, if you don't mind, I'd like to get back to bed.'

'Of course. Sorry.' My cheeks burn as I let go. I think I might throw up. 'I don't usually get this drunk, but I got some bad news tonight and . . . What did you say your name was?'

He glowers. 'I didn't.'

From next door, JB starts barking again and my neighbour lets out a deeply aggravated sigh as he yanks my key from his lock. He drops it into the palm of my hand, and I have an experience akin to being struck by lightning as he closes my fingers over the top of it. *Holy hell!* I know it's summer, but it feels really hot out here.

Our gazes lock and time seems to stand still, but when he finally opens his mouth again, all thoughts of my electrical shock are forgotten.

'Please,' he begs. 'Just go home and silence that beast.'

Beast? Heat of a different kind flushes through my body. I'm about to tell him that JB is nothing but a real-life teddy bear, but before I get the chance the door slams in my face.

How bloody rude!

'No need to be an arsehole,' I mutter as I walk the short distance next door.

This time, the lock turns easily and I make a mad dash into the bathroom, cursing Kieran – and Rory's cocktails – and vowing never to drink again.

3

The Caffeine God

I wake with a pounding headache and a puddle on my bedroom floor because I slept through my alarm and didn't let JB out at his usual time.

My black and white bundle of fluff looks up at me from the end of my bed, his expression one of utmost remorse. 'Sorry, buddy,' I say, as I reach for my phone.

I sit bolt upright. It's already quarter past eight and I'm supposed to be at work by eight-thirty. Although I don't remember a lot about last night, my headache tells me it was a big one. I contemplate calling in sick, but it's my day to collect the coffees and if my colleagues feel anything like I do, they're probably in dire need of caffeine as well.

I crawl out of bed and toss an old towel over JB's mess – thank God I don't have carpets – making a mental note to mop the floor later.

'This isn't your fault,' I tell him as I let him out and fill his bowl with food. I down a glass of water and two Panadol, then shower in record time, making sure to scrub all of last night's make-up off my face. I'm usually religious about my nightly routine. Controlling my skin is a lot healthier than trying to control my body, and thus over the last ten years I've become a skincare junkie. I spend almost as much money on oils and serums as I do on books.

As I massage my second cleanse into my face, a memory from last night flashes in my head. *No way!*

I turn the water off and stand there naked in shock.

Was that a nightmare, or did I really meet Mr Mysterious last night?

My stomach squeezes as the memory becomes clearer.

I remember waving goodbye to Janine and Dave and then struggling to get inside. I remember falling into the arms of someone I thought was a burglar, only to discover *I* was the intruder. I remember how angry he looked, but . . . who could blame him? What must he have thought, being woken in the early hours of the morning to find a scantily clad woman trying to break into his house?

More to the point, what in the world can I do to apologise?

I hear my phone ringing in my bedroom and rush to answer. Of course it's Fred, wondering where the hell I am.

'I'm coming,' I promise. 'I just overslept.' I throw the phone on the bed and grab a patchwork skirt and white shirt from my wardrobe.

Five minutes later, puffing from running, I turn into the Grouchy Sailor, a quirky little café halfway between my place and the library that makes what must be the best coffee in the Southern Hemisphere. Honestly, it's to die for. Think caffeine crafted by gods.

My colleagues and I suspect their newest barista, Fabio, *is* an actual god. The coffee was great before he arrived but now it's out of this world. I don't know what secret ingredient he puts in, but you've never tasted anything better.

22

And Fabio certainly looks like a god too. He may be only slightly taller than me, but he has lovely tanned skin, muscles in all the right places and boasts beautiful, thick, black hair long enough that he needs to flick it away from his eyes every few moments. Along with his smoky-blueish silver eyes – I've never seen anything like them before – these attributes paint quite the picture.

'*Buongiorno, bella*,' Fabio sings when I reach the front of the line. 'Same as usual?' His sexy accent makes every word sound like a sweet nothing.

'Yes, please,' I all but simper.

Even if he wasn't one of the hottest guys I've ever met, the way he makes every customer feel like they're his favourite would have my words tripping over my tongue whenever I'm near him. And I'm not the only one affected. Women and men dream about his coffee as much as they dream about him. I know this to be true, not only because the Grouchy Sailor has been busier than ever since he started, but because Fred, Persephone, Janine and Xavier are also besotted with him. We've always taken turns collecting coffees for each other, but since Fabio arrived, we've devised a roster to make sure everyone gets a regular fix.

Xavier is certain Fabio's gay, but it doesn't really matter if he is. My crush is akin to the kind of infatuation teenage girls have for members of boy bands. I know it's never going to go anywhere. Why would someone as hot and charismatic as him look twice at someone as average as me?

'Do you have the cups?' he asks, his hand outstretched towards me.

And that's when I realise I've forgotten the reusable cups and carrier. They're still on my kitchen bench where I left them last night. 'Sorry,' I say. 'Big night at the library.'

He raises a beautiful dark eyebrow. 'At the *library*?'

'Yes.' It really gets my goat that people assume librarians don't know how to have a good time. Don't these people know that books can take you on the kinds of adventures real life can only dream about? 'It was Library Lovers Day. We had cocktails and dancing, and I didn't get home till after midnight. It was wild.'

'I thought yesterday was Valentines Day?'

'*Pfft*. Valentines Day is so last century. Now February fourteenth is all about the books.'

'I'll take your word for it.' He chuckles and grabs some disposable cups. 'So you still have to work after such a big night?'

I nod. 'No rest for the wicked.'

He leans over the counter towards me and lowers his voice to a husky whisper. 'And just how wicked are you, sweet Bee?'

'Wouldn't you like to know?' I retort, a tingle buzzing down my spine. When he talks to me like this I can't help flirting back, even though I know he's the same with all his customers.

Fabio laughs and then focuses on the task at hand. 'Here you are, bella.' As he hands over one of their takeaway carriers, our fingers touch and my heart spikes.

'*Grazie*,' I say, my accent terrible.

It's 8.47 when I leave the café and 8.50 by the time I launch myself through the staff door at work. Xavier, Janine, Persephone and Fred are waiting by the circular counter near the bottom of the stairs, and the library has already been put back together. Even a crime scene investigation unit would be hard pushed to prove the drunken shenanigans that went on here last night.

We don't have a uniform but each of us has kind of initiated our own. Xavier looks as put together as usual in smart camel chinos and a navy polo shirt. Janine is wearing one of her many linen dresses, red lipstick and pearl earrings. Persephone always wears black, her only colour the cool crystals of her necklace and her dyed copper hair, which falls in perfect waves around her face. And Fred is wearing hot pink overalls she picked up from Good Sammie's, with a rainbow-coloured headband.

I've always loved overalls but whenever I wear them, I feel like a frumpy toddler. I also buy a lot of my clothes from second-hand shops but lean more towards funky skirts and hippie-style tops, with comfy sandals in summer and knee-high boots in winter.

'About bloody time,' Xavier exclaims as I hand over his coffee.

'Do you have a headache too?' Janine groans as she takes a sip of hers.

'Killer,' I reply.

Turns out Fred – looking nauseatingly fresh-faced – is the only one without a sore head, but I distract the others when I tell them about my mortifying run-in with my new neighbour last night. I'm still hoping it was a nightmare. 'Any ideas what I can do to say sorry?'

'I'd bake him a cake,' Xavier suggests.

'Ooh, I'd kill for cake right now,' Persephone says. 'Can you make one for us while you're at it?'

'Oh my goodness,' Janine shrieks and we all look at her.

'What?' I ask, glancing around, looking for a rat or something.

She beams as if she's just orchestrated the end of climate change. 'What if last night was your cute-meet?'

'I think you mean meet-cute,' says Fred, downing the last of the green juice she drinks every morning. She might not read a lot of romance, but she hears enough from me to know the basics.

Janine shakes her head. 'Whatever. After you left last night, Bee decided she's giving up on dating apps and is going to find true love organically.'

'I did?' I say at the same time as Fred rolls her eyes.

Xavier, Janine and Persephone all nod and parrot back to me words I'd apparently said last night about dating apps and the blokes on them.

I have to admit, drunk me made a lot of sense.

'You decided,' Persephone explains, 'that you're going to join some classes, go to places you don't usually go and see if you run into someone naturally, like the rest of us did.'

Just because I remember exactly zero per cent of this conversation doesn't mean it doesn't have merit. 'What kinds of places?'

Persephone shrugs. 'I think you mentioned joining a gym.'

Fred makes a face. She's allergic to exercise.

'But maybe now you don't have to,' Janine continues, practically bouncing up and down in excitement. 'Maybe your neighbour is The One.'

Xavier elbows me. 'What's he look like? Is he hot?'

'He's kinda cute,' I admit, my cheeks heating as I remember him looking down at me last night. Even brooding, he looked good. 'He must be well over six feet, *very* broad-chested, and he had a shadow of dark-red stubble.'

'I *love* stubble,' Fred says. 'And I love redheads even more. They're always the best in bed.'

I laugh. 'His hair was pretty messy, but then I did drag him out of bed.'

'Is he single?' Persephone asks. 'About how old?'

I shrug. 'Maybe early-to-mid thirties. And no idea about a partner, but I don't think anyone else lives with him.'

'Guess there's only one way to find out,' she says. 'Bake him that cake, put on your cutest outfit and take it over to apologise.'

Something inside me tingles. Could this really be it? Could Mr Right have moved in right next door?

'It would be a pretty cute story to tell our grandchildren,' I say. 'Granny was dressed as a tart and tried to break into Granddad's house in the middle of the night.'

They all laugh, then Fred glances at her smart watch. 'I hate to break up this fascinating conversation, but do you think we should open up? It's already 9.01 and our regulars are waiting.'

We all finish our coffees as Fred switches on the escalator and pulls back the rope blocking off the stairs. I spend the rest of the workday dreaming about what I'm going to say to my neighbour tonight.

4

The Way to a Man's Heart

On the way home from work, I detour via the supermarket to pick up the ingredients for chocolate banana bread, and then the moment I walk in the door I get baking. Mum calls while I'm mashing the bananas and I put her on speaker. 'Hey, you must have a sixth sense or something. I'm making your banana bread.'

It's her famous recipe – laden with three kinds of chocolate chips – that I'm using as a peace offering. Once upon a time I knew exactly how many calories were in each chip, never mind a slice of cake, and I wouldn't even let the smallest morsel pass my lips.

'Ooh, special occasion?' she asks.

'Sorta. I'm making it for my new neighbour to apologise.' I pop a couple of chocolate chips into my mouth.

'Why on earth do you need to apologise?'

While I measure out the other ingredients, I tell her about the whole front door mishap.

'Oh dear,' she says with a slightly disapproving laugh. 'Didn't Kieran see you home?'

I groan. 'Um . . . about him?'

'What is it?' Mum asks sharply. 'Has he done something?'

'He *didn't* tell me he's married,' I say, tossing the self-raising flour into my mixing bowl.

She gasps. 'What? Oh, darling, I'm so sorry.'

'Yes, well.' A lump forms in my throat. I know it's stupid, but I feel like a disappointment. Mum is a romantic at heart – she was always reading romance novels when I was growing up – and I know she desperately wants her children to find the kind of love she and Dad have. She's ticked off two of us, but my brother Rupert is showing no signs of settling down, and I'm failing dismally.

'Anyway,' I say, not wanting either of us to dwell on this, 'I've decided I'm done with dating apps.'

'You shouldn't give up on love because of one wanker.'

I silently snigger at the word 'wanker' coming from my mother's usually very-clean mouth. 'I'm not giving up. I'm just changing my approach. I've decided to join a gym.'

The moment I say these words, I realise my mistake.

'Sweetheart,' she screeches. 'This is not on you. There's nothing wrong with how you look – it's all on this horrible Kieran person.'

'Mum, relax. This has nothing to do with my weight or anything like that. I'm joining a gym in the hopes of meeting more men naturally.'

'Are you sure that's the reason?'

'Yes,' I promise. Although . . . my thoughts drift to my hot neighbour. If Mum's banana bread works its magic, maybe I won't have to. 'That's just one of the many things I'm going to try to get me out of my comfort zone. I'm thinking of going to a pottery class or something like that, maybe joining some kind of club.'

'Pottery?'

I laugh, because I know exactly what Mum's thinking – I've never exactly been the arts and crafts type. 'Yes, it sounds fun. Remember the scene in *Ghost* where—'

I don't even have to finish my sentence. Mum audibly swoons. 'How could I forget? Is your instructor a man?'

'I have no idea. I haven't even found a class yet.' Time to change the subject before she starts googling male pottery instructors in my area. 'Read anything good lately?'

'Ooh, yes. Since you gave me that Elin Hilderbrand book for Christmas, I've been binging her backlist on my Kindle.'

'I told you she's good.'

'Good?' Mum scoffs at this gross understatement. 'I've fallen in love with Nantucket since reading her novels and I'm trying to convince your father that we need to go on a holiday there.'

'Ha, good luck with that.' I can't remember the last time Dad took a holiday. When we were little, Mum used to force him to take two weeks leave every year and we'd go to Bali or the Gold Coast or even just down to Perth, but once we grew up, the family holiday kind of fell by the wayside. Now Dad only leaves the farm for funerals, stock shows and other agricultural business.

She sighs. 'It's a dream. Did I tell you Phil is having a seventieth birthday party up in Broome later in the year and your father agreed to go?' Phil had been the best man at their wedding. 'It's only two nights, but I'll take it. Can you believe I've put up with your father for four decades?' Love shines through in her voice.

'You deserve a medal,' I tell her. 'You get less than that for murder.'

We chuckle and then chat for another ten minutes or so about what Dad and my two brothers who work with him on the station are up to – 'Justin is trying to convince your father and Brandon to buy a new breed of cattle from overseas' – the latest adorable mischief my nieces and nephews have been up to – 'Sarah decided to run away from home and we found her two kilometres up the driveway, crying because her feet were hurting. Anyway, sweetheart, I've got to go and get Dad's dinner on. Love you lots.'

'I love you too,' I say, and then finish mixing the banana bread.

I put it in the oven, feed JB and heat up a Healthy Choice meal for me. I'm so lost in the latest adventures of Stephanie Plum that I almost jump out of my skin when my phone alarm tells me it's time to check the bread, but it smells divine.

I wrap the still-warm offering in a clean tea towel and carry it next door. My neighbour's front gate creaks as I push it open – how did I not notice that last night? – and the doorbell echoes through the house as I press it.

When no one comes, I try the bell again. Also futile. Could he be ignoring me?

Maybe he's pretending to be out because he doesn't want to have to deal with me again after last night. Or maybe he's just out to dinner with friends or working. After all, he's out more than he's home.

Still, I don't like the idea that someone might have got the wrong impression about me, so I head to my backyard to see if his car is in the carport. There's no front car entrance to our adjoined townhouses, but there's an access lane out the back. I don't have a car myself, choosing to use public transport, my legs or a bike as I rarely go too far, and cars are both expensive and environmentally unfriendly. The fence between our yards is low enough that I can see over it. And there's no car.

As I snoop, JB jumps up beside me, his claws scraping loudly on the fence, and I imagine what our neighbour might think if he catches us. Second impressions might not be that great either.

With a sigh, I go back into the house, put the cake in a Tupperware container and then write a note – *Dear Neighbour. Please accept my apologies for disturbing you. Enjoy the best banana bread you'll ever taste, and I look forward to meeting you again properly. Cheers, Bee (from next door)* – and sticky tape it to the top of the container, which I leave on his front porch.

Back at my place, I open my laptop and type 'local pottery classes' into the search bar. I'm guessing there might not be many straight men attending such a class, but at least it will give me something to fill the time when I'll no longer be swiping on the apps.

5

Opposites Attract

Since those years in my teens when I exercised almost to the point of death, the only exertion my body gets is my daily dog walk, which means I've never been inside a gym before. The moment Fred and I walk into the one around the corner from the library, I start to panic.

The background music is almost drowned out by the grunts and groans coming from the people beyond the reception area.

'We're here to join,' Fred tells the young, perky-looking blonde woman behind the counter. Behind her, on shelves, are rows and rows of protein supplements and shakes. 'Can you tell us about your membership options, please?'

If the smell of sweat mixed with Lynx deodorant isn't enough to put me off, this woman gives it her best go as she looks us up and down. Fred, of course, is in the cutest little rainbow Lycra shorts I've ever seen and a matching crop top, which she bought when she decided to get into running with her brother Waylen. The running didn't last long – not for her anyway – so she's excited to have another opportunity to wear the outfit. Her look gives Perky Blonde a run for her money.

Me? I dug deep into my wardrobe to find some cotton shorts and have thrown on a baggy old T-shirt to match. My sneakers are sandy from all my beach walks.

After finishing her assessment, Perky Blonde decides to direct her conversation to Fred, going through several options. I zone out and look beyond reception to the actual gym space. I'm shocked by the number of people here; it seems after work on Friday afternoon is a popular time to work out. I'd thought it might be a quiet time to ease myself in, but no such luck.

And, even if any of the men I see racing on the treadmills or pumping iron show any interest in me – highly unlikely when there are lookers like Fred and Perky Blonde present – I doubt we'd have much in common.

'Fred,' I whisper, tugging on her arm.

Perky Blonde, who I now notice is wearing a name badge that says 'Sheena', looks annoyed at the interruption.

'I don't want to do this,' I whisper. I'd rather be alone than put myself through this kind of torture.

Fred shrugs. 'Okay, if you're sure,' she says, then turns to Sheena. 'We've changed our minds. Have a good night.'

Sheena is no doubt glad to see the back of us.

'Thank God,' Fred says as we head towards the pride and joy that is her vintage orange Mini. 'You know I'll do anything for you, but did you *smell* that place?'

'Gross,' I agree.

'Besides, just thinking about all that exercise made me hungry. Let's get pizza and go to your place. I wanna check out that neighbour of yours.'

'Just promise not to be embarrassing if we do see him?'

'Who, me?' she asks as we reach her car.

I laugh. 'And no flirting with him either. If anyone is going to get involved with my neighbour, it's me.'

'You know I'd never. Girlfriend Code and all.'

I smile, beyond blessed to have a friend like Fred. It was a lucky day we sat next to each other in our very first lecture at uni. I must admit that during that first conversation I wasn't sure we were going to click. Fred and I are opposites in so many ways, which was blatantly clear from the get-go. She is a self-confessed extrovert, whereas I tend towards introversion until I get to know someone well. She spoke and I listened, partly in awe of her confidence and style, while also terrified by it.

By the time the lecture started I knew much of her life story – she has a brother who was studying law and she is very close to, but parents they merely tolerate. Said parents were divorced because her father was a 'controlling arsehole', but her mother was a slow learner and on her third marriage to another not-very-nice guy. As a result of our very different home situations, I'm a sop for love and Fred is more than sceptical, but we respect our differences; in fact, they complement each other. And of course we both share our passion for books.

Once we have our pizza – pepperoni, the only meat Fred eats – we head to my place. JB is ecstatic at our arrival and the smell of our dinner.

'Let's eat outside,' Fred suggests, hoping to get a glimpse of Mr Mysterious. This time of year eating outside at night is perfect, as long as we spray ourselves liberally with mosquito repellent.

There's no car in the carport next door, but we'll have the perfect vantage spot if he does come home.

We eat the pizza from the box to avoid dishes and drink Diet Coke from cans and I scold myself as I think about the fact that

Fred can eat twice as much pizza as I do and not gain an ounce. I know such thoughts aren't healthy, but occasionally they still intrude. When we're done, my neighbour still hasn't come back and Fred is getting cranky.

'I told you, he's out a lot,' I say, grabbing the empty box as JB jumps about trying to steal it. 'I'm just going to put this in the recycling bin.'

On my return, I see Fred at the edge of my backyard, peering over the fence. 'What are you doing?' I shriek, half-laughing, half-terrified he'll come home and catch her.

'Looking for clues.' She lets out a loud sigh and returns to the porch, slumping into one of my uncomfortable plastic outdoor chairs.

I reach for my Diet Coke. 'Did you find any?'

She shakes her head. 'Nada.'

We're both quiet for a moment, then she says, 'I suppose there are other options besides serial killer or drug dealer.'

'Oh? Do enlighten me.'

'He could be a pilot.'

'That's not very exciting,' I complain. 'Although the free travel would be fabulous.'

She laughs. 'What about secret agent?'

'Or maybe . . .' I click my fingers. 'He's an Olympic swimmer in training.'

'Nah.' Fred shakes her head. 'It would account for his early hours, but if he was seriously training, he'd probably be in bed by now.'

I concede her point and we spend the next half hour laughing as we road test a whole host of other possibilities until Fred gets a notification on one of her dating apps and announces she's off to meet some guy called Griffin.

'Have fun,' I say.

The good thing about not having a date of my own is that I can climb into bed and finish *Tastes Like Shakkar*. Things were just getting steamy between Bobbi and Bunty when I had to force myself to close the book last night, and I can't wait to get back to them.

'I'm not that bad,' I tell JB the following morning.

He's glaring at me from his worn spot on the couch as I shove my vacuum back and forth, singing along to my favourite playlist on Spotify. Normally, I listen to audiobooks while doing my housework but the narrator of my current book has a voice like Janice from *Friends*.

I feel like a rockstar on stage as I bellow 'Holding Out for a Hero', a song I first heard when Mum introduced me to *Footloose*. We might have lived far from civilisation, but she was big on teaching us all about the 'classics' at our weekly family movie night.

JB starts barking, leaps off the couch and rushes to the front door. I yank my earbuds out, turn off the vacuum and go to see who's there.

Through the glass I make out a tall, well-built man with messy, slightly-darker-than-strawberry-blond hair.

The Neighbour!!!

Hadn't I just been singing about needing a hero?

I'm about to open the door when I realise I'm wearing another pair of old shorts and the oversized, so-old-it's-holey T-shirt that I wore to walk first thing. I haven't even showered yet, but at least I'm not showing as much bare skin this time.

I tighten my ponytail, pinch my cheeks the way heroines in old novels do, and open the door.

A friendly 'hi' escapes my mouth before I realise Mr Mysterious is glowering.

'Do you always screech like a banshee this early on a Saturday morning?'

Screech? Banshee? Was I really singing that loudly? Mr Saunders never complained. Then again, he did wear hearing aids.

My neighbour's scowl grows as he pushes JB – who is trying to sniff his crotch – away. I've got to admit that even pissed off, this man is something to behold. Not classically hot like Fabio, but sexy in a boy-next-door-best-friend's-brother kinda way. He reminds me of someone, but I can't quite pinpoint who. 'And please control your damn dog. It's bad enough having to listen to it barking all day without it molesting me as well.'

This guy's heart must be made of pure stone because I rarely meet anyone who can resist my dog's fluffy face, floppy ears and adorable puppy eyes, even when he is overstepping the boundaries of personal space.

'His name is John Brown,' I snap. 'And are you always this unpleasant?'

My nasty neighbour shrugs and I can't help admiring his ridiculously broad shoulders. He's wearing a tight black T-shirt that pulls over his pectoral muscles, reminding me of the men I saw at the gym last night. 'Only when I'm woken up by crazy women at all hours of the night.'

His biting words put a quick dampener on my lust. I fold my arms across my chest. 'What's your excuse today, then? The sun's been up for hours.'

'Maybe so, but haven't you heard of a weekend lie-in?' He pushes his hair off his forehead, giving me an even better view of his glaring eyes. 'And good manners?'

Good manners? I can't believe his audacity. 'It's also good manners to thank someone when they go out of their way to bake for you.'

He blinks. 'The banana bread was from you?'

'Yes. Didn't you read the note?' Maybe he's illiterate as well as boorish?

'There was no note.'

My jaw tightens. Now he's trying to *gaslight* me? 'Oh yes, there most definitely was. It was taped to the top.'

He shakes his head decisively. 'Nope. No note. Must have blown off or something.'

'And still no thank you, either.'

'Thanks.' It sounds like this word comes at a great cost to him.

'You're welcome. I hope you liked it,' I say sarcastically. I have a good mind to bake him another – this time with arsenic in it.

'I gave it to my grandmother. She said it was good. I don't really have a sweet tooth.'

Pity. He could use some sugaring up. 'Do you have a name?' I ask. 'I'm Bee.'

'You mentioned that the other night. Hard to forget a name like Bee. Just Bee? Or does it stand for something? Like Beyoncé.'

'No.' I shake my head – if he didn't sound so patronising, I'd think he was trying to make a joke. 'Bridget. Bridget Jones.'

I don't know why I tell him my whole name; I'm usually reluctant to admit it to anyone, but he's got me so unnerved, it just slipped out. I wait a beat for him to make a joke – do I wear granny undies too, or when was the last time I made blue soup? – but when he doesn't, I feel slightly less hostile towards him.

'That's why I was dressed as a playboy bunny the night we met,' I explain.

'I think you mean *morning*,' he deadpans. 'And I have no idea what you're talking about.'

'You don't know who Bridget Jones is?'

'I thought *you* were Bridget Jones.' He looks exasperated with this conversation, but I'm flabbergasted – I can't recall meeting anyone who doesn't know my namesake. Guess I can tick movie reviewer off our list of possible careers for him.

'And what about you?' I persist. 'Do you have a name, or shall I forevermore call you my grouchy neighbour?'

'You can call me whatever the hell you want, just don't do it to my face,' he says, and then storms out my gate, walks the two metres to his and disappears inside.

'Oh, I will,' I yell, and slam the door behind me.

Not only do I sing at the top of my lungs while finishing my vacuuming but this time, I ditch my earbuds in favour of my Bluetooth speaker, which I turn up as high as it will go as 'Accidentally Kelly Street' begins.

I guess I won't be getting romanced by my neighbour after all.

6

The Psychopath Next Door

'Bee met her new neighbour,' Fred announces first thing Monday morning as we gather in the staffroom. She's wearing a neon pink short-sleeved blouse and orange flared pants like some relic from the 1970s that would look ridiculous on anyone else.

I'd called her the moment I'd finished cleaning, and we'd bitched about the psychopath next door for almost two hours.

Janine's eyes brighten as Xavier hands her the coffee he's just collected from Fabio. 'Well, go on. What's he like?'

'Yes, don't keep us waiting,' Xavier says, finally taking a sip of his own coffee and not noticing as he spills a drop on his smart, blue-checked business shirt. Persephone isn't here, as she and Nick flew to Fiji for a kid-free week where they planned to do nothing but have sex and lie on the beach drinking cocktails. *Lucky her.*

'He's definitely a serial killer. Or some kind of nutcase,' I declare.

Janine frowns. 'How do you know?'

'Because he doesn't like dogs,' Fred says before I can.

I glare at her – this is my story – as the others recoil and gasp.

Xavier presses a hand against his chest. 'What the actual fuck?!'

'JB rarely barks – only if someone knocks or he hears a cat outside – and I've never had any complaints, until now.'

'Maybe your neighbour's scared of dogs,' Janine suggests, tucking a strand of her flyaway silver hair behind her ear. 'My grandson's terrified.'

'It's not just the dog thing.' I tell them about the singing complaints, his permanent evil eye, his phony thanks, and him basically telling me to never speak to him again. 'Not to mention the fact that he mowed his lawn yesterday morning at seven am. Talk about petty.'

I'd spent the rest of my Sunday plotting various acts of retaliation. I may even have googled 'Ways to annoy your neighbour'.

Fred slaps the lid back on her now empty green-juice bottle. 'Now I've had time to digest the situation, I think the important thing here is that he's hot. Hotness covers all manner of sins.'

It's okay for her – she's not the one living next to Norman Bates. 'Maybe in your world, but I believe kindness is more important than looks.'

She shrugs. 'Not when it comes to flings.'

I think about the sexy stubble on his chin that I noticed while he mowed, and then I come to my senses. 'I don't want one-night stands or a fling, I want—'

She holds up a hand. 'I know, I know, but honestly you don't know what you're missing out on. Boys can't hurt you when you only want one thing from them.'

Although I've heard Fred say a variation of this many times, I often wonder how she lives like that. Is it really possible to protect your heart in such a way?

Xavier wipes some froth off his moustache. 'You could always have a fling with the neighbour while you're waiting to run into Mr Forever. Better than going without.'

'Thanks for your concern,' I assure them, 'but I'll be okay. Some of the best orgasms I've ever had I gave myself.'

They all look at me as if my dog has just died.

Xavier digs his phone out of his pocket. 'What's his name?' He's an excellent social media stalker.

'He refused to give it to me,' I say.

Janine shakes her head. 'Oh, this is no good. He doesn't sound very neighbourly at all.'

'Sounds like he's hiding something to me,' Xavier says.

Fred nods, the spikes of her short, black hair dancing. 'I agree. Maybe he's a paedophile recently released from prison.'

We all shudder, but thankfully we can't dwell on this possibility any longer because the library clock chimes, letting us know it's time to open.

As Janine goes into her office, Xavier to the children's section to prep for today's Rhyme Time session, Fred to the counter to start processing the crates that have just arrived from the state library containing all our exchanges and reserves, I head to the stairs to open up. There are always people waiting for us, and even before I pull back the rope, patrons are charging down the escalators like they're running from a fire. I like to think it's because they've stayed up late to finish a book and are desperate to get a new one, but the truth is that many of our regulars come here because they have nowhere else to go. We have our fair share of homelessness in Fremantle and it breaks my heart, but I love that our library is a safe haven for all.

I'm sending emails to publishers, putting in requests for author talks later in the year, when Fred peers over the top of my computer. 'You busy?'

'That depends on what you need.'

She laughs. 'Xavier's still on lunch and I've got a woman out there who's looking for a book rec for her teenage daughter.'

I almost leap out of my seat – nothing gives me more joy than pimping books.

Fred chuckles. 'Her name's Laura. She's in the YA section. She has really short, funky, blonde hair and she's wearing a mask. Oh, and a vacant look in her eyes as if she's just seen a ghost.'

I make a beeline for the YA shelves and spy the woman in question immediately. At this time of the day this area of the library is almost deserted, but also Fred's description is spot-on. The woman's hair is so short it looks like it's recently been shaved.

'Laura?' I ask as I approach. 'I'm Bee.' I offer my hand and she hesitates, then takes it briefly. 'I hear you need help finding some books.'

She nods as she digs sanitiser out of her bag, squirts a generous amount onto her palm and rubs her hands together liberally. 'Yes, for my daughter. Lola.'

'That's a beautiful name. How old is Lola?'

'Fifteen.'

'Fun age.' Although I smile, I'm remembering when I was fifteen. Not the most enjoyable year of my life. 'And is there any particular reason you're looking for a book for her?' Lots of parents come into the library wanting help to get their teens off screens.

Laura pales for a moment, then fiddles with the Tiffany chain around her neck as she replies. 'She's in hospital for a while. And she's bored. When she was little, she really loved books and I thought . . . well, I *hoped* maybe I could find something to distract her.'

'I'm sorry. Do you mind me asking why she's there?' I don't mean to be rude, but I don't want to give Lola a book that might be triggering. If she's got mental health issues, we'll steer clear of *13 Reasons Why*.

'She's got leukemia.'

Oh my goodness. My heart squeezes. Now I understand why Laura looks like she's seen a ghost and why she flinched when I offered my hand. How awful. I want to say I'm sorry, but such words feel empty. 'Has she got any hobbies, favourite sports to watch or play? Knowing a bit about her will help me find the perfect book.'

'Are boys a hobby?'

Despite the mask, I can tell she's smiling. I laugh. 'Definitely.'

'To be honest, I was wondering if you have any books that aren't too depressing but can help her feel like she's not alone in this. Most of the kids in her ward are a lot younger than her.'

'That must be tough. So you want books that deal with teens having cancer?' I clarify.

She nods. 'But I don't want them to be too depressing. Is that asking too much?'

'No, I think I have a couple of perfect novels to start her on.' As I pluck *Zac and Mia* and *The Last Days of Us* off the shelves, I add, 'I spent two years of my teens in and out of hospital as well, and reading stopped me going insane.'

I don't say it quite literally saved me.

'What were you in for?' she asks.

When I tell her, she surreptitiously looks me up and down and frowns slightly. I'm used to this reaction when I share my illness with people – I look well now and I'm not skinny, so they think I must be lying about how bad I was.

I know I'm one of the lucky ones, but in some ways, I'll always be in recovery.

'These novels are both set in Australia. *Zac and Mia* is actually set in Perth, so hopefully Lola will really be able to relate.' Thinking of what Laura said about boys, I also grab a copy of *Better Than the Movies* by Lynn Painter, just in case she needs something without cancer.

Laura follows me over to the self-serve check-out where I help her with her books and give her one of our 'Welcome to Fremantle Library' tote bags.

'Thanks,' she says. 'I can't remember the last time I came here. Life seems so busy these days, I no longer have time to read.'

I try not to gasp at these tragic words, unable to imagine ever not *making* time to read. If anyone needs the escapist magic of books right now, it's Laura. 'Will you let me get a book for you, too?'

She looks uncertain but I hold up my finger. 'Wait right there.'

Then, before she can reject my offer, I head straight to general fiction and scan the shelves, waiting for a novel to call to me. This is my most favourite part of my job – finding the right book for the right person – and I don't like to boast, but I'm a master at it. I run my finger along the spines and can almost feel the magic jolt into my body when I spy *Someone Else's Shoes* by Jojo Moyes. I read this not long after it came out and absolutely loved it. Jojo's novels are so popular, it's rare they aren't borrowed, so I take the fact it's on the shelf as an omen that I've chosen the right book.

'Maybe you can read alongside each other,' I say as I hand her the extra book. 'Come back and let me know how you both go.'

'I will,' she promises.

Once she's gone, I head back to the office to get on with my task until whatever comes first – lunch or another lost reader needing direction.

Every day at lunchtime, I go home to let JB out for a break in the garden. Today as he sniffs at something by the fence, I peep over it to check for signs of life. Aside from a willie wagtail dancing up and down the verandah step, there's nothing. My neighbour's car isn't in the carport, so he must be at work or wherever he goes when he's not at home acting like Oscar the Grouch.

I see one of his curtains is slightly open and I'm considering going around to look in his window, when I hear the sound of the Australia Post motorbike out the front. JB abandons his pursuit of a white butterfly and races back through the house. I follow him inside to finish my sandwich in the air conditioning.

When it's time to head back to work, I check my letterbox and am disappointed not to find a book-sized package. I know I work at a library and have all the books in the world at my fingertips, but I can't help that I want them in my house as well, and often find myself ordering random books after reading about them online late at night. If I hadn't inherited this place, no way I could afford my habit, but hey, there are worse things I could spend my money on. Drugs, for instance.

Which, if I wanted, I might be able to buy from my new neighbour.

I can't get the thought out of my head that I might be living next door to an actual criminal. Why else would he refuse to tell me his name?

At the thought of him, I glance next door and my heart skips a beat at the sight of an envelope sticking out from his letterbox. A cunning thought lands in my head, and I steeple my fingers and wriggle them like an animated villain in a Disney movie. I'm not usually the type to break the law, but it's not like I'm going to *open* his mail; I just want to see his name.

My heart pounds and, feeling as if I'm planning to break into the Louvre and steal the Mona Lisa, I walk over to where an identical letterbox to mine sits on his wrought iron fence. The lid groans with rust as I lift it, and then my fingers are on the bounty.

Victory!

At that moment, his front door opens and I look up to see the devil himself standing there. He's wearing black pants and a light blue T-shirt, and his hair is as messy as it usually is when he's just climbed out of bed. It seems weird that I know what this man looks like when he's just woken up. It's also weird that I'm thinking such thoughts when he's glaring at me like he wants to make me his next victim.

'What the hell are you doing?'

I swallow. Will he believe me if I tell him I mistook his letterbox for mine?

'Um . . .' Another gulp. 'The previous owner's daughter asked me to check in case anything still comes for him.'

If possible, his emerald-green eyes narrow even further. 'You don't think she'd have asked *me* to do that?'

'I . . . I . . .'

'Because she did.' He marches forward, snatches the mail out of my hand and looms over me. 'So how about you tell me the truth, *Bridget?*'

'Okay. Fine. I was trying to find out your name.'

This seems to amuse him – his eyes widen, and I think he almost smiles. 'Why? Interested in me?'

OMG. Is he serious? 'I just want to know who to report to the police for indecency if you mow the lawn half-naked again.' I hadn't mentioned that bit to my colleagues because if Fred had heard what he looks like shirtless, she'd have lost her mind.

'Pretty sure I can mow the lawn in my *own* backyard in my birthday suit if I want.' He turns and starts back towards his house, calling over his shoulder, 'By the way, everyone calls me Sully.'

Sully? I blink and then laugh. 'Like the big, cute, furry blue monster in *Monsters, Inc.?*'

'That's the one,' he says without even looking back. 'Goodbye, Bridget.'

No one calls me that – not even my mother – and something about the way he says my name sends a shiver down my spine.

Whether it's a good or bad shiver, I can't quite tell.

7

Love Isn't a Character Flaw

Once a month I finish work early and go see my counsellor. After my lunchtime encounter with my neighbour, I'm still feeling on edge and couldn't be more pleased that today is that day.

Aisha works from home in a gorgeous old federation house only a few streets from mine. The stone bricks, red tin roof and iron lacework on the verandah look like something from a painting, and the hanging baskets filled with flowers always make me smile. I ring the bell and less than thirty seconds later it opens.

'Good afternoon, Bee,' Aisha says, hitting me with her dazzling smile as she gestures for me to come inside.

'Hello,' I reply, already feeling the tension leave my limbs.

Aisha was born in Nigeria and wears bright patterned dresses that she orders from designers back home – I don't think I've ever seen her in black – and she always accessorises with huge dangly earrings and multiple bead necklaces that make a click-clacky noise when she moves. I can't tell how old she is, but considering I've been seeing her for almost five years, and she's been practising for over thirty, I'm guessing she's in her mid-to-late fifties.

I can only dream of looking that good at her age.

'How hot is it today?' she says as she leads me into her office, which is also a plethora of colour, and thankfully air-conditioned.

'It's awful.' Even though I grew up in sweltering temps, I much prefer winter. Nothing better than snuggling up under a blanket with a hot Milo and a book.

She nods as I flop down into her comfy couch. Other therapists I've been to have had hard, uncomfortable couches as if they didn't really want you to get too comfy, but Aisha's couch is like a fluffy cloud that almost swallows you whole when you sit in it.

'How was your Christmas and New Year?' she asks, picking up the pen and paper with which she always seems to take a zillion notes. She was away all of December and January, so this is our first session of the year.

I sigh, wondering where to start. 'Christmas was lovely,' I begin. Being home with my family always is. 'And then I met this guy who I really liked not long after.'

She listens, making all the right noises, as I tell her about Kieran and feeling that he might be the one, only to be blindsided when I received the text message from his wife.

'Oh, Bee, I'm so sorry that happened. How did it make you feel?'

I know she's asking if Kieran's betrayal led me to any harmful thoughts about my own self-worth, about my body. 'You mean aside from totally stupid and humiliated?'

She gives me a look of reproval. 'We both know you're not stupid.'

'No. I've been eating normally,' I say, knowing this is a victory.

For someone who likes to be in control, being dumped is one of the worst things that can happen to you – it's why I usually take my time getting to know someone before I allow my heart to become involved. Clearly, I stuffed that up royally with Kieran.

'But I can't help feeling that something's wrong with me. Either I'm a magnet for douchebags or give off some kind of signal that I'm naïve and easily taken for a ride.'

'Being trustworthy and optimistic about love isn't a character flaw,' Aisha says. 'You need to focus on the fact that you're better off without men like Kieran in your life.'

I nod. 'The whole experience has made me reassess my approach to finding love. I'm not going to try so hard to find someone. I'm just going to put myself out in the community more – try new things and hopefully meet new people.'

Aisha smiles. 'I think taking some time away from dating apps is a great idea. Yes, some people have success with them, but they can also be very damaging, and we both know you need to prioritise your mental health. I think you'll find that experimenting with new hobbies and making friends without expectations will help you learn more about yourself as well. I can't wait to hear about these adventures.'

'I can't wait to have them,' I say, not sure what else I *want* to learn about myself. I've been through a lot of therapy in my life, and I think by now I know myself pretty well.

She smiles again. 'And how's work at the moment?'

'Work's great – I've been planning our events schedule for the year, and we've got some great authors scheduled. But there is one other thing slightly bothering me.'

Aisha leans her head forward, interest piqued, and I continue. 'My neighbour.'

'Oh?'

I tell her about my weird interactions with him so far, and she laughs at the bit about me mistaking his house for mine on Valentines Day.

'Sorry.' She straightens her lips. 'Go on.'

'It's okay.' Even I can admit that part was funny. 'I know that wasn't a great start to our relationship, but I tried to apologise and . . .'

She listens intently as I tell her about our interactions since then. 'I don't know what to do.'

Aisha frowns. 'Why do you have to do anything?'

I blink. 'We're neighbours. I just—'

'You're a friendly, kind and happy person, Bee, and as we know, not being liked can be triggering for you. But you don't need to be friends with everyone, and I think it would be better for your own wellbeing if you just wrote this guy off as a lost cause. Don't let his rudeness get to you.'

Easy to say – she's not the one that has to live next door to him. 'But what if it's not just rudeness? Something about him unnerves me.'

This makes her frown. 'What do you mean?'

I shrug. 'I can't quite put my finger on it. It's just the way he looks at me or something, and he hates my dog.' Just talking about this has the hairs on the back of my neck rising.

Aisha takes a moment. 'If I were you, I'd just limit your inter-actions to a wave if you see him in the garden. And if you ever feel uneasy, call someone to come be with you. He's probably just a cranky bastard, but you can never be too careful when it comes to safety.'

8

The Things We Do for Love

Xavier has bought new workout gear specifically for tonight. He picks me up for my first kickboxing class after going home to change and then drives us to the venue, about ten minutes away – long enough for me to get jittery.

'You're thinking about chickening out, aren't you?' he asks as we turn into the car park. After the gym visit, I'd told him I wasn't sure about this, but he'd convinced me a class would be much more social.

'No,' I lie, my stomach twisting as I see two gorgeous women climbing out of the car next to us, carrying boxing gloves. 'Should we have brought our own gloves?'

'Nah, this is a beginner class. They supply them.'

I swallow and climb out of the car, already working up a sweat from the thought of going inside. If I want to meet a guy offline, then it means stepping out of my comfort zone, but I wouldn't have been brave enough to come alone.

The moment we walk inside, a terse looking, muscly woman with dark hair pulled back in a high, tight ponytail greets us as we approach the desk. 'New?' she barks.

Xavier turns on his natural charms. 'Yes, hello. I'm Xavier and this is my friend Bee. I called up yesterday to enquire.'

She hands us two clipboards and directs us to fill in forms. We sign waivers agreeing not to sue if we break our legs or, worse, our necks, and I wonder if true love is really worth it as I head into the main space with Xavier. It looks terrifying – the floor is tiled with blue exercise-mat squares, and the walls are painted with large quotes along the top. *I'm fast. I'm pretty. I can't possibly be beat* and *Do or do not. There is no try.* One side of the room has a row of black punching bags, with floor-to-ceiling mirrors on the other. In the corner there's an actual boxing ring where two hot guys are sparring.

The few other people already here are all barefoot and either punching the bags or skipping. I'm glad to see they're dressed in shorts and daggy T-shirts just like me, although a couple of them must have been here before because they've got the gym's logo on their sleeves. Eminem is blaring loudly from speakers in the corner, not quite drowning out the guttural noises of the people punching.

We dump our things in the cubicles at the back and grab some skipping ropes from a hook on the wall to warm up. While Xavier skips like someone who was the Jump Rope for Heart school champion, my heart rate barely shifts as I merely try not to trip. Coordination was never a talent of mine.

The music suddenly fades, and a deep voice interrupts my half-hearted attempts. 'Alrighty. Let's get started.'

I look up to see the hot guys have climbed down from the ring and are now standing at the front of the room. The punching bags and skipping ropes are abandoned, and everyone forms rows across the room facing the two men. I convince Xavier to hang out at the back, figuring I'm closer to the door if I need to commando roll out of here.

'Now you're all warmed up, fifty push-ups.'

What? I look in horror at Xavier. Surely this is a joke. What beginner can do fifty push-ups?

When I realise I'm the last one standing, I snap to the floor and into a plank, but even before I attempt to lower myself, my arms are shaking. Miraculously, I manage seven.

'Now, grab some gloves and pair up,' says Hot Guy One.

I follow everyone over to the glove container, screwing up my nose at the aroma of stale sweat that emanates from it and almost gag when I slip my hand into a pair of them to find them wet. *Ew.*

'These are gross. Do you wanna get out of here and go get a drink?' I whisper to Xavier as everyone partners up.

He shakes his head. 'Uh-uh. You're not getting out of this that easily. Besides, a little second-hand sweat never hurt anyone.'

I'm not sure that's true, but I follow him back to our spot anyway.

The hot guys, who insist on us calling them Kru – and threaten us with a hundred burpees if we don't – shout out things like 'right kick, left kick, cross, jab, back kick, hook'. At first, I struggle to keep up. I'm having flashbacks to school PE, but after a while, I start to catch on, right-kicking and left-hooking with the rest of the group.

'So are we gonna come back next Thursday?' Xavier asks when it's finally over and, sweat still pouring off our foreheads, we make our way back outside to his car.

I'm surprised to discover I might actually want to. 'That depends on whether I can walk tomorrow,' I say with a laugh as I slide into the passenger seat.

I may not have met a man but in the end, despite more exertion than I've had in years, I almost enjoyed myself. There's something kind of therapeutic about martial arts.

In another effort to meet Mr Right organically, Fred has conned Xavier and Rory into hitting the local pubs and clubs with us Saturday night.

She and I get ready at my place – her haranguing me over how long it takes to do my make-up, saying it's cutting into valuable drinking and scoring time. Fred is barely wearing any make-up and of course she looks gorgeous in a figure-hugging white dress with cut-outs on each side of her waist, accentuating her tanned skin. Me? After much deliberating, I've finally gone with a short denim skirt, a halter-neck black top and sparkly silver heels I splurged on with birthday money from my parents last year but haven't worn yet. I've also blow-dried my hair for the occasion.

When I finally feel happy with my look, we walk down the street to meet the boys at the National Hotel. We're going to have drinks and dinner on the rooftop bar and then see where the night takes us.

'I love it here,' Rory says, leaning back and wrapping his arm around Xavier's shoulders. They're dressed almost identically in fashionable dark jeans and floral shirts. 'What a view.'

I have to agree. From the roof, you can sometimes see right across to Rottnest and right now, with the sun setting over the Indian Ocean, our view looks like an orange and purple postcard. Only enhanced by the smell of the sea on the gentle evening breeze.

'Never mind the view.' Fred claps her hands as if calling a meeting to order. 'We're not here to admire the bloody sunset. We're here to find Bee a man.'

'Sorry.' Rory sits up straight again, looking chastised, then lifts his Aperol Spritz and points it towards someone waiting to order a drink. 'What about him?'

We all swivel to look.

I've got to admit, he's good-looking in a nerdy kind of way – slightly long, wavy brown hair, black glasses and a geometric-print shirt buttoned right up to the collar – and, as someone who loves books, I'm not opposed to nerds. 'He's not bad.'

'Go.' Fred practically pushes me off my seat.

'What?' I shriek, my stomach twisting. 'You want me to go over to him?'

She laughs and squeezes my hand. 'Yes. How else do you plan to strike up a conversation? Just imagine he's someone at the library wanting a book rec. You'll be fine.'

I suppose she's right. This is what we're here for. I take a fortifying gulp of my drink and smooth my hands over my skirt. 'Wish me luck.'

'Good luck,' Rory and Xavier say in unison.

'You don't need luck. You're Bridget Effing Jones!' Fred cries.

I chuckle. 'Thanks, Winifred Darling.' We only call each other by our full names in serious situations.

She blows a kiss to me and I feel her and my other friends' eyes bore into my back as I walk the short distance to the corner bar. My belly is doing some kind of gymnastics and I'm thinking I should have redone my lipstick before approaching my potential husband. Oh well, too late now. I'm too scared of Fred to retreat.

'Hi.' I try to sound casual as I sidle up beside my target and offer a friendly smile.

He pushes the glasses up his nose and that's when I notice his wedding ring. My heart sinks. *Of course.* I smile as I lean past him to grab a napkin, pretending that's why I was here all along.

'Married,' I say as I slump back into my seat.

My friends all utter their commiserations and quickly move on to finding me another target, yet almost everyone here is already with someone and after a few more knockbacks, Fred decides it's time to move on.

'That's it.' She downs the rest of her bourbon and Coke. 'We're not making any progress here. Let's go grab some beers at Little Creatures while we're waiting for the clubs to open.'

I screw up my face. Not because I don't want to go to Little Creatures – it's the after I'm less than enthused about. I was hoping I might have had luck *before* we got to the dancing in clubs stage of the evening, because I've never seen the appeal of nightclubs. They always have a weird smell and are so loud you can never maintain a proper conversation. Don't get me wrong, I like to party, but when I say I like to party, I mean stay home and read books.

And yes, I do have that on a T-shirt!

'Behave,' Fred says, grabbing my hand. 'Remember, this isn't my idea. You're the one who wants to pick up in such an antiquated way.'

The boys follow us out of the bar and we crowd into the tiny elevator. On the street we weave through couples and families and other dinner-goers as we head down High Street and then around the edge of the Esplanade towards the ocean. We can't walk directly through the park as there's a circus in town, and the Big Top, all its entourage and side-show games are taking up most of the grassed area.

'Remember when this place used to be a crocodile farm?' Xavier asks as we finally reach the massive shed that houses Little Creatures.

'No,' I say. 'Did it really?'

He nods. 'Well before your time, I guess. Must have closed sometime in the late nineties. You'd have been a mere babe in your mother's arms back then.'

I sometimes forget that Xavier and Rory are in their late thirties and early forties, but I guess that's the joy of being an adult – age doesn't come into friendship so much.

'Enough reminiscing,' Fred declares. 'Let's get some beers and find Bee some guys.'

'Um, I only need one,' I reply, thinking of some popular Why Choose or Reverse Harem novels I've read lately. Having a group of men devoted to you might be good on the page, but it sounds like a nightmare in real life.

Inside the brewery, it's loud, with pop music and voices battling to be heard over the top of each other, and it smells unsurprisingly of beer. We take our drinks back into the front garden area and miraculously find seats. Immediately, Fred starts scanning the crowd.

'Okay,' she says. 'What about the guy with the wavy brown hair at ten o'clock? He has a bit of a Jensen Ackles vibe going on.'

'Hubba hubba,' Rory says and Xavier laughs. They're both massive *Supernatural* fans. 'Jensen Ackles is my hall pass.'

Fred nudges me. 'Go over, walk past him and then drop something so obviously that he'll have to pick it up.'

'Or, better still,' Xavier shrieks, 'spill your drink on him, then grab some serviettes and start drying him. Always works in the movies.'

'And books,' I agree, recalling all the meet-cutes I've read involving spilled drinks and inappropriate groping under the guise of helping mop up the mess, but my cheeks burn just thinking about how mortifying doing that on purpose would be. I shake my head.

'I'm not sure that trying so hard is any different than being on the apps. The whole point of going off them is to leave my love life to Fate.'

Fred raises an eyebrow. 'How is going to kickboxing and joining groups, et cetera, leaving it to Fate? I thought we were trying to engineer a meet-cute here?'

'Bee's right,' Xavier says, and I shoot him a grateful smile. 'Kickboxing, like tonight, is just about expanding the potential pool – she won't meet anyone sitting at home on the couch reading.'

'More's the pity,' I say, and Fred laughs.

'That's why apps were invented, but I get your point. Let's just drink and have fun and see what happens.' She guzzles the last of her beer. 'Who wants another?'

We all nod, and she goes off to grab more drinks.

'How's your manuscript going?' I ask when she returns.

Her eyes sparkle. The only thing Fred loves talking about more than her sexual escapades is her writing. Whereas I can't imagine a better job than being a librarian, Fred is hoping that one day she'll be able to call herself a novelist and write for a living. 'So good. I've just got to the bit where my main character realises that her roommate is a cannibal.'

'What? But isn't she sleeping with the roommate?' Every Monday Fred updates me on what she wrote over the weekend. I've been begging her to let me read it, but she's such a perfectionist that she refuses to show me her masterpiece until she's written the whole thing.

Xavier and Rory's eyes widen at my question, but Fred just nods with glee. 'Yep. Him and the guy next door and a woman she works with at the funeral parlour. Sometimes all three of them at once.'

Rory frowns. 'What genre is this book?'

Fred waves her hand dismissively. 'It's genre-busting. I don't want to be confined by boring conventions.'

'Fair enough,' Rory says and then takes another sip of his beer as Fred continues to give us a blow-by-blow account of what her feisty main character, Ana, is getting up to. I'm not sure what's more fun, listening to her talk about the crazy stuff happening in her book or watching the guys trying to keep up.

'Okay,' she says, glancing at her Apple watch when she's finally finished giving us the rundown. 'It's time to go dancing!'

Reluctantly I finish my beer and follow my friends out into the night, where we head to a club Fred promises us has great music and isn't full of underage teeny boppers. 'The last thing you want is to be hit on by a sixteen-year-old.'

I don't know whether it's the drinks I've already had or the fact that I've decided to stop actively looking for Mr Right and just go with the flow, but I actually find myself enjoying being on the dance floor with my friends. This club plays music from the eighties and nineties, and although I wasn't born when most of the songs were released, they're so well known that I can't help singing along loudly with Xavier, as Rory and Fred impress us with their moves.

It isn't long before the inevitable happens and Fred finds herself dirty dancing with a long-haired guy in sparkly silver pants, a tight white T-shirt, red suspenders and big silver hoops in his ears. It's not an outfit most people could get away with but on him it works, maybe because he's one of the best dancers I've ever seen and watching him move *that* body in *that* outfit is mesmerising. The rest of us grab another drink and go rest our feet, content to just enjoy the show.

'This is Enrico,' Fred says, dragging him over to greet us after a while. Sweat glistens on both their foreheads but they still look like models. 'He's a trapeze artist with the circus.'

Ah, now that explains a few things.

As Xavier asks Enrico how he got into show business, Fred pulls me off to the side. 'Enrico has offered to give me an after-hours private tour of the Big Top.'

'Is that a euphemism?' I ask, raising an eyebrow, pretending to be appalled.

She grins. 'It damn well better be, but if you don't want me to leave, I'll ask him for a raincheck.'

I shake my head. 'No, you go. I'm more than ready to call it a night anyway.'

'Thanks. You're the best.' She gives me a super-quick hug.

'I know. But make sure you're safe, okay?'

In reply, Fred winks – 'Always' – pats her little cross-body bag, which I know is full of condoms, and then slips her arm through Enrico's. 'Come on gorgeous, let's go see your Big Top.'

9

Homicidal Thoughts

At 6 am I'm ripped from sleep by an ear-piercing sound.

Jolting up in bed, I sniff the air. Is it my fire alarm? This is the last thing I need after a late night and too much alcohol. JB looks at me from where he's curled up at the end of my bed, but I'm relieved to find I don't smell any smoke.

It's only when I'm fully awake that I realise the noise is coming from the other side of my bedroom wall and it sounds like the kind of bedside alarm clock you find in country motels that haven't made it into the twentieth century yet.

Figures that my grumpy neighbour would use something like this. But why isn't he turning it off? Surely if it's this loud on my side, it must be ten times worse on his.

Uttering obscenities that would make my mum wash my mouth out with soap, I try to drown the sound out by clamping my pillow over my head. When that doesn't work, I sit up and bang my fist against the wall.

'Turn off your bloody alarm!' I yell but there is no reply, only the incessant noise.

Not caring that I'm wearing shorty pyjamas, haven't washed

my face, brushed my hair or done my make-up, I storm out the front door and almost barrel into an elderly couple on an early Sunday morning stroll as I strut next door. 'Sorry!'

I jab my finger on Mr Grumpy's doorbell and don't remove it. The annoying ding-dong battles with the alarm still blaring from inside.

Of course, my neighbour doesn't come.

After about two minutes, rage coursing through my body, I head back to my place and go out the back. JB races ahead of me and, as he cocks his leg against a tree, I peer into Sully's backyard. His carport's empty.

What the hell? He's not even home!

I feel like crying or breaking into his house to turn off the alarm myself, but I don't want to be arrested. Then again, I think I'd have a pretty good case in court.

I'm sorry, your Honour, but that noise would cause anyone to snap.

However, I'm all bark and no bite, so I head for the shower, which miraculously drowns out the noise and calms me a fraction.

When I emerge all clean and shiny, the alarm is still going. I wonder if I can call the police about such a thing, but instead I clip JB's leash onto his collar and head down to Bathers Beach for a dose of much-needed serenity.

Aside from a few eager swimmers and a couple of seagulls, the beach is almost deserted and I relish the peace, fresh air, and sea breeze. Now that the alarm isn't overpowering my thoughts, I suddenly realise that I could have snuck around to the fuse box and turned off the power. What an idiot! But if the blasted alarm is still going when I get home, that's exactly what I'll do.

After fifteen minutes, I whistle to JB, who is splashing in the water, and head back through the old Whaler's Tunnel so I can make a detour past the Grouchy Sailor. I don't usually splurge on café coffee on the weekend, but after the late night and annoyingly early morning I deserve a treat.

As I walk down High Street, my phone beeps with a text from Fred: *Did you know it's possible to have sex on a trapeze?*

A photo from somewhere up high, looking down at the big top ring with mini pony-jumps and sawdust, followed by an eggplant emoji, accompanies her messages.

I gasp. *You didn't?*

Well, to be honest, I was busy hanging on for grim life, but Enrico is very talented. And strong.

My mind boggles. *At least, one of us got lucky last night! What are you up to today?*

Writing. Of course. I admire her dedication – I'm not sure I could work all week and then spend hours on the weekend at a laptop tapping out words. *You?*

Reading, reading and more reading. And after that maybe some more reading.

Really, what else are Sundays for?

Her laughing emoji lands just as I arrive at the coffee shop.

'Bella.' Fabio's sexy voice and gorgeous smile are almost as therapeutic as the beach. 'What a pleasant surprise. You're up early this morning.'

I nod. 'Not by choice. I was rudely awakened by my neighbour's alarm, and I didn't get home till late, so I'm exhausted. Can I have an espresso instead of my usual latte, please?'

'*Non c'è problema.* Anything for my favourite customer.' He winks. 'Did you have a hot date or something?'

That he thinks such a thing possible makes me glow inside. 'No, I was just out with friends,' I say while he works his magic at the coffee machine.

'Lucky friends,' he says as he hands over my coffee, and I relish the connection as our fingers brush against each other.

If a simple accidental touch can make me feel so good, I can only fantasise about what sensations a more intimate interaction might invoke. Hoping he can't read my mind, I thank him for my drink and flee outside to collect JB.

Miraculously, Sully's alarm has stopped when I get home, and I'm in a much better mood after my encounter with Fabio, so I climb back into bed with Meghan Quinn's new book, delighted that the hero and heroine are just about to get down and dirty. As I read, I can't help but replace Meghan's characters with me and Fabio. One hand holding the book above my head, I slide down onto my pillow and creep my hand down to my knickers.

As the heroine's pleasure builds within her, so does mine.

'Oh, *God*!' I cry, visualising Fabio glancing up my body, hunger in his eyes as he devours me.

We're both so close.

'Yes. More. I need more!' I shriek, reading the dialogue aloud, and imagining it's Fabio Meghan's describing as the hero in the novel licks his lips and kneels buck naked on the bed in front of his partner. As he thrusts into her, I toss aside the book and reach into my bedside drawer for the vibrator Fred gave me for my birthday last year.

I'm building up to a beautiful crescendo when a loud noise begins in Sully's back garden.

Thump. Thump. Thump.

My whole body freezes.

Thump. Thump. Thump.

What the flip is he doing now?

Telling myself I don't care, I close my eyes, hoping to get back to business, but the moment is ruined.

Throwing back my sheet, I climb out of bed, straighten my clothes, then march outside and over to the fence. On the other side I see Sully dribbling a basketball up and down his back path, occasionally pausing to shoot it into a hoop. Was that there before or did he buy it specifically to annoy me? I definitely don't recall Mr Saunders having one. Although when he lived here, I never had reason to look over the fence.

'Training for the Olympics?' I shout angrily, unsure whether they even have basketball in the Olympics.

He looks over to the fence and scowls. 'Just trying to drown out the noises coming from your place.'

Oh my God. He can't be serious. Surely he didn't hear what I was getting up to with Fake Fabio in my bedroom?

He smirks. 'Sounded like you were quite enjoying yourself.'

A blaze of heat races up my neck to my face. The cheek of him.

I want to jump over the fence and murder him with my bare hands, but instead I yell, 'I was!' as I storm back into my house.

I hear his evil chuckle just before I slam the door.

It's the first time he's shown any signs of possessing a sense of humour and, of course, he's laughing at me.

10

Caterwauling

Monday night, I'm just sitting down to a microwave dinner, a rom-com from a debut Aussie author that came into the library today splayed out in front of me, when the most horrendous noise I've ever heard starts up next door.

My fork freezes halfway to my mouth. 'What the fresh hell is that?' I ask JB as he launches himself at our shared kitchen wall and starts barking like there's a rat trapped in there.

I thought the continuous *beep-beep-beep* of the bedside alarm was bad, but that has nothing on this. It sounds like Sully has got himself a cat and is inflicting torture on it. As JB's paws scratch against the wall, leaving marks, I consider reporting my neighbour to the RSPCA, because even if he isn't in there doing unspeakable things to some poor animal, he's definitely torment-ing mine.

Once again rudely interrupted while reading, I snap the book shut and turn on my TV – something I rarely do – in the hope of distracting me from Sully's noise and JB's barking. I don't even care what's on, yet all that succeeds in doing is adding to the cacophony. I rub my temples, feeling another headache coming on.

This street used to be peaceful, my house a sanctuary.

Since Sully moved in, it's been anything but!

Discarding my dinner, I go out the back, creep over to the fence and peer into his yard, hoping he's left a curtain open so I can catch a glimpse of what the heck is going on in there. Words can't come close to describing how awful the sounds coming from inside are. Either he's watching some weird porn or he's attempting to play some kind of unfamiliar instrument.

I suppose I could just go over there and find out, but then he'll know I'm annoyed and I don't want to give him the gratification.

Instead, I press record on my phone and stretch my arm over the fence, getting as close to the source as possible. I've got about thirty seconds captured when the sound abruptly stops.

The back of my neck prickles and I duck.

My pulse racing, I stop recording and run back to my place. JB, thinking it's a game, chases after me, darting between my legs and almost tripping me. When we're both safely inside, I send the soundbite to my friends and family.

Does anyone know what this is?

Wednesdays aren't usually my day for coffee pick-ups, but Persephone still isn't back at work. Apparently she picked up some nasty bug on the trip and has been vomiting ever since, so I do the honours and get my Fabio fix a day early.

'Hey, can I play you something?' I ask as I reach the front of the queue and hand over our cups.

'What do you mean?' His expression is the closest I've ever seen to him frowning, and I realise how crazy I must sound, but Sully is driving me bonkers.

I quickly fill him in on the weird noise that began next door on Monday night. 'So far no one has been able to tell me what it is.'

My mum suggested the bagpipes. Fred and Xavier went a little wild over the idea of my neighbour parading around in a kilt – both agreeing that kilts make any man ten times hotter – but Dave ruled that out. His family is from Scotland, and he said even learners don't sound *that* terrible.

Fabio leans across the counter towards me, and I can't help noticing how good he smells. 'Let me hear it.'

I press play on the soundbite of the cat-strangling, thankful that there isn't a queue behind me. His brow furrows in deep concentration as he listens.

'Sounds like a ghost in the *acqua* pipes,' he declares once it's ended.

I can't quite tell if he's serious, but I suppose it's always possible that Mr Saunders is haunting the place.

'Hmm, maybe.' As strange as it sounds, a ghost might just be the most logical explanation.

'Why don't you just ask him?' Fabio asked, going back to the task at hand.

I snort – 'My neighbour and I aren't exactly on good terms' – and then give him a very brief run-down of our interactions, minus what I was doing to provoke the basketball incident.

'This man sounds like a *giocare*,' Fabio says, accentuating every vowel. I don't know what that means but it sounds offensive, and I like it.

I nod. 'I should have asked the people I sent round to his house to investigate.'

'What people?'

'Just after I got home from work yesterday, I had two people knock, peddling some kind of religion. I told them I didn't have time to talk but that my neighbour was sad and lonely, but also very shy, so not to give up on him because he desperately needs meaning in his life.'

Fabio chuckles as he pours frothy milk into the cups.

'Judging by the shouting that followed, I'm guessing they woke him up.' Of course, I'd paid for it almost immediately, because the cat-strangling started up again.

'I'm not sure who to feel sorrier for – your neighbour or those poor people. Aren't you scared of what he's going to do to get back at you for that?'

'Whatever he tries, it can't be as bad as what I've organised.' I pause for effect before delivering my evil plan. 'I'm holding a karaoke party at my house on Saturday night.'

If Sully doesn't like *my* singing, wait until he hears Janine and Dave do their rendition of 'Summer Nights'.

'Remind me never to get on your bad side, bella,' Fabio says, chuckling as he pops the last cup in the tray.

'You could never be on my bad side,' I tell him. 'I'd have to find a new barista then, and we all know you're the best.'

He beams and blows me a kiss. 'Grazie, bella.'

'Hey, why don't you come to the party?' I suggest. 'The more vocal cords, the better, and you'll know most of the people as they're all regulars here.'

'I'm so sorry, but I've already got something on.'

My heart sinks. Of course he has. He'll probably be having hot sex with his even hotter boyfriend.

I can't believe I asked him anyway. What was I thinking?

He might be polite when I'm here but we're not friends. His rejection is a stark reminder that while he might be the star of all my dirty dreams, I'm nothing more than another customer to him.

'No worries,' I say, eager to get out of the café and put this embarrassing scenario behind me.

The highlight of an otherwise frustrating week is when Laura comes into the library and seeks me out in the adult fiction section. I recognise her immediately.

'Lola loved the books,' she shrieks and then slaps her hand over her mouth. 'Sorry.'

I smile. 'It's okay. The days of libraries being deadly silent are long gone. You should be here tomorrow morning when we have thirty-odd toddlers in for Story Time.'

'Sounds terrifying.' She visibly shudders. 'I was wondering if you could recommend some more novels. The . . . the cancer ones were good, but she really liked the other one, about the movies. Have you got anything else by that author?'

'We sure do,' I say, gesturing for her to follow me. I pluck *The Do-Over* and *Mr. Wrong Number* from the shelves and notice an Elena Armas shelved incorrectly.

'What's that?' Laura asks as I tuck it under my arm to take back.

'*The Spanish Love Deception.* It has a cult following on TikTok, but it's supposed to be in the adult romance section.'

'Do you think Lola would like that too? The cover is fun.'

I nod. 'It's very popular with teenage girls, but I've got to admit it's a little bit steamy.'

'I'll take it,' Laura says, plucking the book from me and popping it onto her pile. 'I'd rather her be getting her sexual education from books than porn.'

'I agree. I'm always saying we should make teenage boys read romance novels at school.'

Laura chuckles. 'I love it, although I'm not sure my son would.'

'And what about you?' I ask. 'Did you get a chance to read the book I gave you?'

She nods, looking a little sheepish. 'I finished it in a few days. Not much housework got done in that time.'

'It's practically a sin to waste time vacuuming and ironing when there are so many good books in the world.'

'The book was so relatable – I loved both the main characters – and it's funny you chose that one, because I once accidentally switched shoes with someone myself.'

'Oh, really?' I ask.

'Yeah. Years ago, I was at an interschool swimming carnival and took the wrong bag home from the changeroom. Mum spent ages trying to track down the real owner, and when she did, it turned out to be the daughter of someone she went to high school with. They reconnected and are still friends today.'

'That's so cool.'

Laura smiles. 'Do you have any other recommendations for me?'

'You might regret asking me, because if there's one thing I always have, it's book recommendations.'

As we trawl through the fiction shelves, I ask her more about Lola.

Laura tells me that Lola was diagnosed with acute lympho-blastic leukaemia late last year and has been in and out of hospital for chemotherapy ever since. 'She has intensive times where she's an inpatient for about a week, and then has some time at home to rest and recover before the next session.'

'Is she still able to go to school in between?'

Laura shakes her head. 'Not yet. The risk of infection is too high and she's very tired. She'd never last a whole day, but the school have been great about giving her just enough work to keep her on track but not overwhelm her, and her friends have been keeping her updated with the gossip and visiting her when possible. Once this induction period is over, her chemo will be more spread out, so maybe then she'll be able to go back part-time.'

I make a mental note to look up the prognosis for Lola's cancer. I might not have met her but she sounds sweet and Laura is so lovely, I can't bear the thought of her losing her daughter. 'I really hope she likes these books as much as the others, and I hope you enjoy those.' I nod at *The Invisible Husband of Frick Island* by Colleen Oakley and *Eligible* by Curtis Sittenfeld. 'They're two of my favourites.'

'I've no doubt.' Laura smiles. 'Thanks, and see you next time.'

I head back to the desk, where I'm halfway through unpacking new books, with a spring in my step. Aside from giving recommendations and converting new readers, this is one of the best parts of my job. It's like Christmas, going through the box and thinking about which of my favourite patrons I'm going to recommend all the different novels to.

11

Everything Can Change in a Moment

The party is supposed to start at seven and my guests arrive promptly.

'Is he home?' Fred asks as she dances through the door. There's a guy I don't recognise right behind her, but he's wearing a T-shirt that reads, *The book was better than the movie*, so I approve.

'I think so,' I say as I usher everyone inside, JB so excited he doesn't know who to greet first. 'His car's there and he was out back playing with his basketball this arvo,' I say, as I usher everyone inside.

The karaoke machine I've hired is set up in my living room, which is only just big enough to fit everyone. I considered putting it out the back, but my porch is tiny and besides, this time of the year the mosquitos would drive us insane.

'What can I get you all to drink?' I ask.

Persephone waves a hand in the air. 'Plenty of time for drinking. Presents first.'

It's then I realise that as well as alcohol and plates of food – Rory can't go anywhere without bringing dessert – they're also holding gifts.

'You didn't need to bring anything. It's not my birthday.' Although who doesn't like presents?

'Isn't this a piss-off-the-neighbour party?' Persephone says, thrusting her present at me. When I nod, she adds, 'Well, parties equal presents. And this one is particularly appropriate for the occasion.'

Curious, I unwrap the paper and pull out what looks like a baby mobile with little moons, stars and suns made of metal hanging from it. It's *very* Persephone. 'Windchimes?'

She smiles widely. 'Yep. Xavier told us that when their neighbour got some, it almost made Rory homicidal.'

Rory nods and visibly shudders. 'Nasty things.'

I'm confused until I open Janine's. In a funny not-coincidence, she too has given me windchimes – hers are an upside-down triangle of dragonflies, with tiny bells beneath each one. They're stunning.

'Persephone tells me the dragonflies symbolise transformation and rebirth,' Janine says.

'And I thought that was a load of bollocks,' Dave says with a shake of his head, 'so I bought you these.' He hands me a box.

'Thank you,' I say, chuckling as I pull yet another set of windchimes out of the box.

'When Xavier told us he was going to get you some to help annoy *your* neighbour, we decided we should all do the same,' adds Fred. 'After all, what's more annoying than one set of windchimes?'

'More than one,' everyone choruses.

By the time I've finished unwrapping everyone's gifts, I have chimes made of metal, wood, glass, shells, porcelain and even some made from a bunch of old cookie cutters. Eight sets of windchimes all up.

'Thank you.' I grin. 'I love you guys so much.'

'Here, give them to me,' Dave says, holding out his hands. 'Nick and I will hang them up for you. Back or front?'

'Why not half and half?'

He chuckles – 'I like your style, young lady' – and he and Nick head outside, while the rest of us crack open the drinks and get stuck into the singing.

'I googled a list of the most annoying karaoke songs,' Persephone announces, holding up her phone. 'Let's get this party started.'

'How can our singing not have lured the beast out of his lair?' Fred asks from over by the fence where she, Rory and Persephone are blatantly staring into Sully's backyard.

Her latest hook-up, Ricky, who is doing a PhD in Marine Biology, is currently playing UNO with Dave, Xavier and Nick on the back patio. He fits in well with our little gang, but I'm not silly enough to think that means anything. Sometimes I feel like Fred is ticking off an imaginary list of book boyfriends – just this year she's been with a jock (trapeze guy), a single dad, a bad boy and even a phlebotomist, who I'm calling her vampire. Ricky is your typical hot professor with a side of cinnamon roll – only she doesn't read romance.

'Are you sure he's home?' Persephone calls to me, before sipping from a water bottle. She's still not feeling a hundred per cent so is steering clear of alcohol tonight. 'I can't believe I gave up Netflix and Chill for this.'

I have to agree – it has been an uneventful evening. We've gone through Persephone's 'Most Annoying Karaoke' songs list three times – crooning 'My Way' by Frank Sinatra, 'American Pie', 'Steal My Sunshine' and many more as loudly as we can – and nothing. I'd been hoping when the singing started, Sully would growl obscenities and shout threats at everyone so they could see what I have to put up with, but there hasn't been one sound from next door. No cat strangling. No basketball. Not even a flicker of his curtains.

'Maybe he went out,' Dave suggests.

'But his car's still there,' I counter.

'He could be at his girlfriend's or something,' Nick suggests, then shouts, 'UNO!'

'No way,' Ricky grumbles. 'Are you sure you're not cheating?'

'Maybe Persephone put a hex on you.' Dave laughs – he finds the fact that she identifies as a witch hugely amusing.

I shake my head, wanting to focus on the real problem here. '*That* guy does *not* have a girlfriend.' Who in their right mind would put up with him?

'I reckon he's messing with you,' Persephone says, looking up towards the roof. 'Do you have security cameras? We could check them to be sure he hasn't left.'

'No.'

Janine rests her wineglass on my outdoor table. 'Living here all by yourself, you really should have cameras.'

'I can sort some out for you through work,' Nick offers. 'Get you a special deal.'

'Good idea,' Persephone says, then clicks her fingers at him. 'Come on, we're going home. I told the babysitter we'd be back by eleven.'

I hug her as she picks up her bag. 'Sorry we didn't even get a glimpse of him.'

'Hey, don't mind me, I'm just tired,' she says, squeezing my hand.

They leave and Fred and Ricky follow soon after.

Janine, Dave, Xavier and Rory stay to help me clean up and put my house back together.

'I really like Ricky,' Xavier says with a sigh as he unplugs the karaoke machine.

'Me too,' Rory says.

'Don't get attached,' I warn with a smirk.

They both laugh, then Xavier says, 'His talk of his PhD got me thinking.'

'Oh?' Rory and I ask in unison.

'Yeah, I'm wondering if I should do a Masters or something. I figure having another piece of paper will increase my chances of promotion.'

'Are you after my job?' Janine calls from the kitchen where she's loading the dishwasher. Her jokey tone indicates she's not threatened.

'As if you'll ever retire,' Dave says, something like bitterness in his voice.

'Just because you're ready to play golf three times a week and sit around at home watching footy doesn't mean I want to waste my golden years doing the same.'

'That's not what I want—'

Xavier, Rory and I look anxiously at each other, like three kids whose parents are fighting, but this turns out to be the least of our worries when we hear a shattering noise.

'Dave! Are you okay?' Janine shrieks.

The rest of us rush into the kitchen to see Dave's hand against his head. One of my dinner plates is in pieces on the floor.

I look to Janine. 'Did you throw that at him?'

Dave shakes his head. 'Sorry . . . Got a . . . headache.' His words are slurred despite the fact that he's only had a couple of beers, and I realise that he must have dropped the plate.

'Dave?' Janine says again, her voice high-pitched.

'Maybe sit down?' I suggest, but when Dave tries to cross to the table, he stumbles.

Xavier and Rory catch him and lead him over, helping him into a chair.

'Can you smile?' Xavier asks.

Dave attempts to do so but only one side of his mouth lifts.

'Okay.' Xavier nods. 'Now what about raising your hands?'

Again, Dave tries to follow the instruction and fails. Only one arm lifts properly.

'Oh, God,' Janine says, her face turning pale as she cottons on – she and Xavier are the library's first aid officers. 'You think he's having a stroke?'

'I think we should call an ambulance just to be on the safe side,' Xavier replies gravely.

As we wait for the paramedics, Dave's symptoms only get worse, and as Janine sits close and whispers that he's going to be okay, I pray like crazy that she's right.

12

Noise-cancelling Headphones

After learning that Dave did have a stroke Saturday night, we're all surprised to see Janine when we arrive for work on Tuesday morning. She looks exhausted – there are grey bags under her eyes, and she's not even bothered with her lipstick.

'It could be worse,' she explains. 'The doctors say he has a good chance of a near-full recovery. There'll be lots of rehab; he won't be home for another week or so, and even then he'll require care, so I'm afraid I've had to put in for a few months' family leave.'

Although this isn't a shock, we all give a little gasp, because Janine *is* this library. It's her energetic and bubbly personality that makes it so fun to work here – that and the books, of course.

'Do they give you enough leave for that?' Xavier asks, always with the logical questions.

Janine scoffs. 'Course not. I'm going to take some of my long service leave as well.'

My heart breaks for Janine, and for Dave, who must feel helpless.

'Is there anything we can do?' Persephone asks. 'Drop round some meals? Clean the house? Mow the lawn?'

'Thank you,' Janine says, 'but I think all that's covered. What I need from you lot is to keep this place running. I'm sorry, Xavier, but I'm hoping you'll take charge. There's no budget for a replacement for me, but hopefully some of the casual library assistants won't mind a few extra shifts.'

He nods. 'Don't worry about anything. I promise I'll take good care of this place for you. We all will.'

The rest of us mutter our agreement, and then Janine looks to me. 'Don't suppose you've read *Horse* by Geraldine Brooks, have you?'

I shake my head, wondering what this has to do with anything.

'It's the next Bookstars novel,' she says. 'You should have plenty of time to read it before book club next week, but I can also email you my notes.'

Is she kidding? Speedreading is my other superpower. 'You want *me* to take over the Bookstars?'

She nods and I choke up a little.

The Bookstars, as they call themselves, are the members of our senior citizens' book club, which happens in the library every second Wednesday afternoon. They're Janine's pride and joy and I feel honoured that she'd trust me with them.

'Xavier is going to have enough on his hands,' she says, 'and Persephone doesn't read enough fiction.' She's our non-fiction librarian, obsessed with all things true crime, self-help and new age. 'And Fred . . .' Janine looks apologetically at her.

Fred laughs. 'I say what I think and swear too much to be let loose on the OAPs.'

We don't let her near the under-tens either.

'You don't mind, do you?' Janine asks me. 'If you don't like the books I've chosen for the next few months, I'm sure the Bookstars won't mind a few changes. Just nothing too racy – years ago we read

Fifty Shades of Grey because the members wanted to know what the fuss was all about, and we had to use the defibrillator on Lorna.'

Xavier winces. 'I remember that.'

The truth is I might be more comfortable discussing E.L. James than the likes of Geraldine Brooks and Margaret Atwood, but I'll put my all into this role. 'I'm sure the books you've already chosen are fine and I wouldn't want to upset the group by bringing in a whole new list of books. They'll already be upset enough about me replacing you.'

'Aw, sweetheart. They'll love you.' Janine's voice is rich with emotion. 'And it'll be easier leaving them, knowing they're in such good hands. Thank you.'

'It's my pleasure.' I'll just have to remember not to wear any low-cut tops on Wednesdays, so as not to encourage Edgar.

'Good. That's settled, then.' She lets out a deep, slow breath. 'I'm going to stay for a few hours and wrap up some things before I leave you all in the lurch.'

While everyone goes about their jobs, I head to the shelves to grab the next few Bookstar books. Even if I'm slightly scared of the members, I'm determined to be prepared.

I work till close that evening, and the way JB greets me as I walk through the door, you'd think I've been gone a month, not merely since lunchtime.

'It's lovely to see you too,' I say, bestowing a hundred cuddles on him.

After letting him out for a pit-stop, I take a quick shower before pouring myself a glass of wine to drink in bed while I start reading *Horse*. I've barely settled myself under the sheet – it's still too hot for more than a light covering – when Sully's horrendous noise starts up next door.

Not again. This can't be a coincidence – he must have heard me come in. I no longer have any doubt that he's doing this to annoy me.

JB gives me a look that says he too has had enough, then jumps down off the bed and slinks out of the room. I know he's heading for the pantry – he's recently discovered it's the most soundproof place in the house. I'm not sure whether it's because I'm already feeling unsettled after everything that's happened with Dave and Janine, the fact that I can't relax without JB at my feet, or that one human can only put up with so much cat-torturing before they snap, but I've had e-bloody-nough!

Throwing back the sheet, I launch myself out of bed, march into the kitchen and pop my head into the pantry. 'Come on, Puppy Stuff. We're going to see the neighbour.'

As if he understands, JB gives me a look of terror and/or awe, but he opts to stay in the pantry until the deed is done.

Thump, thump, thump!

My hand stings as I pound on the door and wait for Sully to hear, but of course this is a futile hope. If I can't hear myself think, how is he supposed to hear me?

Giving it next to no thought, I put my hand on the knob and turn. It opens! Before I know it, I find myself stepping right into his living room to find him standing in the middle of it, his back to me. He's kind of swaying, and although I can't work out what exactly he's doing, I can confirm the sound isn't a ghost. He's definitely the one making it.

Holy sugar. What the hell am I doing? Is it breaking and enter-ing if the door is unlocked? My heart pounds.

I'm frozen, deliberating what to do next when the noise shudders to a stop and Sully turns to face me, the warm breeze from the open door alerting him to my presence.

His eyes widen. 'What the hell are you doing in my house?'

It's déjà vu from the night we met.

'I . . . I . . .' What on earth is wrapped around his torso?

'Have you been drinking?' he asks.

He must have the nose of a hound. 'Only a few sips of wine – not that it's any of your business. More to the point, what are *you* doing?'

'What am *I* doing?' His gaze drops to my legs, bare from mid-thigh down as I stand there in my shorty (really short) pjs and tank top (no bra) that Mum and Dad gave me for Christmas.

I swallow. Why didn't I think to cover myself before I stormed over? Still, I refuse to let what Sullen Sully may be thinking about my size 14 thighs distract me from my mission.

'Yes, what is *that*?' I point to the thing tied around his chest like some kind of medieval torture device. 'And what are you trying to do with it?'

'These,' he says, 'are bagpipes. And I'm trying to learn how to play them. At least I was before I was rudely interrupted.'

I can't help myself. I laugh. 'No, they're not. I've seen bagpipes before and if someone sold those to you and said they were, then I'm sorry to say you were ripped off.'

He sighs, lifts a hand and runs it through his hair. 'These are Northumbrian bagpipes.' Before I can say anything, he adds, 'Smaller than Scottish ones, and quieter too.'

Quieter? What a joke. And, far less sexy. Also – sadly – Sully is not wearing a kilt, but board shorts and an old Quiksilver T-shirt, so I'm not sure exactly what the point of them is. 'Well, whatever they are, can you find somewhere else to practise them? I'm trying to read and it's impossible with you making such a noise.'

In reply, Sully unclips the ugly thing and puts it down on his coffee table. I think I've won, until he says, 'Wait there,' and heads into what I presume is his bedroom – our houses are carbon copies of each other. I've barely got time to snoop before he returns and hands me a pair of giant headphones.

'What are these for?' I ask.

'They're noise-cancelling.'

This is his solution? 'And you're giving them to me?'

'No, I'm showing them to you. These are mine. They work a treat – I left a five-star review on their website when you had that god-awful karaoke party.'

I *knew* he was home. This victorious thought only lasts a second.

'Get yourself a pair and my music won't bother you,' he adds.

'Music?' I snort out a laugh. The man's delusional.

Sully glares at me and snatches the headphones back. 'Now, do you mind?' He gestures to his front door, which is still wide open.

Without another word, I flee – I suppose I should be grateful that he doesn't call the police.

You'll never guess what? I text Fred all the details as I head back to my place.

So, does this mean he's a musician? she replies. *That would account for the weird hours he keeps, and the grouchiness. All rock stars have a chip on their shoulder.*

I laugh so hard that JB emerges from the pantry and looks at me, his head cocked to one side.

Well, if he is a musician, he's a horrendous one! When I asked him to stop, he suggested I buy soundproof headphones.

The bloody nerve of him!

I know. I have a good mind to buy some and send him the bill.

13

When Hell Freezes Over

Thursday night, post kickboxing, I'm flicking through the mail while making eggs on toast for dinner. As usual, there's nothing exciting – junk mail and an official-looking letter from the Fremantle Shire. It's not rates time, so I tear it open and frown at the letterhead of the environmental health officer.

My jaw drops open as I read.

Dear Ms Jones

I'm writing to let you know that we have received a complaint from a nearby resident who says they are being disturbed by noise from your home resulting from an excessive number of windchimes.

I have today investigated this accusation and discerned that there are multiple windchimes hanging around your property, which is definitely excessive and falls under the category of noise pollution. The shire asks that you remove all but two of the offending items or we will be forced to take further action.

Thank you for your cooperation in this matter. I will return early next week to ensure this request has been carried out.

Yours sincerely,

M. Roper – Environmental Health Officer, Fremantle Shire.

The toast pops as I screw up the piece of paper.

This means war!

I'm still annoyed when Xavier hands out the drinks the following morning.

'What's up your nose?' he asks.

'Sully put in a noise complaint to the Shire about her,' Fred explains. I'd been on the phone half the night ranting to her about it.

Xavier's eyes widen. 'Wow. So did you take them down?'

'Hell no!' I've always been a rule follower and pride myself on being a good neighbour, so it took a lot of willpower not to imme-diately obey the authoritarian request, but . . . 'I refuse to kowtow to The Grouch Next Door. No one else has a problem with them, and even I'm starting to quite like them.'

Okay, that's a lie – the incessant clanging and tinkling has got so much into my head I hear them even when I'm not home – but I ordered some of those expensive noise-cancelling headphones from Officeworks last night and they are due for delivery today, so hope-fully I can put up with them a little longer for the greater good.

'That's my girl!' Fred grins as she lifts her green juice in a toast. 'Take that, Sullen Sully. So what are you going to do to get back at him this time?'

'Well, I did a little research this morning . . .' They all lean in eagerly; no librarian can resist an investigation story. 'It turns out Sully's breaking the law with his ghastly attempts at learning the wannabe bagpipes. Local regulation states that you're not allowed to practise a musical instrument in a domestic residence for more than an hour a day and only between the hours of 7 am and 7 pm Monday to Saturday, and 9 am and 7 pm on Sundays.'

'Oh dear,' Xavier says. 'I'd better warn Rory – sometimes he plays the piano late at night when he can't sleep.'

'I'm going to report *him* to the shire for noise pollution – two can play at that game.'

'That's good. But is it enough?' Fred clicks her fingers. 'I've got an idea. You could sign him up to all sorts of junk mail catalogues – his letterbox will be inundated, and he'll never be able to prove it's you.'

'You're terrible!' I squeal. 'But I love it. When I was little, Mum joined us up to this Sunday School via correspondence – I wonder if that's still a thing. Maybe the Lord can teach him about loving thy neighbour.'

Persephone snorts out a laugh. 'Do places even send physical catalogues any more? I thought everything was online.'

I shrug. 'I don't know, but you bet I'm going to find out.'

'Maybe you should just leave him be,' Xavier suggests.

I glare at him. 'You were the one who came up with the wind-chimes idea!'

He nods. 'Yes, but you have to live next to the bloke, and neighbourly disputes can get ugly. You could just bake him another cake and propose a truce.'

'Good idea,' I say. 'When hell freezes over.'

Later, Xavier is on lunch and Fred is weeding the collection of damaged books when I call over to her and ask, 'Can you watch the desk? I need to pee.'

She nods and I head to the staff bathroom.

As we don't have a huge number of employees, it's rare to bump into anyone else in here, but when I enter, one of the cubicles is already occupied and there's a pungent aroma of vomit.

I clear my throat. 'Um . . . is everything okay in there?'

'Yeah, fine,' moans a voice.

'Persephone?' I think of the croissant she scoffed earlier and all the other food I've seen her devouring lately. *OMG!* Is this how she stays so thin after birthing two babies?

I lock the door, so we won't be interrupted.

'Bee, what are you doing?' she asks as she hears the click.

'How long has this been going on?'

She flushes and then the door opens. I'm expecting denial but instead she says, 'About six weeks,' and then crosses to the sink to wash her mouth.

Okay, so not that long. *Good.* And it's also a good thing she isn't denying she has a problem. 'I can help you,' I say. Only Fred knows about my history, but I'm prepared to share it with Persephone if it can help.

'Why?' She looks at me. 'Do you know a miracle cure for morning sickness?'

Morning sickness? I start to laugh as relief washes over me. 'You're pregnant?!'

'Yes.' She looks at me like I've grown three heads. 'What did you think was going on?'

'I . . . Never mind.' Now is not the time to explain, so I throw my arms around her. 'Wow! Congratulations!'

'Hush.' She glares at me. 'Nick and I agreed not to tell anyone until three months. Honestly, I thought you lot would have guessed when I stopped drinking coffee and didn't drink any booze at your party, but for a bunch of librarians, you can be a bit thick.'

I chuckle. 'Well, we didn't know you were trying.'

'We weren't, not that I'd have told you if we were. *Some* things are private.' She places a hand on her stomach. 'This little bundle was a surprise.'

I raise an eyebrow. 'How's Nick dealing with that?'

'He needed a three-day lie-down when we first found out. We thought we were finished breeding and the light at the end of the sleepless nights and Duplos spread over the floor was in sight, but he's come round and now we're both excited.'

'I'm so glad,' I say, giving her a quick hug. 'So happy for you both. When are you due?'

'September sixteenth.' She gestures to the door. 'I'm ten weeks, realised when we were on holiday. But now that you know, I may as well tell the others. This last month trying to keep mum has been hell!'

I4

Once in a Blue Moon

'Oh my,' I say as Fred and I step inside the bustling Freo Markets on Saturday morning. As usual, it's jam-packed with people, conflicting noises of chatter, buskers and stall owners calling out bargains. I inhale the scents of spices, sizzling meat, incense, scented soaps and coffee beans, just a few of the enticing aromas and mouth-watering delicacies on offer. 'I always forget how much I love this place.'

'Me too,' Fred says as she starts towards a stall selling Sin Gin.

'Hey, we're supposed to be looking for a gift for Janine.' After everything she's been through this last week, we decided to buy her a little pep-me-up. 'Besides, isn't it a bit early for alcohol?'

'It's always five o'clock somewhere in the world,' Fred tells me, before fluttering her eyelashes at the big burly guy with dark-brown dreadlocks behind the gin counter. 'What do you recommend?'

'A little bit of everything,' he replies with a wink.

Before I know it, I too am sampling the seven deadly sins made by one of Perth's many artisan distillers. When I was a kid, I thought only grandmas drank gin, but now . . . 'Wow. That's delicious,' I say, downing a shot of Pride.

Fred leaves with the gin guy's phone number and I leave with a bottle of pink gin, because I always feel guilty for not buying something after I've sampled it.

After half an hour of ambling around, oohing and ahhing over handcrafted earrings, sampling dozens of hand-made creams and face lotions, and buying a book-scented candle in a gorgeous glass jar for Janine, Fred exclaims, 'All this shopping has worked up an appetite. Fancy an Eggspot?'

'When do I ever not fancy an Eggspot?'

Fred laughs as we wander into the food hall. We place our orders at the counter and then step back out of the way to wait for our numbers to be called.

'So do you have a date tonight?' I ask.

It's rare Fred has a free Saturday night, which is why we often hang out during the day, but I don't hear her reply because my heart shoots to my throat and I almost swallow my tongue as I recognise the man joining the queue to order.

Grabbing Fred's arm, I drag her into the clothing store behind us.

'Ouch,' she says. 'Have you lost your mind?'

'It's him! Sully,' I whisper-yell. 'He's at the Eggspot counter.'

'What?' Fred spins around to take a look. 'Which one?'

'He's second in the queue,' I say as the elderly gentleman before him steps aside and Sully moves forward to place his order.

'OMG. He's way hotter than you made out!'

I slam my hand over her mouth. 'Shut up! He'll hear you.'

She shakes me off and peers around a row of what Mum would call hippy skirts to take a better look. 'Holy mother of Mary. He's spectacular.'

'Really? You think he's *that* good looking?'

'How can you not?'

'Well . . . he's no Fabio.'

She rolls her eyes. 'No one is as hot as Fabio, but personally I like a guy that's a little more real, slightly rough around the edges. Rugged.'

Sully doesn't appear to have shaved and probably doesn't wash his clothes; I swear he's wearing the same T-shirt and shorts he was wearing the other day to clean the roof.

'I certainly wouldn't mind him roughing me up a little,' she says, giggling. 'I'm going to use him for inspiration for a character in my book. Ana is getting a little bit bored with the cannibal.'

'How can you get bored with a cannibal?' I ask, hoping to distract her from Sully.

'He doesn't look like a psychopath,' she says, ignoring my question.

'How would you know what a psychopath looks like?'

A guy behind the counter calls our numbers in quick succession.

I thrust my ticket at Fred – 'You collect mine' – and she flounces forward.

I don't know why I'm nervous – perhaps it's just that I wasn't expecting to see him here, or that I don't want him to catch a whiff of the alcohol on my breath.

Does gin even smell?

He already thinks I'm a loony alcoholic.

Why do I even care what he thinks?

Oh, no. Fred's turning towards Sully. From my hiding spot, I can't see her face, but I know by the way she tucks some of her hair behind her ear that she's entering flirt mode. I can see his face though, and his expression tells me he isn't much impressed.

'You're right. What a tosspot,' Fred says as she returns.

I take my food from her. 'What happened? What did you say?'

'I asked him if he was new around here or a tourist as I hadn't seen him before. When he grunted "new", I asked if he wanted to grab a drink sometime, and do you know what he said? He *said*, "I'd prefer not." What the hell does that mean? He'd be lucky to have a drink with me.'

'He would be,' I say, managing not to laugh because I know she doesn't find this funny. Only once in a blue moon does a single guy turn Fred down.

Then again, we don't know he's single. Either way, I'm pleased it's not just me he's rude to. 'I hope you weren't really considering going out with him. Your loyalties are supposed to lie with me.'

'They do. But I thought it might be good for you to have a girl on the inside. Anyway, I need to go home and write.'

'Good luck.' I kiss her on the cheek. 'Hope you get all the words.'

When I emerge, Sully has disappeared but I'm stealth-like as I leave the markets, not wanting to run into him again. I go home and eat my Eggspot, which tastes utterly to die for. I can't believe I once had the willpower to deprive myself of such delights.

Afterwards, I curl up with JB on the couch to read Lucy Score's *Things We Hide from the Light*. I've lost track of how many times I've read it but it's the perfect weekend read, never failing to make me smile.

If only I could find a boyfriend like Nash Morgan.

15

Rumpelstiltskin

'Bee, phone call for you on line two,' Xavier announces, coming over to the borrowing desk where our regular, Edgar, who refuses to learn how to use the self-serve check-out kiosks, is waiting with some DVDs.

To be honest, the way he talks to my chest makes me uncomfortable and I'm grateful when Xavier offers to take over. 'How are you today, Edgar?' I hear him say as I move away to answer the call.

'Hello? Bridget speaking.'

'Is that Bridget *Jones*?' The deep voice on the other end of the line laughs. 'How's that diary of yours going?'

My jaw tightens as I close my eyes. I can't be rude because for all I know this man is someone higher up in the WA Library Service or a borrower. 'Yes, how can I help?'

'My name is Mark Roper, the local environmental health officer.' Suddenly I've forgotten the way he scoffed at my name, delighted he's responding to me so quickly. I only sent my email Friday afternoon. 'I'm calling regarding your complaint against Dr Sullivan at 3A.'

Dr Sullivan! Internally I squeal, then, thinking quickly, say, 'Oh, you mean James?' He looks like a James, right? And *doctor*? Aren't doctors supposed to be good people?

'No, Dr Michael Sullivan.'

Michael? Sully doesn't look like a Michael, but I can't help grinning. I feel like I've just guessed Rumpelstiltskin's name.

'Oh, yes, sorry,' I say, 'that's what I meant.'

'Well . . . I'm afraid, Bridget,' he replies in a tone I don't like at all, 'there's not much I can do about your complaint without any evidence.'

What?! I stop smiling. 'But I sent you the soundbite via email. What more evidence do you need?'

'The recording was time-stamped 5.48 pm and was only twenty-three seconds. Local regulation states a person is allowed to play an instrument before seven pm on a weeknight as long as it's not for more than one hour all up.'

What? I can't believe this. 'But he went much longer than that; I just stopped recording. He's constantly playing that ridiculous thing at all hours of the day. And for way longer than an hour all up!'

At least it certainly feels that way.

'Please don't yell,' Mark says. 'I'm sorry if you don't like what I'm telling you, but unless I have evidence that Dr Sullivan is violating local regulations, there's nothing I can do about it.'

'What kind of evidence?'

Mark sighs. 'I suggest you keep a logbook, recording whenever you hear the music – day, time, how long it goes for. Bring me your records after a couple of weeks and we'll speak again. By the way,' he adds, when I think he's about to hang up, 'I went around to investigate your accusation this morning, and noted that you haven't removed any of your windchimes – I assume you received my letter last week?'

'Yes.' I'm half-furious, half-terrified of his authority. What exactly is the punishment for ignoring official shire requests?

'And will you be taking them down?'

'Of course. Sorry.' Suddenly feeling nauseous, I rush to get the words out. 'I've been busy.'

'I'll check again tomorrow afternoon,' he threatens, before finally disconnecting the call.

Enraged, I immediately log on to my computer and sign Sully – or should I say Michael? – up to receive Ezibuy, Innovations and Pottery Barn catalogues. Who knew so many businesses still send promotional material via snail mail? When Fred first suggested the catalogue thing, I'd registered him for a few, but, after my telling off from Mark Roper, a few now doesn't feel nearly enough.

The moment I arrive home from work, I begin taking down the windchimes, one by one, starting out the back. I'm not tall enough to reach them without standing on a chair and as I do so, I almost topple off.

My squeal alerts Sully, who is on the other side of the fence faffing about with his damn basketball. 'You need any help with that?' he calls, his tone soaked with smugness.

'No, thanks, *Doctor*,' I say as I give him the finger.

Even from this distance I can see him frown, and his baffled expression brings small joy to an otherwise infuriating day.

16

What a Load of Bollocks

I've just finished setting out the Arnott's biscuits and making sure the urn is working, when the door of the function room opens and in hobbles the first book club member. She has glossy grey hair in the kind of cut most old women seem to favour, is neatly dressed in a pale pink, short-sleeved blouse and a calf-length, black corduroy skirt and is walking with the aid of a bright pink stick. I've seen her before, but don't know her name.

'You must be Bee,' the woman says in a strong English accent as I walk over to greet her. 'Janine sent us an email saying you were taking over.'

'Yes.' I smile and offer her my hand, which she accepts in her soft papery one. 'And you are?'

'Daisy Norman. Lovely to meet you.'

'You too. Where's that accent from?'

'The northeast of England. I'm a Geordie,' she says, in the same manner as one might say they're a Nobel Prize winner.

Over the course of the next ten minutes, the rest of the group arrives and sits in the circle of chairs I set out earlier. As they sip tea and munch biscuits, I ask them to introduce themselves to me, making a mental note about each person in the hope it'll help me remember their names.

Daisy immigrated with her Irish husband in the early sixties. Barbara, a retired languages teacher, is also English, but from the south, which she clearly thinks is better than the north. Her outfit is almost identical to Daisy's, and I think they must both shop at Sportscraft, like my mum. Ronice and Sue, the youngest of the group – late sixties, at a guess – tell me they're later-in-life lesbians. I smile. Do they want me to congratulate them or something? Ronice grew up in Southern Cross, then married a fisherman from 'these parts', and Sue proudly informs me her great-great-great-great-great grandfather was one of the original convicts at Fremantle Prison.

Then there's Olga, a Russian seamstress who wears her greying hair in a tight bun and peers at me over her wiry glasses in a slightly terrifying manner; Rose, who is tiny with a sunny smile and glowing cheeks; Kerry, a sheep farmer from Kojonup who moved to Perth when her husband died and her daughter took over the property; Lorna and Beth, who are both softly spoken; and of course Edgar – our only man – who has positioned himself in the seat next to mine.

'Just so you know, I'm not here to read the books,' he informs me. 'I'm here to meet the ladies.'

At this there are some tsks, a few scoffs and a couple of giggles from his fellow Bookstars.

I raise my eyebrows as he wriggles his unruly white ones. Is he flirting with *me*?

'That's no good on my watch,' I tell him. 'This isn't craft morning at the CWA – you either read or you're out. And speaking of books,' I add before he can object, tapping my copy of *Horse* on my lap, 'how did everyone find this one?'

'Magic,' Barbara exclaims, clutching her copy of the book to her chest. 'In my opinion, Geraldine Brooks can do no wrong.'

Although I wasn't particularly excited about the prospect of reading it, I have to agree – the story and the writing captivated me, and now I want to read some more of Brooks' backlist.

There are murmurings of agreement from everyone except Olga and Sue.

'I've never been a fan of horses,' Olga grumbles, 'and this horse is supposed to be zee most famous horse in America, yet nobody has ever heard of him? *Pfft.*'

'Well, that aspect is true,' Daisy objects, 'and one of the parts I found most fascinating. It just shows how important documenting history and important people is – or in this case, horses – or they are forgotten. We need to learn from the past.'

Sue shrugs. 'Never mind the horses, what about the fact that a white Aussie woman has written a book about Black slavery in America?'

'What's the problem with that?' Edgar asks, before taking a bite of what must be his fifth Iced VoVo.

'What's the problem with that?!' Sue glares at him as she throws her hands up in the air. 'Such a typical white middle-class man thing to say. Haven't you heard of Own Voices?'

He shakes his head but I'm impressed that Sue has.

'This story should only have been told by a Black American,' she says.

'That's ridiculous,' Olga interjects. 'Does that also mean a Black author can't write about white people? Or men can't write about women? Everyone is too precious zees days.'

Oh boy. I knew that the Bookstar discussions sometimes got heated, but this is happening quicker than I imagined and I don't fancy playing referee between Olga, Sue and poor Edgar, who hasn't even read the book.

Thankfully, Lorna saves the day. 'I don't know about all that political stuff, and I was never a horse girl myself growing up, but I really enjoyed the love story between Theo and Jess.' She places her hand against her chest and smiles.

'That was my favourite part too,' I admit. 'I believe any novel, in any genre, is enhanced if there's a romance subplot.'

Almost everyone agrees, but then Kerry turns the focus onto me. 'Speaking of romance, do you have a boyfriend?'

Such a personal question startles me, but before I have a chance to answer, Sue adds pointedly, 'Or girlfriend?'

Kerry looks towards my hand. 'I take it you're not married or engaged, because you're not wearing a ring.'

'My Beryl didn't always wear a ring because she was a jeweller,' Edgar says, rubbing biscuit crumbs off his chin. 'The machine she used to polish jewellery would sometimes catch on it, so it was too dangerous.'

Rose, who is sitting on his other side, pats his hand briefly, and I notice his eyes glistening with emotion. This obvious love for his late wife blindsides me, as I'd never have guessed Edgar to be so romantic, or monogamous.

'Um . . . what were we talking about again?' I'd rather a war break out between the Bookstars than get personal with them. 'The famous horse?'

'No.' Barbara dips another Kingston biscuit into her tea. 'You were telling us about your love life.'

'I was?' I let out an incredulous laugh. 'Well, that's hilarious because I don't currently have one!'

This is clearly the wrong thing to say. All thoughts of *Horse* are forgotten, and the book club members spend the rest of the hour grilling me.

They ask about my family.

'Well, I grew up on a station in the Pilbara, and my parents and two of my brothers are still up there. Brandon and Justin are married and live on houses on the property with their wives, Elsie and Kara, and their kids.' I smile at the mention of my nephews and nieces. The youngest is just a baby and I'm obsessed with her. 'Then there's Rupert. He's the youngest after me and has always been a little bit wild. He joined the army straight out of school.'

'My grandson is also in the army,' Beth mentions. 'Maybe they know each other?'

I try not to laugh – does she know how big the army is? 'Maybe.'

'You must miss your family living so far away,' Barbara says. 'Or at least, I bet your mother misses you.'

I nod. 'I do, and she does, but Mum and I talk on the phone all the time and she's kept very busy working alongside Dad and the boys, and helping with the kids.'

Next the conversation moves on to hobbies. Rose is obsessed with gardening, Daisy is a knitter and into puzzles, Kerry lists too many things for me to remember, Lorna enjoys hiking – 'or at least I did when my legs worked better' – Edgar likes watching movies and lawn bowls, Sue and Ronice are bargain hunters, Olga tells us about her beloved Chihuahua and that she races mobility scooters. I didn't even know that was a thing. Beth is very involved with her church, and me?

I shrug. 'I know it's my job, but reading is also my biggest hobby. But I've recently started kickboxing and I'm enjoying that more than I imagined.'

We talk a little about travel. Ronice and Sue are planning a trip around Australia next year, so they're interested to hear about my year of backpacking between finishing school and starting uni. 'I worked in roadhouses and pubs. Growing up on the station, we didn't get many holidays and apart from a trip to Bali, I'd never been outside of WA, so I wanted to see what the rest of Australia had to offer. My favourite spot was Tambourine Mountain in Queensland.'

But the thing they're most interested in is my love life. They can't believe I don't have a whole host of suitors.

Edgar shakes his head. 'What's wrong with the young men today?'

'You're not on those terrible app things, are you?' Olga asks, scratching her bun.

I shake my head. 'Not any more.'

Somehow the Bookstars manage to inveigle the embarrassing end to my last relationship from me.

'But that's only one bad egg,' Daisy says, shaking her head. 'You shouldn't let him make you bitter.'

'It wasn't just Kieran,' I say. 'My longest relationship before that also ended because he wasn't honest with me, and most of the guys I've dated just got bored and ghosted me.'

'Ghosted?' a few of them ask.

'It means they just stopped calling or replying to my messages,' I explain.

All the Bookstars shake their heads, appalled by this generation's behaviour.

'To be honest, I'm starting to wonder if I'm cursed because of my unfortunate name.'

Rose frowns. 'I think Bee's a lovely name, or is it short for something?'

'It's short for Bridget. And my surname is . . . Jones.'

The recognition dawns on their faces like a Mexican wave.

'Like the movie!' Edgar sounds excited that he knows this.

I don't even bother to correct him. 'Anyway, maybe like the other Bridget, I'm destined to fall for players and two-timing charmers, while my friends all turn into Smug Marrieds. Excepting Fred, that is.'

'*Bridget Curssse*,' Olga hisses. 'What a load of bollocks!'

I shrug. 'Maybe, maybe not. Now, please can we spend the last few minutes talking about the book?'

17

A Bunch of Nonnas

'*Buongiorno*, bella,' Fabio exclaims as he claps eyes on me on Thursday. 'You look tired today.'

I make a mental note to take a leaf out of Janine's book and wear a brighter lipstick tomorrow. 'I'm a little emotionally exhausted,' I say as I hand over the cups.

'Reading too many novels late into the night, or is that neighbour giving you trouble again?' The milk steamer whirrs loudly as he talks.

'No, it's not Sully this time. It's work.'

'Work?' Fabio looks confused. 'How can working with books be stressful?'

Although I smile, I'm slightly annoyed at his insinuation that my job is easy. Most people have no idea what being a librarian entails – it's a lot more than just reading and checking out books. 'It's not the books that are the problem . . .' I glance around just to make sure none of the Bookstars are in the café. 'It's the people.'

'Ah, *sì*, I can relate.' He grins as he pours the milk into Xavier's flat white. 'Not all my customers are as lovely as you.'

I laugh coyly as a warm heat floods my body. It's impossible not to glow when Fabio says something lovely. Since giving up the apps, I've had no male attention aside from JB and, as adorable and affectionate as he is, it's not quite the same.

'What are these borrowers doing to aggravate my bella?'

His bella. For a moment I forget what we're talking about. Oh, that's right. I tell him about the Bookstars. 'I was really looking forward to taking over the book club, but let's just say they're a handful.'

He pauses what he's doing as if he's itching to hear my story. 'Seniors, you say? You mean old people?'

'I doubt they'd like to hear you calling them old, but yes, the majority are retirees.'

Fabio's eyes dance in amusement. 'Don't tell me you can't handle a bunch of nonnas?'

'Hey,' I exclaim, 'you have no idea – they're more exhausting than doing Rhyme Time with toddlers.'

'How so?' he asks, placing the lids on our cups.

'Yesterday I left feeling like I'd adjudicated a high school debate and then been subjected to the Spanish Inquisition,' I say, ready to settle into the story when a middle-aged woman behind me glares at us. 'Fabio, the usual.'

The woman – who I now notice is dressed in a traffic infringement officer uniform – doesn't even say please, but the best barista on the planet doesn't glower at her like I want him to.

'I'm sorry, Karen,' he says with a warmth she definitely doesn't deserve. 'I'm on it.'

'Thanks, Fabio,' I say. 'See you soon.'

He offers me a beguiling smile. 'I can hardly wait.'

*

Not long after the library opens, one of our assistants finds me at the computer where I'm scheduling Facebook and Instagram posts for the next month.

'Are you busy?' he asks. 'There's a woman called Laura and her daughter wanting to talk to you.'

My heart leaps at this news. After a couple of weeks of recommending books for Lola, I'm excited I'm going to meet her, and I'm so glad to hear she's out of hospital. I squirt some sanitiser onto my hands, knowing how important it is for her not to catch any germs, and head out.

'Laura,' I say as I approach them, 'so good to see you. And you must be Lola?'

The blonde-haired teenager is tiny – more like the height and size of a ten-year-old – and I know from talking to Laura that she's wearing a wig. Her face is gaunt and masked, her jeans are hanging off her and, despite it being warm, she's wearing a jumper that also looks too big. She nods brightly. 'Yes. Hi. I'm so excited to meet you.'

I smile back. 'The feeling is mutual. How'd you go with the latest books?'

'OMG. *The Spanish Love Deception*! I love it. I've read it like four times already.' She presses both her hands against her chest, and, despite the mask, I can tell she's grinning. 'I'm in love with Aaron. I wish he was real. Do you have the next in the series?'

I laugh; her enthusiasm is infectious. 'Yes, I think so, but if not, we can order it in. And I know that feeling. I have several book boyfriends too.'

She giggles. 'Who's your fave?'

'Ooh, such a hard choice. It's a toss-up between Gus from *Beach Read* and Brendan from *It Happened One Summer*. I love a grumpy guy. In fiction, of course,' I clarify, thinking of my neigh-bour. 'Nothing worse in real life.'

'I'll need to get both those books, like, yesterday.'

Laura puts her hand on her daughter's shoulder and smiles. 'Lola really wanted to meet you in person to say thanks for all the joy you've brought her.'

'Yeah, I think I'd have, like, *killed* myself if not for your books.' I see Laura flinch at the words, but Lola seems oblivious. 'Can I have a look through the shelves?'

'Sure.' I point in the direction of the romance section, because we've established that she's a girl after my own heart. 'Knock your-self out.'

Laura lets out a deep sigh as Lola heads over there, slower than someone her age should. I can only imagine how exhausting it must be having a child in hospital long-term and I make a mental note to call my mum later and remind her how great she is for taking such good care of me and never giving up when I was ill. She sacrificed so much to be there for me, and while I might not have appreciated it then, I do now.

'She's so fantastic. You must be so proud,' I say. 'And great news that she's out of hospital. The treatment must be going well.'

'This is only a brief escape – she's got a couple of weeks before we start the next phase and so she's spending some time at home – but yes, the doctors are confident that the chemotherapy will work.' She sighs and glances over to where Lola is lost in the back cover of a book. 'Thank God. I don't think I could cope if . . .' Her voice drifts off and she shakes her head. 'Anyway, I can't thank you enough for what you've done for both of us these last few weeks. The books have kept us going during a really tough time. Sometimes, when Lola has been too tired to read herself, I've read aloud to her, just like I did when she and Leo were little.'

I feel such warmth in my heart hearing about this special time she's had with Lola. 'That's so great.'

Lola interrupts us then, holding up a copy of *My Roommate Is a Vampire*. 'Is this any good?'

'I haven't had the chance to read it yet,' I say.

Lola hugs the book to her chest. 'How many can I borrow?'

'As many as you like,' I say with a smile.

Even if we had a limit, I wouldn't make her stick to it.

18

Officially a Wanker

After another weekend of Sully torturing cats, shooting hoops and mowing his lawn – which he's definitely doing to annoy me because it's barely grown from last time – I'm delighted to get back to work on Monday, so much so that even the sight of Edgar lurking in the DVD section is welcome.

At least I can do something about him.

I grab a copy of *Lessons in Chemistry* by Bonnie Garmus and head over to him. 'Morning, Edgar,' I say brightly.

He turns and blinks rapidly, clutching his selection of films to his chest. 'H-h-hello, Bee.'

He sounds scared of me. Perhaps I came on a little too strong last week, but what's the point of attending a book club if you don't read the books?

Holding up the book and smiling widely, I say, 'Wasn't sure if you'd managed to get a copy of our next read yet?'

Edgar shakes his head. 'I . . . uh . . .' He looks like he's about to cry.

My heart squeezes. *Oh, God*, what have I done? I have no idea how to handle weepy old men. I glance down at his selection of films – *Top Gun: Maverick*, *Knives Out* and *The Boys*. 'I loved *Knives Out*. Everything about it is perfect – the writing, the acting, even the music.'

His expression brightens. 'It's brilliant. This is actually a rewatch.'

We spend a few minutes discussing our favourite parts of it and other movies we both enjoy. Although I'd always rather be reading than watching, at least one in five dates I go on seem to involve going to movies, and whenever my brother Rupert is in town we have a movies and pizza night. Then I finally broach the topic I originally intended.

'Have you read *any* of the Bookstar books?'

Edgar doesn't meet my gaze, his thick black spectacles slipping down his blotchy nose as he looks to the ground. 'To be honest, I'm not much of a reader.'

'So why are you part of the book club?'

Now that I'd spent that hour with him, I wasn't sure I believed his line about being there for the ladies. Surely if it's about picking up women, he could do it someplace else. There must be a dating app for seniors. And he clearly has a social life, because he mentioned playing lawn bowls.

He sighs deeply as if I've cornered him. 'My Beryl was the reader. She used to come here twice a week and borrow half-a-dozen books. Always had her nose in a novel, and we'd talk about whatever she was reading over breakfast. Near the end, when she couldn't come by herself, I'd bring her in her wheelchair and . . .' He pauses and wriggles his nose as if warding off tears again. 'When she died, coming here made me feel like I hadn't lost her completely.'

Damn. Now Edgar isn't the only one close to tears. How had I never noticed this elderly couple? Did Janine know his story? If so, she could have warned me.

'I'm so sorry,' I say, reaching out to touch his arm. 'How long ago did she pass?'

He finally meets my gaze. 'Six months. Hardest six months of my life. We did everything together. That's why when I heard about the Bookstars, I thought maybe hearing the women chat about books – about the plots and the characters the way Beryl used to – would make me . . .'

He doesn't finish his sentence, emotion getting the better of him.

As he digs into his pocket for a neatly pressed, blue handkerchief, I blurt, 'You can keep coming. It doesn't matter if you read the books or not.'

How I'm speaking around the tennis-ball sized lump in my throat, I have no clue.

'Really?' Edgar looks up at me like I've just offered him a million dollars.

I nod – 'I'll see you next Wednesday' – and then hurry to the office to grab a tissue.

I'd almost forgotten my act of signing up Sully to receive catalogues until I arrive home for lunch to see such a large bunch of them sticking out of his letterbox that the flap can't even close. I can't describe the immense glee this brings me.

That so many have arrived on one day makes my evil plan even sweeter.

I'm humming as I open the gate, but even before it clinks shut, Sully's front door opens, and I struggle to contain giggles as he strides towards his letterbox. He's so tall, it only takes two steps.

Lingering, I bend down to reposition one of my beloved gnomes, angling my head to watch his reaction as he yanks out the A4-sized envelopes. 'That's a lot of catalogues you've got there.' I deserve an Oscar for keeping a straight face. 'Not very good for the planet. Haven't you heard of online shopping?'

I'm rewarded by his signature scowl as he storms back into the house and am grinning ridiculously as I head into mine.

I hug JB, let him outside, make myself some beans on toast and then sit down to eat on the back verandah. It's starting to cool now, but after being in the recycled air of the library all morning, I'm enjoying the freshness.

My bliss is short-lived. I've barely had two bites of lunch when JB rushes over to the fence and starts barking. Sully's 'music' has kicked off again.

I storm back inside to the kitchen bench where I've left the logbook Mark Roper recommended I keep, and pick up my pen. So far, my records look like this:

LOG BOOK Tuesday
7.14 am 31 minutes
1.10 pm 17 minutes
6.48 pm 12 minutes

LOG BOOK Wednesday
7.01 am 22 minutes
11.14 am 33 minutes
6.55 pm 5 minutes

Every single entry adds up to exactly one hour – unless he's sneaking in some sessions when I'm out – and he never plays outside of regulated times.

LOG BOOK Saturday

9.01 am 15 minutes

10.56 am 9 minutes of pure torture

1.10 pm 7 minutes. Now he's moved into the backyard and is playing shirtless.

3.52 pm 21 minutes

6.51 pm 7 minutes

The only thing I can assume is that Mr Roper warned him.

Grr. Talk about men sticking together. I throw the pen across the room, the buzz I'd got from seeing the catalogues in Sully's letterbox withering away. Is there even any point to this?

All I've proved is that my neighbour is officially a wanker!

19

The Great Gnome Kidnapping

'What's that?' Fred asks as I dig out my key to open my front door on Wednesday evening. She's dragging me along to some book launch tonight at the Norfolk Hotel, and since my place is closer to the pub, she's getting ready here before we go.

'Huh?' I glance down to where she's pointing at my welcome mat and see an envelope sticking out from under it. On the front in cut-out newspaper letters, like you see in bad crime movies, is the word 'RANSOM'.

'What the fuck?' Fred's words echo my thoughts.

Handing her my key, I tear open the envelope and yank out a piece of paper, also covered in cut-out letters.

IF YOU DON'T PUT AN END TO THE CATALOGUES,
THE GNOMES GET IT.

Enclosed with the threat is a photo printed on cheap paper of three of my darling gnomes tied up with rope. Somehow, he's managed to nab my favourites – a gnome on a stack of books, one sitting on the toilet reading and the other with his pants down and the word 'Welcome' scrawled across his bum.

'I can't believe it,' I cry, whirling round to see if any others are missing. I survey my bright flowers in pots and the gnomes I'd inherited from my grandma scattered around them. All present except the three in the photo.

'What's going on?' asks Fred.

I thrust the letter and photo at her and immediately start gathering my remaining gnomes. 'Open the door. We need to get all these'—and the ones out the back—'inside now. And then I'll need your help to bury Sully's body.'

'You think *he* did this?' Fred chuckles as she reads the letter.

'Of course it's him,' I say, my arms already too full of gnomes. There'd been more catalogues in his letterbox yesterday and at lunchtime today. Perhaps I did go a little overboard, but I didn't think they'd all arrive so quickly. 'You don't think I have *two* psychos trying to make my life a living hell, do you? And it's not funny.'

As she opens the door and JB bursts out, excited we have a visitor, she says, 'To be fair, you're trying to make his life hell too and it is a *little* funny.'

'Whose side are you on?' I deposit the first load of gnomes carefully on the kitchen table, then head back outside.

'Yours, of course,' she says as I pass her in the doorway. 'I reckon he likes you.'

I pause and glare at her. 'What?! How do you get *that* from *this*?'

'Didn't your mum ever tell you that when a boy's mean to you it's because he's secretly crushing on you?'

'Yes, and she was wrong.' Plenty of boys were mean to me growing up – I think about the awful taunts from the boys at our brother school about how fat and ugly I was – and none of them had the hots for me. They were simply cruel. 'And Sully's not a boy. He's a man.'

She wriggles her eyebrows at me suggestively. 'Oh, believe me, I know. I saw, remember?'

'And you also decided he was a tosspot, which this proves.'

Fred shrugs and starts picking up gnomes. 'This is theft, you know. You could report him to the police.'

'Trust me, if I didn't think they'd laugh me out of the station, I would.'

JB's confused as we go back and forth into the house carrying the gnomes, but when they're all safely inside, I give him his dinner and then Fred and I get ready to go out.

About an hour later, we're at the pub and I'm at the bar ordering us drinks, when a shadow appears on the stool beside me.

'Fancy meeting you here, bella.'

'Fabio!' Suddenly, my evening is looking up. It's my favourite barista carrying a takeaway pizza box.

He grins back at me. 'Are you here on your own?'

'No.' I point towards the stage, which is set up with a mic ready for the festivities and where Fred is talking to some people from her writing group. 'One of Fred's friends is launching their debut book.'

'Cool.'

'What are you doing here?' I ask.

'Thought I'd grab something for dinner.' He taps the box, then tries to catch the bartender's eye for both of us. It doesn't work. 'Speaking of books, how'd your book club with the nonnas go today?'

I chuckle at 'the nonnas'. 'Do you mainline ginkgo biloba or something?'

He gives me a blank look. 'Ginkgo what?'

'It's a supplement that helps with memory,' I explain. 'How else do you remember everything that's happening in all your customers' lives?'

'Want to know a little secret?' He leans closer and whispers, 'I only remember things about my very favourite ones.'

I roll my eyes – knowing he says things like this to everyone – but internally, I'm giddy. His voice is so sexy, I swear I could have an orgasm just from listening to it. 'Anyway, we haven't had another book club yet; it's only every second Wednesday.'

'I see.' He looks weirdly disappointed.

The bartender finally notices us. 'What can I get for you, mate?'

Fabio gestures to me. 'The lady's first.'

'Thanks.' I smile, and then order a bourbon for Fred and a glass of prosecco for me.

When my drinks arrive, Fabio requests a sixpack of beer to go and then turns back to me. 'So I guess most of the nonnas in your book club are poor, which is why they use the library.'

I shake my head. 'No, I think some of them are rather wealthy, actually. A lot of them are widows and retired professionals. Many of them buy the books rather than borrowing them, but they come to the library to socialise and meet like-minded people.'

'I see.' He opens his mouth as if to add something, but the bartender returns.

'Enjoy, mate,' he says, passing Fabio the beers.

'Well,' Fabio says. 'It was good seeing you, Bee. Bye.'

'You too,' I say, grabbing the drinks off the bar. I'm shocked he remembers my name – I honestly thought he called me 'bella' because he didn't know it.

We're both about to go our separate ways when he asks, 'Is Bee short for anything?'

'Um.' My heart squeezes. I'm torn between feeling chuffed that he cares enough to ask and mortified that now I'm going to have to tell him. I could make up something like Brooke or Bree Jones, but I don't like deception of any kind.

'Bridget,' I say eventually. 'Bridget Jones.'

Sure enough, his eyes widen with recognition and then he laughs. 'No way? Like Bridget from the movie? The one who runs through the street in her knickers?'

'Actually, it was a book first,' I reply. 'And that scene was only in the movie.'

I could write a thesis about the differences. Once I was old enough, I made it my mission to learn everything I could about the fictional character I was named after – literary and film versions. Most people don't even know there was a book between *The Edge of Reason* and *Bridget Jones's Baby,* called *Mad About the Boy.* In this book – spoiler alert – Mark Darcy died, but that was conveniently forgotten when the film company decided to make the baby movie, in which he is miraculously alive.

'It's a good movie,' Fabio says eventually. 'I like Bridget. She's funny. And sweet. Like you.'

OMG. I feel a jolt of pleasure somewhere deep inside – did Fabio just call me sweet? – and immediately forgive his clichéd response.

He hits me with another breathtaking grin. 'Anyway, best be off. Goodnight, Bee.'

'Goodnight, Fabio,' I reply, hoping I don't sound like I'm swooning too much.

20

Tit for Tat and All That

Thursday night, I'm getting ready for kickboxing when my phone rings.

'Hey, Mum.' I put my phone on speaker so I can finish tying up my sneakers.

'Hello, sweetheart. How's things with you? And how's Dave?' Mum has met my 'city parents' on her visits to Perth and they got along like a house on fire.

'He got out of hospital yesterday actually. Physically he's going well, but Janine says his spirits are low. We're all going over to their place on Sunday to try and cheer him up.'

Mum sighs. 'Poor man. I can only imagine how your father would be in the same situation. I'll order Dave a gift basket of goodies and send some flowers for Janine. And how's things with your neighbour?'

'You'll never guess what he's done now.' I tell her about The Great Gnome Kidnapping, as I say goodbye to JB and start walking towards the gym.

'That man sounds unhinged,' she says. 'I'm not sure I like you living next door to someone like that. I think you should cease the catalogue thing, and are you sure you shouldn't report him to the police?'

'No.' I laugh. Although Fred had suggested it when he'd first stolen my gnomes, she'd been joking. I'd been angry, but now I had to agree with her – it *was* kind of funny. 'Tit for tat and all that.'

Mum doesn't sound convinced. 'Just be careful, sweetheart.'

'I will,' I promise, not wanting her to lie awake at night worrying about me. She did enough of that in my teens. And I know she hates that we live so far apart and she can't just drop round every five minutes to check on me. 'How's things with you and Dad, anyway?'

'Oh!' Her tone switches from concerned to animated. 'That's why I was calling, actually. We've decided to renew our vows for our fortieth wedding anniversary in April – the weekend following Anzac Day. I know it's quite short notice, but we'd dearly love it if you could be here with us.'

'That's great, Mum.' I predict *she* decided this and Dad is just going along with it. I'm sure I heard him say years ago that renewing vows was only for show ponies but forty years! I guess that's worth celebrating.

'We'll pay for your flight and the boys will all be there. I've just got off the phone with Rupert. Even he thinks he can get away for a few days. And of course, feel free to bring a *friend*.'

'It'll just be me,' I tell her, knowing when she says friend, she means a boyfriend. I could drag Fred up with me, but I'll need to ask her to look after JB.

I make a mental note of the dates so I can put in a request for leave. Anzac Day is a Thursday, which means if I take Friday off as well, I can leave Wednesday night and have a lovely long weekend at home. Although I was home at Christmas, that seems like months ago now, and I can't wait to hug my parents and get in some quality snuggle time with my nieces and nephews.

'Thanks so much for coming,' Janine says, opening the door to me, Fred, Xavier and Rory on Sunday morning. Nick's car is already parked in the driveway, so I guess he, Persephone and their girls, Samantha and Sabrina, are already here.

'You know I'm always up for a party,' Fred replies as she steps inside.

I give Janine a hug and hand her a box of handcrafted chocolates I bought from the markets this morning. 'It's so good to see you.'

The men agree as they each kiss her on the cheek. Xavier is carrying a bottle of bubbles and a sixpack of beer, while Rory has brought a pavlova for dessert.

Janine thanks us and leads us through their open-plan house, past walls full of family photos and kids' paintings out into the garden, where Persephone and Nick are sitting with Dave at an outdoor table beneath a large eucalypt tree that provides shade for much of the backyard. Theirs is your traditional Aussie quarter-acre block. They could have subdivided it and made a fortune, but they much prefer the space for their grandchildren to run amok.

'Well, hello strangers,' Dave says, his words slightly slurring.

Although Janine has warned us about Dave's condition, I'm stunned. He's like a shell of his former self, but we're all determined not to let our shock show on our faces. As we sit down to cinnamon scrolls, ham and cheese croissants and enough fruit to feed the monkeys at Perth Zoo, we talk about everything but the stroke and its impact on their lives. We toast when Fred tells us she's almost finished the first draft of her manuscript and is definitely going to submit it to publishers by the end of this year, and Persephone when she tells us her ultrasound yesterday revealed they are having a boy.

She beams. 'Nick is ecstatic. He was worried about being even more outnumbered.'

He beams right back at her. 'You know I wouldn't have minded another princess.'

We pass the ultrasound photo around, everyone making oohing-and-ahhing noises as we brainstorm names for their son. As their daughters are both named after famous witches, we throw around characters from some of our favourite books.

'Merlin?' I say.

'Gandalf.' This from Rory.

'Prospero' is Janine's idea.

'Ooh, what about Oz,' Xavier suggests. 'You know, from The Wizard of Oz.'

'That's very cool,' Fred says, and Persephone agrees, but in the end, Nick decides he quite likes 'Harry'.

When Persephone puts the photo away, Janine says, 'And everything is really okay at the library?'

Although we miss her presence immensely, we reassure her that we've got everything under control.

She smiles. 'I'm glad to hear it, because . . . I have an announcement to make.' She looks to Dave, who gives her a lopsided grin in reply. 'I'm retiring.'

'What?!' I exclaim.

The others look equally horrified.

She reaches over and takes Dave's hand. 'It's time. The last couple of weeks have made me reassess my priorities. You know I love my job, the patrons and of course you crazy bunch, but I love

Dave more, and it's time to pursue some of our lifelong dreams. We're buying a caravan and setting off on a trip around Australia as soon as possible.'

The way Dave is at the moment, I'm not sure he'll be able to enjoy a round-Australia road trip that much, but perhaps she just wants to give him something to look forward to and get better for. I'm happy for them, but gutted for myself. My real mum is already far away and now my surrogate mum will be as well.

Persephone is the first to find words. 'Wow. Well, we'll sure as hell miss you, but congratulations.'

I begrudgingly add my well wishes, as do Xavier and Fred.

'Thank you,' Janine says. 'I wanted you lot to hear it from me before we tell the rest of the staff. The good news is that I've recommended to the Shire that Xavier take over from me permanently as library manager, and . . .' She looks at me. 'And if he gets the position, I hope you'll put in for his job, Bee. You'd be the perfect replacement.'

'Me?'

She nods. 'Yes, *you*.' She looks at me in that motherly way she has. 'I know Fred wants to concentrate on her writing and Persephone will be going on leave again, not to mention the fact that you're the very best person for the job. You know books better than anyone I've ever met – you are good with people, no matter their age, race or gender. Even after one session, the Bookstars are already messaging me your praises. So what do you say?'

I'm torn between immense sadness that Janine's absence is going to be permanent and excitement for the possibility of furthering my career. Of course I've thought about a promotion before, but the truth is, I didn't want to leave Fremantle Library and my colleagues who are practically family, so I put it off for future me to deal with.

'I say I'm definitely interested!' I announce with a grin.

'Wonderful.' Janine raises her glass and we all toast to the future.

Conversation about where exactly they'll go on this once-in-a-lifetime trip follows and I can't help catching some of Dave and Janine's excitement as they mention destinations they've always wanted to go to, like Hahndorf village in South Australia, Coober Pedy, Port Arthur and the Dog on the Tuckerbox.

Having been to many of these spots myself, I promise to provide them a list of must-see places along the way.

'Are postcards still a thing?' Fred asks, finishing her second glass of bubbly. 'If so, I want one from every location.'

'Send them to the library,' Xavier suggests. 'We'll put them up on a wall, so the borrowers can follow your trip as well. They'll love that.'

After a couple of hours, Dave starts to tire, so we make our excuses to leave.

When I get home, I spy another envelope peeking out from beneath the doormat and pick it up excitedly. There were yet more catalogues in Sully's letterbox when I arrived home Friday afternoon. I'm curious, and perhaps a tad nervous, to see how he's responded.

I bite my lip, as I slip my finger beneath the seal to open the envelope and find a photo of my gnomes perched on a bookshelf stacked full of well-loved paperbacks. *Wow*. I'm almost certain I didn't see such shelves in Sully's house, but maybe they're in one of the bedrooms. If this was a phone image, I'd enlarge it so I could see what kind of books he likes to read – you can tell so much about a person from their shelves – but instead I pop the photo on my fridge, happy that even though my gnomes aren't with me, they're safe.

If Sully's a reader, as the evidence suggests, then he can't be *that* terrible.

21

Books Not Boys

The following week everyone arrives promptly for Bookstars, including a couple of women who weren't here last time. After they've briefly introduced themselves to me, I launch right in.

'I hope you all loved *Lessons in Chemistry* as much as me,' I say, 'because if you didn't love the dog Six-Thirty, I don't think we can be friends.'

I expect a few dissenters – the way Janine tells it, they never all agree on a book – but it's like they don't even hear my question. Instead, Barbara stretches over Rose, who is sitting between us, and hands me a piece of paper. On it is the name James and a phone number.

'What's this?'

'Some of us were talking about you at Mall Walkers the other morning and we decided to find you a man.'

'You what?!'

'You're too young to be alone,' Daisy says. She is sitting next to Edgar.

'I'm not alone, I've got a dog.'

'You're not a lesbian, are you?' Sue sounds hopeful. 'I said we should bring phone numbers of women as well, just in case.'

Oh, God. How sad is life when you need a bunch of old women to take your dating into their hands? This might be even worse than dating apps.

I cough out a laugh. 'You're all very sweet, but I don't need your help to find men. And,' I remind them, 'we're here to discuss books, not boys.'

Once again they ignore me and instead, as each of them pass me more names and numbers, they bicker about who has the most eligible, single grandsons or godsons or nephews. Only when I agree to hear quick pitches from all of them about why their candidate would be best suited to me do they agree that we can chat about the book.

Kerry tells me about her nephew, Jack – good name – who's a cop. 'Detective, actually. Because of all the shiftwork he does, he finds it hard to meet anyone, but he's an absolute catch.'

Daisy makes a strong case for her grandson, Mikey. She shows me a photo that must be decades out of date, as she tells me he's now thirty-six. 'Recently separated, poor love. His wife had an affair.'

'That's awful,' I say. Nothing I hate more than cheaters, but I wouldn't want to be anyone's rebound girl.

'Do you want to have kids?' Olga barks. Every time she speaks, I feel like I'm a schoolkid about to get in trouble from the principal.

'I think so,' I say, then realise my mistake and quickly add, 'but I don't need a man for that these days, you know.'

Edgar's brow creases. 'How the heck would that work?'

Ignoring him, Olga hauls herself out of her seat and waves a photo in front of my face. 'My godson, Aleksei, is very good with the babies.'

Aleksei is the spitting image of Matt Preston – tall and broad like a giant – and he looks more like he'd *eat* babies.

'Lovely.' I fake a smile. I might want love but not so much that I'm prepared to put myself in the hands of these crazed matchmakers.

After five more photos and insistence from Sue and Ronice that I should consider switching teams if I want to find a love who truly understands me, we *finally* start talking about the book.

Afterwards, when everyone is refilling their cups of tea and nabbing the last of the Iced VoVos, I tap Edgar on the elbow. 'Can I steal you for a second?'

'I'm sorry I didn't give you any numbers,' he says, scratching his head, 'but I don't have any single relatives your age. I'd take you on a date myself, but truth be told, I'm just not over Beryl yet. Not sure I'll ever be.'

'That's okay.' I manage not to laugh as I draw a copy of *Killing Floor* by Lee Child out from behind my back. I bought it myself because the library copies are always out and the reserves list ridiculously long. After finding out about his wife, I'd called Janine and asked her to tell me anything else she knew about Edgar. I had his library history, which confirmed his love of action movies, but I wanted to glean as much about him as possible. After much consideration – it was a toss-up between Child's Reacher and Matthew Reilly's Jack West – I'd gone with the first because Janine told me Edgar had always wanted to visit America.

'I got this for you,' I say, offering it to him.

He recoils slightly and looks at the book like it's a baby crocodile about to snap off all his fingers. 'I thought you said I didn't have to read to come?'

'You don't,' I promise. 'This isn't for Bookstars.'

He frowns, still not accepting the copy. 'What is it, then?'

'It's a novel about an ex-army cop who roams around America, taking odd jobs and finding himself in dangerous situations that he ends up investigating. Honestly, I think you'll love it.' Before he can object, I add, 'And since I'm allowing you to stay in the group, despite not reading the texts, I think it's only fair you give it a try.'

He lets out a long, loud sigh, then grumbles, 'Okay then, girlie, I'll give it a few pages.' I wince at being called 'girlie'. If anyone else did this to me, I'd probably bonk them over the head with the book, but I'm so pleased I've got Edgar to at least take the book, I let him off.

'But don't go getting your hopes up,' he adds.

Oh, I'm not *hoping* anything, I think as he tucks the book into his satchel and heads off to the DVDs. I *know* he'll be back for more.

Fifteen minutes later, I'm reshelving books when Daisy hobbles up beside me. 'Excuse me, dear?' she says in her strong English accent.

'Hi. Is everything okay?' I hope she hasn't sought me out to continue her argument for why I should give poor, broken-hearted Mikey a call.

'Oh, yes, everything's fine. I'm just heading off, but wanted to let you know that I won't be here for the next couple of sessions. I'm having a hip replacement next Wednesday.'

My gaze drops to the walking stick she always uses. 'Thanks for letting me know. I hope it goes well.'

'Me too. The only good thing about this stick is that it doubles as a weapon if need be, but I'll be glad to be rid of it.'

I laugh, imagining all too well that Daisy wouldn't be afraid to use it if anyone attempted anything untoward with her.

22

Giddy-up

'Whereabouts in Italy are you from?' I ask Fabio as he makes our coffees on Thursday morning. He's always asking about me and I know next to nothing about him.

'You been to my country?'

I shake my head.

He smiles wistfully. 'It is a magic place. So many incredible *artistes*, such beautiful architecture and history. Not to mention wine. I know you Aussies think Margaret River and the Barossa are wonderful, but nothing compares to Tuscany.'

Somehow he manages to talk with his hands while also making the drinks. It's a beautiful thing and I could sit here and watch him all day.

'I'll put it on my bucket list. I was planning a trip overseas, but Covid put a spanner in the works and I'd almost forgotten it was possible. Maybe it's time to start planning a trip. I could take some time off, go visit all the libraries in Italy.'

'You wouldn't miss your own library? And the nonnas?' The twinkle in his eye tells me he's teasing me.

'They'd kill you if they heard you calling them that.'

'What's wrong with nonnas?'

'Nothing, but most of them don't like to consider themselves old. Even Lorna, who just turned ninety-five.'

'How many of them are there?' Fabio asks as he snaps the lids on our cups.

'Um . . . there's twenty-one registered, but about half usually turn up.'

He lets out a surprised sound. 'That's quite a lot.'

'Yes. Which is why every second Wednesday, I'll need a double shot.'

'I think I can manage that,' he says, smiling as he hands over the drinks. Our fingers brush in the exchange. 'So, what were they like yesterday?'

I quickly tell him about the phone numbers they'd pushed on me.

He laughs. 'And are you going to ring any?'

'Hell no.'

'Because you already have *ragazza*?'

Oh, God, his accent is so damn sexy. 'What's that?'

'Boyfriend,' he clarifies.

It's my turn to laugh. 'No. No boyfriend.'

'Good.' He takes a pen from behind his ear, then reaches for my hand – the one not holding the drinks – and scribbles a phone number onto my skin. 'You'll call me then? We'll go on date.'

Am I still asleep? I stare at the digits on my hand, then blurt, '*You* want to go out with *me*?'

He opens his mouth to reply, but another customer arrives, all but shoving me out of the way, and I have to act quickly to keep from dropping our drinks.

'Bye, bella.' Fabio smiles despite our rude interruption, then makes a phone sign with his fingers and presses it to his ear.

I hurry out of the café, my heart beating as if I've just run a half marathon in stilettos.

I'm puffing when I arrive at the library and give Xavier his coffee. He kisses the cup.

Persephone looks longingly at our drinks and then takes a sip from her can of ginger ale. Apparently, it's good for morning sickness. 'The least you could do is not flaunt it in front of me.'

Fred chuckles, sipping her morning green juice. Then she frowns, staring at me. 'Are you okay? You look like you've seen a ghost.'

'Fabio just asked me out.'

'What?' they exclaim at once.

I don't blame them. I'm *still* in shock.

I hold up my hand to show them. 'This is his phone number.'

'Wow.' Xavier shakes his head. 'I could have sworn he was gay.'

Fred holds up a hand. 'Hang on . . . back up a moment. How did this happen?'

'I was telling him about the Bookstars, then he asked if I had a boyfriend and then he did this.' I hold up my hand again; it's still shaking. 'And told me to call him.'

Fred palms her hands against her cheeks. 'Oh my God, oh my God, oh my God. This is so exciting. I can't believe you have the spunky barista's phone number. What are you waiting for?'

'I can't call him now! He's working and we're about to open.'

'But you are going to call him, right?' Persephone asks, her brow furrowing slightly.

My stomach clenches at the thought. There's a war going on inside my head. Part of me wants to, but the other part of me can't believe this is actually happening. 'Um . . . I don't know. Why would he be interested in me?'

'Ah duh, because you're hot as hell,' Fred says, and Xavier and Persephone nod in agreement. 'And funny, and kind, and smart. And cuter than a doll with your bouncy caramel ponytail and ever-present smile. He's obviously a clever guy who knows a good thing when he sees it.'

'But he's Italian.'

They all laugh.

'What's wrong with Italians?' Xavier asks.

'Nothing. But what if he wants to go back there one day? I could never leave Australia. Living hours away from my family is bad enough.' Getting involved with someone like him seems like setting myself up for heartache right from the beginning.

Persephone gives me a reassuring smile. 'You don't know he wants to go back. Plenty of Italians live here. Don't write anything off; it's amazing what people do for true love.'

Fred nods. 'Besides, why do you have to take everything so seriously? Every guy you go out with doesn't have to be husband material. So what if he might go back to Italy one day? The man's got fun written all over him, and if anyone deserves a bit of fun, it's you. Besides, didn't you want to meet someone organically? Well, this could be it!'

'She's right,' Persephone says.

Xavier nods in agreement. 'Yeah, and even if he's not The One, maybe you can have some fun with the Italian stallion while wait-ing for Mr Right.'

'Giddy-up.' Fred mimes riding on a horse.

'You guys are ridiculous,' I say, my insides quivering at the thought. I can't even imagine having the confidence to take my shirt off in front of him, never mind my underwear. But even worse is the thought of ruining the good thing we have going: amazing coffee with a side of friendly flirtation. 'What if it ends badly? Then where am I gonna get my coffee?'

'If you turn him down, things might get awkward anyway,' Xavier says, always the voice of reason. 'Besides, we can collect the coffees, so really, what have you got to lose?'

When he puts it that way . . . I glance at the numbers scrawled on my skin and feel my pulse thumping beneath them. 'Okay, I promise, I'll give it serious thought.'

'If you don't ring him, I will!' Fred says, peering down at my arm as if she's trying to memorise his number.

'Behave,' I warn her, hiding my hand behind my back so she can't see it.

On my lunch break, I notice Sully's letterbox stuffed with catalogues again and there's another envelope just visible under my mat.

I'd never admit this to Sully, but I'm really starting to enjoy these little glimpses into my gnomes' 'holiday'. This time there's a note alongside the photo of my gnomes – lounging in a hammock far too big for them – and again it's written in letters cut out of newspapers and magazines.

Doesn't he have anything better to do with his time?

I'M BEGINNING TO THINK YOU DON'T GIVE A DAMN ABOUT
THESE GNOMES AS THE CATALOGUES ARE, IF ANYTHING,
INCREASING.
FOR THEIR SAKES . . . I HOPE I'M WRONG!

I snort, and then giggle. Something tells me that maybe Sullen Sully has a sense of humour after all.

Before heading back to work, I peer over the back fence to check if he's home. His car isn't there, so I'm confident he's out when I sneak into his front courtyard and leave my own note under his boring doormat.

HOW ABOUT YOU RETURN MY GNOMES IN ONE PIECE AND THEN I'LL SEE WHAT I CAN DO ABOUT THE CATALOGUES.

Maybe I shouldn't have admitted on paper that I was indeed responsible for his overstuffed letterbox, but I want him to know that I'm not going be blackmailed by Mr Grumpypants.

Besides, I'm kinda having fun!

23

Too Good to Be True

On Saturday morning Fabio is waiting for me at the top of the dunes on Bathers Beach. It's a beautiful autumn day – not too hot, not too cold, no nasty breeze – and he's dressed in smart navy shorts and a short-sleeved pale blue shirt, open low at the neck so I can see the hair on his chest. Weirdly, it's much lighter than the hair on his head. He's carrying a large wicker basket and, with the crystal blue sea shimmering in the background, he looks like he's stepped right off the cover of a European travel brochure.

His face lights up with a smile as I approach. 'Bella! You look . . .' His gaze skims my body, taking in the buttery-yellow sundress that ends just above my knee, before he mimes a chef's kiss. '*Bellissimo.*'

'Grazie,' I manage, warmth flooding me at his compliment. I'd spent hours deliberating between this dress and a floaty top with denim capris, but his approval tells me I went with the right outfit. 'You look pretty good too.'

He turns his attention to my faithful sidekick, who is tugging on his leash, desperate to make a new friend. When I finally worked up the courage to call Fabio on Thursday evening, he suggested

brunch on the beach, weather permitting. I'd asked if he'd mind if
I brought JB along and he said he'd love that as he missed his own
dogs back in Italy.

JB is so excited to meet Fabio that when Fabio stoops down to
stroke him, he pees on the sand right near his feet.

'I'm so sorry,' I gush, dragging him back. As if I wasn't nervous
enough already!

But Fabio simply laughs. 'It's fine.' He pulls JB into an actual
hug, allowing him to smooch him with his sloppy tongue.

Be still, my heart. Is it weird to wish I was my dog right now?

'What breed is he?' Fabio asks, pulling back from the kiss.

'A sheepadoodle. He's a cross between an Old English sheepdog – you know, like the Dulux paint dog – and a standard poodle,
or as my brothers say, a bitza.'

'*Beet-za?*' he asks in his drool-worthy accent.

Despite my nerves, I can't help thinking how he'd sound in
bed, talking dirty to me.

'It means he's not a purebred,' I say, hoping he isn't a mind reader.
I don't want him to think I'll be easy – if there's one thing my last
few 'relationships' have taught me, it's that rushing into sex is never
a good thing. Whatever Fred thinks – or says – I plan on getting to
know Fabio properly before taking things to an intimate level.

'How long have you had him?'

'He was a present from my parents when I moved into my own
place. Ever since I read this picture book when I was little about an
Old English sheepdog, an old woman and a black cat, I've wanted
a dog like that, but they're hard to find in Australia, and the mixed
coat is a little easier to manage too.'

'Can I give him a treat?' Fabio asks.

I nod, and he pulls out a rawhide bone from his pocket, then hands it to JB. The dog's tail starts wagging even more furiously. 'I think you've got a fan for life.'

Fabio chuckles and then gestures towards the beach. 'Shall we go find a spot so I can feed *you*?'

With salty air wafting on the breeze and JB tugging at the leash, we walk a little way up the coast, past a couple of kids playing – their harried-looking parents trying to luxuriate in what might be the last warmish day of the year – and find a quiet spot on the sand. Fabio removes a tartan rug from the basket and spreads it out while I let JB off so he can go for a paddle.

'Take a seat, bella.' He gestures to the rug as he starts to unpack the food. There's croissants, a tub of sliced melon and strawberries, and also champagne flutes and a bottle of prosecco.

'This looks very romantic,' I say, knowing that whatever happens between us long term, this will likely go down as the best first date in history. Or at least my history.

'This?' He expertly pops the bottle. 'This is just a standard Italian picnic. Wait till I show you *real* romance. The French think they're the world's best lovers, but we Italians know the truth.'

The way he says 'lovers' leaves my insides feeling as if I've just stepped off the Gravitron at the Perth Royal Show.

'Your English is very good,' I say as he hands me a very full glass. 'Did you learn it at school?'

'*Sì*. Did you learn a language?'

I shake my head. 'Not really. I did do French in high school but I missed a lot of the classes.'

I wonder if he'll ask me why, and if I'll tell him – this is usually information I save for after I've been seeing someone for quite some time – but he simply lifts his glass in a toast. 'To weekends, good company and *amore*.'

I clink my glass against his and can't help but smile. What Aussie man would even nonchalantly mention the word 'love' on a first date?

'Here, have a cornetto,' he offers, lifting one of the trays.

'I thought they were croissants,' I say.

He chuckles. 'No, these are far superior. The French say they invented croissants, but it was actually the Austrians.' A fact I already know. 'And cornettos are Italy's version, much better, much sweeter. Try one. I made them just for you.'

'You *made* them?'

He nods, spots of red appearing on his cheeks.

Even after all these years my instinct is always to say no to such food in front of a hot guy, but I fight it because I know it's silly and I also don't want to offend him after he went to this much effort. I should be able to manage one if I do what I did when I was first recovering my appetite, which is tackle it in tiny pieces.

'Thank you,' I say, taking one.

He looks at me in anticipation as I rip off a little chunk and pop it into my mouth.

The sugar melts on my tongue and immediately I forget my hang-ups. 'Oh, my giddy aunt. They're freaking amazing.'

He beams in a way to rival the sunlight behind him. 'Told ya.'

'Okay. What's wrong with you?' I ask through another mouthful.

'What do you mean?'

'You make the best coffee I've ever tasted, you read, you're nice to my dog, you're . . . not harsh to look at—'

Fabio smirks. 'Are you saying I'm good-looking?'

I roll my eyes at his interruption – as if he doesn't know. '*And* you can bake. You're too good to be true.'

'Oh, bella, you are very good for my ego, but I'm by no means *perfetto*.'

I narrow my eyes at him. 'Prove it. Tell me all the things that aren't so great about you.'

'How long have you got?'

I lift the bottle of prosecco and angle it towards him. 'As long as it takes for us to finish this?'

'Okay, bella. This is something I've never admitted to anyone . . .'

As he leans closer, I hold my breath in anticipation.

'I was obsessed with Pokémon cards as a kid and still collect them. The last packet I bought was only last week.'

I blink. 'That's . . . a little geeky, but kinda endearing, so I'm not sure it counts.'

Fabio sighs, runs a hand through his thick hair and looks off into the distance as if struggling to come up with something. 'Okay,' he announces eventually, 'but I fear if I tell you, you are going to run into the ocean and drown yourself rather than spend another second in my company.'

I raise an eyebrow, intrigued.

'When I was little, I accidentally killed my sister's goldfish because I wanted to see how long it could survive out of water. Turns out, not long at all.'

'Oh my God.' I slap a hand over my mouth. 'What did you tell her?'

'I didn't. I raced down to the pet shop, bought another one with my pocket money and put it back in the tank before she came home. She never noticed the difference.'

'That's terrible,' I exclaim, trying not to laugh.

'Told you.' He hangs his head. 'There is a dark side to me I cannot deny. So, bella, is this romance over before it's begun?'

I tease him by pretending to deliberate on the issue, then, 'That was a long time ago, so if that's the worst thing you've ever done . . . I'm willing to overlook it.'

'Phew.' He wipes the back of his hand against his brow theatrically. 'Now, your turn.'

'Huh?'

'I've told you some terrible things about me; it's only fair you repay the favour.'

I laugh. 'How long have you got?'

In reply, he tops up my glass with more prosecco.

Oh dear. 'Are you trying to get me drunk so you can have your wicked way?'

Fabio looks hurt. '*Non.* I just want you to have a lovely brunch.'

Chastised, I smile at him. 'I'm sorry, of course not.'

While JB frolics in and out of the water, Fabio and I share all our bad habits, failures and foibles. It's like a competition where we're trying to one-up each other on who is less of a catch.

After telling him I often read the last chapters of books first, am a bit of a hoarder (okay, *a bit* might be an understatement), can't tell my left from my right, spend far too much time stalking old boyfriends on Facebook (which he tells me he's not on), talk loudly in my sleep, buy more books than I can afford, never mind read, and believe Jane Austen Day should be a national holiday, we're both laughing our heads off and I'm sure an impartial judge would award me the winner.

Being so down on yourself is surprisingly therapeutic.

'I'm having a wonderful time with you, bella,' he says, and suddenly the easy banter between us seems like ancient history as my insides tighten and my lips tingle.

The look in his eyes tells me he wants to kiss me and as much as I don't want to rush things, I can't help wanting to know if he tastes as good as he looks. Against my better judgement, I lean into him.

He takes my lead, cupping my face with his hands and, as he draws my lips to his, I decide this might just be the best first date I've ever been on.

24

The Terminator

Floating on air is such a cliché but it's exactly how I feel as I walk home from the beach, the memory of our kiss replaying in my head. I thought Fabio might try to invite himself back to my place, but he was the perfect gentleman, thanking me for the date and asking if I enjoyed it enough for another. What kind of question was that? I'd need my head read not to say yes.

Since he arranged the first date, I told him date number two is on me and that I'll text him the details once I've done a little investigating. There are so many things I love around Freo and I'm excited to introduce him to them, but I need to check times and available dates first. I'm googling what night the prison does their spooky evening tours as I walk into my courtyard and am so distracted, I almost miss another note.

If not for JB sniffing madly at the mat as I get my key out of my bag, I probably would have.

'What's this?' I say to him as I pick up the envelope and take it inside.

I dump my bag on the hallway table, kick off my sandals, then rip it open, excited to see what my gnomes are up to today, but my heart shudders at the photo inside.

No! My whole body goes cold. This can't be real.

Two of my gnomes are standing side by side and in front of them is a large bowl with a hundred or so tiny pieces of broken colourful ceramic.

How could he?!

I slump back against the wall and slide to the floor. My phone shaking in my hand, I call Fred.

'Hey, girlfriend,' she sings. 'How was the date? I want *all* the details!'

'He— he— he killed her.'

'What?' she shrieks. 'Fabio *killed* someone?'

'No. Not Fabio,' I rush, stupid tears filling my eyes. 'Sully.'

'What the fuck? I'm coming over. Lock your doors.'

She disconnects and I stare at the photo. I can't believe he'd actually do this. JB is right beside me, nuzzling my face, licking the tears from my cheeks, and I pull him close, burying my head in his soft fur.

Five minutes later, Fred lets herself into my house and drops to the floor beside me. JB must sense something is wrong because he doesn't leave my side to try to lavish her with love. 'What's going on?'

I thrust the now-crumpled photo at her. 'He killed Veronica.'

'Oh, thank God,' she breathes, and I suddenly realise that I'd made it sound like he'd murdered an actual human.

'Sorry, I didn't mean to scare you.' I sniff, the shock wearing off a little now. For all I'd joked about Sully being a psychopath, the truth is I'd been starting to warm to him this last week or so. 'I know it's stupid to be so upset over a garden gnome, but she was my favourite, one of Gran's and one of the few I actually had a name for.'

Fred pulls me into her side, strokes my head like she's thirty years older than me, not three months, and kisses the top of it. 'You're not stupid. That man's a lunatic.'

'I know. What kind of doctor kidnaps and tortures gnomes? Shouldn't he be saving lives or something?'

Fred frowns. 'Perhaps he's not a medical doctor. Maybe he has a PhD in something worthless like astrophysics.'

I chuckle. I'm not sure astrophysicists would agree that their work is worthless, but she might have a point about the PhD.

'Do you know if he's home?' she asks.

When I shrug, she pushes off the floor and marches out through my front door. Seconds later I hear her banging loudly on his. 'If you're in there, you better come out here and deal with me, you monster!'

There's no response.

'The wanker isn't home. Or if he is, he's hiding from me,' Fred announces on her return.

I swallow. 'Do you think I *should* report him to the police? I mean, I thought this was just neighbourly fun, but if he can kill a gnome, what else is he capable of?' I pull my dog to my chest. 'What if he does something to John Brown?'

'If he does something to John Brown, I will break into his house while he sleeps, rip off his toes one by one and shove them down his throat.'

Despite the situation, I laugh. Sully is almost twice the size of Fred. She might be feisty, but he could eat her for breakfast.

She sinks to the floor beside me and squeezes my knee. 'I'm not sure the cops will want to waste time with something like this when they're dealing with domestic abuse, drug dealers and people scamming the elderly.'

'You're right,' I say with a sigh. 'I'm just going to cease all contact with him, and I'll cancel the catalogues too. It'll probably take a while for them to stop, but if I beat him to his letterbox, I might be able to remove them before he murders Archie and Betty as well.'

'If you're really worried, why don't you and JB come stay with me for a bit?' she suggests. 'At least until the catalogues are well and truly finished.'

'You don't think Waylen will mind?' I ask, not opposed to the idea at all. I'm probably overreacting, but with the Terminator living right next door, my home no longer feels like the haven it once did.

'It'll be fine. He loves you and John Brown. Everyone does.'

'Not everyone,' I say, nodding towards the wall behind me. 'But thanks. If you're sure. That would be great. Just for a few days.'

Fred helps me pack a bag and JB's things and then we stuff it all into her Mini. I didn't pack much, but the car is so small, it's still an effort to fit the three of us inside.

'So,' Fred asks as she pulls away, 'how was your date?'

'It was lovely,' I say, happy to think about fabulous Fabio rather than what I'd come home to. 'We talked and laughed and ate and drank prosecco—'

'And blah, blah, blah. Please tell me you're getting to the good part.'

'Do you mean the part where we kissed?'

She squeals as she swerves around a corner far too quickly. 'Was it hot?'

'Well, I don't want to kiss and tell, but . . . yes.' My body heats at the memory and I absentmindedly touch a finger to my lips. I can't remember the last time I kissed someone like that.

'And after the kiss . . .' she pries. 'Did you get down and dirty in the dunes?'

'No.' I snort, knowing that this is not outside the realms of possibility for Fred. 'After my last few relationships, I want to take this one slow. I want to make sure I really know someone before I take things to the next level.'

'And Fabio's happy with that?' Fred asks.

'He'll have to be. I don't want a man who doesn't think I'm worth waiting for.'

She shakes her head. 'I'd be tapping that man till his cock fell off, but whatever floats your boat, sista.'

I laugh, but the truth is I'm terrified of being hurt again, and this seems the best way to protect myself.

25

Worse Things

Edgar is one of the first patrons through the door on Monday morning and he looks like a different man. He's not hunching as much as usual, and there are smile lines around his eyes I never noticed before.

He waves the copy of *Killing Floor* in the air as he approaches me at the desk. 'I don't know what you put in this, girlie, but it's addictive. I told myself I'd read two pages a day to tell you I'd tried, but then I couldn't stop! Read until four o'clock Saturday morning.'

'That's wonderful,' I say, warmth radiating from my heart right through my body. There's nothing like the thrill of introducing someone to the joy of reading.

'I came in yesterday to tell you, but they said you weren't working until today.' He opened the book and pointed at the page with a list of the other Reacher books. 'I need them all. Pronto.'

I gesture for him to follow me to the crime section. 'Let's see what we've got on the shelf.'

Unfortunately, we only have books five and fifteen available. 'I can order in the rest for you.'

He looks like I've told him someone has died.

'It shouldn't take too long for some others to come in, but if you're really desperate, you could always try New Edition on the corner of High Street and Henry Street or Elizabeth's, the second-hand bookshop on South Terrace and Victoria Street.'

I grab him *Echo Burning* and *Worth Dying For*, then say, 'You know, there's another author I think you might like while you're waiting for the others. Michael Trant is from WA, and he's written a couple of crime novels about a dog trapper in the outback.' Before he can protest, I add, 'Lee Child said he loved the first.'

'Well . . .' Edgar puffs out his chest a little. 'If it's got Lee's seal of approval, then you'd better give me those too.'

Both grinning, we head to the counter, and I show Edgar how to use the self-serve check-outs. 'But I'm always here if you need help.'

'Thanks, girlie. Oh, and I'd better give you this one back,' he says, thrusting *Killing Floor* at me.

'Oh, no, that one's not a library book,' I say. 'I bought it especially for you as our copies weren't available. You can keep it.'

He beams. 'Really? You're a gem. How much do I owe you for it, then?'

I shake my head. 'Consider it a present.'

Seeing his face light up over the book is payment enough.

When I come back from lunch on Thursday, I spot Laura perusing the general fiction shelves and go over to say hi.

'Lola not with you today?'

She shakes her head. 'We're back in an intensive chemo stage, so she's in hospital again. It's taking a bit out of her. Even reading's been an effort the last few days, but I got a notice that one of the books you ordered for her was in, and she begged me to come get it, so I thought I'd see if I could find anything for myself while I was here. Ever since you got me reading again, I don't seem to be able to stop.'

'There are worse things to be addicted to,' I tell her.

'Oh, I'm addicted to some of those too. Pretty sure my body is half caffeine at this stage.'

I laugh.

'Do you have any other recommendations for me?' Laura asks. 'There's so much choice, I don't know where to start, but your picks so far have been amazing. I'm still thinking about *The Paper Palace*.'

'Isn't it fabulous? Have you read any Marian Keyes?'

Her eyes light up. 'I used to love her, pre-kids when I had time to read.'

'She's a freaking literary genius.' I grab *Grown Ups* and *The Break*, which should keep her busy for a while, and then say, 'Have you thought about trying audiobooks for Lola? I can set you up so she can borrow them through the library from home – or the hospital. You just need internet access.'

'You mean talking books?'

I nod. 'They're super popular now and she can listen to them on her phone, which means if she's tired and you're not around to read to her, she can still be entertained.'

'Wow. That sounds wonderful.'

'Awesome.' I smile and lead her over to the desk to set up BorrowBox. 'The only problem is some of the books will have a long wait, but I can provide recommendations for ones that are available.'

Laura sniffs, emotion filling her eyes.

'Are you okay?' I ask, touching her arm.

'It's just . . . you're being so kind to us.'

'Lola's a great kid, and I meant it when I said I'd do whatever I can to help her. And you.'

'Thank you.' Laura bites her lip, then says, 'Look, I'm sorry if this is out of line, but . . . I was wondering, would you like to come for lunch at our place in a couple of weeks when Lola is home again? Totally understand if you're busy or it's not something you're comfortable with, but I'd love to have you over to say thanks, and I know Lola would appreciate hanging out with someone cooler than her family for a change.'

Me, cooler? How could I say no to that? And anyway, I don't want to. 'I'd love that,' I say.

'Lovely.' She smiles and we exchange numbers so we can organise a date. 'Of course, you're welcome to bring a partner if you have one.'

I think of Fabio, but we've only been on one date, and it will be easier to focus on Lola if I'm on my own. 'It'll just be me.'

'I'd better be off, but thanks for the audiobooks and I can't wait to tell Lola about lunch.' And then she surprises me by leaning in and giving me a hug. 'It'll give her something to look forward to.'

'I'm looking forward to it just as much. Tell her I said hi and I can't wait to see her when she's home again,' I say, feeling a weird closeness to this woman I've only met a few times.

Then again, I guess bonding over books will do that to people.

26

Scared of the Dark

I meet Fabio out the front of Fremantle Prison for our second date. This is possibly my favourite place in our whole historic neighbourhood. I love everything about it, from the grim limestone gatehouse to the eerie history of what happened between its walls, especially the tales of the Catalpa Escape and Moondyne Joe.

When my brothers and I were kids, we'd come to Perth to stay with Gran and Grandpa, and after the first time they took us here, I constantly begged them to take me back.

And it's even better at night.

'Evening,' I say, my stomach flipping as we close the distance between us.

Will he kiss me? Will he kiss me? Will he—

He kisses me – the kind of kiss of long-lost lovers who haven't seen each other because one of them has been away at war. 'Hello, bella,' he says when he finally pulls back. 'So where are we going tonight?'

Grinning, I gesture to the prison behind us, then grab his hand. 'Come on.'

He doesn't budge. 'You're taking me in there? To gaol? I just thought we were meeting here.'

I laugh. 'It's not a gaol any more, and I'm not going to hand-cuff and lock you up.' The moment I say that I realise how it sounds, and I blush. 'Trust me, you're going to love it.'

He swallows, his skin going pale under the lights as if he might be about to be sick.

'You're not scared of the dark, are you?'

He shakes his head. 'But I am scared of ghosts.'

I have to bite my lip to stifle a smile, because he sounds serious. 'Do you really not want to go in there? We could just go have a drink or something?'

'No,' he says firmly. 'You planned this, and I will be brave.'

'I promise I'll protect you,' I say, slipping my hand into his.

In the gift shop, as I angle my phone to show our tickets, Fabio whips his wallet out of his back pocket. 'I should pay you for these tickets.'

I wave away his chivalrous offer, while secretly loving it. 'No, my choice, my treat.'

A smiley woman with shiny white teeth instructs us to wait in the courtyard. 'Anders will ring a bell when the tour starts.'

We look at some of the displays as we wait and I notice at least three other women checking out Fabio.

Sorry, girls, he's all mine.

Before long, a tall, lanky man with near-white hair appears. 'Everyone, grab a torch from my bucket and head on into recep-tion,' he says in a Scandinavian accent.

Reception is the actual room where prisoners were first received in the prison and we all sit on a bench while Anders starts his spiel.

'Welcome to Fremantle Prison, where tonight I will take you on a journey to explore the darker side of its history . . .'

Anders explains that on arrival prisoners were made to strip naked, put their old possessions in two white bags and then sit on 'that there bench with their naked bottoms waiting to be searched'. We all shudder and hope the bench has seen a lot of bleach since those days.

'Now, follow me through the shower block, but stay close. These walls echo with tales of loneliness, pain, suffering, riots, executions gone wrong, escapees, innocent men (and some women) unjustly punished and, of course, guilty, terrible people getting their just desserts.'

I feel a chill pass through my body, but tell myself it's just the cool evening wind. Anders tells us a tale about a brutal murder of an inmate right out here on the grass between the front part of the prison and the foreboding cell blocks looming beyond.

Fabio's grip tightens on my hand and he doesn't let go as we enter the first cell block, where Anders talks about the Holy Bucket. 'The inmates did their business in these right up until the prison closed in 1991, and they were often used as weapons as well as toilets.'

A piercing whistle sounds, and we all jump and shriek as some-one explodes out of one of the closed cells.

'What are you all doing milling about in here when there's a riot going on out there?' she yells at us, and we make our way through one tiny cell that opens up into a sparse, concrete exercise yard, half-laughing, half-spooked.

The only signs of life out here are a dozen or so massive cockroaches, but Anders assures us there are many lingering spirits we might not see but feel as we move through the prison.

The rest of the tour is a combination of sombre stories and laugh-out-loud moments when more actors jump out of dark corners, trying to scare us. We visit the execution yards, the solitary confinement cells and even the morgue, which has an odd smell despite not having been used for decades.

'That was amazing, bella,' Fabio exclaims when Anders dismisses us and sees us out of the prison, so they can 'lock up the ghosts for the night'.

'Really? You liked it?' I'd been a bit nervous after his reaction at the entrance.

He nods. 'Best date I've been on. Let me buy you a drink to say *grazie*.'

'Okay,' I say – I haven't had enough of him yet, 'but only one as I've got work tomorrow.'

'One drink,' he agrees, and we head just round the corner to the Norfolk Hotel.

Fabio buys a beer for himself and a white wine for me and I decide this is my chance to delve deeper. I want to know about his family, his childhood, his hopes, dreams and values. I want to know what makes him tick.

'You mentioned you have a sister?' When he nods, I add, 'What's she like? What does she do? Did you say you were twins?'

'*Sì*. Francesca is five minutes older than me and never lets me forget it.'

As I sip my wine, he tells me she's in hospitality and does shift-work at posh city hotels. While soapies were her thing as a kid and teen, she's now obsessed with reality TV, swimming and Korean boy bands, which she plays loudly when she gets ready for work and drives Fabio insane.

'Hang on. Does she live here too?' I ask.

'*Sì. Sì.*' He grins. 'We live together. Our mother was a single woman – our *padre* left her when she was pregnant – and not too long ago she died of cancer.'

'I'm so sorry.'

'*Grazie*. There were too many painful memories in Italy, so Francesca decided she wanted to live in Australia for a while – she was massive fan of *Home and Away* as a teen – and I decided to join her.'

'You must be very close,' I say, surprised they knew about Summer Bay in Italy. 'But why WA? I'd have thought if she was a *Home and Away* fan, she'd have wanted to live on the East Coast?'

He shrugs. 'That's Francesca for you – impossible to predict. What about you? Do you have *fratelli* or *sorelle*?' He lifts his beer to his mouth.

'Three brothers,' I say, guessing the translation. 'All older. We're all named after characters from books my mum loved.'

There's Brandon from *The Flame and the Flower* by Kathleen E. Woodiwiss, Justin from the pages of *Playing the Odds* by Nora Roberts, and finally Rupert, who is of course Mum's tribute to Rupert Campbell-Black from Jilly Cooper's Rutshire Chronicles.

'That's funny,' he says. 'Your dad didn't want a say?'

I laugh and shake my head. As if Dad ever has a say in anything but the station.

We talk about the library for a while, how much I love working there and that I might even be getting a promotion soon. I tell him about my superpower – matching books to people – and he asks what book I'd pick for him.

'Do you like reading?'

He nods. 'Of course. Who doesn't like reading?'

I'll admit this confession throws me a little. It was hard enough controlling my little crush when he was a demi-god who made heavenly coffee and had an accent that had every woman swooning, but men who read are my kryptonite.

'Are you comfortable reading novels in English?' It was one thing speaking a foreign language, quite another being able to read or write it, but my powers didn't stretch to foreign books.

'Uh . . .' He pinches his thumb and forefinger together. 'I would like to get better.'

I don't even have to think about it. 'I know the perfect book for you. I'll bring it next time we catch up.'

We finish our drinks and when Fabio asks if I want another one, it takes all my willpower to resist. 'Not tonight – work in the morning – but thank you for a wonderful evening.'

In reply, Fabio leans across the table and kisses me hard on the lips. 'The pleasure was all mine. Shall I drive you back to your place?'

'Actually, I'm staying at Fred's for a while, so I was going to get an Uber.'

He frowns. 'Something wrong with your place?'

I tell him about Sully and the gnomes.

'*Grazie a Dio*. I'm so sorry you feel unsafe in your own place.' He squeezes my hand. 'I'll drive you to Fred's.'

27

The Total Package

Saturday morning is my third date with Fabio and I spend ages getting ready. I try not to bother Fred while I'm deciding what to wear and how to do my hair because she's writing, and also, all she'll want to talk about is the possibility of me and Fabio doing the horizontal mambo.

It *is* the third date after all.

In the end, I go with slim fit jeans, sparkly silver sneakers and a lightweight jumper with books on the front that says, 'I have no shelf control.'

Despite my dithering, I'm still ready early, so make the most of the time by freshening up my résumé. Xavier has an interview next week for the manager role and once he's appointed, they'll advertise his job, so I need to be ready to apply. Although a promotion wasn't on my radar until a few weeks ago, I'm now super excited about the possibility of being able to put more of a personal stamp on the library. I've got so many ideas and think we can do even more than we're doing now to help our local community, especially the homeless. Fred and I have been talking about the possibility of a movie night once a week during the winter, where people can enjoy some entertainment out of the cold and we'll also provide a hot meal. We heard about one library in Tamworth that allows the homeless to sleep in the library once a week, and the Mount Gambier library offers a service for women in domestic violence home situations, but we both think it's good to start with something smaller and build from there.

Aside from pimping books, there's so much more we could be doing to help and I'm excited as I type my vision into my cover letter.

Finally, I shut my laptop and go say goodbye to Fred. I find her fast asleep on her bed, Aunty, her cat, sprawled on top of her.

'I thought you were supposed to be writing,' I scold, startling her awake.

'What?' She sits up quickly and rubs her eyes.

I laugh. 'Words going well?'

Fred groans and flops back against her pillows. 'Dreadful. I have writer's block. Kill me now.'

'I thought you didn't believe in writer's block?'

She narrows her eyes at me.

I bite down on another chuckle. 'I'm heading to Fabio's now – is it still okay if I borrow your car?' She nods, and I add, 'I'll see you in a few hours.'

'Don't come home on my account,' she says with a wink, and then frowns. 'You're not taking a book, are you?'

A library copy of *Legends & Lattes* is poking out the top of my handbag.

'Fabio asked me to recommend him something.'

Fred hoots. 'Is that some form of foreplay?'

I don't justify her crude question with an answer, instead looking to JB, who followed me in and is trying to nudge Aunty awake. 'Come on, JB, let's go.'

'You don't have to take him. He's welcome here with me,' she offers. 'Wouldn't want him cramping your style.'

'Thanks,' I say, 'but Fabio loves him and told me to bring him along.'

She sighs. 'Fine. Leave me all alone and go have fun with lover boy.'

As I leave her room, she's already reaching for her phone, and I bet she'll find someone to take her mind off her writer's block this afternoon.

JB and I climb into Fred's Mini and I follow my phone directions to the address Fabio gave me in East Fremantle. I'd imagined two glorified backpackers would live somewhere small and slightly shabby, but this house is larger and nicer than I pictured. Maybe the customers give Fabio a lot of tips. I can't dwell on this for long, because now that we've stopped, JB is jumping around the car, desperate to escape and explore this new terrain. I grab a hold of his leash and then open my door as he skips to the ground over the top of me.

When I look up, Fabio is standing right in front of us in all his deliciousness. Tingles flood my body as I gaze at him in dark jeans, a white long-sleeved tee and an apron the colours of the Italian flag tied around his waist. How patriotic!

'Bella,' he exclaims, plucking JB up into his arms. I'm not sure whether he's talking to me or the dog, but when I clear my throat, Fabio closes the distance between us and, still holding JB, kisses me on both cheeks, before lingering slightly longer on my lips. 'You look *bellissimo*!'

'Thank you,' I say, my cheeks *and* mouth tingling.

Fabio takes my hand and leads us into his house, where he unclips JB's leash and plops him on the ground.

'Maybe we should keep him on there,' I suggest. 'I don't want him destroying your house.'

Fabio waves away my concern. 'He'll be fine. Let him suss out his surrounds while we eat. I hope you're hungry.'

'Famished.'

'Excellent.' He takes my hand, pulling me into the house and leading me down a coffee-coloured hallway into an open country-style kitchen. 'I'm making ricotta pancakes. An Italian speciality.'

'Sounds delicious. Is Francesca here?' I ask, glancing around the kitchen as if maybe she's hiding in a cupboard.

He turns on the gas stovetop and places a frying pan upon the flames. 'No, she's working today.'

'Pity, I was hoping to meet her,' I say, my stomach churning a little at the knowledge that we're alone. Aside from JB, we don't have a chaperone. I'm unsure whether I'm excited or nervous about this prospect.

Fabio grins. 'Plenty of time for that. Now, can I get you a drink? Coffee or orange juice? Wine?'

'Juice, please.'

'Coming right up.' A moment later, he hands me a glass with freshly squeezed juice and ice and then gets stuck into cooking the pancakes.

While he cooks, we chat about the funny customers he has at the café and some of the more interesting regulars that come into the library, but honestly, watching him cook – his arm muscles bunching as he whisks the egg and milk into the flour mixture – is a little like watching porn. A man who cooks is almost as much of a turn-on as a man who reads books. JB arrives in the kitchen in the middle of the show, and Fabio pauses to fill him a bowl of water.

The dog, exhausted from his house inspection, collapses onto the wooden floorboards at my feet.

When Fabio has made a stack of thick, fluffy pancakes, he leads me into the lounge room.

I'd thought a rug, cornettos and prosecco on the beach were romantic but they have nothing on what greets me in here. Flames are crackling in the open fireplace. The coffee table, which sits between two plush leather couches, is dressed in a crisp white linen tablecloth and set like a Michelin-starred restaurant with shiny silver cutlery, white china plates and sparkling crystal glassware. There's also a slim crystal vase in the middle, with one red rose emerging from it. On a little silver tray to the side is a bowl full of berries and another smaller one of whipped cream.

'Wow. This is . . .'

'Too much?' he asks at my shocked expression. 'I just wanted to make this special for you.'

'It's beautiful,' I say, blinking back tears. 'I don't think anyone has ever done anything like this. Thank you.'

He beams – 'I told you we Italians were romantic' – then gestures to the cushions on either side of the coffee table. 'Please, take a seat before the pancakes get cold.'

I do as I'm told, and Fabio puts three pancakes on my plate and then adorns them with berries and a dollop of cream, before doing the same for himself.

'Eat,' he instructs.

I close my eyes and moan as I experience my first mouthful. It tastes even better than it smells. When I open them, I find him staring at me, a delighted smirk on his face. 'Good, hey?'

'Better than good. What did you put in these? Can't just be ricotta that makes them this fluffy and rich.'

He taps the side of his nose. 'If I told you, I'd have to kill you.'

I laugh and fork off another mouthful, praising God that I can now, mostly, enjoy food like this without berating myself about it. Thankfully JB is so worn out that he doesn't even try to con us into sharing. 'Who taught you to cook like this?'

'My mamma,' Fabio says sadly. 'She was an excellent cook. She had a dream to own her own *ristorante*, but . . . it wasn't meant to be.'

'I'm so sorry. You must miss her so much.'

He nods. 'But enough about me. Tell me about where you come from?' He gets stuck into his stack.

'The nearest town is Port Hedland – not that small, there's about fifteen thousand people – but our station is a hundred kilometres south.'

'Did you go to school there?'

'No, we did School of the Air in primary school,' I say, explaining what that is. 'And I boarded in Perth for high school.'

I'd much rather hear about growing up in Italy, but he's fascinated about the outback. 'Were there lots of snakes?'

I laugh, share a few stories of close encounters we had growing up and then ask him if there was any dangerous wildlife where he lived.

He shakes his head and tells me briefly about the tiny coastal village he comes from, but quickly turns the conversation back on me. 'Why do you live in the city if all your family are up north?'

'My younger brother isn't,' I say, 'and to be honest, I was never much of a country girl. I like the station in small doses, but I spent most of my time hiding inside reading books.'

He chuckles.

'As long as I can remember I wanted to be a librarian, and there were more opportunities here. My gran left me her house when she died, just after I finished uni, and then not long after that the job came up at Freo library and I love it. Which reminds me, wait here.'

I rush back into the kitchen where I left my bag and retrieve *Legends & Lattes*. 'Here's the book I promised,' I say, handing it to him.

He frowns down at the cover, which is the original self-published version with a green orc and her pink succubus on it. It's still my favourite.

'It's about an orc who gives up her life of breaking heads for money and decides to open a coffee shop instead, in a place where no one knows what coffee is. Trust me, you'll love it. I'm never wrong when it comes to matching books to people.'

He raises an eyebrow and then puts the book aside.

'Did you always want to be a barista?' I ask and then realise that might sound judgy. 'I mean . . . you're so good at it. Do you want to own your own coffee shop one day or something?'

'That's the dream,' he says, before reaching for another pan-cake. The man has an insatiable appetite. I'm so full I'm not sure I'll be able to eat for a week!

'Will it be in Australia, Italy or somewhere else entirely?' Yes, this is a loaded question, but if I'm going to risk my heart to this man, I want to know what else I might have to sacrifice. Could I move to Italy if that's what he wanted? Leave my beloved family and friends?

'My goal is to have the first Italian café on Mars,' he declares.

'Mars?!' I laugh, pretty sure he's joking.

'*Sì*. Why settle for being the best barista in the world when I can be the best barista in the universe?'

'True.' If anyone can achieve such lofty heights, it's Fabio.

'Speaking of coffee,' he says, getting to his feet and picking up our now empty plates, 'can I make you one?'

'Will it be as good as the ones you make at the Grouchy Sailor?'

'Better,' he scoffs. 'This will be proper brewed Italian coffee.'

'In that case, yes, please,' I say, standing to help him.

'No, no, no.' He all but pushes me onto the sofa. 'You relax.'

I stroke JB, who is still resting peacefully on the floor, as I look around the room. It's a lot less cluttered than my place, yet with indoor plants and a couple of fabulous art-deco lamps, it has a homey warmth that Sully's house lacks. I shake my head – why am I letting Sully intrude into my thoughts right now? – and admire two large art prints on the wall. One is of a sophisticated woman sipping a cocktail with the word AMALFI across the top and the other has a similar woman eating coffee and cake, cute scooter by her side and a castle-like building in the background. PORTOFINO, reads the title.

'Here you are, bella,' Fabio says, delivering my drink in a small, glass mug. He sits beside me and sips his own drink.

'So what will you call your coffee shop?' I ask. 'Heaven's Brew? The Cosmic Grind? Bean Me Up?'

A rumble of deep laughter bursts from his mouth as he almost chokes on his coffee. 'You're too funny,' he says. 'Now I feel boring to admit I was joking. I actually studied cyber security at university.'

'Really? Like ethical hacking and stuff?'

'Sì.'

'So why are you making coffee for a living? Not that I think there's anything wrong with that,' I clarify. 'But you must be pretty damn smart. Don't you get bored?'

He shrugs one shoulder coyly, but I can tell he's underselling himself. And I have to admit, I've always had a bit of a thing for nerds.

'After our mamma died, Francesca convinced me to get away for a while, to go travelling with her, and I was feeling a bit burned out from work, so I decided a break for a year or so might do me good.'

I nod. 'That makes sense. I must admit I had you pegged as someone more arty than techy.'

'Why?'

'Because you're good with your hands,' I say, my gaze drifting to the way his long fingers curl around the glass mug.

He smiles teasingly. 'You think I'm good with my hands?'

'What I meant . . .' I say as heat rushes to my cheeks, 'is that you're a great baker, and your coffee art is some of the best I've ever seen.'

He leans a little towards me. 'Only *some* of the best?'

Next thing I know we're kissing again, and I have no complaints. The man knows how to use his mouth. I lean into him as he deepens the kiss even more.

Somehow, I find myself lying on the couch, my head against the arm rest, his beautiful hard body stretched across me, our legs entwined and his hand teasing the bare skin beneath my jumper. I try to relax and enjoy myself as his hand slides up my stomach and cups my breast, but my brain screams a warning: *Too much, too fast.*

But this is your third date.

Shut up, Fred. Despite my hormones and Fred's voice trying to overrule my head, I know I'm not ready for this yet. We may have had three dates, he may be lovely and unbelievably hot, but I don't even know his middle name. Or exactly how old he is. Not to mention his favourite colour.

'I'm sorry, I can't do this,' I say, tugging at my jumper.

Fabio looks horrified. 'Bella. I'm . . . I'm so sorry.' He rakes a hand over his gorgeous face. 'I misread the situation. I thought there was – how do you say it? – a spark between us.'

'It's not you.' I rush to reassure him, my cheeks burning in mortification. He looks so vulnerable, and I can't have him thinking there's anything wrong with *him*. 'I've had the hots for you since the day we met, but I'm scared. No, not just scared. I'm bloody terrified.'

He frowns and then takes my hand, rubbing his thumb gently over my palm. 'What are you scared of, bella? You can tell me. I won't judge you.'

Oh, Lord, he's so sweet. 'I'm scared of being hurt and made a fool of again,' I confess, unable to look him in the eyes as I think about how I've fallen victim to a long line of losers. Tears prickle my eyes. How pathetic must I sound?

'Bella.' He brings my hand to his lips and kisses my fingers gently as he looks right into my eyes. 'Everyone is scared of love.'

'Maybe,' I concede, although I'm not sure I believe that. 'But some people have better luck. I'm a magnet for cheats and liars. I thought I might have found the one earlier this year and it turned out he was just like the rest. So I promised myself I won't rush into a relationship or sex . . . Until I really know the person. I'm sorry.'

My heart halts as I wait for him to dismiss me – and I try to tell myself if he does, he's not the man I need – but he smiles and squeezes my hand. 'Oh, bella, there is nothing worse than a broken heart.'

'You sound like you speak from experience?'

The light that is always in his eyes dims for a moment. 'I do. I too have been cheated on. It is why I left Italy and came here to join Francesca on her adventure. My long-time girlfriend slept with my best amigo.'

'Oh, God, I'm so sorry.' At least none of my boyfriends had ever done that.

'I too didn't think I was ready, but then we start chatting and you . . .' He presses his hand – still joined with mine – against his chest. 'Get into my heart.'

I blink, unsure any sweeter words have ever been said. At least not to me.

'So I want you to know,' he continues, 'that I care about you, bella. I'm happy for us to take our time.'

'Thank you.' I smile as warmth and relief fills me. 'But . . . are Italian women stupid? What kind of idiot would cheat on you? You're the total package.'

'As are you, bella,' Fabio says, looking right into my eyes like they are hot springs he wants to dive into. 'As are you.'

28

Or Else!

On Monday, I'm sitting at the desk, opening the red satchels of books from the state library courier service and dreaming of yesterday with Fabio. He's so easy to be with, and the more time I spend with him, the more I want to.

'I'm not paying you to stare into space,' Xavier sings as he arrives beside me. He's just finished Rhyme Time with parents and babies, followed by a session of Story Time with pre-schoolers. If I'd just had his morning, I'd need a stiff drink, but he's riding on his usual high. It's a pity he and Rory don't have kids, because they'd both make such good dads.

'You're not paying me,' I retort, poking out my tongue. 'The shire is.'

'True, but until anyone says otherwise, I'm your boss and that stack won't unpack itself.' His tone is teasing.

'Yes, boss,' I say, rolling my eyes as I open the next satchel. Inside are some of our books returned from other libraries and a couple more for Daisy Norman, from the Bookstars. I'm about to put them on the collections shelf when I remember she told me she was having an operation last week. I find her number in the system so I can call and leave a message.

'Hello. Daisy Norman speaking.'

I'm surprised when she answers – I never pick up an unknown number – but Lord, I love her accent.

'Oh, hi, Daisy. It's Bee calling from the library. I'm sorry, I didn't mean to bother you, I was just going to leave you a voice-mail to say your books are here and I'll keep them on my desk until you're well again.'

'Oh, pet, how precious of you. Thank you.'

'You sound well,' I say. 'How'd the operation go?'

'Not bad, but I've picked up a bit of an infection, so the doctors are insisting I stay for another few days. Which books are in?'

I list them all and she gives a little shriek at the mention of the latest Finlay Donovan.

'That's splendid. Such a fun series. Have you read it?'

'No,' I say, 'but I will now. What hospital are you at?'

'St John of God in Subiaco.'

'Would you like me to bring them to you?' I ask before I can think better of it. It's an easy train ride and a manageable walk to the hospital from there, but I tend to avoid hospitals. 'That's if you're up for visitors.'

'Oh, are you sure? That's so very kind of you. I could get my grandson to drop in and collect them, but he's very busy with work and is already taking such good care of me.'

Although my chest is a little tight at the prospect, I tell her it would be my pleasure and promise to bring her books straight after work.

Just after 5.30 pm, I get off the train and start towards St John of God. The closer I get, the more laboured my breathing feels. It's a miracle I've managed to avoid visiting hospitals since leaving as a patient for the final time nine years ago, but when Persephone's baby arrives, I'll want to go visit her. This can be a practice run.

I step inside the foyer, which reminds me more of a fancy hotel than a place that takes care of sick people. I decide to pretend I'm visiting Daisy at the Ritz or something. This only works as far as the lift. When the doors peel open and a gaunt-looking man in a wheelchair is pushed out by a woman who might be his daughter, my stomach turns, and I contemplate running.

At least he's old, I think; being gaunt in old age is entirely different to looking like a skeleton in your teens. I force myself into the lift, which smells like disinfectant, flowers and stale cigarette smoke, and push the button. Mere seconds later, the doors open again and I step out into Daisy's ward. Two nurses in navy scrubs barely glance up as I pass the desk. Trying to ignore the sounds of beeping machinery, I force myself down the corridor to her room. The door is partly open, but I knock and call out her name before going inside.

She smiles broadly as she sees me and her bag of books. 'Bee, you absolute pet.'

'Hello, Daisy,' I say, ignoring the medical paraphernalia as I approach her bed. She's in the middle of her dinner, so I put the bag on the bedside table. 'How are you feeling?'

'Better now you've brought me those. I finished my last novel yesterday and nothing on TV has grabbed me. It's all reality shows about people marrying strangers and renovating houses.' Her smile morphs into a frown. 'Are you okay?'

'Hospitals make me uncomfortable,' I confess.

'Oh dear. I would never have insisted you come if I'd known.'

I manage a smile. 'You didn't – I offered.'

She nods. 'Well, would you like to stay for a cup of tea – or do you want to get out of here quickly?'

'Actually, tea would be nice,' I say, sitting on the visitor's chair. 'Thank you.'

As if on cue, an orderly rolls in the tea trolley and we take our cups from her gratefully.

'Do you want to tell me about the aversion to hospitals?' Daisy asks. 'I've been told I'm a good listener.'

I swallow and then take a quick sip of tea. 'I was sick in my teens and spent a lot of time in hospital – not good memories – so I've avoided them ever since. It's silly, really.'

She shakes her head. 'I think it's perfectly understandable. Are you well now?'

'Yes.' I smile. 'Thank you.'

'No, thank *you*, pet. Now I'm even more grateful to you for bringing the books.'

'I'm glad I did,' I reply. I'm unsure whether it's the sweet tea or her calming personality, but I'm starting to relax. 'I'd die if I didn't have anything to read.'

She chuckles. 'Well, *die* might be a slight exaggeration, and if you hadn't said you were coming, I'd have asked my grandson to bring me some old favourites from home, but I'm very grateful that you did.'

'Mitch, was it?' I ask, remembering the photo she'd shown me.

'No, Mikey.' She beams at the mention of him.

'Does he live with you?'

'No, but he's staying at my place at the moment, taking care of my cat, and he makes sure to come in and visit his old Gran daily.'

'Is Mikey your son or daughter's child?'

'My daughter's. My late husband and I only had one child. Sadly, Joanne and her husband aren't with us any more – a car accident when Mikey was in his early twenties. His younger sister was in the car as well. We lost all three of them.'

My heart goes out to Daisy and her grandson. I can't imagine how I'd survive if I lost my parents and my siblings in one fell swoop. And parents aren't supposed to outlive their children. 'That's just awful.'

'We're all each other's got now. His parents would be so proud of the man he's become. In fact . . .' She taps her phone to check the time and grins. 'He should be here any minute.'

And . . . *that's* my cue to leave. I put my now empty teacup back on the table and stand. 'Thank you so much for the tea and the—'

'Oh, I was hoping you could stay to meet him,' she interrupts, and I think of her and the other Bookstars conspiring to set me up.

Perhaps I should mention Fabio – so much has happened since the last book club – but I don't want to jinx things by calling him my boyfriend.

'That would have been lovely,' I lie, 'but unfortunately, I've got somewhere else I need to be. Call me at the library if you end up being here longer or need a home delivery when you're discharged.'

She sighs. 'Well, maybe next time, pet. You have a good evening.'

'You too,' I say as I exit her room and head down the corridor to the elevator.

I'm downstairs and passing the hospital gift shop when I see a familiar figure up ahead going into the café.

OMG, it's Dr Michael Sullivan!

Guess he's not a fake doctor after all.

I could follow him into the café and expose him to any colleagues or patients who might be there, but I've never liked being the centre of attention, and if I start demanding he return my other two gnomes pronto, everyone will stare at me.

Like *I'm* the psycho one!

Instead, I wait until he's at the counter, and then peer stealthily around a wall to scrutinise him. He's more dressed up than I'm used to seeing him – wearing smart jeans and a navy polo shirt, stubble closer cut than before, and it appears as if he might even have run a brush through his hair – but still very casual for a doctor. Perhaps he's popping in to check on some patients after a round of afternoon golf.

I shudder at the thought that Sully might have golf clubs in his house. Could they be what he used to smash poor Veronica to smithereens?

Something inside me snaps. I don't need to make a scene, but I'd be a fool to give up this opportunity to confront my deranged neighbour in a safe space.

I move just out of sight and wait, trying to work out what I'll say, until he comes out.

'Dr Sullivan,' I call, hurrying after him as he starts briskly towards the elevators carrying two takeaway slices of chocolate cake. The other must be for a colleague. Nice gesture. Good to know he's not a total bastard to everyone.

He turns around at the sound of my footsteps and I halt quickly, falling just short of slamming into him. We're face to face, even closer than our previous encounters. So close I can smell his spicy deodorant.

'Bridget? Are you stalking me?' he asks, stepping back as he bestows upon me his perpetual scowl. Did no one ever read *When the Wind Changed* to him when he was a child?

'Stalking you?' I snort. 'I'm not the criminal here. If you must know, I was visiting someone and I happened to see you, so I decided it was as good a time and place as any for us to have it out.'

He raises a thick eyebrow. 'How did you find out I'm a doctor?'

'I don't reveal my sources and I don't care if you're the doctor for the King of England, if you don't deliver Archie and Betty back to me immediately, I will make sure everyone here knows what an absolute jerkface you are!'

Jerkface? I cringe.

'You name your gnomes?' he asks, his tone droll.

'Yes, and while you're at it, you can hand over all those pieces of Veronica as well.' I might not be able to stick her back together, but at least I can give her a proper burial. 'Or else!'

His lips twitch in obvious amusement. 'Or else what?'

I narrow my eyes at him. 'Or *else* I tell your colleagues *and* patients exactly what kind of musically untalented, lower-than-pond-scum kind of lowlife you are.'

Before he can respond, I turn and storm out.

Of course, now if he doesn't give back my gnomes, I'll have to follow through on my threat, and that thought terrifies me.

29

The Bane of my Existence

Thump. Thump. Thump.

I've barely been asleep for ten minutes when a sound wakes me up. For a moment I forget where I am and wonder what Sully is doing shooting hoops at this time of the night, but then screams and moans join the cacophony, and my eyes widen. Fred was still out on a date when I went to bed and if the sounds coming from her bedroom next door are anything to go by, said date must have gone pretty well.

I sit up, switch on the bedside lamp and scramble to find my noise-cancelling headphones. Hopefully listening to my new audiobook, *The Sweetest Revenge* by Lizzy Dent, will help drown out the noise. Fred often recounts her sexcapades to me but it's one thing listening to her talk about them after the fact and quite another being privy as they happen. I don't know how Waylen can stand it – especially considering he's so straitlaced and proper.

As the sounds of the narrator fill my ears, I turn off the light and lean back. JB shifts from the bottom of the bed and tries to bury his head under my pillow, and I wonder if anyone has invented headphones for dogs.

*

I yawn as I wander home at lunch time the next day for my daily check of Sully's mailbox. It's been hours since my morning coffee and I'm starting to fade. It's partly Fred's fault that I'm so tired and partly Lizzy Dent's – her story stopped me from falling back to sleep, as I was desperate to find out the ending. I wonder if I'll ever tire of reading about other people falling in love.

I'm relieved to find only one catalogue in Sully's letterbox and stumble inside, deciding to forgo food for a quick powernap in my own bed. Oh, how I miss my mattress. I'm in the middle of a blissful dream – yes, it might just involve a sexy Italian barista – when the doorbell rings. *Argh!* Who on earth would be visiting at this time of the day? Deciding it's probably religious callers again, I roll over and try to immerse myself back in the dream.

Thankfully, whoever it is doesn't ring again.

Forty-five minutes later, my alarm goes off and I haul myself out of bed to head back to the library.

What the hell? I blink twice as I open my front door and almost trip on a bucket full of broken, colourful ceramics.

'Veronica!' I bend down and snatch her up – all the shattered pieces of her – clutching the bucket to my chest like it contains the ashes of a very dear friend.

There's an envelope nestled among the broken pieces.

Scowling, I take my poor broken gnome inside to join my other gnomes and then rip open the envelope.

UNTIL THE CATALOGUES HAVE CEASED COMPLETELY . . .
THIS IS ALL YOU'RE GETTING.
BTW, I SHOULD PROBABLY INFORM YOU THAT I DON'T WORK
AT ST JOHN OF GOD, SO IF YOU STORM IN THERE THROWING
AROUND ACCUSATIONS ABOUT ME, YOU'LL LOOK STARK

RAVING MAD. AND THEN I WON'T BE THE ONLY ONE WHO
THINKS SO!

What? Dr Psycho's calling *me* stark raving mad. I curl my
fingers into my palms, my nails digging into my skin, as fury
courses through me. This man is the bane of my existence!

If he doesn't work at that hospital, then what was he doing
there? And who was the other piece of cake for? Of course, he could
be bluffing. But I have his full name, so I can google him. I can't
believe I didn't think about this before. Why didn't Fred? And we
call ourselves librarians! I blame him for not telling me his name in
the first place and befuddling me.

My fingers dash across my phone screen as I walk back to work.
There aren't any links to social media, which doesn't surprise me.
Sully doesn't seem the type to air his laundry – dirty or otherwise –
but LinkedIn provides the goods.

Dr Michael Sullivan has been a Royal Flying Doctor for the
past five years.

A flying doctor? I can't help but be impressed. Living as remote
as my family do, we had to rely on the flying doctors more than
once when I was growing up. In fact, if it weren't for them, my
brother Justin might not be alive today. At least now I know why
Sully goes out at all hours of the day and night – he's a shiftworker.
And one who cares for the vulnerable at that.

How bad can he be if he helps people for a living?

Before taking to the skies, Sully was at Charlie Gairdner
working in Emergency, and he completed his medical degree at
UWA. I do some quick maths, estimating his age from when he
graduated high school, working out that he must be thirty-six or
thirty-seven.

The most interesting thing is his profile picture – it's like his much happier doppelganger. There's no doubt it's him, but in place of his perpetual scowl is a sunny smile, visible in his eyes as well as his mouth. I can almost feel his warmth emanating off the screen and wonder what it would take to get him to smile at me.

I recoil at my own traitorous thought and silently scold myself.

Even if there is a more human side to Sully, that doesn't mean I want to get to know it. Some things are unforgiveable and in the short time we've known each other, he's done more than a few such things.

I have a bucketful of poor Veronica to prove it!

30

Welcome to the Bookstars

'Okay, everyone. Grab your drinks and let's get started,' I say. Today we're discussing the newest Kristin Hannah. 'This is a juicy novel with so much to unpack, and I don't want to waste a moment.'

I hear Olga mutter about me being so much bossier than Janine as they all load up their plates with biscuits and migrate towards the circle of chairs. Edgar is settling into his seat beside me when the door opens and in strides Fabio.

'What are you doing here?' I blurt, my heart doing a little blip at the sight of him.

'Isn't this the book club?' he asks, throwing his come-hither smile around the circle.

I actually hear a few old dears whimpering, and I don't blame them. Just one look at him in jeans and a simple black hoodie and I'm whimpering too.

'It sure is,' Rose exclaims. 'And who, pray tell, are you?'

He offers her his hand. 'I'm Fabio. Pleasure to meet you . . .?'

'Rose,' she supplies, giggling like a schoolgirl. 'Are you here to join us?'

Fabio gives me a smile that melts my inside. '*Sì*, I am.'

'Goodness, are you Italian?' Lorna pats the vacant seat beside her. 'Welcome, sexy. You can sit right over here next to me.'

'I'm sorry,' I tell him, struggling to curb my smile. 'But this group is for seniors. We have other book clubs you can join though. There's a fantasy group, a true crime group and a couple of evening groups that read general fiction like us and are always keen for new members.'

Fabio stands his ground, leaning back into the seat and folding his bulky arms over his wide chest. 'Are any of those others run by you?'

I shake my head; I'd tried to get a romance group going once but no one around here was willing to admit they read it.

'In that case, I want to join this one,' he confirms.

The older women simper on my behalf, and I try not to swoon – it's sweet that he's doing this to spend time with me, but there's no way I'll be able to concentrate on intelligent conversation with him only a few feet away. 'Not possible, I'm afraid. This group's for old people.'

'Excuse *me*,' Kerry exclaims. 'Who are you calling old?'

'Yeah,' Lorna echoes. 'We're seniors, thank you very much. And very nimble ones at that,' she adds, wriggling her eyebrows suggestively at Fabio.

Oh Lord.

'Let the boy join,' Edgar mutters. 'It'll be good to have another bloke around here.'

'Stop being a stickler for the rules, Bee,' Rose says.

I let out an exasperated sigh – I know when I'm fighting a losing battle – and gesture to the spare chair. 'Fine. Welcome to the Bookstars.'

'Thank you.' He has no idea what he's getting himself in for as he grins. I see Lorna's already shifted her chair even closer to his.

'Right, who enjoyed the book?'

'Are you single?' Ronice asks, totally ignoring my question and giving Fabio a look that says she'd be willing to switch teams again for him if he is.

'Um . . .' He glances over at me and my insides twist; we haven't officially said what we are to each other. I raise an eyebrow at him.

'Our Bridget is single,' Sue informs him, looking my way. 'And you clearly both love books. Always good to have something in common.'

'Is that right?' he says. 'I'll bear that in mind.'

I clear my throat. 'Do you think we could talk about *The Women* now?'

A few of the Bookstars look chastised, but any proper discussion is almost impossible. Fabio hasn't read the book and keeps interrupting my attempts to get a good discourse going. Most of the female members seem to have lost the ability to speak and all Edgar wants to talk about is his new love affair with Jack Reacher.

After time is officially up, everyone heads to the afternoon tea table to finish off the biscuits, the women still flocking around Fabio. If they weren't all fifty-or-so years older than me, I'd worry I had competition. Instead I find it kind of sweet and even a little bit sexy.

As much as I'd like to stay and watch them all try to monopolise his attention, our hour is up and I have work to do. They're all so enamoured by him that nobody notices me leave, but Fabio finds me half an hour later to say goodbye. 'That was fun. Thanks for letting me join the club.'

'You didn't exactly give me a choice.'

He shrugs and lifts his hand to tuck my hair behind my ear. 'Is it my fault if I can't get enough of you, bella?'

I roll my eyes, while inwardly glowing. 'You shouldn't be able to sweet-talk so well in a second language. It's unfair. Although,' I admit, 'I liked having you there as well. However, if you insist on coming again, *I'm* going to have to insist on a few ground rules.'

'Such as?' he asks with the cutest, most earnest expression.

'Um . . .' I struggle to think of any. 'You must always read the book, and you're not allowed to distract from the discussion.'

'I'm a distraction for you?' he teases.

My cheeks heat. 'Not to me! To the nonnas.' But I can't help smiling.

'I thought we weren't supposed to call them that?'

'*You're* not. I can call them whatever I like because I'm in charge, which means I can kick you out if you become a disruption.'

'I promise to be on my best behaviour,' he whispers, leaning forward and kissing me on the lips.

I pull back quickly because PDAs are frowned upon in the library, especially by employees. 'Are you busy tonight? I was wondering if you want to come see an ABBA cover band at the Norfolk with Xavier, his husband Rory, Fred and probably some guy she's just met. You can bring your sister if she's not working. I'm dying to meet her.'

His face falls. '*Fanculo.* I'd love that, but I just told Edgar I'd go to lawn bowls with him.'

'Lawn bowls? With *Edgar?*' Although I'm disappointed, I can't help my amusement. It looks like the nonnas weren't the only ones moving fast in there. 'I didn't know you were a bowler or knew Edgar?'

'I'm not. We just got chatting and he told me he used to go with his wife, but hasn't been back since, because everyone else goes in pairs. I thought he'd feel more comfortable if I go with him.'

I press a hand against my heart. 'That's so sweet. Of course, you must go.'

'You could come with us?' he suggests with a sexy smile.

'Thanks, but I wouldn't want to be your third wheel.'

'What about tomorrow night, then? You could show me some more of the sights of Freo.'

I'm about to say yes when I remember I've got my monthly appointment with Aisha, followed by kickboxing. 'Sorry, I can't tomorrow, but what about Friday?'

He nods – 'It's a date' – and I'm already making plans in my head. Maybe we could do an escape room and then finish with drinks at Darling Darling.

When Fabio leaves – after borrowing *Mad Honey* which is the next Bookstar novel – Fred pounces.

'What the hell was your hot barista boyfriend doing in there?' she hisses, earning her a side-eye from a mother who is sitting in a nearby beanbag reading her toddler the classic that is *Burglar Bill*.

'*Shh!*' I laugh and lead her towards the magazine section, which is always quiet. 'He's joining the book club. He likes books and wants to talk about them.'

In reply, Fred throws back her head and laughs loudly. 'Bull crap. He's just trying to earn brownie points so you'll let him into your pants!'

31

The Plot Thickens

I can't wait to tell Aisha everything that has happened since the last time I saw her – the escalation of Sully's insanity, the possibility of promotion at the library and, of course, what's been happening with Fabio. As I turn into her garden, the front door opens, a man walks out of the house, and I almost swallow my tongue.

It's not just any random man but Dr Michael Sullivan. Did my thoughts conjure him?

I consider scrambling behind a bush, but it's too late, he's seen me. I panic – my heart beating too fast – as our eyes lock, then I tell myself to stop being silly. What does it matter if he knows I'm seeing a therapist? Knowing you need help is a sign of strength, not weakness and, anyway, I don't care what he thinks of me!

'Bridget?' He looks as surprised to see me as I am to see him, and before he can accuse me of something untoward again, I say, 'Don't go assuming I'm stalking you – I've got an appointment with Aisha.'

'Good for you,' he says. 'I assume you found Veronica?'

My eyes narrow. 'Yes, I did.' If he expects me to thank him, he's going to be gravely disappointed. 'And you'd better not have done

anything to Archie or Betty. I'm doing my best to stop the catalogues and those poor gnomes are innocent in all this.'

'Archie, Betty and Veronica . . .' he muses. 'You an Archie
comics fan?'

'None of your business,' I snap.

He simply nods and I can't help noticing how wrecked he
looks. His eyes are bloodshot with dark bags beneath them.
He's probably burning the candle at both ends. He glances at his
watch as if he has someplace else to be, and I realise one of us is
going to have to step off the path or turn sideways to let the other
past. Part of me wants to stubbornly stand my ground, but my
conscience won't allow it now I know he has such an important
job. Every minute standing here pissing me off is one less he could
be saving lives.

While my mind is racing with thoughts, the door opens again,
and we both look to see Aisha waiting in the doorway.

'You coming in, Bee?' she calls.

Sully steps aside so I can pass. 'See you round, *neighbour.*'

If not for his sarcastic tone, it would be the nicest thing he's ever
said to me.

'Hopefully not,' I reply, catching a whiff of that nostril-teasing
spicy scent as I stalk past him. How can someone so deranged smell
so good?

'What was Sully doing here?' I ask the moment Aisha closes the
door behind us.

She ushers me into the front room. 'You know I can't speak to
you about another patient.'

'He's a patient?' *Interesting.*

I don't know why the thought didn't cross my mind that Sully
might be in therapy too, because being a flying doctor must be

a stressful occupation. He probably sees all manner of traumatic things in his work.

'No comment,' Aisha says as I lower myself into her cloud-couch. It's still warm and the knowledge that he was sitting here only minutes earlier sends shivers down my spine. 'How do *you* know him?'

I'm about to tell her that it's unfair to expect me to answer her questions about him when she won't tell me anything, but maybe if I do, we'll get talking and she'll let something slip. 'He's my neighbour.'

Her eyes widen. 'Not *the* neighbour?'

'Yes,' I say. 'The one who tortures me with his terrible bagpipe practice.' I'd told her about that at last month's appointment. 'And he also kidnapped my gnomes and even killed one of them!'

'He did what?'

'He smashed one to pieces.' I fill her in on the whole gnome fiasco and tell her about our altercation at the hospital. 'I was a bit freaked out by his behaviour, so I moved in with Fred.'

Nothing I've ever said before has appeared to shock Aisha, but the look that flashes across her face indicates she's surprised by all this.

She takes a deep breath. 'And are you still living with her?'

I nod and Aisha frowns and folds her hands in her lap. 'I really don't think you need to fear Michael. He's a good guy.'

'Um . . . did you hear nothing? He *killed* Veronica.'

'I must admit that does sound out of character, but then again, you did torture him with an onslaught of junk mail.' She gives me a look of reproval and I remember her advice just to wave occasionally.

But whose side is she on? I've always felt so comfortable with her, but now I know he sees her too, I feel almost violated.

'That may be so,' I say, 'but surely violence is never the answer?'

She gives me an exasperated look. 'Bee. It was a gnome. For all you know, he accidentally dropped it.'

'Oh, no, no,' I all but shout, 'Veronica's demise was no accident. It's a good thing Sully's seeing you, because I'm telling you, he's not right in the head.'

Aisha offers a benign smile, clears her throat and asks me if there's anything in particular I'd like to chat about this month.

'You mean *aside* from why Sully was here?'

Her return expression is school-principal stern.

I sigh and sink further back into the cloud. 'Well, I might have made progress in conquering my fear of hospitals.'

My period arrives on Friday morning, along with the killer headache that often accompanies it. Somehow I make it through the day on painkillers, but I'll have to cancel my date, and, after another broken sleep due to Fred's late-night shenanigans, I also decide it's time to move back home. After all, Aisha doesn't think Sully is truly a threat and I *do* trust her. I'm in no state to do anything except curl up in my *own* bed with a hot water bottle on my stomach and JB by my side.

When I text Fabio telling him I'm not well, he replies almost instantly: *Bella! What do you need? I bring you chicken soup or tissues? Anything!*

I'm so emotional, his message brings tears to my eyes. *That's so sweet, but I'm okay. I don't need anything and I wouldn't be very good company right now.*

I shouldn't be surprised when just after seven o'clock that night my doorbell rings and I find Fabio standing on my porch holding a paper shopping bag. Under his other arm is a package that looks and smells suspiciously like fish and chips. I didn't think I felt very hungry, but the aroma makes my mouth water.

'What are you doing here?' I blurt crankily.

He smiles. 'I wanted to make sure you're okay. And I brought gifts.'

Reluctantly, I tighten my dressing gown around my waist and let him in. As comfortably as if he lives here, he heads into my lounge room, JB harassing him for the food on his way. I follow to see him dump the contents of the paper bag on the table.

My eyes boggle at the sight of tampons, sanitary pads, pain-killers, a microwavable wheat pack and a large block of Cadbury's chocolate.

'Have you eaten?' he asks.

I shake my head – I didn't even have the energy to pull out a microwave meal – then gesture to the spoils on the table. 'How did you know?'

Holding the takeaway high out of JB's reach, he puts his arm around my waist and draws me close. 'I have a *sorella*, remember?'

'Fish and chips are my perfect comfort food,' I say into his chest, not mentioning that even now, I rarely let myself eat them.

'Then let's get them into you.' He fetches water from the kitchen and then we sit next to each other on the couch, dinner between us, laughing as we try to ward off JB.

Like magic, after a few mouthfuls, I'm feeling slightly better and decide it's time to dig a little deeper into Fabio. By the time he leaves tonight, I want to know enough about him that I'd be able to pass a green card interrogation.

'What's your middle name?' I ask before biting a crispy chip in half.

'Bruce.'

I almost choke on the chip. 'What?!' Bruce is about as un-Italian as you can get. 'You're not serious? With a first name like Fabio, I thought it'd be something like Giuseppe, Lorenzo or Ricardo.'

He laughs and shrugs one shoulder. 'My mamma is a big fan of Bruce Willis. What about you? Do you have a middle name?'

I nod. 'Elinor.'

'Is that after a movie character like Bridget?'

'Bridget is after a book character,' I remind him. 'And Elinor is a character from *Sense and Sensibility*, which is also one of my mum's favourite books.'

Fabio takes a gulp of wine. 'So your mamma is as big a reader as you?'

'Yes. She always has a novel in hand, the latest Nora Roberts or Jude Deveraux. She says books were her friends when she moved to the back end of beyond to marry my dad. She reads in bed, while watering the garden or cooking the dinner – one hand on the hose or wooden spoon, the other holding her book – and she reads on long car journeys if Dad's driving and while he watches TV.'

According to family lore, my first name was originally going to be Elinor, but in hospital Mum read a new release called *Bridget Jones's Diary* and told my father to put Bridget Elinor Jones on the birth certificate form instead.

To be fair, she didn't know then how much of a classic the book would become, that there would be sequels and movies, and that it would inspire a whole boom in the 'chick-lit' genre. She simply thought it was a nice name and the character made her laugh when the sore nipples I gave her made her want to cry. I was five before she really realised what she'd done – that was the year the movie came out, and we all know what happens to a book when it's made into a movie.

Suddenly even people who would never read chick-lit knew about the trials and tribulations of Bridget Jones. She became a fictional icon, and I became a laughing stock. That's when my family started calling me Bee, although in their teens my brothers found it hilarious to call me BJ and sometimes it still slips out.

'If you have *bambinos*, would you follow your mamma's naming tradition?' Fabio asks, and my ovaries quiver at the way he says this word.

'I've never really given it much thought.' I want to have kids one day, but my focus has been more on finding someone to share that experience with rather than naming imaginary babies. 'What about you? Do you want children?'

He nods enthusiastically. '*Sì, sì*, I want to give my mamma lots of bambinos.'

Hang on . . . his *mamma*? My grip tightens on my glass. 'I thought you said your mother was dead?'

Fabio blinks, then shakes his head slightly. 'She is, but . . .' He glances solemnly at his hands. 'She always wanted to be a grandmother – she'd have loved to spoil and cook for grandchildren. I know me having them would make her happy.'

'That's beautiful,' I say, sniffing back emotion.

He smiles softly. '*Grazie*.'

At the sound of a car door slamming outside, JB wakes from the dead and rushes over to the back door, barking furiously at it.

'That'll just be my neighbour,' I say with a dismissive wave of my hand.

'*Dio Mio!*' Fabio pushes back his chair and crosses to the window. 'You mean your evil neighbour?'

I laugh at the way he's peering out the window like a little old lady on neighbourhood watch.

'Do you want me to go next door and have a talk with him, man to man? Tell him to stop bothering you?'

'No, but thank you,' I say. 'I'd much rather you keep talking to me.'

And talk we do. When the fish and chips are gone, we crack open the chocolate. I learn Fabio's favourite food ('lasagne but not how the Aussies make it'), his favourite colour (yellow – 'such a *contento* colour'), what music he likes (mostly bands I don't know) and his age (twenty-five).

I tell him I'm twenty-eight in September. 'Does that make me a cougar?'

He throws his head back and cackles, then his expression grows serious. 'Our age gap doesn't worry you, does it, bella?'

'No.' I swallow. 'But I am wondering . . . how long are you planning on staying in Australia?' I don't want to freak him out, but as sexy as he is, I know my heart and body are linked, and casual dating isn't for me. Before I fall entirely for Fabio, I want to know there is at least potential for something long-term.

'That depends . . .' He smiles at me and does that thing where he tucks my hair behind my ear. I love the intimacy of the gesture and the warm way it makes me feel.

'On what?' I whisper.

'On if I meet someone who makes it worthwhile staying. I do love it here, but sadly, I'm only on a working visa.'

'You sure that's not what you want from me? A green card?' I ask, half-joking, half-serious.

He frowns again. 'Do you really have that low an opinion of me, bella?'

'Of course not.' I squeeze his hand and then rest my head against his shoulder. 'I'm sorry. I just have trust issues, but they're on me, not you.'

'I get it. You're scared of getting hurt. I can't promise what the future holds, but I can promise you this – I really like you. I would stay in Australia for *amore,* and I would never hurt you on purpose.'

We share another near-perfect kiss and, although I do feel like I know him even better after tonight, although it would be so easy to take his hand and lead him into my bedroom, I'm still not quite ready to take that next step. Fred would think me insane and maybe I am, but I still can't shake the feeling that this is too good to be true – that *he's* too good to be true.

Just a little bit longer, I tell my cranky libido as we finally bid him goodnight.

If this is meant to be, it will be worth the wait.

32

Two Teaspoons of Sugar

Another order of books arrives for Daisy on Monday afternoon, and I give her a call to check in. 'It's Bee from the library. Just seeing how your hip and your need for books is going. Are you home yet?'

'Bless you, pet. Yes, I'm home and hoping to make it to Book-stars next week, but I'm not sure whether I can sit that long just yet.'

'I'm glad to hear you're home,' I say. 'Would you like me to drop your books around after work?'

'Oh, pet. Are you sure? I don't want to put you out, but I have to say, a visitor would be nice.'

'It's no trouble at all.' I checked her address and know she's only a few kilometres away from my place. 'See you in a couple of hours.'

Daisy's garden is delightful. Her front yard overflows with native shrubbery and there are cute little statues throughout – not gnomes, but cherubs and small animals. I press the bell and am smiling at the cane rocking chairs on the front verandah complete with crocheted throw rugs when the door peels open and Sully fills the frame. My stomach flips.

'Sully?' I splutter.

He blinks. 'Bridget?'

You know when you swallow nothing, choke on air, and erupt into a wild coughing fit? That's the only way I can describe how I feel. We stare, our open mouths mirroring each other; he appears to be as flabbergasted as I am by this whole situation.

Eventually, we speak at the same time.

Me: 'What are you doing here?' Maybe he's Daisy's doctor.

Sully: *'You're* Gran's librarian?'

Gran? Of all the coincidences! I can't believe it.

'And you're Mikey.' Dr *Michael* Sullivan. That's why he was at the hospital.

'Only Gran calls me that,' he says warningly, and I can understand why. Mikey sounds like a five-year-old boy, which of course means I'm going to call him that from now on.

'Mikey! Is that my librarian friend? Don't leave her standing there on the doorstep.'

Sully aka Mikey aka the Psychopath Next Door glowers at me, then calls over his shoulder, 'She's just dropping off the books.'

Maybe he's scared I'll tell Daisy about his transgressions. She obviously thinks the sun shines out of his arse.

'I can say hello,' I say firmly and loud enough that his grandmother can hear me.

'Splendid,' comes Daisy's accented voice from further in the house.

At Sully's scowl, I say, 'Don't worry, I won't stay long. I've got to get home and walk my dog.'

'How is the beast?' he asks as I step inside the house, which is toasty warm compared to the autumn breeze outside.

I glare at him. 'He's great. A total darling, especially since I've been staying at my friend's place, so we haven't had to listen to you torturing those pipes every day.'

'You wouldn't have had to anyway – I've been staying here since Gran had her op, taking care of Moose while she was in hospital and looking after them both now.'

Seriously? All this time I'd been hiding away at Fred's, Sully hadn't even been at home!

'I have to say,' he adds, 'it's a lot more peaceful here than at my place.'

There's a *lot* of things I want to say to that, but I don't want to argue at Daisy's house, so I swallow the instinct to fight. 'Who's Moose?'

'You'll meet him in a moment. Gran's just in the lounge room, last door on your left off the hallway.' He gestures down the corridor, and it sounds like he's speaking through a mouthful of sand.

Sully walks behind me, and we emerge into a lovely sunny room, with embroidery in frames on the walls, photo frames on all available surfaces, indoor plants and a row of get-well cards upon the mantelpiece, a fire roaring beneath it. But most appealing are the floor-to-ceiling bookshelves taking up one whole wall.

'Bee,' Daisy exclaims from her position in a green velvet armchair. In an identical one on the other side of the room sits a massive fluffy black cat, who I assume is Moose. He narrows his yellow-green eyes at me suspiciously.

'Hi, Daisy. How are you feeling?' I ask, popping the books on the coffee table beside her.

'I can't complain, but it's lovely to see you.' She gestures to the sofa. 'Take a seat and tell me what I missed last book club. Sully, go make us some tea.'

As he obediently disappears, I lower myself onto the sofa.

'Well, what do you think?' she whispers, her eyes bright as she nods towards the door Sully just left through.

'It's lovely,' I say, purposely misunderstanding her question as I glance around the room. 'Is the embroidery yours? My grandma used to embroider and whenever I came to Perth to stay with her as a child, she'd teach me some stitches.'

Daisy waves away my question with her hand. 'Never mind the embroidery. I'm talking about Mikey. Isn't he just adorable? Such a good boy. And much better looking than Olga's Alex. Everyone says Mikey looks exactly like Prince Harry. That ex-wife of his has rocks in her head. Who cheats on someone as good-looking, smart *and* kind as him?'

I honestly don't know what to say – there are two sides to every story and if Sully treated his wife anything like he treats me, then who can blame her for cheating? – so I just smile. It's then I realise the bookshelves are the ones from Sully's ransom photo. My heart hitches. This must be where he's been hiding Archie and Betty.

'Mikey's a doctor,' she continues, 'but he's taken a few weeks off to care for me. Staying with an old, needy woman is not exactly the holiday he deserves, poor love. He has to go back to work soon but says he'll arrange his roster so he can bring me to book club.'

'That's sweet of him,' I say, the words feeling like rocks in my throat.

'Actually, Gran,' Sully calls from the kitchen, making me real-ise he's heard every word she's said so far – thank God I didn't agree that he was hot. 'Bridget and I already know each other. She lives next door to me.'

'You're neighbours?' Daisy claps her hands together. 'How wonderful.'

'That's one word for it,' Sully says as he returns to the room, carrying a tray with a teapot, three dainty china cups and a pile of melting moments.

I'm impressed – I'd expected him to just boil water and throw teabags into mugs.

'Bridget's been collecting my mail for me,' he says, narrowing his eyes at me as if warning me not to say anything bad as he puts the tray on the coffee table and begins to play mother.

'It's been my pleasure,' I reply, hitting him with a sickly sweet smile. 'And *Mikey's* been assisting with my gardening.'

'It was getting a little *cluttered*. How d'you like your tea?'

'Black, no sugar. Some of us don't need sweetening up.'

He raises an eyebrow and dumps two teaspoons of sugar into my cup before thrusting it at me.

'Thanks,' I spit.

'Is that why you wanted to watch *Bridget Jones's Diary* a while back?' Daisy asks.

Sully's cheeks go red. 'Um.'

He wanted to watch *Bridget*? Now this is a fascinating development.

'Well, isn't this grand?' Daisy beams, oblivious to my smirk and Sully's obvious discomfort. She reminds me a little of Lady Violet Bridgerton, desperate to marry off her eligible sons and daughters. 'I knew you two would get along like a house on fire.'

'Oh yeah, we're practically besties,' Sully says as he hands me my cup. 'We both love music. Don't we, Bridge?'

Bridge? My grip tightens on my cup. 'Yes, we do. Although our tastes are slightly different.' I have some, which is more than I can say for him.

'Have you heard Mikey playing the bagpipes?' Daisy asks as Sully carefully hands her a cup of tea and then turns back to pour his own. 'He won't let me hear him yet.'

'I have had that pleasure, and I've never heard anything quite like it before.'

I feel Sully's narrowed eyes boring into me as Daisy adds, 'My late husband made them.'

'Wow,' I say, feeling only slightly bad. 'He *made* them?'

She nods proudly. 'He was very good with his hands, as well as being a talented piper. He made six sets – sold four and kept one for each of the grandchildren. Sadly, he died before he could teach either of them.'

Sully takes her hand and I can't help noticing the tenderness between them. The way he dotes on his grandma is in complete opposition to the image I've formed of him, of some emotionally-barren, empty shell of a human being.

But then again, they are all each other has.

Could grief be why Sully is so grumpy and antisocial? And maybe also why he sees Aisha? I can only imagine how I'd react if I lost almost my whole family – not to mention his wife – and I feel tiny pieces of the wall I'd built around my heart where he's con-cerned starting to chip off.

'Would you like a melting moment?' he asks, jolting me from my thoughts.

Not wanting Daisy to think me rude, I accept. 'Thanks.'

I realise that unless he moves Moose, the only place for him to sit is on the sofa. Next to me. And I get the feeling Moose rules the roost and wouldn't be relocated even if the prime minister came to tea. Sully's so large that when he lowers himself onto the sofa, there's barely any space between us.

My eyes drift to his thighs and boggle at the thickness of them, not to mention the length of his legs. Sitting next to him, I feel almost dainty, which is something I rarely feel and perhaps why

I find myself imagining those strong legs wrapped around my waist as he . . .

What the heck? What on earth am I doing, thinking such things about a man I don't even like while his grandmother is sitting less than a metre away? Not to mention the fact I have a boyfriend.

I shove the biscuit into my mouth in an effort to distract myself. 'Wow. These are delicious,' I say, barely conscious enough to taste anything.

'Sully made them,' Daisy tells me as Moose rouses and jumps off the armchair.

'You bake?' It's hard to imagine Dr Michael Sullivan wearing an apron and sliding hot trays out of an oven.

'Don't sound so surprised.' He smiles at Daisy. 'I learned from the best.'

'All men should be able to cook as well as women, if you ask me,' she says.

'I couldn't agree more.' I pop the rest of the biscuit into my mouth and then reach out to pat the cat as it stalks past me.

Moose lifts a big, black paw and swipes me, hissing as his claws dig into my skin.

'Youch,' I cry, pulling back my hand.

'Moose,' Sully scolds, scooping him up and holding him against his chest. Immediately, the cat begins to snuggle into him and purr. I can feel the smugness radiating off Sully. At least I know he doesn't hate *all* animals, but this one might deserve it.

Moose definitely warrants the title of Beast more than JB.

'I'm so sorry, pet,' Daisy says. 'I should have warned you. Aside from me, Moose only likes men. And he adores Mikey, but then again, everyone does.'

'Not me,' I almost say, 'and his ex-wife doesn't sound all that fond of him either,' but instead I simply nurse my throbbing finger and wonder if it's too soon to make my escape.

'Shit.' Sully dumps Moose on the floor. 'You're bleeding.'

'Oh dear,' Daisy exclaims. 'I'm so sorry. Mikey, go fetch a bandaid and some antiseptic cream.'

'I'll be fine,' I say, trying to stop the blood – how sharp are that cat's claws? Perhaps I need a tetanus shot – but Sully is already on his feet and heading out of the room.

Daisy makes kissy noises at the cat, who prances over and jumps into her lap. 'I can't believe you and Mikey are neighbours,' she says, stroking Moose like he isn't a vicious animal. 'What a lovely coincidence.'

Sully returns with a first-aid kit and reaches for my hand. 'Let me take a look.'

'It's fine,' I protest again, pulling it out of his reach.

'Bridget,' he says, sounding exasperated.

Annoyed, I thrust out my hand and suck in a breath as his warm ones take hold of it.

'Hmm . . . it's quite deep,' he muses, dabbing an antiseptic wipe over it, 'but I think you'll live.'

'Is that your professional opinion, Dr Sullivan?'

In reply, he wipes Savlon over it and then expertly whips open a bandaid before wrapping it slightly too tightly around my finger. I hope his bedside manner is better with actual patients. 'There.'

'Thank you,' I say through gritted teeth and then stand. 'Well, it was lovely to see you, Daisy, but I must be getting home to my dog.'

'But you haven't finished your tea,' she objects.

'Gran,' Sully says, 'if she's got to go, she's got to go.'

Daisy sighs. 'Okay, then. Thanks so much, pet.'

'You're welcome. Hope to see you back at the library soon.' I give Moose and Sully the evil eye as I start out of the room. When Sully follows, I add, 'I can see myself out.'

But he isn't having any of it.

'Maybe I can have you both round to Sunday lunch when I'm properly on my feet again,' Daisy calls as he ushers me down the hallway.

'That would be lovely,' I lie.

'Thank you for not saying anything about the gnomes,' Sully whispers as he opens the front door.

I narrow my eyes at him and glance back into the house. 'Are they here?'

He nods. 'I'll drop them back to you tomorrow.'

'You'd better,' I order. 'Or *else*.'

And this time he knows my threat isn't empty. If he doesn't return Archie and Betty in one piece, then his beloved Gran will hear some harsh truths about her *precious* grandson.

33

A Not So Happy Birthday

The next morning, I'm wrangling large silver balloons with the numbers four and zero, when I open my front door and almost trip over three gnomes sitting on my welcome mat.

I gasp. After spending most of the night messaging with Fabio, I'd almost forgotten my ultimatum to Sully.

But *three* gnomes? What the heck? There's Betty sitting on the loo reading, Archie baring his butt, and, miraculously, Veronica perched on a stack of books. A lump of emotion rushing to my throat, I bend down and snatch her up, scrutinising her from top to bottom, but I can't find so much as a scratch on her.

Sully was obviously messing with me. What kind of person does that?

It's then I notice Betty is perched upon a white envelope. I carefully pick it up and take them all inside. 'Look who's back, JB.'

I have to be careful not to drop the gnomes and the balloons as I navigate past JB to the kitchen, where I put everything down on the bench, then read.

THANKS FOR THE LOAN. I'M SORRY TO SEE THEM GO.
I WAS GROWING KIND OF FOND OF THEM.

'Thanks? And *kind of fond of them?*' I say aloud.

Who knew Dr Sullen was capable of developing feelings, never mind admitting them?

I'm feeling grateful and almost softening towards him until I remember the only reason he returned Archie, Betty and Veronica is because he was scared I'd dob him in to Granny.

At least now I know *his* kryptonite!

My phone beeps in the bag hanging over my shoulder and I know before looking that it's Fred: *Where the hell are you? And did you get the balloons?*

I shove it back in my bag; replying will only slow me down.

'Bye, JB, see you at lunch,' I say for the second time that morning and then sprint towards the library, hoping Xavier won't get there before me. Fred will be furious if I ruin our surprise.

'Thank fuck,' she shouts, throwing up her hands when I burst through the staff door five minutes later, sweating and panting like I've just been chased by a crocodile. She grabs the balloons out of my hands. 'What happened to you? Xavier will be here any moment.'

'Sully returned my gnomes,' I say as I follow her and Persephone to the main counter, which they've already covered in streamers and tiny black and silver stars.

'He listened to your threat? What a Granny's boy.' Fred cackles, positioning the four and zero so that the birthday boy will see them the moment he arrives.

'What threat?' Persephone asks, rubbing her belly in the way all pregnant women seem to constantly do.

We fill her in on my visit to Daisy – which of course I'd messaged Fred about – and her eyes widen when I get to the bit about Sully being her grandson.

Persephone shakes her head. 'But Daisy's a delight. And from what you've said, Sully—'

'Even serial killers love their grannies,' Fred says, standing back to look at her handiwork.

Before we can say anything else on the matter, we hear the click of the staff door again and all line up in front of the desk, shouting, 'Surprise! Happy birthday, Xavier,' as he appears.

'Thanks, peeps,' he says, half-smiling, but it's too late – we already noticed the glumness written all over his face.

'What's wrong?' Persephone asks, handing him his coffee from Fabio.

'This isn't because you've hit the big four-oh, is it?' Fred tsks. 'Not everyone gets to such a grand old age.'

'I'm not worried about that. I plan to grow old totally ungraciously and I agree every year on this planet is a blessing.'

'But?' we all ask.

'I didn't get the job,' he says. 'They've given it to some woman from a north of the river library.'

'What?' We screw up our noses.

Not only at this gross misjustice, but the thought of someone from *north* of the river coming in and telling us how to run our precious library is horrifying.

My heart sinks. And I guess I won't be getting a promotion either.

'I think we should stage a protest,' Fred declares, stamping her foot.

'Or better still,' Persephone says, 'when she gets here, we'll freeze her out and refuse to do anything she says. We'll make her life hellish, so she quits before the first week is out.'

'I love it,' Fred exclaims, and I shake my head, but Xavier doesn't even laugh. I've never seen him so gutted.

'I spoke to Janine,' he says, 'and the good news is that her replacement is well respected in the WA library system – Janine's met her a few times at meetings and said she's super passionate about her job – so I guess that's something.'

I reach out to squeeze his arm. 'I'm so sorry. This more than sucks, but the timing is the shittiest.'

'Thanks, Bee,' he says, and although he smiles, it's not the kind of smile anyone should have on their birthday. 'Thanks to all three of you. I really appreciate this surprise. You are the best colleagues anyone could ever ask for.' He opens his arms. 'Group hug?'

The four of us embrace and we stay there until Xavier sniffs. 'Suppose we better open up.'

34

Terms of Endearment

Although Laura told me not to bring anything for lunch tomorrow, I can't turn up empty handed, so I've decided to take Mum's famous chocolate banana bread.

I'm listening to the next Bookstar read – *Mad Honey* – and mixing the bananas into the flour when I realise JB hasn't come back in since I let him outside when I got home from work. It's been raining today and the last thing I want him doing is digging in the mud and dragging his dirty paws all through my house. My carpets are still recovering from the last time that happened.

With a sigh, I pause my baking.

'Baby dog,' I call as I switch on the verandah light and scan the backyard. My eyes boggle as they come to rest on what looks like Sully and JB having a friendly chat over the back fence. JB's paws are up against the fence and Sully is rubbing the fur beneath his neck – or maybe he's trying to strangle him. 'What are you doing?' I demand, pulling out my earbuds as I march over like a protective mama bear.

'Just having a little chat with John Brown. Weird name for a dog.'

'No, it's not. He's named after a classic literary character. Didn't your parents ever read you *John Brown, Rose and the Midnight Cat*?'

He shakes his head.

'It's only the best picture book ever written.'

'Big call.'

'Anyway,' I say, annoyed, 'I thought you didn't like dogs?'

He looks at me like I'm crazy. 'What made you think that? Only psychopaths don't like dogs.'

'Well, you called him a beast. And . . . kind of acted like a psychopath.'

'Bridget.' He sounds frustrated as he runs a hand through his thick, messy hair. 'It was the middle of the bloody night. He'd been barking his head off, and then you turn up on my doorstep and try getting into my house. I think most people would have been cranky in my position.'

'When you put it that way . . .' I pout.

He *almost* smiles. 'And, sure, I might have called him that again when you visited Gran, but now I think of it more as a term of endearment.' He ruffles JB's fur again. 'Who's a gorgeous, big beasty-beast?'

Beasty-beast? I can't help but smile and when Sully looks up and catches me, I feel something shifting in the air between us. Daisy's right – he does look like Prince Harry and that isn't a bad thing.

'How *is* your gran?' I say, slightly flummoxed.

'She's doing really well,' he says as JB drops down to the ground and starts sniffing something in the dirt. 'I'm just trying to make sure she doesn't overdo things.'

'Are you moving back home now, then?' I ask, when what I really mean is, *am I going to have to start wearing my noise-cancelling headphones again?*

'Not yet – just came to check my mail.' He raises his eyebrows. 'Although I think she's planning on kicking me out soon. Gran's a very independent woman, likes her own space.'

'Speaking of Daisy . . . thank you for returning my gnomes.'

'Didn't have much choice, once I realised Gran knew you. She'd kill me if she thought I was teasing you.'

'*Teasing* me? I think you might mean tormenting me.'

'I'm sorry.' He looks like he's stifling a smile. 'I didn't know you were that attached to a few garden ornaments, but isn't that a bit pot calling the kettle black? You started the torture with that godawful karaoke party and those deafening windchimes. I might have been able to forgive you for those if it wasn't for the catalogues.'

'Um . . .' I'm outraged. 'Are you forgetting your bagpipes? If they aren't classified as torture, I don't know what is!'

He puts a hand to his chest as if deeply offended, but his eyes are smiling. 'Ouch. Is that why you had the karaoke party?'

I meet his gaze head-on, refusing to admit guilt or give in to the urge to apologise.

The air seems to crackle a bit between us. Although that could be the log fire coming from the house on the other side of me.

'No comment,' I say eventually.

The laughter coming from his mouth is so alien it disarms me. 'Well, I should probably be getting back inside.'

He nods, then clears his throat. 'I was thinking . . . since you and Gran are friends and we're neighbours, maybe we should agree to end our shenanigans. What do you say to a truce?'

Truce? I take a moment, pretending to hesitate as I stare at his large, outstretched hand, then, just as he begins to pull it back, I reach out and snatch hold of it. 'Okay. Truce.'

His shake is firm and when we let go, I immediately jump back, mildly flustered from this unexpected interaction.

'See ya round, Bridget,' he says as I start towards my house.

'Bye, *Mikey*.' I wave my fingers at him and laugh when he scowls back.

35

Lola's Library

Laura and Lola live in a gorgeous two-storey house in North Fremantle, and as it's a lovely autumn day, I ride there rather than catch the bus.

The door opens as I'm securing my bike, and a tall man in his mid-forties with a near-bald head and funky black spectacles greets me. I know this must be Laura's dad and that he's not naturally balding; Laura mentioned that the rest of the family had shaved their heads when Lola started to lose her hair.

'You must be Bee,' he says, offering his hand. 'I'm Luke. Laura's just popped to the shops because she forgot cherry tomatoes for the salad or something. Come in. Lola's so excited to see you.'

I hand him the choc banana bread. 'Hi, nice to meet you. I made this for you guys.'

'Thank you.' He ushers me into a house that's both stylish and modern. The ceilings are high, and the décor is light and Hamptons-like but also homey, with large family photos on the walls and lots of indoor plants.

'You have a beautiful home,' I say.

'Can't take any credit for it, I'm afraid. Laura's brother is an architect and she's an interior designer; this is all their doing.'

I follow him down the wide hallways to an open plan kitchen-living-and-dining area, where he nods towards a large corner couch, accentuated with what must be a dozen shabby-chic cushions. I spy Lola lying among them, a throw rug over her as well.

'Lola, you have a visitor,' Luke announces. When she doesn't even stir, he chuckles. 'Can't hear us for the AirPods. She's had them permanently attached to her ears since Laura told her about those talking books. Think we've got you to thank for that.'

I smile. 'Sorry.' But I can tell he's not annoyed in the slightest.

He goes across to his daughter, taps her on the shoulder. 'Bee's here.'

'OMG! What are you doing here?' She yanks her AirPods out of her ears and leaps up to throw her arms around me.

Her excitement is akin to JB's every time I come home, but unlike anything I've received from an actual human. 'Your mum invited me for lunch. Hope that's okay?'

'You kidding? Best day ever.' She grabs my hand and pulls me onto the couch beside her. 'I'm listening to *Anna and the French Kiss* by Stephanie Perkins. How have you not introduced her to me before? This is so good.'

'Isn't it amazing? I've reread that book so many times. And the best news is, there's two more books in the series.'

'I know. I've already reserved *Lola and the Boy Next Door*. If only there was a cute boy living next door to us.'

I laugh, feeling a buzz shoot through me that I have given her so much joy during a difficult time. Once an author came into the library and spoke about how sometimes they felt their job wasn't important compared to doctors, teachers, people researching cures for cancer or those fighting climate change, and I told them about all the readers who tell me on a daily basis about certain books that have helped them through tough times or made them feel seen. I might not even be here myself today if it wasn't for a very special book, and although novels don't have the power to cure cancer, taking Lola's mind off her illness and treatment is definitely a gift.

'Can I get you a drink?' Luke calls from the kitchen. 'Maybe a glass of wine?'

I nod. 'Thanks. That would be lovely.'

Lola and I chat books non-stop. I tell her I'm reading the latest from one of my auto-buys, Abby Jimenez, and she recounts the plot of *Anna and the French Kiss* despite the fact she now knows I've read it numerous times. There's barely a breath between our sentences until Laura returns from the shops. She hugs me hello and apologises for being out when I arrived.

'I've made Lola's favourite for lunch,' she says. 'A pumpkin, spinach and fetta quiche. Hope you're hungry.'

'That sounds delicious. Is there anything I can do to help?'

'Summon my son back from the depths of the ocean?'

I clearly look confused because they all laugh, then Lola explains, 'Leo is out surfing. Mum told him to be home an hour ago.'

'Ah, I see.'

'Do you have any siblings, Bee?' Luke asks as he puts a jug of cold water on the already laid table.

I tell them about my three older brothers and how I always wanted a sister.

'Me too,' Lola says. 'Are your brothers as annoying as Leo?'

'They were when we were growing up, but now we're all adults, I quite like them. Most of the time.'

Laura glances at her watch and sighs. 'We'll have to start without him.'

Just as we've all settled into our seats, a boy of about twelve or thirteen who hasn't grown into his lanky body hurries in, dripping water and sand all over the floor. Like his parents, his hair is short, although it looks like his is growing back faster.

'Leo!' Laura exclaims. 'What time do you call this?'

'Sorry, Mum, the waves were unreal!'

She points to a staircase. 'Go. Shower faster than the speed of light.' Leo hurries upstairs and Laura turns to me. 'I'll introduce you properly when he doesn't look like a sea urchin.'

I laugh as we start passing around the quiche, salads and warm bread rolls. Leo returns in record time and piles his plate high with food.

'Did your brothers eat your parents out of house and home when they were teenagers?'

'Lucky for them we all went to boarding school, so they only had to feed them in the holidays.' Not that my mum would ever have complained about any child of hers eating, not when it took such an effort to get me to so much as nibble on a piece of fruit.

We slip into easy conversation – Lola's family feels similar to mine. They joke and tease each other, but the love is palpable between them. Leo clearly looks up to Lola, and I think how unfair it would be if cancer stole his older sister from him.

The thought brings tears to my eyes, but thankfully no one notices because Laura distracts us all. 'Who wants dessert?'

'Please tell me you made apple pie,' Leo says, dutifully starting to clear the empty plates from the table.

Laura shakes her head. 'No, today I made your sister's favourite.'

He groans but I'm delighted to discover that Lola's favourite is sticky date pudding, because it's mine too, and if the amount Leo eats is any indication, he's not *that* disappointed.

I can't help noticing that Lola barely manages a few small mouthfuls. She's picking at her food like I used to.

'The chemo has affected Lola's appetite,' Laura explains.

Lola screws up her nose. 'Nothing tastes how it should any more. I'm sorry, Mum, I've had enough.'

Laura reaches across the table and squeezes her hand. 'It's okay, sweetheart. There's plenty more sticky date in your future.'

Lola quickly pulls back from her mother. 'When Bee's finished, can I show her my bedroom?'

'That's up to Bee,' Luke says. 'She might be sick of us by now.'

Lola looks to me. 'Are you sick of us?'

I shake my head and answer truthfully. 'Not at all.'

Five minutes later, I find myself in Lola's orange and purple haven. There are lots of soft toys, candles, trinkets and a trumpet on a stand by the window. 'Do you play?' I ask.

She shrugs as she sits on the bed and draws her knees up to her chest. 'Used to. I haven't had the breath for it since getting sick.'

Before I can work out what to say to that, she asks, 'Do you have a boyfriend?'

I blink as I lower myself into the armchair opposite the bed, picking up a teddy so as not to sit on it. 'Um . . .' I hug the bear to my chest. 'I think so. We've only just started seeing each other.'

Her smile widens as she leans back into the pillows. 'What's his name?'

'Fabio.'

Lola snorts. 'What? Like the romance cover model?'

'I'm surprised you know about him.'

'My grandma is mad for Mills & Boon. She has all these old novels and always jokes to my granddad about Fabio being the love of her life.'

I laugh and make a mental note to find an old M&B with the other Fabio on the cover for myself. 'Well, my Fabio is even better looking than the famous one.'

'Wouldn't be hard. I think the famous one is a bit creepy. I'm not one for guys with long hair. Not to mention the fact he must be ancient by now.'

'Very true.'

'So do you think your Fabio is The One?' Considering Lola's favourite genre is romance like mine, I'm not surprised she believes in this concept.

'I don't know,' I say, picking at a purple bow wrapped around the bear's neck. 'It's early days, but he's really lovely.'

'Tell me about him. I want to know *every*thing.'

'Well, he's Italian, so he has this super sexy accent,' I begin, amused by this interrogation.

'Can I ask you a personal question?' she asks after I've told her everything I can about Fabio.

When I nod, she blushes. 'Is sex in real life as good as it is in novels?'

I don't know whether to be honest with her – that so far, my sexual experiences have been anything but – or lie and tell her yes. Oh, don't get me wrong, it's not that they've been awful, but mostly they've been messy and a little bit awkward, definitely not anywhere near the realms of the explosive meetings of souls that happen in romance novels.

'Well, I haven't actually slept with him yet,' I admit, hoping her mother doesn't mind me talking about sex to her teenage daughter.

'What are you waiting for?' she asks.

'I want to get to know him properly first.'

She sighs. 'Probably a good idea, but to be honest, being sick has made me impatient. I want to know all the things and feel all the things. Please tell me you've at least kissed him.'

Now I'm the one blushing. 'Yes, we have kissed.'

Lola squeals. 'And was it good? Actually, I can tell just by your face that it was.'

'Yes,' I agree, thinking she could be the little sister I never had. 'It was good.'

She's quiet for a moment, and I can tell something's bothering her.

'What's up?' I ask.

She inhales and exhales slow and loud. 'I've never kissed a boy.'

'You're only fifteen. I hadn't kissed a boy at your age either.' In fact, due to my illness, my first kiss didn't happen till my early twenties. 'There's plenty of time.'

'But there might not be,' she whispers, meeting my gaze. 'I'm scared I'm going to die without ever having even kissed a boy. Without ever experiencing all the things I read about – first kiss, first love. Sex.'

Oh, Lola. My heart cracks and there's that lump in my throat again.

'You're *not* going to die,' I say forcefully, rushing over to sit beside her on the bed. I've done my research and, according to Laura, Lola's doctors say she has a good chance of a full recovery. I pull her into my side. 'That's why you're having chemo. You're going to kick cancer's butt and show it who's boss, okay?'

She leans her head against my shoulder. 'Okay. I guess I'll give it my best shot then.'

'That's my girl.' I pat her knee. 'Now, I know you've never kissed a boy, but what about crushes? Any hot guys in your year?'

Her smile grows. 'Yeah, but he barely knows I exist and, even if he did, he's probably forgotten me now because I've been away so long.'

'What's his name?'

'Mason.'

She tells me all about him – he's apparently tall, dark and dreamy with the most gorgeous black curls you'd ever know – but when she finally yawns, I think it's time to go. I know that she often needs an afternoon nap.

'I'd better be getting home,' I say, pushing to my feet. 'Text me when you've finished *Anna and the French Kiss*. You're gonna love the ending.'

'Bee?' she asks as I reach her bedroom door.

I look back. 'Yeah?'

'I know I'm not going to die, but I've been thinking. If I did, I've done nothing in my life that's important.' I open my mouth to tell her that she's brought joy to her family's life and mine, but she holds up her hand. 'Please, let me finish.' I nod and she continues. 'Have you heard of Make-A-Wish?'

'Of course. They're an organisation who grants wishes for sick kids.'

'Well, Mum applied to them for a treat for me, but I don't want a trip to Disneyland or to meet a K-Pop star like lots of the little kids do. I want to do something meaningful with my wish.'

I nod, feeling way out of my depth. 'Any ideas?'

'I was thinking how Mum had to get books from the library to bring to me in hospital, and that not every sick kid will have a parent able or willing to do that. There are some books in one of the play rooms at the hospital, but everything there is for little kids and most of the books are old and falling apart. I'd love to set up a proper library at the kid's hospital for all ages, with the latest releases in every genre.'

'That sounds like a fabulous idea.'

'Do you think you could help me?'

I nod. 'I'd love to.'

'I was thinking we could ask Make-A-Wish to donate money to that instead of sending me to see Mickey Mouse.'

I laugh at the way she rolls her eyes on these last two words. 'Are you sure?'

'Yes. Mickey is almost as creepy as the other Fabio, and I want this to be my legacy. Maybe we can call it Lola's Library or something.'

'Okay, well, I'm happy to help on one condition.'

She eyes me warily, but nods.

'You don't speak about your "legacy" ever again. You're going to be here for years to come to make sure your library keeps running, to keep sharing your love of books with other kids. Maybe you'll even become a librarian like me.'

She giggles and thrusts out her hand. 'I'd like that. Okay, it's a deal.'

As we shake, I tell her I'll start researching the logistics straight away. 'Have you told your parents about this?'

'Not yet.' She yawns again. 'Mum's so busy taking care of me. I wanted to see if you thought it was a good idea and if you'd be willing to help first.'

There's a knock on the door and Laura pops her head into the room. 'Just wondering if you'd like a cup of tea or coffee, Bee?'

'No, thanks,' I say. 'I'll be off in a moment, but first, we have something we want to talk to you about.'

36

Water off a Duck's Back

'*Buongiorno,* bella!' Fabio is the first to arrive for book club and he strides straight over to where I'm setting up the afternoon tea, dumps a white cardboard box on the table and pulls me into a kiss.

Wow. 'Afternoon, Fabio.' I grin when we finally pull back, thankful that no one else is here yet. I nod towards the box. 'And what do you have there?'

He lifts the lid to reveal a beautiful cake that makes our usual Arnott's family pack pale in comparison. 'Cherry and chocolate torte. For the nonnas and you.'

'Don't tell me you made that?'

'*Non*, not this. I bought it from a bakery.'

At that moment, Rose bustles into the room and eyes the cake. 'Is that for us?'

Fabio nods. '*Sì*, I bought it to say *grazie* for welcoming me to the group.'

'Isn't he a gem?' Rose blushes as she swats him playfully with her handbag.

'He's not too bad,' I say with a smile as the rest of the Bookstars flock into the room.

Everyone gushes over the cake, which we've put aside for after, and once they all have their cups of tea, I call them over to the circle. As they're taking their sweet time getting to their seats, Sully and Daisy arrive. I'm surprised to see her back so soon. She's still using a walking stick but is moving much better than she was.

'Welcome back,' the other Bookstars exclaim, Lorna, Rose and Barbara halting on their way to sit down, greeting their friend instead. 'We missed you!'

Sully glances over them to meet my gaze. 'Where does Gran usually sit?'

I point out a spare seat. 'And a lovely afternoon to you too, *Mikey*.'

'Michael,' he corrects, his cheeks reddening slightly.

I shrug one shoulder – 'Isn't that what I said?' – then address Daisy. 'How are you feeling?'

'Fabulous, sweetheart. Like a new woman. Don't need this blasted stick any more, but Mikey insisted it was safer when I'm out and about.'

'Good idea.' I clap my hands. 'All right, everyone, let's get started.'

As usual, the women all fight to sit next to Fabio, and Sully makes sure Daisy is settled. 'I'll just be in the library,' he tells her, then looks to me. 'Come get me if she needs me.'

'You're welcome to join us.'

He shakes his head. 'Thanks, but I'll leave you to it.'

'Right,' I say as he departs. 'Let's have a show of hands. Who loved *Mad Honey*?'

Half the room's hands shoot up in approval.

'I'm guessing the rest of you weren't so keen?'

'I was enjoying it until halfway,' Lorna says, 'but then it lost me.'

Barbara frowns. 'Me too. I don't see why every second book that gets published these days has to be about transgenderism.'

'Don't be so transphobic,' Sue snaps, glaring at her.

'I'm not scared of trans people,' Barbara retorts, glaring right back. 'I just worry about such young children being given hormone blockers and having surgery, when most kids and teenagers can't decide what their favourite colour is or what job they want when they grow up. What if they change their minds?'

'I tend to agree with you,' Lorna begins.

But Ronice rides right over the top of her. 'Gender isn't something you change your mind about willy-nilly. It's about who you are deep inside.'

I glance at Fabio across the circle and our gazes meet, our brows raising in synchronicity. It's like we're communicating without saying a word.

'What did you all think about the beekeeping element?' Fabio asks.

I shoot him a smile, grateful that he's diverted this potentially divisive discussion.

'Bored me to tears,' Edgar announces, his eyes drifting across to the cake. 'In fact, the whole book did – this Pee-cult woman has nothing on Lee Child.'

Barbara gives an irritated huff. 'It's Pee-co.'

'You *read* the book?' Even though he didn't enjoy it, I feel like a proud mum.

'I did.' He shakes his head. 'Waste of my bloody time. I'm hoping the next book is better.'

'Well, I enjoyed it,' Kerry says, dipping a Nice biscuit into her tea. 'I learned a lot about beekeeping and it challenged my thinking, which I always like.'

The Bookstars discuss the significance of the bees and whether they were an essential part of the story. In the end, we mostly agree that they were a bit of overkill.

'To me,' Rose announces, 'Olivia was like one of those people at parties who only want to talk about one thing.'

'Perfect character assessment,' Kerry agrees. 'And what was with the romance with the cop?'

Lorna giggles and glances at Fabio. 'Ooh, that was the best part. I love romance novels, don't you?'

He grins – 'Of course, romance makes the world go round' – then winks at me.

My insides tighten and heat flushes right up to my neck, but thankfully no-nonsense Barbara barrels on. 'But this *isn't* a romance novel, so that felt a bit tacked on. I could never work out whether it was supposed to be a thing or not?'

'I think that kiss near the beehives was a pretty clear indication,' Sue says, narrowing her eyes at Barbara.

Oh, Lord, it's clear she hasn't forgiven her for her earlier comments, and I feel another disagreement coming on. If we're going to argue about kisses, the least we could be doing is reading a proper romance novel, and this gives me an idea. Janine did say I could put my own stamp on the Bookstars, and now they've got to know me, maybe they'll trust me to choose a book.

'I know we're reading *A Man Called Ove* next and *The Talented Mr. Ripley* after that, but since many of you have enjoyed the romance elements in the books so far, I'm wondering if you'd allow me to choose the book after that? Spoiler, it's going to be a romance.'

Olga looks at me suspiciously. 'Please don't tell me you are going to choose something trashy by Nicholas Sparks or that tragic book *Me Before You*.'

'Actually,' I say, '*Me Before You* isn't a romance novel. To be classified as a romance, a story must have a happy ending.'

Olga blinks. 'Well, the main character . . . I can't remember her name . . .'

'Lou,' Rose supplies.

Olga nods approvingly. 'That's right, *Lou* – she had a happy ending in the next book, did she not?'

I nod, surprised she knows this, considering what she just said about the first book. 'It might not have been your typical romance, but I guess she did. She sought help for her grief and through that—'

'And,' Rose interrupts, 'I guess Will got his happy ending too, because he got what he wanted and maybe the next life was even better for him?'

Kerry scoffs. 'You believe in an afterlife?'

'I do,' I pipe up. 'I'm not really religious' – despite the correspondence Sunday school Mum made us do – 'but I'm sure there's something after . . . this. And I love the idea that if you don't get a happy ending in this life, maybe you get the chance to try again in the next.'

Even Kerry and Olga look a little misty-eyed at my words – I guess all of them are closer to the next life than I am, and maybe they like the idea of having a do-over.

'Well, I think reading a romance is a splendid idea.' Lorna twists the long gold chain around her neck between her fingers.

'Me too,' Beth says. 'There's already enough tragedy in the world. I like the sound of a guaranteed happy ending.'

The rest of the group, even Edgar, agree to give my choice a chance; the only problem is now I have to work out what to pick. There are so many great romances, but would they prefer something sweet like *Virgin River*, or do I go a little more risqué with *The Love Hypothesis* or one of Christina Lauren's?

'Do you want me to get you another cup of tea and a slice of the cherry and chocolate torte?' I ask Daisy as the rest of the Bookstars make a mad dash to the afternoon tea table.

She insists she's okay to help herself.

'Okay, I'll just go let Mikey' – that nickname still feels awkward on my tongue – 'know we're done.'

Fred grabs my arm and yanks me out of sight as soon as I emerge from the book club room. 'I don't want to alarm you, but Sully is lingering in the crime section looking all serial-killer-ish.'

I laugh. Nothing ever gets past her. 'It's okay, he's—'

'I'll bet he's picking up tips or looking for new ways to innovate his side hustle.'

'It's okay,' I say again, louder this time. 'He drove Daisy here.'

She sighs as if disappointed. 'I guess I won't kick his no-good arse out, then.'

As Fred flounces back to work, I head over to the crime section, feeling a weird, wobbly sensation in my gut as I spy my neighbour with his nose in a book. Maybe I'm hungry – hopefully there's some torte left when we go back. 'Hi, *Mikey*.'

He looks up and scowls, snapping the book shut. 'If you call me that one more time, you will seriously regret it.'

'I thought we'd made a truce?'

'Like rules, truces can be broken,' he says.

I nod towards the copy of *Gone Girl* he's holding. 'That's a good book.'

He shoves it back onto the shelf. 'Wouldn't know. I'm not much of a reader. Just killing time.'

I recoil as if he's just stabbed me in the heart. *Not much of a reader?* Just when I was beginning to warm to him. 'You don't read at *all?*'

He shrugs. 'I read the odd bio, medical journal, and I've read a zillion textbooks in my time, but fiction bores me, to be honest.'

He sounds so condescending, and I feel my nails curl into my palms. I don't mind the occasional biography myself – I read *Spare* by his doppelgänger – but fiction is *not* boring.

'Let me guess, you haven't read a novel since high school? What was it that ruined fiction for you? *Far From the Madding Crowd? The Grapes of Wrath? The Scarlet Letter?*'

He neither confirms nor denies my guesses. Could be he's just one of those stuffy intellectuals who think reading for pleasure is a waste of time.

Either way, I can't resist the challenge, and stare at him as I try to get a read on his vibe so I can pick the perfect book, but the guy is hard to decipher. I'm not getting anything more from him than the usual grumpy arrogance.

Wait. Our gazes lock. There's something else there too.

I scrutinise him further, trying to look past his six-and-a-half (at least) feet of pure muscle, three-day shadow, strong jawline and unsmiling emerald eyes to find the essence of him. But all I feel is a tiny tug low in my belly.

Oh. God. No!

'Why are you looking at me like that?' he asks, taking a step back.

I swallow and try to focus again. 'What's your favourite movie?'

'*Inception.*'

I nod in approval. I don't usually need to ask questions to pick a book, but I'm clutching at straws. 'Television show?'

'Um . . .' He scratches his head. 'Probably *Underbelly.*'

'Old school,' I say; my dad also loved it. 'And what about travel? Beach or country? Overseas or Australia?'

'Country, I guess. I live near the beach, so can see it every day if I want. And probably Australia. I wouldn't say no to an overseas holiday, but I've seen so much of the country from the air, it would be good to have a chance to explore some of it properly. What's all this about?'

I ignore him. 'Would you prefer to laugh or cry?'

'What kind of third degree is this?'

I hit him with my sternest expression.

He holds up his hands as if I'm about to shoot. 'Okay, okay, probably laugh if I have to choose, but both can feel good.'

'Hmm.' I stare at him for another long moment; the answer seems like a word on the tip of my tongue.

He takes another step back. 'I think I'm going to go find Gran.'

'No!' I shriek, grabbing his arm, relieved the epiphany finally hit. 'I've got it!'

He looks down at where I'm holding him. 'Aren't you supposed to be quiet in a library?'

I let go. 'No, that's no longer a thing. Come on.' I gesture for him to follow me towards the general fiction shelves, too excited for what I'm about to give him to be embarrassed about touching him.

A, B, C . . . Even after all these years, I still say the alphabet in my head when I'm shelving or looking for a book. And there it is, right between Emma Dakin and Casey Daniels – surprisingly, I've never read either of them. 'Here.' I thrust *Boy Swallows Universe* at him. 'Guessing you don't have a library card?'

He shakes his head as he stares at the novel. 'This doesn't look like non-fiction.'

'It's not. What you don't know about me is that my superpower is turning non-readers into bookworms.'

He's still staring at the book like it's a vial of poison. 'What if I don't want to be a bookworm?'

'Humour me. I *dare* you to read that and not enjoy it!'

This makes him smirk. 'Is that right? You think you know me that well after a few banal questions?'

I look him dead in the eye. 'I might not know you . . . but I know books.'

'So what's it about, then?' he asks, glancing back at the cover, as if he couldn't just flip it over and read the blurb.

I never tell anyone about the books I choose for them, preferring to let them discover for themselves. 'Read it and you'll find out. Now, come on, I need to get you registered.'

Miraculously, Sully doesn't object and five minutes later, I'm handing him his new card and showing him how to use the self-serve check-outs when Fabio sidles up beside us.

He places a hand on the small of my back in what feels like a slightly possessive move. 'I was wondering where you'd got to, bella.'

Does he think Sully is competition? Somehow, I manage to withhold a laugh. We're barely on speaking terms, but there's definitely a standoffish vibe between them. Sully is probably just annoyed by the interruption, but this might be the closest I ever get to two men fighting over me, so I can't help but bask a little in the moment.

'I was just helping Mikey with a book,' I say, smiling as I lean into Fabio. 'Please tell me there's some cake left.'

Sully glares at the nickname, but I'm getting so accustomed to his scowl that it's like water off a duck's back.

'You might just be lucky,' Fabio says as he takes my hand and leads me back into the book club room.

37

Aunty BJ

Mum is waiting with a massive sign – Welcome Home Bridget – as I step into the tiny arrivals hall at Port Hedland airport along with a sea of miners in bright orange hi-vis uniforms. She does this every time and it's mortifying, but also always makes me cry.

I throw my arms around her – the cardboard banner crumpling between us – and enjoy the familiar warmth and squishiness of her. She was a lot thinner when I was younger, but my eating disorder made her abandon years of yo-yo dieting and now she carries her love of cake around her middle proudly. She's not fat, but she's not skinny either – just like me. Her hair, once the same caramel colour as mine, is now slightly greying and tied back in a sensible ponytail.

'Darling!' She squeezes me hard and then pulls back to scrutinise me as usual. Her smile falters. 'You've lost weight! I knew I should have come down there after that bastard broke—'

'Mum, relax. I'm fine. I'm not starving myself and I'm not heartbroken. I'm just a little more toned because of the kickboxing. Remember I told you about that?'

She doesn't look convinced but nods. 'Do you have luggage?'

I shake my head and indicate my backpack. 'Just carry-on.'

It's much warmer up here; even in the winter it rarely gets below 27 degrees during the day. Apart from the jumper I've got on and the dress I'm wearing for my parents' vow renewal ceremony, I didn't bother bringing much as I still have a few old things at the homestead.

'Lovely. Let's get you home, then. Dad and the boys are desperate to see you. And Sarah has been asking all week, every couple of minutes, when Aunty BJ is coming.' Mum shakes her head. 'It's driving Kara batty.'

'Then we better hit the road,' I say as we walk out into the warm air and over towards Mum's faithful old Landcruiser, once white, but now permanently tinged reddish-brown due to the colour of the dirt up here.

I left work at lunchtime to catch my mid-afternoon flight, so the sun's still shining high in the sky as we head out of the airport car park and drive the forty-five minutes it takes to get home. I can't stop smiling as I look out the window at the familiar deep-red earth and bottle-green shrubbery on the sides of the wide, sometimes bumpy highway, and Mum prattles on about everything that's been happening lately.

I'm definitely back in the Pilbara. There are stunning cliffs and deep gorges with glittering, turquoise waterholes you can swim in, like those found in Karijini National Park, but the region is so vast that all these natural beauties are hiding far from the main highway. All I can see right now is endless dusty plains with the occasional barren hill in the far distance. Every now and then a massive road train with two or three trailers zooms past us. Even the Landcruiser feels tiny in comparison, and I think that they'd probably blow Fred's Mini right off the road.

'We have a very sweet new worker,' Mum tells me. 'He's a real gentleman, only twenty-five but very mature, and very handsome . . .'

She could not be more unsubtle, and I decide to return the favour. 'That's great, Mum, but I'm not in the market for your matchmaking this trip.'

'Oh?' she asks hopefully.

'Yes,' I say, biting down on a smile. I hadn't planned on telling my family about Fabio yet, but I don't want her trying to set me up with some poor guy. 'I've recently started seeing someone.'

She squeals and demands to know everything about him. As I talk, I glance down at my phone, wondering if he's messaged me yet, but we're out of range and I won't be able to receive or send messages till we're on the station.

'Well, he does sound rather nice,' Mum admits, 'but I hope he won't whisk you off to Italy to live.'

'It's early days, but I get the impression he'd quite happily stay here. His mother died a few years back, he doesn't know his dad, and his sister lives here at the moment too.'

Mum makes the right noises, and our discussion of my new romance reminds me I need to pick her brain. 'You know Janine's book club? Well, I've convinced them to read a romance novel but now I can't decide which one to choose.'

'Ooh, how exciting,' she says, doing a little jig in her seat. 'Do you want something contemporary or historical? A new release or a classic?' When she says classic, I know she's not talking about Dickens or Brontë, but the likes of Jude Devereux, Lisa Kleypas or Susan Elizabeth Phillips.

'I'm honestly not sure.'

'Hmm . . . What about *Heroes Are My Weakness*, by SEP?'

Told ya. 'Yeah, that's a good one, but I'm not sure I'll be able to find enough copies in the state library system.'

'Guess that answers our question about whether you need recent or a classic.'

After tossing around titles by Emily Henry, Tessa Bailey, Julia Quinn and, of course, Colleen Hoover to name but a few, we both shout at the same time, '*The Switch.* Beth O'Leary.'

Yes, it seems so obvious now. Although I preferred her first novel, *The Flatshare*, this one will be perfect for the Bookstars because there's an octogenarian romance as well. Lorna will love it, and there should be plenty of copies available to order from the inter-library loan system.

'Thanks, Mum. You're the best,' I say just as a kangaroo jumps in front of the car, causing her to slam on the brakes. She's used to such interruptions and drives on unshaken as the animal bounds off.

Eventually we turn into the gravel track that leads to our station, and I'm greeted by a herd of red Droughtmasters off to one side.

'Whatever you do,' Mum warns, 'don't ask Dad and Justin about the new cattle. They're still bickering about the pros and cons of introducing a new breed, but I've forbidden them from talking about work this weekend.'

The old Landcruiser clunks over the cattle grates as we head the few kilometres towards the homestead and, when we pull up in front of the house I grew up in, there's a whole welcome party waving. Justin, Brandon, their wives – Kara and Elsie – and my four nieces and nephews, the youngest strapped to Brandon's chest in a baby carrier. They've come from their houses on other parts of the station for a welcome dinner, and Rupert arrived earlier in the week so he's also here.

After hugs all round, during which Dad's kelpies attempt to get in on the action, my four-year-old niece, Sarah, who has the Jones trademark caramel-coloured hair but her mother's tight curls and looks like something out of a Raphael painting, latches onto my hand. 'What took you so long to get here, Aunty BJ?'

I glare at my oldest brother, Brandon, who has taught all the kids to call me this, despite my mum's and their mums' best efforts not to. It's fine now when they have no idea what else BJ stands for, but I shudder to think about the day they learn.

Sarah's mother, Kara, plies her from me. 'Give Aunty *Bee* some space. She probably wants to go get freshened up.'

If it weren't for the fact that I'm desperate to check my text messages, I'd let Sarah come with me, but instead I promise to play hide and seek with her later and then head into my old bedroom to dump my bag, change into shorts and a T-shirt and, yes, to check my phone.

Nothing much has changed in here since I went off to boarding school at thirteen. There are posters of dogs on the wall and my bookshelf is crammed full of *Baby-Sitters Club*, *Nancy Drew*, and *Sweet Dreams* novels, which were handed down from my mother.

Five messages from Fabio are waiting for me when I flop down onto my old single bed – at least Mum's updated my doona cover from *My Little Pony* to a more grown-up floral print – to read them.

Have a safe trip, bella, and lots of fun with your family xx
Missing you already. Xx
How long are you away again? Xx
Send me a photo of the cows xx
I'm going to bowls again with Edgar tonight, but call you later? Xx

I smile as I tap out a reply, then put on my boots to head outside to take photos. I've barely set foot into the garden, full of native plants that thrive up here without much water, when I'm accosted by Sarah, her brother Eddie and my other nephew, Campbell. Eddie has the same colouring as Sarah, but Campbell has a mop of bright red hair, inherited from Elsie, and a dusting of the cutest freckles across his nose.

'What you doing, Aunty BJ?' Sarah demands, her chubby little hands perched on her hips. Although the boys are both two years older than her, it's clear who's in charge. They stand behind her nodding their heads, reminding me of the people who stand behind politicians during press conferences.

I drop to my knees and pull them into a group hug. 'God, I miss you three.'

Sarah is the first to extract herself. 'You still haven't told us what you're doing!'

I chuckle. 'I thought I'd take some photos for a friend. Wanna help?'

Three little heads nod gleefully at me, and it isn't long before I realise the error of my ways. When I said help, I meant tag along, but they squabble over my phone, taking turns snapping pics. I'd planned on sending Fabio a photo of the garden and maybe a panoramic shot of the horizon to give him an idea of the rough, dry terrain and rich blue skies that were the backdrop of my childhood, but instead he gets one of a snakeskin, a broken gate and Sarah's new boots.

'Shall we send your friend some cows?' Eddie asks, jumping up and down a bit like JB.

'Yes,' I say, taking his and Campbell's hands. Sarah leads the way, my phone still in her grasp and I wonder if I'll ever get it back.

Thank the Lord she can't read, just in case Fabio sends me anything risqué.

When we finally head back, I'm exhausted and hungry, so I'm
pleased that dinner is almost ready. We eat at a long table on the
verandah, and as the dishes of corned beef and vegetables are passed
around, there's never a pause in conversation. The boys are on their
best behaviour – no one mentions cattle – and Rupert entertains us
with tales from the army. Of course, Mum tells my family about
Fabio, and they all delight in his name.

'So you're the *other* Bridget,' Rupert says, leaning back in his
seat, a bottle of beer in one hand, 'and he's the *other* Fabio.'

'Sounds like a match made in heaven,' Elsie declares, struggling
to eat while holding six-month-old Martha on her lap. She lasted
all of five minutes in her highchair.

I hold out my hands. 'Do you want me to take her for a while?'

'You sure?' Elsie's beautiful chestnut eyes brighten at the
suggestion.

'I'd love to.' We do the baby swap and Martha snuggles into
me, wrapping her tiny fingers around my hair. She's changed a lot
since I first met her at Christmas and is much more communica-
tive now, but she still smells divine with that sweet clean smell of
babies. I feel my biological clock skip a beat as I think about the
way Fabio says 'bambinos'.

'How's things with that neighbour of yours?' Dad asks, wiping
a bit of white sauce from his thick beard.

I've already told Rupert about Sully in our weekly phone calls
and Mum's obviously told Dad, but I fill the others in. 'I think we
just got off to a rocky start. He's not that bad.'

After dinner Justin, Brandon, Kara and Elsie take the kids home
to bed, and I sit with my parents and Rupert out on the verandah,

drinking beer and playing cards, until Dad declares he's hitting the sack. I help my brother clear up the kitchen, the dishwasher already whirring from when we loaded it earlier.

'So what's this Fabio guy really like?' Rupert asks. 'Is he good enough for my little sis?'

I roll my eyes. 'Will anyone ever be good enough?'

'Hell no!'

We both laugh, then I say, 'Still no great romance for you?'

He snorts. 'If anyone ever wins my heart, I promise you'll be the first to know.'

After giving my brother a hug – something I don't realise how much I miss until I feel his arms wrapped around me – I retreat into my room to call Fabio. We talk until after midnight when he finally calls it a night because he's helping Rose with her garden in the morning.

'Rose from the Bookstars?' I ask, surprised.

'*Sì.*'

'Do you know her? I mean, outside book club?' Maybe she also gets her coffee from the Grouchy Sailor.

'*Non,* but last club she told me she loves to garden but is struggling with some of the heavy work. Her family don't have time to help her.'

'Surely they could pay someone?' Although it's very sweet that Fabio has offered to give up his Friday afternoon to do this, especially when he gets up so early for work.

'Rose doesn't like strangers coming into her garden. I told her I help my mamma with her flowers back in Italy. It's really no trouble.'

*

On Saturday afternoon the homestead is brimming with people for the vow renewal ceremony. Rupert and I had been put to work helping Mum scrub the house from top to bottom – not that it really needed it, as she's always been militant about cleanliness and tidiness – but it's worth it to see the smile on her face as she welcomes family, 'neighbours' – who live many, many kilometres away – and old friends who came up yesterday and have pitched tents and caravans in the paddocks. It's a testament to my parents that so many people have travelled here to watch them celebrate their love.

Dad has even donned a suit for the occasion, and Mum's wearing a gorgeous, emerald-green silk wrap dress from Sacha Drake, which she told me cost more than her wedding dress. Totally worth it – I've never seen her look so pretty or so happy as she stands at the top of the verandah steps, holding my dad's hand. They're both glowing like newlyweds, the celebrant officiating the service slightly off to the side. The rest of my family and the many guests are standing in the front garden watching, and it's impossible not to smile as my parents share honestly about the highs and lows of forty years of marriage.

Baby Martha starts to cry when Dad mentions the fire that swept through our property in 2002, in which they sadly lost a lot of cattle, but miraculously Sarah is on her best behaviour through all the speeches.

Mum gets choked up and Dad hands her a hanky she folded and ironed for him earlier as she talks about the joy of becoming parents and then grandparents. 'Honestly, I couldn't have asked for a more wonderful husband, and I'm so proud of the beautiful family we created together.'

After the ceremony, everyone is given champagne – Dad splurged and bought real French stuff, the kind they had on their honeymoon in Paris – so that my father can raise a toast to my mother.

'Julie,' he says, looking at Mum like she's not only the only woman in the Pilbara but the whole world, 'I don't know what I did to deserve you and I probably don't say it often enough, but I count my lucky stars for the day we met and you agreed to be my girl. I love you so much. So to say thank you and to celebrate forty wonderful years of waking up next to you, I got you a little something.'

I look to Rupert standing beside me as Dad hands Mum a silver envelope, but he shrugs. We all watch silently as she opens it and then gasps.

'Oh goodness, you didn't!' She throws her arms around my father and then waves the contents in the air over her shoulder. 'I'm going to Nantucket!'

'Where?' Rupert asks, but I'm grinning too much to respond. *Well done, Dad.*

I'm so happy for Mum and super jealous, not just of the trip to the island that's been on my bucket list since I read my first Elin Hilderbrand novel, but of their love. It's what I've wanted since the moment I was old enough to understand it.

Of course, I think of Fabio. Could he be the one that finally claims my heart?

Next comes a lovely afternoon tea of fancy sandwiches and delicious cupcakes, and I have the same conversation over and over again with close family and people I knew growing up.

'Yes, I'm doing well.'

'Yes, I'm eating now.' People can be so rude and intrusive.

'Work is good.' I tell lots of folks about the Bookstars.

My phone beeps in my pocket and I surreptitiously slip it out, excited but not surprised to see another message from Fabio.

We've been messaging almost non-stop since I got here and have talked for hours every night.

How's the party going? xx

Great. xx

I send him a few photos of my parents during the ceremony and a smiley selfie of me in the red, pink and silver maxi dress I'd bought especially for the occasion. Mum's right; I have lost weight, but I'm more toned than thin, and I feel stronger than I have in years. Kickboxing might not have led me to Mr Right but now I can't imagine not doing it.

You look beautiful, bella. *hot flame emoji* *Very sexy dress.*

'Bridget!' At the piercing voice of Dad's sister, I lift my face from the screen. 'What are you doing hiding away in the corner?'

'I'm not hiding,' I reply, leaning forward to kiss her on the cheek. 'How are you, Aunty Andrea?'

She sighs loudly – 'Ah, well, can't complain' – and then proceeds to do exactly that, telling me about her arthritis and her irritable bowel syndrome.

I try my best to listen attentively and make the right noses, although I'm desperate to get back to my phone. I tell Aunty Andrea I need to go to the ladies, and escape inside to reply.

Thanks. What are you up to?

Nothing much. Just missing you and wishing I was there. xx

I miss you too, I text back.

It's true. As enjoyable as this weekend has been, it feels much longer than a few days since I've seen Fabio and I can't wait to see him again.

38

Knickers in a Knot

Usually, I'm sad saying goodbye to my parents at Port Hedland airport, but by the time the plane touches down in Perth late Sunday afternoon, I can't get out of it fast enough. I order an Uber as I'm hurrying through the terminal and text Fred while I'm waiting for it to arrive.

Hey, babe . . . do you mind keeping JB another hour or so? I want to go say hi to Fabio.

Is 'go say hi' code for something else?

I grin. *Maybe.*

Then take your time. Ride that Italian stallion. Giddy-up!

I'm still laughing when a shiny red Mazda SUV pulls up in the Uber pick-up zone and the driver gets out.

'I can't believe this,' Sully says.

Him and me both. I'm standing here, my mouth open like Michael from Mary Poppins as my brain tries to make sense of what I'm seeing. What kind of doctor drives for Uber on the side?

Maybe one who has a gambling habit and is in a lot of debt? Or he really *is* a serial killer and does this to find his victims. *I knew it!*

Before I realise what he's doing, Sully takes my backpack and throws it in the boot. As he strides back to the driver's side and climbs in, I scramble into the back seat, wondering if I should have sat in the front.

'You have a beard in your driver photo,' I say accusingly as I click my seatbelt and Sully turns his key in the ignition.

'Yeah, grew one last year, but got sick of it. You're not going home?' he asks as he glances at my destination address on the screen in front of him.

'I'm heading to my boyfriend's place,' I say smugly.

'Right. The guy from the library?' Sully's tone is scathing and I remember the way he and Fabio eyed each other off.

'That's the one.' *I've been visiting my parents for four whole days and we're desperate to bonk each other's brains out.* I smirk to myself, wondering what he'd say if I said this out loud, but he doesn't respond as he joins the row of cars waiting to escape the airport mayhem.

'This car is nice,' I say, only because I loathe uncomfortable silence.

'Thanks.' He doesn't meet my gaze in the rear-view mirror. 'By the way, I finished the book.'

My heart rate spikes in anticipation. 'And?'

'And that's eight hours of my life I'll never get back.'

What?! I frown. 'You didn't enjoy *Boy Swallows Universe*?'

'It was a bit long-winded and disjointed. And the main character was rather whiny.'

'*Whiny?* You didn't like Eli Bell?'

'I suppose I felt sorry for him and his brother, but what exactly is the book supposed to be? A saga? A coming-of-age story? A crime novel? And some of the scenes were so unrealistic. Maybe a better editor could have fixed it.'

'Right.' I'm fuming. 'So, after reading one novel, you know better than one of Australia's bestselling authors and some of the country's most experienced editors?'

'Hey, don't get your knickers in a knot,' he says. 'It's just a book.'

But it's not just a book, it's *me*. This feels like a personal insult, and I swallow as stupid tears come to my eyes. Sully isn't just telling me he didn't like *Boy Swallows Universe*; he's telling me I failed. And when it comes to books, this almost never happens.

After that we don't say a word to each other. The drive from the airport to Fremantle is about forty minutes, but feels like forty weeks. I spend time scrolling Goodreads on my phone, trying to work out where I went wrong while he stares resolutely at the road ahead. Not once do I catch him looking in the mirror to see what I'm up to.

Finally, he slows the car in front of Fabio and Francesca's house in East Fremantle. 'Here you are. Have a good day.'

I almost jump out of my skin at the sound of his deep voice. Never mind the fact I'd forgotten where I was going. I'm not sure I'm in the mood for this any more – but I'm here now.

And no way am I asking Sully to take me home instead.

'Thanks,' I say as I unclick my seatbelt but he's already out the car, grabbing my bag from the boot. Despite the fact that he's doing this when far too many Uber drivers don't bother, I have a good mind to give him a one-star rating.

Sully looks briefly towards the house as he hands me the bag, before getting back into the car without so much as a goodbye.

Someone really needs to teach that man manners.

My stomach tightens as I hang my handbag across my body, hitch my backpack onto my shoulder and approach the front door. I wanted to surprise Fabio, but is turning up unannounced really such a good idea? The drive with Sully appears to have unnerved me and I'm dithering when the front door opens.

'Hello? Can I help you?' asks a woman in her mid-twenties, with dark, wavy hair piled up in a high ponytail and the kind of make-up you usually only see on beauty influencers. She's all dressed up as if she's heading out, and I guess she must be Francesca. Her English is as impeccable as her brother's.

'Um . . .' I smile nervously. 'I'm Bee. Fabio's . . . ah, girlfriend.'

'Oh.' She blinks, but recovers quickly, her pink-painted lips curling into a smile as she pulls me to her and kisses both my cheeks one after the other. '*Piacere di conoscerti!* Is he expecting you?'

'No. I've been away for a few days and I thought I'd surprise him. Is he home?'

She grins and nods back inside the house. 'He's in the kitchen making dinner. I'm just on my way out. Have *fun*.'

I follow the music coming from the back of the house to find Fabio listening to Birds of Tokyo as he chops onions. I'm impressed by his choice of Aussie music and take a moment to admire his butt in low-slung tracksuit pants, before clearing my throat. 'What are you making?'

'Bella!' Fabio spins around, the shock on his face morphing into what I think is joy at the sight of me. He closes the distance between us and kisses me hello. 'Did you let yourself in?'

'No. I met your sister as she was heading out.'

'Ah. I see.'

'So . . . I guess that means we're alone,' I say, winking suggestively.

His hands still on my hips, he tilts his head to the side, half-frowning, half-smiling. 'Are you saying what I think you're saying?'

I nod. 'I missed you over the weekend, and I'm ready.'

He doesn't reply – not with words anyway. Instead, he makes a growly guttural noise as he turns around, switches off the hot plate and then turns back to me and plunges his hands into my hair, dragging our faces together.

At the taste of his mouth on mine, I *try* to push all thoughts of my pesky neighbour and his aversion to books out of my head and succumb to the moment I've been fantasising about all weekend.

A moment we're both so desperate for, we have it right there on his kitchen floor.

39

Fabio-lous

After sex and spaghetti, I call an Uber to take me back to Fred's, and Fabio kisses me goodnight. 'See you soon, bella.'

'Night, Fabio,' I reply, thanking my lucky stars the Uber driver isn't Sully.

At Fred's, I let myself inside with the spare key that lives under a turtle statue on the front porch. At the sound of the door, JB thunders down the corridor and throws his large, fluffy body at me.

'Hey, baby dog,' I say, dropping to my knees for a slobbery snuggle. 'I missed you too.'

Fred appears a second later, dressed in bright green flannelette pyjamas and hot pink Ugg boots. 'Well?'

'Well, what?'

She perches her hands on her hips. 'Don't play coy with me. I've been waiting long enough for this. Was it Fabio-lous?'

I scoff at her pun and shrug as I straighten, JB still dancing between us. 'It was . . . nice.'

'*Nice?*' She screws up her face – 'Oh, boy. That sounds like we need a glass of wine' – and turns towards the kitchen.

I leave my bag by the door and follow her, waving as I pass Waylen sitting on the couch, laptop on his knees and SBS news playing on the TV in front of him.

'Does he ever stop working?' I whisper to Fred.

She rolls her eyes as she grabs a cask from the fridge – her favourite wine comes in a box from Aldi – and two glasses from the shelf above the stove. 'I think he was born with a laptop in his hands.' She points to the table and miraculously JB takes the command. 'Tell me everything. Was Fabio a dud, then? Often the best-looking blokes are.'

'No,' I say, feeling bad for Fabio as I take a chair. 'He was very skilled – he did all the right things – but I was kinda distracted.'

Fred hands me a very full glass and sits across the table with an identical sized one. I was counting on her driving JB and me home, but I might have to sweet talk Way. She takes a sip of wine and then frowns over her glass. 'What on earth could have distracted you from that man-god?'

I tell her about Sully collecting me from the airport.

'Hang on . . . I thought he was a doctor?'

I shrug. 'So did I. Maybe he's both?'

She snorts. 'How many doctors do you know who have the time or need for a side hustle?'

'I don't know any other doctors, but stop fixating on the Uber thing, that's not what put me off my game.' Although I agree, it *is* weird. 'I don't think I told you, but last Wednesday at book club I found out Sully doesn't read fiction.'

Fred tsks. 'Why am I not surprised?'

'Anyway, I chose him a book—'

'Of course you did.'

'Will you just be quiet and let me finish?' I beg.

Chastised, she lifts her glass to her mouth and drinks.

'I gave him *Boy Swallows Universe*' – a book that even Fred, who rarely strays from fantasy, enjoyed – 'and he tore it to shreds.'

She shrugs. 'Just confirms he has no taste. Give up on the guy. He's clearly a lost cause.'

'How long have you known me?' I ask, running my hands through JB's fur, desperately seeking comfort.

Fred sighs. 'Let's see, must be about seven or eight years?'

'Exactly,' I say, 'and how many times have you known me to recommend a book to someone that they didn't love?'

She takes a moment, and then concedes, 'Zero.'

I nod. 'What if I've lost my superpower?'

At this, she rolls her eyes. 'This is *not* a reflection on you. Don't let this tosspot get under your skin any more than he already has. Not only has he made your life a living hell for months, now he's ruined your first time with Fabio.'

'He didn't ruin it. It wasn't *terrible*. Although Fabio's kitchen floor was rather hard and cold.'

'You did it on his kitchen floor?' she shrieks.

I put my finger to my lips and laugh, not wanting Waylen to hear about my sex life. 'Enough about me. Did you have any sexy shenanigans on the weekend?'

'Nah, I've been busy writing.' She gestures to her pyjamas. 'Haven't even got out of my PJs.'

I pretend to sniff and wave my hand in front of my nose. 'So that's what the smell is in here.'

'Haha.' She grins. 'But even if I do smell, it's worth it.'

'Oh my God.' I wrap my fingers around my glass ready to make a toast. 'Did you finish *How Not To Catch Feelings*?'

She raises her eyebrows smugly. 'Maybe.'

I leap up from my chair and throw my arms around her. 'Why aren't we drinking bloody champagne? This is the best news. When can I read it?'

'Hold your horses, Bridget Jones,' she says, chuckling as she extracts herself from my grip. 'I have to edit it first.'

'But, Winifred Darling, I can help you with that. People never see their own mistakes anyway.'

She shakes her head. 'I'm not talking about a proofread, I'm talking about a proper edit – this is a very messy first draft. There are snatches of scenes and notes for me to fill in the gaps everywhere. It won't even make sense to you. I need to check for character inconsistencies, that the plot makes sense, that the sex scenes are plausible, that—'

'Okay, okay, I get it. But please hurry up.'

'I'll do my best,' she promises and then pours the rest of the bottle into each of our glasses.

We toast anyway, and then I say, 'Are you excited to meet our new boss tomorrow?'

40

Water under the Bridge

'Bee slept with Fabio,' Fred announces to Persephone, just loud enough for other library staff to hear, as we head into the book club meeting room just after 8 am. Some people here aren't even working today but we've all been summoned to greet our new boss.

'Shut up.' I glare at Miss Sex Positive, who doesn't understand that not everyone wants their sex lives made public, then take a sip of the coffee I'd collected from Fabio, because Xavier – who usually does the honours on Mondays – wanted to be here before Ursula arrived to welcome her and make a good first impression.

Persephone flops into a chair and sighs as if she's already done a whole day's work. 'Ooh, go, girl. What was it like?'

'I'm not kissing and telling.' I laugh and quickly change the subject. 'Anyone seen a glimpse of Ursula yet?'

They shake their heads, then Persephone grabs my hand and puts it on her stomach as I take the vacant seat beside her. 'Do you feel that?'

I think I'm supposed to be experiencing a kick but I shake my head. 'Sorry.'

Persephone repositions my hand. 'What about now?'

'Um . . .' I should lie but I've always been terrible at it.

'Oh, never mind.' She scowls and pushes away my hand as the chatter around us falls silent.

Xavier has just entered the room with a giant of a woman who is dressed a lot like Mary Poppins – long black skirt, long black coat and black hat – but is giving off strong Agatha Trunchbull vibes. Mary Trunchbull. I giggle. We all sit up straight and I tell myself to give her the benefit of the doubt – just because she's not Janine and looks slightly terrifying doesn't mean she isn't lovely. Until she opens her mouth.

'I'm Doctor Ursula Alcott, your new leader, and I run a tight ship,' she declares, speaking right over the top of Xavier as he opens his mouth to introduce her.

He shrinks back against the wall, and I feel terrible for him – it should be *him* taking the library reins.

Ursula starts telling us about her 'impressive' experience and her 'acclaimed' PhD, an exploration of library as place. She talks about her critical theoretical approach, grounded in historical research, and someone called Walter Benjamin's theories of modernity, and blah, blah, blah. Her voice is so monotone that I find myself drifting off, lifting my takeaway coffee to my mouth and daydreaming about Fabio handing it to me not long ago. After last night, I felt so much closer to him and—

'And there will be no more drinking on the job,' Ursula shouts.

I startle and coffee splashes out of the hole in the lid onto my top. Of course, today of all days, I'm wearing an ice-pink shirt. As the liquid seeps into the fabric, I feel my colleagues staring at me, and it's like I'm back in high school being told off by a teacher, only

I never got in trouble at school, *and*, until today, I was second-in-charge of these people.

Persephone pats my knee in a show of support.

'Sorry,' I mumble, my cheeks hotter than my coffee.

I'm rewarded with another terse glare from our new overlord before she continues. How can *this* be the woman Janine told us about?

Finally, mere minutes before opening time, she finishes by letting us all know that she's excited to be making changes and will be going over each section of the library with a fine-tooth comb to find areas that need improving. She doesn't even tell us to have a good day as she marches out of the room and leaves us all staring at each other in shock.

'What just happened?' I whisper.

Fred says, 'Was that a fucking joke? I can't believe she told you off like that in front of everyone, Bee. I almost threw my drink bottle at her.'

'She won't last long,' Persephone promises, caressing her bump. 'I'm going to put a hex on her.'

Usually, I'm a sceptic like Fred; I've never really believed Persephone had any powers – until I met her, the only witches I knew were from *Harry Potter* – but by the end of Mary Trunchbull's first day, I very much hope I'm wrong.

Today was without a doubt the longest and worst day of my working life. Within the first twenty minutes of opening, Ursula had implemented a no talking unless absolutely necessary rule. She's old-school and believes libraries should be places of silence. I'm back home, pouring myself a rare but much-needed glass of weekday wine, when the doorbell rings. JB bounds down the hallway and I follow him, glass in hand, ready to dismiss whoever it is as quickly as possible – unless it's Fabio bringing me ice cream and commiserations after my whiny text messages about our new boss.

I take a sip, pull back the door to reveal Sully, and inwardly groan. Of course he finds me drinking alcohol on a Monday night. Better not tell him I also had the better part of half a bottle with Fred last night or he'll be reporting me to Alcoholics Anonymous.

'Was I breathing too loudly or something?' I snap.

'Huh?' He looks confused and maybe a little nervous as he shakes his head. 'No. I just . . . I wanted to explain why I'm driving Uber, not practising medicine at the moment.'

Oh. I'm taken aback. 'You don't owe me any explanations.'

'I know, but . . .'

'But you don't want me to tell Daisy about your side hustle?'

He nods sheepishly. 'If she knew the truth, she'd worry, and that's the last thing I want her to do.'

I stare at him, at the concerned expression on his handsome face. I could tell him I'm not that cruel, that I don't want to cause Daisy any undue stress either, or that what he does is none of my business, but the truth is, I'm curious. After months of speculating, I can't resist this opportunity to find out more about him. 'Do you want to come inside?'

Sully deliberates a moment before nodding.

'Would you like a glass of wine?' I ask as I shut the door behind us.

'Um . . .'

'I don't make a habit of drinking on weeknights, but I had a terrible day.'

He holds up his hands. 'Hey, no judgement here. And yes, please, I'd love a glass.'

I nod down the hallway towards the kitchen, and he follows me.

'Wow, your place really is the exact opposite of mine,' he says as he glances around. 'Although I'll admit, yours is much nicer.'

'Thank you,' I say as I grab another glass and pour. Polite small talk between us feels so odd. 'I inherited it from my grandparents, but I'm slowly putting my own touch on it.' I pass him the drink. 'Are you renting, or did you buy the house from Mr Saunders' estate?'

Our fingers brush awkwardly as he takes the glass. We both look away. 'Thanks,' he says. 'Just renting for now, while I . . . uh . . . work a few things out.'

I gesture for him to sit with me at my small dining room table. When I have friends here, we always sit in the lounge room or out on the verandah, but Sully is not my friend and the formality of the table seems more fitting. JB hovers next to his chair and lets his head fall into Sully's lap.

Sully chuckles, gives him a neck rub, then asks, 'Did your grandparents live here long?'

'All sixty-two years of their marriage.'

'Geez, that's an impressive innings.'

I nod. 'My brothers and I used to stay with them in school holidays, so I feel like I've lived here most of my life in a way as well.'

'Where did your family live?'

'On a station in the Pilbara. We actually had the flying doctors land there a couple of times. One of them saved my brother's life.'

As if he didn't even hear me, Sully glances around at the gnomes still occupying many of my surfaces. 'Have you always collected gnomes?'

Done with the small talk, I raise an eyebrow and fold my arms across my chest. 'Daisy said you're recently separated. Is the Uber driving anything to do with that?'

He lets out a long, deep sigh. 'Not exactly. It's more to do with my work.'

I lean forward – 'As a flying doctor?' – wondering if he had a malpractice suit against him or something.

He nods. 'I haven't been able to work for a while. I'm suffering from PTSD.'

'Oh.' I don't know what I'd been expecting but not this. 'I'm sorry, that must be tough.' My words sound so inane, but what else am I supposed to say?

'Thanks, but I'm not telling you this because I want you to feel sorry for me. I just wanted you to understand why I was driving Ubers and why Daisy can't find out.'

'Why exactly are you driving Ubers? Surely you have paid sick or stress leave?'

He nods. 'Yeah, but not enough, and anyway, it got pretty boring hanging around home – even worse for my mental health – so at the beginning of the year, I signed up for Uber. It's been good. I can choose my own hours, it's not stressful and I've met some interesting people.'

'I can imagine. I've met some interesting Uber drivers myself – one even tried to sign me up to a pyramid scheme.'

He clearly finds this amusing, but something is still bothering me.

'Don't you think your grandma would want to be there for you, to support you?'

Sully adamantly shakes his head. 'There's nothing she can do to help, and she's been through so much – first the loss of my parents and sister, then only a few years later, my granddad. I'm all she's got. She was upset enough when my marriage ended, and I don't want her to worry that I might let this thing beat me and leave her too.'

Is he telling me he's been suicidal? My heart squeezes. I wonder if his family tragedies somehow contributed to his PTSD, but I refrain from commenting. 'So that's why you're seeing Aisha?'

He smiles genuinely. 'Yeah, she's great.'

I nod. 'Do you mind me asking what caused it?'

He takes another sip of wine and I see his other hand drift to JB as if he too finds comfort in touching him. 'Well, it was building up over a number of years. Sadly, I'm not unique in the medical system – most of us are overworked and stressed with the high patient load and long hours – but for me, there was one thing that finally did me in.'

He goes quiet for a long while and just when it gets awkward and I think he's not going to tell me, he says, 'I was called up to the Kimberley. A pregnant woman from a remote station – probably not unlike the one you grew up on – had gone into early labour. Despite being thirty-four weeks, it was all looking pretty straightforward but, as you'd know, they don't have neonatal facilities up there, so our job was to get her to King Eddie's, hopefully before birth.'

I sit on the edge of my seat, a terrible dread filling my belly as he continues.

He takes another long breath and a sip of wine, then continues. 'She went into labour on the plane. Not ideal, but I've delivered babies before, even pre-term ones, and it was her third child, so she was in good spirits. She gave birth to a little boy, but as he was so early, the flight nurse and I were concentrating on keeping him alive, and we missed some vital signs in the mother. She'd gone a bit pale, but I didn't notice until she started having breathing difficulties. We gave her oxygen as I tried to work out the issue.

'The nurse was notifying the hospital that the mother was in a bad way and would need immediate intervention when she went into cardiac arrest. That's when I guessed it was an amniotic embolism.'

I don't know what that is but decide now is not the time to ask.

'I couldn't save her. She died as we touched down in Perth.'

Oh, God. My chest grows tight at the anguish on his face and in his voice. 'But surely you don't blame yourself? You didn't cause the embolism. It's just a terrible, tragic situation.'

Sully shakes his head. 'I had everything at my disposal that I needed. I *should* have been able to save her.'

But I'm not having any of this. 'How many people have you saved who might not have made it if not for you?'

'Quite a few. And that mother wasn't the first patient I lost in the air, but even if, logically, I know I did my best, something broke inside me then, and I couldn't bring myself to go back.' He downs the rest of his wine. 'So there you have it. I'm a mess.'

I grab the bottle and top up his glass – he looks like he needs it. 'Have you had dinner yet?'

'No.'

I can't believe I'm going to ask him this, but . . . 'I've got a pizza in the oven. Only a supermarket one' – I grabbed it on my way home because I couldn't be bothered to cook – 'but you're welcome to share it if you like.'

He looks surprised. 'You sure?'

I nod, and get the pizza out of the oven, give JB a treat bone so he doesn't try and steal some, and suggest we migrate into the lounge room. Now Sully has shared such a vulnerable part of himself with me, I feel myself softening towards him.

'I get why the flying doctors might not be for you, but why not get a job in a normal hospital with all the resources at your fingertips?' I ask as we dig into the pizza.

'I can't explain it, but I don't trust myself,' he says. 'I still have nightmares about what might have happened if I'd noticed she was in trouble earlier, if I'd done something differently. Maybe a better doctor could have saved her. PTSD isn't rational.'

'Is seeing Aisha helping at all?' I ask.

'I think so, slowly; she's given me some good techniques to use whenever the dark thoughts threaten to overwhelm me.'

'Such as?'

His lips twist up into a smile. 'Well, learning an instrument was one. Taking up a sport. I thought I'd brush up my basketball skills before I joined a team.'

Okay, now I feel terrible for all the horrible thoughts I had towards his pursuits. 'You're actually getting a lot better at the pipes,' I tell him, 'but I'm afraid I'm not qualified to comment on the basketball.'

He laughs.

'Do you think you'll ever go back to medicine?'

'Anyone ever tell you that you ask a lot of questions?' he says.

I shrug but smile. 'My house, my rules. You were the one who came over here to talk about this.'

'Touché.' He grabs another piece of pizza but answers before he bites. 'I don't know. I quite like driving Ubers, but I don't think I want to do it forever. Can I ask you a question?'

I raise an eyebrow at him. 'That depends on what it is.'

'Why are *you* seeing Aisha?'

I take a bite of pizza, buying time as I contemplate whether I want to tell him. If anyone had asked me a month ago if I'd ever bare my soul to The Grouch Next Door, I'd have laughed in their face. Maybe it's the long, tough day and the alcohol that has my defences crumbling but, weirdly, after everything he's shared with me, it feels only fair to be honest.

'I had anorexia in my teens,' I tell him and then down the rest of my wine.

I still feel slight shame admitting this to strangers, which Sully pretty much is. He's the first man – aside from my dad, brothers and medical professionals – who I've ever spoken to about this. I haven't even told Fabio yet. Many people think eating disorders are brought on by vanity, and thus don't deserve the same kind of understanding you'd offer someone who had cancer or even a broken leg, but Sully looks at me with nothing but compassion. Probably because he's a doctor and knows better than most.

'I'm so sorry to hear that. But you're recovered now?'

'Yes. For almost ten years.' I smile because this is something I'm so grateful for. Some of the girls I met during treatment weren't so lucky. Many others are still probably battling – the full recovery rate is only around twenty per cent. 'I'll never be one hundred per cent comfortable with my body – what woman is? – but most of the time, I don't feel like we're in battle any more.'

'That's good,' he says, and I'm glad he doesn't offer some platitude about my looks.

'It was a long journey. I spent a lot of years in and out of hospital.'

'Were you in PMH?'

I nod.

'That must have been tough with your family up north.'

'It was . . . for my mum more than me. She had to leave the station a lot. I was already at boarding school, so I would have been away from home anyway.'

'Have you've been seeing Aisha all that time?'

I bite my lip, wondering how much I want to tell him. 'No. I had a relapse about four years ago.' Just after I broke up with Tim. 'This time I knew the signs and I didn't want to succumb again, so I found a local therapist. Speaking to Aisha once a month is healthy for me. We don't just talk about my eating disorder now; we talk about everything. I should probably tell you, I told her about all the terrible things my new neighbour was doing.'

His eyes widen in amusement. 'Terrible things *I* was doing? I thought we'd already established that you were the instigator and I'd never have kidnapped your gnomes if you didn't bombard me with junk catalogues.'

'Hey,' I exclaim. 'Wash your mouth out with soap. *Sunday School Weekly* isn't junk, you heathen!'

We both laugh so loudly that JB looks up from the floor and cocks his head as if he's wondering what's so funny.

'Besides,' I say, 'I would never have stooped that low if you hadn't complained about me to the council.'

His eyes bulge and he shakes his head. 'What?'

'The noise complaint. About my *windchimes*.'

'I never complained about your windchimes,' he says with so much conviction I believe him.

I blink. 'But if you didn't do it . . .'

'Must have been one of the other neighbours,' he finishes with a smirk. 'I wondered why you suddenly took them down. To be fair, if I didn't have my noise-cancelling headphones, those things would have been enough to drive me to commit a crime.'

'One greater than murdering gnomes?'

'Hey, you know I didn't do that. And when the catalogues kept increasing, I didn't know what else to do to make you stop.'

'So,' I clarify, 'the pipe practising and the basketball playing and the mowing the lawn at the crack of dawn . . . none of those things were done to aggravate me?'

He shakes his head. 'What on earth did you think of me?'

'You don't wanna know,' I say, feeling like the biggest idiot on the planet.

'I'm sorry. We probably didn't get off to the best start. I can see why you might have assumed I was doing those things.'

'You reckon?'

'I apologise for barging over and yelling at you about your morning singing, but I was sleeping particularly badly at that time, and I just snapped. Then because of that, I thought you were an early riser, so wouldn't mind me mowing the lawn.'

'Are you sleeping any better now?'

He nods. 'A little, but if I really can't sleep now, I just get up and drive.'

Something occurs to me. 'How did you know I was responsible for the catalogues?'

'Because they were addressed only to Sully and, believe it or not, I don't have a whole host of enemies.'

I'm mortified. I want to drop my head into my hands and cry, but instead I say, 'What must you have thought about *me*?'

He grimaces apologetically. 'That you had a few screws loose.'

I cringe. 'I'm so sorry.'

'Water under the bridge,' he says. 'I didn't lie when I said that I started to have fun with those ransom notes. Probably sad to admit, but they were the most interesting thing happening in my life.'

My phone pings with an incoming text message and I grin when I see it's from Fabio.

'Your boyfriend?' he asks, and I tame my smile as I nod.

'Well, I'd better be going.' He stands and shoves his hands in his pockets. 'Thanks for the pizza. And for listening.'

'No worries. Any time,' I say, and I find that I actually mean it. I always wanted to be friends with my neighbour, in case of a sugar emergency or anything. Then I remember Sully telling me he doesn't have a sweet tooth. Maybe he doesn't even have sugar.

JB and I see him to the door and as I open it, I ask, 'Did you really hate *Boy Swallows Universe*?'

'I just found it tedious,' he says apologetically.

I nod, defeated. 'Night, Sully.'

'Night, Bridget.'

He's almost at my front gate when I call out, 'What was your favourite thing to do when you were a kid?'

He laughs – 'Play video games!' – and lifts his hand to wave as he heads over to his house.

My phone beeps again: *What you up to, bella? Feel like a visitor? xx*

I smile at the message and quickly type my reply: *Only if you pick up gelato on your way! xx*

41

Put a Hex on Her

Mary Trunchbull stands over me, hands perched on her hips and a glare on her face as I hang up the phone at my desk Tuesday morning. 'Was that a personal call?' she literally spits.

I resist the urge to wipe my face, not wanting to anger her any more than I already have. More than everybody has. Every little thing we do seems to be wrong. This morning, Persephone purchased a new book about Testudines for one of our regulars, an autistic young man who is captivated with all turtles, and Ursula gave her a verbal warning for wasting library money on one person.

'No,' I say. 'I'm helping one of our young borrowers and her mum try to get a community library off the ground in the kids' hospital. She's got cancer and I was just talking to the community liaison officer at—'

'Your responsibility is to *this* library, not to any extracurricular activities. From now on, please use your own time for such matters.'

Before I can object and explain that this project might not be specifically linked to Fremantle Library but serving the community is part of our role as librarians and Lola *is* one of our borrowers, she thrusts a piece of paper at me. 'I want you to take all these off the shelves ASAP.'

I blink at the list of books, which at a quick scan includes many of our most popular novels and a lot of my personal favourites. 'Is this for a display or something? Do you think one of the assistants could do it? I've got—'

Once again, Ursula interrupts me. 'I'm asking *you* to do it. You clearly don't have so much on your plate since you can find time for *extra* things.' She nods disapprovingly towards the phone. 'And no, it's not for a display. We're not a department store.'

I take another look at the list, trying to work out if the books have anything in common. 'Then what is it for?'

She sighs as if she really doesn't have time to waste on my petty questions. 'That is a list of books we need to remove from circulation immediately.'

'What? But why?' I'm pretty sure half of them will be borrowed anyway. Even though Agatha Christie's been dead almost fifty years, her books still have lots of holds on them.

'Because they are not suitable for public distribution. We are not here to promote witchcraft or promiscuity.'

'We're banning books?!' This can't be real. 'Is this an instruction from the government or Library Board?'

She shakes her head. 'No. I'm branch manager of this library and that means I don't have to consult anyone else for small operational decisions.'

'But this isn't small,' I argue. 'You can't censor what people want to read.'

'*Bridget.*' She speaks like someone losing patience with a small child. 'I have already found you on a non-work-related phone call today, and now you're contradicting me? Are you *asking* for a verbal warning?'

I feel my face flush with fury. 'No, Ursula,' I say, resisting the urge to scrunch the list up and throw it at her.

As I go about my business, piling book after book into a trolley, Fred raises an eyebrow at me, but I can't risk talking to her yet. Ursula might only have been here a few days, but in that time she's never taken a lunch break and rarely seems to need to pee either, and if she sees us chatting, we'll both be in trouble.

The moment I escape the library for lunch, I pull my phone out of my bag and text Xavier, Fred and Persephone: *Emergency meeting tonight.*

Thank God, comes Xavier's quick reply. *Where?*

Darling Darling? Persephone suggests.

We all reply with a thumbs up. It's not the quietest place for a meeting, but it is our favourite.

I go home after work to feed JB, let him outside and then quickly drop off a book for Sully.

'Well, hello,' he says when he pulls back his front door. 'This is a pleasant surprise.'

I thrust a library copy of *Tomorrow, and Tomorrow, and Tomorrow* by Gabrielle Zevin at him. When he said he liked video games, I immediately knew what book to get him. 'I promise, this is the book for you!'

His lips curve into a smile as he glances at the cover and then back to me. 'That's what you said about the last one.'

As if I'm not cranky enough already! 'Sorry, can't chat. Got somewhere to be, but just read the bloody thing!'

I don't know what happened the first time, but I'm sure I've got it right now. Sully will relate to the gaming backstory in this novel as well as the medical stuff, and who knows, maybe it'll remind him what he's missing.

'Good to know you're not a quitter, Bridget,' he calls as I hurry back out of his courtyard. 'I'll start it tonight.'

I run almost all the way to Henry Street – my colleagues would have gone straight from work, and I don't want to miss out on any bitching about our new fascist boss.

There's nothing more than a small sign on the outside wall to signal the existence of Darling Darling, a hole-in-the-wall establishment also known as the 'pirate pub', but when I slip inside, it feels like I've gone back in time to the 1800s.

The pub is dimly lit, with ropes hanging from limestone walls, exposed timber beams and rafters, the furniture is all made from weathered leather or wood, and the floor is covered in peanut shells, which are the only snacks you can get here but also happen to be free. Tonight I'm greeted by a pirate playing a fiddle and singing 'What Shall We Do with the Drunken Sailor?' Almost all the other patrons are singing along, most of them drinking negronis or old fashioneds made by a bartender with a ripped shirt, a messy beard and scruffy long hair barely kept back by a black bandana. All except my colleagues, who I spy in the back corner, gathered around a wine barrel.

And my heart sings. Janine is with them!

I launch myself at her, wrapping my arms around her neck. 'Please change your mind and come back. I know you want to go grey-nomading with Dave, but we need you.'

'Oh, honey.' She strokes my hair. 'Even if I wanted to, I couldn't. I've resigned and taken my retirement. We've put a deposit on the caravan. Let me buy you a drink instead.'

It seems a small consolation, but I accept, and Janine orders my favourite – a Salty Dog. As I'm taking the first sip, Fred says, 'Did anyone else hear Mary Trunchbull' – of course I told my friends the nickname and they all immediately adopted it – 'tell that baby to stop crying today? Then she said to the mother that if she couldn't control her child, she shouldn't bring her to a library.'

'No way!' Xavier looks ropable. We're a haven for mothers and kids, and even on non-Story Time or Rhyme Time days, the kids' section is always full of toddlers pulling books off shelves and harried-looking parents taking a few moments to relax.

'*And*,' Persephone adds, nursing a glass of lemonade, 'she told Victor he couldn't just sit around in the magazine space all day. She actually said, "This is a library, not a homeless shelter."'

If the situation wasn't so dire, I'd laugh at her perfect mimicry of Ursula's awful, grating voice, but Victor is one of our regulars. 'Doesn't she know libraries are supposed to be places where everyone feels welcome?'

Janine frowns – she'd always maintained libraries are homes away from homes, where anyone can come to feel safe, accepted, educated and entertained. 'This sounds very much out of character, from what I've heard of her.'

'That's not the worst of it,' I say, noticing I've already drunk half my cocktail. 'She asked me to remove a whole bunch of books she deems inappropriate.'

'What?' my colleagues exclaim in unison.

I nod. 'Anything with offensive language, sexual promiscuity, graphic violence, witchcraft . . . the list goes on.'

'She can't do that,' Fred says, her knuckles whitening around her rum and Coke. 'This isn't America.'

I look to Janine. 'I'm glad you're here, because you know more about her job than any of us. Please tell me Fred's right. Ursula doesn't actually have the right to do this, does she?'

Blessedly, Janine shakes her head. 'No. She could probably remove any of the books Fremantle Library specifically bought or received for donation if she wants, but definitely not anything in the state library circulation. Are you sure that's what she was doing?'

'Definitely,' I say, feeling the rage whirring up inside me again. I need to take a deep breath before I continue. 'The question is, what can we do about it?'

'Firstly,' Janine says, reaching for a couple of peanuts, 'a couple of you should approach her together. Tell her you are putting those books back on the shelf and if she tries to censor any more without Library Board permission, then you'll report her to her boss at the council. I'm sure that'll halt her in her tracks.'

'Okay.' I nod; I love a plan. 'Who wants to come with?'

Xavier raises his hand. 'I'll do it. I'm assistant manager – not that you'd know it.'

'Thank you,' I say. 'Let's speak to her before the library opens tomorrow. How'd you go with her today?'

Xavier sighs. 'When I asked her which character she'd be dressing up as for National Simultaneous Storytime next month, she said she wouldn't be dressing up and that none of you are allowed to either. As children's librarian, I can if I really think it's necessary.'

'What the fuck!' Fred yells, so loudly that even over the noise of the fiddle, the other patrons look over at us. 'Like hell she's telling me what I can and can't wear.'

I bang my fist on the table. 'Me either.'

'Relax, everyone,' Persephone says, cracking another peanut shell. 'She won't last long. I've put a hex on her.'

'No offence, Persephone,' Fred snaps, 'but I think this requires more than you playing around with a few herbs and crystals and shit.'

Persephone barely bats an eyelash. 'O ye of little faith.'

42

TGI Weekend

I wake to Fabio's lips dusting across my forehead.

'*Buongiorno*, bella,' he says, smiling down at me as I open my eyes. 'I didn't mean to wake you, but I couldn't resist kissing you goodbye.'

He's hovering above me in his work uniform and I can't help thinking about the first time I saw him. I'd thought him hot then, but his attractiveness has grown even more as I've got to know him properly. His kind and caring nature only amplifies his appeal.

'Do you really have to go?' I groan, catching his hand and pulling him to sit beside me. I can hear the wind howling outside, rain slapping against my tin roof. It's perfect stay-at-home-and-watch-a-movie weather. 'Why don't you take a sickie and come back to bed. It's much nicer under here than it is outside.'

He runs his thumb over my cheek – 'Tempting, bella, but I can't let down the boss' – and kisses me again on the forehead.

I sigh. 'Fine. Go be a good person. Go make the best coffee in the world for other women, but don't forget, if Ursula comes in, make sure you spit in her drink.'

'I promise,' he says with a chuckle. 'I let JB out the back and gave him his breakfast, so you just relax and take it easy until you have to go to the hospital with Lola.'

'Aw, thank you.'

'You deserve it after your week.' Fabio grins, then stands again.

'What are you up to after work?' I ask, already missing him.

'More gardening at Rose's place – if the weather improves. Almost got that jungle under control.'

I pout jokingly. 'You're not cheating on me with Rose, are you?'

His laugh is so loud it echoes around the room. 'Well, she does make a great cup of tea, but she has nothing on you. Why don't you come help me with her garden when you're finished with Lola?'

I grimace and shake my head. As much as I enjoy his company, the last thing I feel like doing on my weekend is ripping weeds out of dirt in the rain. 'Why don't you just call me when you're finished?'

He nods and starts towards my bedroom door.

'After you've showered,' I add, admiring his cute butt in his black work chinos as he swaggers out.

Seconds after I hear the front door open and close, JB lands on my bed.

'Argh,' I squeal. 'You're soaking.'

In reply, he shakes his head, splattering rain all over me.

'Lucky I love you.' I grab my phone off the bedside table to check the time. There are still hours until Laura is coming to collect me, so I grab *Finlay Donovan Knocks 'Em Dead*, lean back into my pillows and start to read. After Daisy was so excited over *Finlay Donovan Rolls the Dice*, I'd borrowed the first book in the series and now I'm onto the second. She was right – they are as good, if not better, than Stephanie Plum, and I can't wait to talk to her about them.

*

It's still raining when Laura is supposed to pick me up, so I wait on the front porch, trying to ignore JB's whining from inside. I hate leaving him on weekends, but this is important, and there's no way Mary Trunchbull will let me take time off for Lola's project during the week.

I glance next door, wondering how Sully is going with the new book. It's only been three days since I gave it to him, and I've been busy in that time – plotting with my colleagues about how to get rid of Ursula, emailing various people about Lola's Library and, most evenings, hanging out with Fabio or Fred – but I'm desperate to know what he thinks. Sadly, there's no sign of him. I guess he's out driving. Before I can ponder this further, a black Tesla pulls up and I spy Lola waving from the back seat. I make a mad dash from the porch to the passenger side and climb in.

'Thanks so much for picking me up.'

'No worries,' Laura replies. 'We're so grateful to have your help with this project.'

'I'm so excited,' Lola says, grinning from the back seat.

I turn to smile at her, always in awe of how chirpy and positive she seems despite the battle she's facing. She looks quite healthy and fresh today – sometimes it's hard to believe that she's actually very ill.

'So how are things going with your new boss?' Laura asks as she navigates through weekend traffic towards the city.

I groan. Laura came into the library on Thursday and Ursula saw us talking and told me off. That was the day after Xavier and I confronted her about her book banning and she'd merely told us if we dared to question her authority again, we'd both be getting verbal warnings.

'That bad, hey?' Laura flicks the windscreen wipers onto a higher speed.

'The woman throws around threats of verbal warnings like rice at a wedding.' I tell them about the books she'd asked me to remove. 'Our assistant manager has sent an email complaining about this to her boss at the shire, but apparently they're on leave until next Thursday. She's put all the *bad* books in her office and keeps them under lock and key, so we just have to wait.'

'She'd better not get rid of any of Lauren Asher's books or Meghan Quinn's,' says Lola and I see her glowering in the rear-view mirror.

'I'll hide them, if necessary,' I promise. 'She's also cancelled half our author talks for the rest of the year. Says they're a waste of budget because people only come for the free biscuits.'

'Geez. Would it help if I made a complaint about her?' Laura asks.

'Maybe,' I say, 'but what would you complain about?'

'Oh, we'll find something, won't we, Mum?' Lola chimes in. 'Hey, maybe we can take the books she doesn't want for *my* library?'

After that I vow to put Ursula out of my mind for the rest of the weekend. Today is about Lola – we're meeting Vicky, who works in the patient and family care section of the children's hospital, to talk further about Lola's idea. I've already spoken to her on the phone, but she wants to hear from Lola before she applies to the necessary departments for permission to move forward. Laura has also spoken to Make-A-Wish and they're keen to help Lola achieve her dream.

Laura drops us right in front of the hospital so Lola doesn't have to walk far, and then goes to find a park. We wait for her just inside the entrance.

'So, spill,' Lola says as she flops down on a bench, slightly out of breath from the short walk. 'Have you slept with the hot Italian yet?'

'Shh . . .' I laugh, glancing around to see if anyone heard her.

'Well?' she prompts.

I'm unable to curb my grin. 'I'm not sure we should be talking about this here.'

She rolls her eyes. 'I've got cancer. I might die. I can talk about whatever the hell I want wherever the hell I want.'

'You're not going to die,' I scold, glad Laura isn't here. 'You promised me, remember?'

Lola shrugs. 'We're all going to die, so you should indulge me and tell me all the details. I can tell you've done it, anyway. There's something glowing about you.'

I laugh. 'I think you're reading too many romance novels.'

'And whose fault is that? Is he a ten? Judging by the expression on your face he's a ten.'

'He's a ten,' I say. It would feel like a betrayal to Fabio to rate him any less.

'Hot damn.' She sighs. 'I need more details. I need *all* the details.'

'Details about what?' Laura asks, appearing beside us like an apparition in the night.

My heart thumps. How much of our conversation did she hear? I wonder what I'm doing allowing a fifteen-year-old girl to pry information about sex out of me, but it's hard to say no to a kid who spends more time having chemo than hanging with her friends.

'Bee was about to tell me how she became a librarian,' Lola lies, flicking the lengths of her blonde wig over her shoulders.

I stifle a smile. She might be sick but she's quick when she needs to be.

'Ooh, that's a story I'd like to hear too,' Laura says, glancing at her watch. 'And we've made good time, so shall we go get a quick drink in the cafeteria before our appointment? You can tell me all about it.'

Five minutes later, I find myself sitting at a plastic table in the hospital café – coffees for me and Laura and a chocolate milkshake for Lola – telling them how books became my life.

'Mum was always reading to me when I was little, but I much preferred to be outside chasing my older brothers around. When they went away to boarding school, I missed them so much. I whinged about my loneliness and boredom and Mum said she could give me more chores, or I could read.'

Lola snorts. 'I know what I'd have chosen.'

'You and me both,' I say. 'So she took me to the library in Port Hedland every couple of weeks and when I ran out of library books, I stole her romance novels. I couldn't get enough of them.'

Laura smiles. 'I wish *my* mother had read romance. She was an English literature teacher and only kept books that were classics or had been nominated for the Booker Prize in our house. No wonder I thought reading boring when I was a kid.'

I chuckle before continuing. 'I didn't have a great time at boarding school when I went away too, and the school library became my refuge. But it wasn't until I travelled around Australia a couple of years after finishing school that I even thought of working with books.'

'What happened then?' Lola asks.

'I met different people in hostels and doing odd jobs, and many of them told me they hated reading. This made me sad and so I made it my mission to find a book that would change their minds. I discovered I had a knack for recommending books that would get non-readers addicted. And suddenly, I knew what I wanted to do with my life.'

Lola twirls the metal straw in her near-empty milkshake. 'That's so cool. I have no idea what I want to do when I leave school.'

'You've got plenty of time to work that out,' I say. 'Who says you need to know by then anyway? You could do what I did – travel and see if something takes your fancy.'

Laura nods. 'Good advice, but right now, it's time to go meet Vicky.'

43

All the Feels

Fabio brings a box of Italian pastries to the Bookstars, and there's no way they're going to last till after our discussion. Now that he's joined, many of the women arrive earlier than necessary and, as I'm finishing setting up the chairs, he's over by the tea table holding court. Watching them hang on his every word makes me feel warm and fuzzy, especially when Rose starts gushing about the miracles he's worked in her garden.

'I could do with some help in *my* garden,' Lorna pipes up suggestively.

I stifle a giggle as Fabio grins at her. 'It would be my pleasure. Let's talk.'

'You don't have a garden,' Barbara exclaims. 'You live in an apartment.'

'I have window boxes,' Lorna snarls.

'I *amoro* window boxes,' Fabio reassures her in his delicious accent. It's so sexy when he drops the occasional Italian word.

'Don't you mean *adoro*?' Barbara asks with a slight frown.

He frowns. 'Isn't that what I said?'

As the other Bookstars wander in, I overhear him arranging to not only help Lorna with her window boxes but also to take a look at some leaky taps at Ronice and Sue's house, help Olga sort out her garage, and go to community choir with Kerry this evening.

'Community choir?' I ask as I sidle over to join them. 'Can you even sing?'

He shrugs and squeezes my hand. 'I guess we'll find out.'

'Will you still be able to find time in your busy schedule for me?'

He leans right in close to me and whispers, 'The hours between midnight and six am are all yours.'

A warm and delicious shiver slides through me just as Daisy arrives, followed by Sully. I wasn't sure she'd still need him to drive her but I'm surprised to find myself happy to see him.

'Afternoon, Bridget,' he says, dipping his head as if he's wearing an invisible hat.

'Afternoon, Sully.' Now that everyone's here, I turn to address the group. 'All right, time to take your seats.'

I'm expecting Sully to wait in the library again, but he settles Daisy in her seat and then commandeers the one beside her.

My stomach does a weird flip as if I'm nervous about him watching me in action.

'Right.' I hold up the book, trying to ignore him and focus. 'I'm so excited about this chat because Fredrik Backman is one of my favourite authors and *Ove* is such a gem of a book.'

Edgar screws up his nose and adjusts his thick glasses. 'I don't know. I found it a bit slow, and that man is a grump.'

I bite my lip to stop from smiling; Edgar reminds me a lot of Ove. They've both lost their wives and yet try not to show pain or weakness.

'Neighbours can have interesting relationships,' I say, daring a glance at Sully to find him smiling at me. It's such a surprise to see a grin rather than a scowl on his face that I find myself blushing and quickly look away.

'Oh, I adored him,' Barbara says, beaming down at the cover. 'I'd love to find me a widower like him.'

'Me too. I cried my bloody eyes out.' Beth sniffs, digging a tissue out of her bag as if she might start bawling again at any moment. 'But I laughed just as much.'

Lorna nods in agreement. 'He's cantankerous, I'll give him that, but I could relate to his pain. I was lost when Stanley died and cranky with anyone who tried to reach out to me. I think that's why the relationship with the neighbours, especially the immigrants, really touched me. Only thing it could have done with is a little romance.'

Sue tsks, saying not every damn book needs romance, and I'm beginning to realise that she's simply an antagonistic person, always looking for an argument.

I quickly throw our first question into the ring, and they all rush to talk at once. Fabio and I exchange secret glances whenever someone says something amusing or totally politically incorrect. When conversation moves on to Ove's plan to end his own life, the discussion gets quite deep and I realise Edgar might not have liked the book because he identified *too* much with Ove.

'Fabio,' I say – he's been quiet throughout, and I hope he may be able to lighten the mood – 'do you have any thoughts to add?'

He ponders a moment, then, 'I really liked Marisol.'

'Marisol?' Kerry frowns. 'I don't remember any Marisol.'

I don't either, although it's been a few years since I read it. Then it hits me. Marisol is from the American movie version – *A Man Called Otto*. I don't usually bother with films of books I love, because invariably they make me cranky, but I watched this one with my parents when I was home for Christmas.

'Did you not read the book?' I ask, irritated that he'd try to pull the wool over our eyes.

He looks sheepish. 'I ran out of *tempo* – I'm not very fast reading English – and it's been a busy couple of weeks, so I watched the movie last night.'

The guilt hits me like a slap in the face. Why didn't I think of this?

'Leave poor Fabio alone.' Beth shifts her chair towards him protectively. 'Unless any of us are prolific in reading Italian novels, then we have no right to criticise. At least he tried, which is more than I can say for some.'

'Hey,' Edgar exclaims, narrowing his eyes. 'I'm reading the books now. Doesn't mean I have to like them.'

I clear my throat and try to regain control of the discussion. Soon enough our time is up and I remind everyone of our next book: *The Talented Mr. Ripley*.

The pastries Fabio brought have all been hoovered up, but there's still the Arnott's family pack and tea and coffee. As usual, no one is in a hurry to leave. Sully hangs back while the Bookstars swamp Fabio again, and I take the opportunity to talk to him.

'Have you read any of *Tomorrow, and Tomorrow, and Tomorrow* yet?'

'I returned it on my way in.'

'Did you *read* it?'

He nods. 'Of course. It was long but . . . I've got time.'

'Tell me you loved it,' I say, holding my breath. He *has* to have loved it. Not only is it a beautiful story about the complexities of friendship and love and overcoming adversity, but the gaming stuff is fascinating. Even I enjoyed it and I've never played a video game in my life.

'It was okay. Sam and Sadie irked at times, and I'm not sure I bought the depth of their friendship. Marx seemed like a good guy, but it lost me when the narration switched to the video game about Emily.'

'But . . . you said you liked video games.'

'When I was a *kid*. And playing them and reading about them are quite different.' He gives me an apologetic shrug. 'I could have read a non-fiction book about that.'

I'm speechless. *Two* misses! This has never happened before. I even managed to get Edgar, who is old and stuck in his ways, addicted to fiction.

'So what's next?' he asks.

I raise an eyebrow. 'You want me to try another recommendation?'

He nods. 'Maybe it'll be third time lucky. Unless you want to admit defeat?'

The twist of his lips says he's mocking me, and I want to march into the library, grab a book off the nearest shelf and bonk him over the head with it, but instead I take a deep breath and think.

'*Bridget!*' Ursula's sharp voice comes from the doorway and I glance over to see her index finger beckoning me in a way that makes me wonder if Persephone isn't the only witch in the library.

I paste a bright – clearly fake – smile on my face as I go over to her. 'Yes, Ursula?'

'What are you doing?'

I open my mouth to tell her but she doesn't let me speak.

'Looked to me like you were flirting.'

'With *him*?' I glance at Sully and silently laugh at the ridiculousness. Why would I flirt with a fiction-hater when I have a sexy boyfriend who not only reads novels in Italian but also wants to read them in English?

'Yes,' she snaps. 'And why are there two young men in this book club anyway? I thought it was for seniors. This better not just be a way for you to pick up!'

'*Excuse* me?' Now it's her I want to throw a book at.

A shadow appears behind me and I know Fabio has come to my rescue. Hopefully he'll use a bunch of Italian swear words to tell her to back off.

'*I'm* here because I drove my grandmother and Bridget was talking to me because I was asking for book recommendations.'

I startle at the sound of Sully's voice; he's the last person I expected to stick up for me.

Ursula opens her mouth – no doubt to threaten *him* with a written warning – but Rose steps forward, getting in first.

'And Fabio is Bee's boyfriend, but that's not why he's here,' she huffs. 'He's my driver and wants to improve his English, so rather than sitting in the car, I invited him to join us.'

It's a blatant lie and I can tell Ursula doesn't believe her, but miraculously she backs down. 'Fine. The men can stay, but Bridget, as book club is over, you don't need to be in here any more. If anyone needs a book recommendation, they can come to the desk.'

As she turns and storms out the door, I have to bite my tongue to stop from poking it at her.

'Well, someone got out on the wrong side of the bed,' Kerry says.

That's if she even has a bed. I'm fairly sure she's not human, so she probably doesn't need to sleep!

I may head back to work, but all I can think about is where I went wrong with Sully's book choice. Perhaps my mistake was not giving him something light – considering he's in a dark place, maybe the themes of the first two books were too much. I rack my brain, feeling the pressure but determined not to fail again. Maybe I need more of a feel-good book, one that's guaranteed to make him laugh.

When it hits me, I can't believe I took so long to think of it. Especially considering the book we discussed today. The online catalogue says we have one copy, but I can't find it anywhere. This isn't unusual; books are often put back in the wrong place by borrowers – once we found *The Joy of Sex* in the kids' non-fiction shelves – and we also get a surprising amount of theft, but I can't help wondering if Ursula might have banished it.

Annoyed, I do a quick scan of the surrounding shelves but reaping no rewards, I detour home via New Edition Book Shop, praying they have what I need.

'Hey, Bee,' the owner says from behind the counter, which is almost hidden by stands of bookmarks, book bags and other book-related merchandise. As usual he has a pen tucked behind his ear.

'Hi, Alan. How's business?'

'Can't complain.' He staples a couple of papers together and puts them off to the side. 'Anything I can help you with today?'

I glance towards the rows of shelves jam-packed with bookish goodness. 'I'm hoping you have a copy of *Anxious People* by Fredrik Backman?'

He frowns as he punches the title into the computer, then smiles. 'Sure do. Would you like me to grab it for you?'

'Thanks, but I can find it.'

I should buy it and get out of here quickly, but I can never come in here without a proper browse. As well as the Backman book,

I grab a copy of the new Mhairi McFarlane and then see a gorgeous hardcover edition of *Lessons in Chemistry* that begs me to take it home. I resist any other additions to my home library and walk back to the counter.

On my way, a table display of language books catches my eye – in particular, *Fifteen Minute Italian*. It promises to teach me in just fifteen minutes a day if I also download the accompanying app. Smiling as I imagine the expression on Fabio's face when I rattle off a couple of sentences in his native tongue, I take it with the other books to the counter.

I see a coffee mug there that says: 'Reading books and buying books are two different hobbies'. 'I'll take that as well,' I tell Alan as he starts to ring up my purchases.

'Planning a trip to Italy or something?' he asks.

'Maybe.' I try to curb my smile. 'My new boyfriend, Fabio, is Italian.'

His eyes widen. 'Not the barista from the Grouchy Sailor?'

'Yes, that's the one.'

He whistles. 'That guy makes the best coffee in town. Please marry him so he doesn't move on. His coffee is like three-ply toilet paper – once you've tried it, you can't go back to anything less.'

I laugh as I tap my credit card. 'I'll do my best.'

At home, I greet JB with the usual fanfare and glance into Sully's backyard. I'm disappointed to see his car isn't there, but go back inside, find an old paper bag to wrap the book in, then write a note: *If this book doesn't give you all the feels, you have no heart.*

I shove the book and note into his letterbox, then download the *Fifteen Minute Italian* app onto my phone.

44

The Wicked Witch from the North

Thursday mid-morning I'm on the desk when Ritik, Ursula's boss from the shire, arrives.

Hallelujah, I think, giving him my biggest smile. 'Morning, Ritik. How can I help you?' Although I know damn well why he's here.

He smiles back. 'I've come to see Ursula. Is she available?'

I nod – 'She's in her office' – and he thanks me before heading that way.

The moment the door closes behind him, I leap up from my seat to find my friends. I haven't been so excited since Marian Keyes announced she was writing another Walsh sisters book. 'Ritik's here!' I all but squeal once I have them all gathered. I don't even care that Ursula's going to be angry, or that I'll probably be the one who has to return all those *nefarious* books to the shelves, I'm just glad we'll have wiped that smug expression off her face.

Persephone palms her hands against her cheeks. 'Told you my hex would work.'

Fred rolls her eyes. 'Or it could be Xavier's email.'

'Who cares,' I say, practically bouncing on the spot. 'The important thing is that he'll put her in her place and remind her she can't control what our borrowers have to read.'

'She's going to be fuming.' Xavier sounds nervous – he doesn't like conflict.

I squeeze his arm. 'Don't worry, we're in this together.'

'I hope he gives her a verbal warning,' Fred snarls. She'd received her first one yesterday for telling someone they didn't have to pay to replace the book they'd left on the bus.

'Surely banning books deserves a written warning,' I say.

They all nod in agreement.

'Half the books we'll need soon for Pride Month displays have been removed,' Fred says.

'Oh, didn't you hear? Displays are banned now too. *We're not a department store*,' I mimic.

'I wonder why she even became a librarian,' Persephone says, rubbing her stomach, which seems to have exploded to basketball size in the last week or so. 'She doesn't seem to like books *or* people.'

When Ritik finally leaves, Ursula storms out and summons Xavier and me.

I'm feeling bold, so I tell her this better be quick as I'm about to go on lunch.

She snaps her fingers at me. 'That's it. I've had enough of your cheek, Bridget. Consider this your verbal warning.'

'What?' I exclaim as we enter her office and she shuts the door behind us.

Neither of us can believe what she tells us. It's like she's gaslighting the both of us. Apparently Ritik confronted her about our accusation, and she set him straight.

She points at the boxes of books stacked up on the back wall of her office – the books she'd made me remove from the shelves. 'I don't know where you got the idea that I asked you to remove these books because of their content.'

'Uh, because you told me.'

Xavier nods and Ursula shakes her head as if we're both imbeciles. 'I told you those books were damaged.'

'But they're not,' I say.

She gestures at the boxes for me to take a look.

Tentatively, I cross over to them. I pick up a copy of *A Court of Mist and Fury* and, sure enough, it's water damaged. I can't believe it. The next book I check has the pages ripped out.

'You did this!' I say, shaking the book at her.

'That's a very offensive accusation,' she retorts.

'Since they are all damaged, I guess you'll be replacing them, then?'

Ursula narrows her eyes and peers down at me – she really is a giant. 'If the money's in the budget, I'll think about it. I don't believe that's any concern of yours anyway.'

I glance to Xavier for back-up – the budget might not be part of *my* job description but as assistant manager, it's definitely part of his – but he looks broken. Defeated. I'm so scared he's going to apply for a job at another library and leave the rest of us all alone to deal with The Wicked Witch from the North.

'Now, I have work to catch up on. You two should be ashamed of yourselves for wasting both mine and Ritik's valuable time.' Ursula points to the door. 'You can see yourself out. And, Bridget, take the five minutes you were late this morning off your lunch break.'

I swear it was only two minutes – I'd got a little caught up talking to Fabio at the café – but I know better than to object.

Persephone appears in the tearoom when I'm getting my bag.
'You okay?'

'Whatever hex you put on Ursula, it's not working,' I say. 'It's
time to up your game.'

45

Definitely a Keeper

The front screen door is unlocked when Fabio and I arrive at Janine and Dave's house in White Gum Valley on Sunday afternoon for Janine's leaving–retirement party. We knock but there's no answer, unsurprising considering the noise coming from around the back. Winter has turned on a beautiful day, and it sounds like the guests are out there making the most of it.

'We'll just go on in,' I say, pushing open the door.

Fabio whistles as we walk down the limestone hallway, and he glances up at the mezzanine level. 'Wow. What a place. Such a perfect combination of old and new. They must have a bit of money.'

'I think they've just worked hard over the years. Plus, they bought this place when they first got married, so it would have been a lot cheaper then.'

'What are they going to do with it now that they're going travelling?'

'They're turning it into an Airbnb,' I say as we walk through their open-plan kitchen and dining area to their massive verandah, which is overflowing with lush greenery in big bright pots. There are outdoor heaters at each end, and Janine's oldest son Steve looks to be burning sausages on a barbecue while Jimmy Barnes wafts from the stereo. Heralding a new adventure in the middle of the backyard – between a Hills hoist washing line and swing set from the eighties – is their brand-new caravan. Most of the guests are gathered around it and Dave appears to be giving some kind of TED Talk. Nick is taking photos like a proud dad, while Persephone pushes four-year-old Sabrina on the swings, a cranky expression on her face and a hand supporting her back as she glares at her husband.

Janine sees us and rushes in through the open concertina doors. 'Bee, thanks so much for coming.' She pulls me into a hug and then turns to Fabio. 'So lovely to see you again.'

'And you too, Janine.' He gives her the bunch of flowers we picked up on the way, then does the Italian thing of kissing her on both cheeks. She blushes as all women tend to do in his company.

'Come on through and meet my husband and the rest of the gang. And help yourself to drinks.' She gestures to the eskies set up not far from the barbecue. 'If you want wine, Bee, there's glasses on the kitchen counter.'

'Thanks,' I say as we follow her over to the crowd of caravan admirers.

Dave pauses his spiel to shake Fabio's hand and kiss me on the cheek.

'You're looking great,' I tell him. It's the truth. He's like a new person compared to when we were last here – the colour is back in his cheeks and he's regained a little weight – and his excitement about their new toy and upcoming trip is all over his face.

'Aw, thanks, Bee. Come have a look inside.'

The moment we step up into the van, three children jump out at us from under the tiny table. I quickly identify them as Samantha – Persephone's seven-year-old – and two of Janine's grandsons.

Dave lovingly taps one of the boys on the back of his head. 'That was only funny the first time, Artie. Now, skedaddle.'

The kids disappear and Dave gives Fabio and me the grand tour. 'Look.' He points to a little shelf by the bed. 'There's even room for some of Janine's favourite books, although I'm thinking of buying her a Kindle so she can bring as many as she likes.'

I smile knowingly, glad he hasn't bought one yet because the rest of us have all put in for one for her retirement gift.

'It's fabulous,' I say, but Fabio really wins Dave over when he starts asking specifics about things that I have no understanding of or inclination to find out about.

I slip out, leaving them to it and head over to Persephone. 'Want me to take over?' I say, gesturing to the swing. 'You look like you need to sit down for a bit.'

'For a bit?' She eagerly steps aside. 'I reckon I need to sit down for a few months!'

'How many weeks are you now?'

She groans. 'Too many and not enough. I swear I'm too old for this.' Then she nods towards the caravan. 'Must be serious if you've brought him to an official gathering?'

'Maybe.' I can't help grinning. 'He's just so sweet and kind.'

'Happy for you, babe.' Persephone sighs and rests her hands on her stomach. 'Just take my advice and use very good protection.'

I laugh, then tell her to go take a seat on the verandah while she can.

As she climbs the few steps, Xavier, Rory, Fred and a tall guy wearing an Eagles beanie emerge from the open back door. They each hug Persephone and then glance my way. Fred waves and then mimes lifting a cup to her mouth with a questioning look.

I nod and she and the guy make their way across with a whole bottle of prosecco. Classic Fred. We all take sips straight from it as she introduces me to Andy – apparently they met at their Monday night writing class.

'She's so talented, isn't she?' He stares dreamily at her.

'Has *he* read your book?' I demand, offended she's let some random see it before me.

'Only the pages I had to share with class.'

'So so so so so good,' he says, and that's when I realise he's stoned.

Ignoring him – he won't last long anyway – I hold up two fingers to Fred. 'I'm giving you a deadline. I want to see it in two weeks. Or else.'

She laughs as Fabio emerges from the caravan and heads over. He knows Fred from the café, but only talks to her briefly before turning to Sabrina, who I'm still pushing on the swing.

'And what's your name?' he asks, stooping slightly.

She tells him, then asks, 'Why do you sound funny?'

He chuckles. 'Because I'm Italian.'

'My friend's mum is Italian,' Sabrina says. 'Can you push me instead of Bee?'

'*Certo minascola,* bella.'

She giggles loudly. Even the under-fives are besotted with him.

'You okay here?' I ask Fabio. 'We want to give Janine her present.'

He nods, and we sneak her away from the party to tell her we have a gift for her.

'Oh, you sweet things. But you shouldn't have bothered.'

'Yes, we should have,' I say adamantly. 'Although we'd prefer it if you weren't leaving.'

Although we all nod, none of us mentions Mary Trunch-bull; we'd promised each other we wouldn't let her taint today's celebrations.

Xavier gestures to the beautifully wrapped box. 'Go on, take a look.'

'My goodness,' Janine exclaims when she opens it to reveal the Kindle. She sniffs. 'I was just telling Dave the other day how much I want one.'

'It's even engraved,' Persephone tells her. 'Turn it over.'

Janine reads out the inscription – *To the best boss ever. You're like our favourite book, one we love so much we return to it over and over again. Despite your faded, curling pages, you'll always have a place on our shelves and in our hearts* – then laughs. 'I don't have to ask who wrote this.'

'It was nothing.' Fred shrugs and takes another mouthful of prosecco. She sure does have a way with words.

After that, we all get proper glasses and toast the best boss we've ever had.

'Food's ready,' Steve calls as his wife helps him carry aluminium trays to a trestle table already overloaded with salads and bread rolls.

Later, when everyone is stuffed full of sausages and salad and tipsy from drinks, I'm sitting on a wooden bench under a massive eucalypt tree with my surrogate mum, watching Fabio have a pretend tea party with the kids.

'He's adorable,' Janine says, clinking her glass with mine. 'Handsome as hell, makes amazing coffee and is good with kids. Rose told me he's been helping a few of them with some chores too.'

I nod. 'He also goes to bowling with Edgar, and Kerry has roped him into community choir.'

She laughs. 'He's definitely a keeper. And how are you and that young girl going with the hospital library project?'

'Not bad,' I say. 'Make-A-Wish has agreed to provide all the shelving, a few beanbags and reading chairs, a cosy rug and a thousand books to start us off.'

'That's fabulous.'

'Yeah, and loads of publishers have said they're willing to donate new releases every month so we can keep the shelves stocked.'

When we thought about logistics, an actual library where people officially borrowed the books was going to be too hard to staff with volunteers, so our new concept is a room in the hospital that runs like a book exchange or street library. Once it's set up, Lola and I will check in once a week to make sure everything is in order and unpack and shelve new donations as they come in.

'That's a lovely thing you're doing, sweetheart,' Janine says when I've finished explaining everything. 'I'm proud of you.'

She pulls me into a hug and as I wrap my arms around her, I sniff. 'Don't or you'll make me cry. I'm going to miss you so much.'

'I'll miss you too, chicken,' she says, patting my back. 'But just remember, I'm always only a phone call away, and I'll be back eventually. Maybe then I can volunteer for Lola's Library as well?'

We hold each other for a long moment, and when we pull apart, I look around for Fabio but can't see him anywhere. He's no longer sipping pretend tea with the kids, and a quick glance doesn't find him talking to any of the other guests either. I feel bad for leaving him alone for so long when he doesn't really know anyone.

'I'm just going to go find Fabio,' I say, standing and heading into the house.

The guest bathroom door is open, so he's not in there. I'm walking around the downstairs area, when I hear a shuffling noise upstairs.

'Fabio?' I call.

A moment later his head appears over the mezzanine railing. 'Hey, bella. Did you know you can see the ocean from the upstairs balcony?'

'What are you doing up there?'

He grins down at me – 'Just having a look around' – then makes his way back downstairs and pulls me into his arms, kissing me hard.

'Come back outside. They're going to have cake soon.' I take his hand, feeling slightly awkward that he's been wandering around Janine and Dave's place on his own and hoping no one else noticed.

'And then can we go?' He leans close and whispers, 'I want to spend the rest of the afternoon in bed, showing you how much I *adora* you.'

A thrill of pleasure goes straight to my core and any irritation I had at him melts away at his sexy words.

'I have no complaints about that,' I say, as I lead him back outside.

46

Channelling Colin Firth

On Monday night, I'm heating up an oven meal for one – Fabio is at bowls with Edgar again – when Sully starts on the bagpipes next door. JB looks up at me from his dog biscuits and I laugh at his forlorn expression.

'Just let me finish dinner and we'll go for a walk,' I tell the dog, whose ears perk up at the W word.

I scoff dinner, put on my puffer jacket and a beanie, then head out into the night, JB bouncing along beside me like it's the first walk he's ever had. We wander through the streets of Fremantle, passing busy restaurants and pubs, and I'm glad I've just eaten or the aromas of French, Italian, Chinese, Indian, Thai and Mexican food would torment me.

While JB pauses every few minutes to sniff around, I listen to *Fifteen Minute Italian* in my earbuds. As I repeat the basic Italian words back to the voice in my ears, I feel like Colin Firth in *Love Actually* when he's walking the streets of London learning Portuguese. Hopefully mine and Fabio's ending is as happy as Jamie's and Aurelia's.

Next, we move on to a few simple phrases – '*Buongiorno.*

Buona sera. Come ti chiami?' – and I repeat the words back to my teacher, but it feels frustratingly slow. Apparently fifteen minutes a day will mean I have all the basics needed for a trip to Italy, but I don't want to be able to ask strangers for directions, I want to be able to impress Fabio by saying something meaningful. And maybe a little flirty.

We turn left off the Cappuccino Strip and head towards the Esplanade. JB loves the park – sometimes he'll pick up a fallen pinecone and carry it all the way home. We're halfway across and all I've seen are a couple of homeless people trying to get comfy for the night when JB starts tugging on the leash. I look up to see a jogger approaching us.

'John Brown!' says a deep voice as the figure gets close enough to recognise.

'Sully!' I reply.

'Evening, Bridget.' Sully ruffles JB's fur.

I frown. 'What are you doing here? You were just at home,' I say accusingly. 'Do you have an identical twin or something?'

He runs a hand through his messy hair. 'Keeping tabs on me, are you?'

'No.' I half-scowl, half-laugh. 'Hard not to know you're home when you're attempting to play that thing you call an instrument.'

He smirks. 'I stopped at 6.59. Wouldn't want anyone to report me to the council,' he says and then glances around the near-deserted park. 'You ought to be careful walking around in the dark alone. You don't know what kind of psychos could be out.'

'It's hardly the middle of the night. Besides, I have JB.'

Sully looks at JB and then back to me, one eyebrow quirked. 'You're relying on this teddy bear to protect you?'

He has a point. JB is more likely to smother someone to death while trying to French kiss them than attack them, but I'm not going to concede. 'You're out here alone as well.'

'I'm big enough and ugly enough to look after myself.'

My eyes drift to his biceps, barely hidden by his long-sleeve tee. Big enough, maybe, but definitely not ugly, especially with the moonlight shining across his chiselled face.

'Well, actually, I'm also an expert kickboxer,' I say. Slight exaggeration but last night my teacher did tell me I'd come on in leaps and bounds. Probably because I've started imagining Ursula's head with every kick.

'Is that right?'

I nod. 'Yep, so don't try anything untoward because I can whip your arse.'

'Thanks for the warning,' he says faux-seriously.

'Anyway, I'm heading home now.'

He nods. 'I'll walk with you.'

'You don't have to. Don't you want to finish your run?'

'I'll shoot some hoops later.'

'*Fabulous*,' I say, and he chuckles so deeply it warms my chilly bones.

As we fall into step beside each other, JB bouncing between us, Sully says, 'I don't think I've ever told you how grateful I am for you being so kind to Gran since her op. Thank you.'

'It's nothing. It's my job to take care of our patrons, and she's a sweetheart. I'm happy to help.'

'Well, we both really appreciate it.'

An awkward silence descends upon us until I can't stand it a moment longer. 'Have you started the new book I gave you?' When he nods, I add, 'How far in are you?'

He shrugs. 'A couple of chapters.'

'And . . .' I should know better by now, but I can't help myself. 'Are you enjoying it?'

'I'm finding it a bit slow, to be honest.'

I halt my strides, yanking poor JB on the lead, and turn to glare at him. 'Slow? It starts with a bank robbery and immediately develops into a hostage situation.'

He nods. 'In theory, that should be pretty exciting, but maybe it's the way the author writes. I dunno, it's a little bit grating or something.'

Grating?! I'm insulted on Backman's behalf. He's one of the few non-romance authors on my auto-buy list.

'I'm sorry if I've offended you, but you did ask.'

'You didn't offend me,' I lie. 'You just need to give it a little longer. Wait till you get to the twist. I guarantee you'll be banging down my door, desperate to talk to me about it.'

Again, he chuckles, although this time it *grates* on me rather than warms me.

I pick up my pace, no longer wanting the company he's thrust upon me. He doesn't appear to be bothered by the silence and makes no attempt at further small talk. Neither do I.

When we get to my gate, I pause in front of it. 'Well, thanks for walking me.'

'My pleasure.' He smirks at my sarcastic tone. 'Have a good night, Bridget.'

'You too, Mikey,' I say begrudgingly as I push the gate open and head towards the front door. It's not a sin to not like a book, but I can't work out if Sully is a particularly hard nut to crack, or if something about him is putting me off my game.

He waits until I go inside before finally walking next door.

I kick off my shoes and flop down on my couch just as a text message arrives from Lola.

OMG!!!!! I just finished listening to Rock Bottom Girl. *I have a new book boyfriend!!*

Ooh yeah, Jake's a good one, I reply.

Honestly, Bee. I never thought I'd be in love with a history teacher of ALL people, but I think he's ruined me for all others. He will have my heart for eternity.

laughing emoji After reading that book, I purposely matched with some teachers on Tinder, but none of them lived up to the Lucy Score hype.

Wow. I've never had a history teacher under ninety-five!!! But . . . TELL ME ABOUT TINDER!

Of course, I don't tell Lola everything – she's far too young to know the whole horrible truth about dating apps – but I do share some of my funniest stories and we end up texting for almost an hour, before she finally goes quiet, and I figure she must have fallen asleep.

Secretly hoping Fabio will drop in post-bowls, I pick up *Finlay Donovan Jumps the Gun* and snuggle under my covers to read.

47

How Not to Catch Feelings

'I'm driving you home,' Fred announces as we both clock off on Thursday afternoon.

'Okay,' I say. 'Any particular reason?'

'You'll see.'

We spend the short drive talking about Andy, who Fred tells me she actually hasn't slept with yet, despite the fact there's so much chemistry between them. She doesn't want to risk things being awkward at their writing class when she tires of him.

'Maybe you won't? Maybe this is the one,' I suggest.

She scoffs – 'No offence, but you know I don't believe in that bullshit' – as she turns into the alleyway behind my house and pulls her Mini into my barely used carport.

JB is so excited to see Fred when I open my back door that he pees on the patio.

'Ew,' Fred screeches.

'Sorry, but he only does it when he really likes someone. Do you want a cup of tea?' I dump my keys on the kitchen bench and turn on the heating.

'Sounds good!'

I make the tea in two bookish mugs as Fred perches on a kitchen stool and pulls a large, gift-wrapped package out of her oversized handbag and places it on the bench in front of her. 'For you.'

'What for?'

She grins smugly. 'Open it and you'll see.'

I do as she says while the teabags brew, and squeal as my fingers close around a thick wad of paper. 'Oh my goodness, is this . . .' My voice trails off as I read the title on the front cover: *How Not to Catch Feelings* by Winifred Darling.

She nods. 'I figured two days was better than two weeks. I printed and bound it at work today when Ursula wasn't looking.'

'That's totally a written warning offence,' I exclaim, tsking jokingly at her.

Fred shrugs. 'Well, hopefully I'll be telling Mary Trunchbull where to shove her job soon.'

I literally cry as I start flicking through the pages, staring at all the rows and rows of words, just absorbing the thickness of what I'm sure will be pure brilliance. 'I'm so damn proud of you. I can't believe you wrote this in only six months, but I wish you'd given me a heads-up. I'd have bought bubbles to celebrate.'

'You can do that when I sign a contract.'

'Deal.' I grin. 'I'll start it tonight.'

'No rush. Although hopefully once you begin, you won't be able to stop. Andy says it's a real page turner.'

'I think you like this Andy guy,' I say, removing the teabags.

'What makes you say that?'

'Because if you didn't, you wouldn't care about things getting awkward after you sleep with each other.'

'Don't be ridiculous,' she says, but I see a hint of pink in her usually pale cheeks. 'You read too much romance.'

I pick up the mugs. 'No such thing as too much romance. Shall we take these into the lounge room?'

She nods and JB follows us in there, curling up on the couch between Fred and me while we dream about what will happen when she's a hugely successful novelist.

'You better not forget me when you're rich and famous.'

'Bridget who?' She laughs and I throw a cushion at her.

When our tea is finished, Fred goes home and I start on dinner. Fabio is coming over, so I'm making more of an effort than my usual microwave meal. I dice an onion and toss it with some oil into the frying pan and am getting some beef strips out of the fridge for stroganoff when there's a knock on my front door.

'You're early,' I say as I peel open the door. 'Can't get enough—'

The words die on my tongue because it's Sully, not Fabio.

'Good evening,' he says, the copy of *Anxious People* in his hand.

'You've finished it?' Slow learner that I am, I can't help my excitement. 'I knew you'd be banging down my door, desperate to talk about it.'

He snorts. 'I wouldn't call it banging, and I'm not desperate. I'm just returning it because I noticed it wasn't a library book. I figured it was yours?'

'Yes,' I say, taking it from him. I'm not about to tell Sully I bought it especially for him. 'Dare I ask what you thought?'

'It was . . . not bad,' he says, tipping his head to one side. 'Interesting premise. Some of the characters were a little over-the-top.'

'Not *bad*?'

'The chapters with the police interviewing the witnesses were pretty good. I did feel sorry for that dude.'

I smile – this is the most promising conversation we've had about a book so far. 'I loved those bits too. And what did you think about the twist?'

He frowns. 'What twist?'

'Uh, who the bank robber actually was!'

'That was supposed to be a twist? I guessed it was them from almost the beginning.'

I narrow my eyes at him, trying to tell whether he's lying. 'Really?'

He nods and I feel defeated. 'On a scale of one to ten, how would you rate it?'

'Maybe six or seven.'

'So, I haven't turned you into a fiction fiend?' Maybe I should give him Fred's book – I might not have read it yet, but if it reads anything like her personality, it'll be all-consuming and addictive.

He sniffs and looks past me. 'Are you cooking something?'

For a moment I think he might be trying to engineer an invitation to dinner – good luck! – and then I smell the burning.

'Shit!' I race back to the kitchen and take the frying pan off the heat just as my smoke alarm starts screaming. The onions are blackened.

Sully grabs a tea towel and waves it at the alarm, while I rush to open the back door. As if the noise isn't bad enough, JB starts barking and trying to jump up and grab the tea towel out of Sully's hands. Finally, just when I think it's never going to stop, the alarm goes silent. And thankfully, so does JB.

'I'm so sorry,' Sully says, putting the tea towel on the bench right next to Fred's manuscript. 'That's my fault. Let me order you Uber Eats or, better yet, cook something for you.'

'Don't be ridiculous. It's fine.' I don't want to have to make small talk over dinner with the only person I've ever failed to convert to reading. 'I've got another onion . . .'

He nods. 'In that case, I'd better be going.'

'I'll see you to the door.'

We walk back down my book-lined hallway, and Sully pauses. 'Why do you have so many books when you work in a library?'

Only a non-booklover could ask such a ridiculous question!

'Some of them belonged to my grandparents, but it might shock you to learn that I'm a librarian because I love reading, so although I do borrow books, I buy all my favourite authors and collect special editions of books I've loved. Besides, a house is not a home without books.'

Yes, this *is* a dig at his sterile residence.

'This is an eclectic collection,' he says, perusing the shelves. 'What kind of books do you enjoy the most?'

'I read everything – it's part of my job to know what's out there. I love a lot of the classics, and cosy crime, but my favourite genre is romance.'

I prepare for the roll of his eyes, some sarcastic remark about romance novels giving women unrealistic ideals about men, but he surprises me by asking, 'Why didn't you try me on one of them, then?'

'Because this isn't about me. I was trying to find a book I thought *you* would like.'

'Who says I wouldn't like romance?' he asks, his tone a little playful. 'You think because I'm separated, I'm bitter about love?'

This is the first time he's mentioned his relationship to me, and I must admit I'm curious. 'You're not?'

He shakes his head. 'I'm sad my marriage didn't work out, but I'm not cynical or vain enough to think that no marriage can.'

His honest confession renders me speechless.

'What's your favourite romance novel, then?'

'Why?' I ask warily.

'Because I want to read it and see why you love it so much.'

I shake my head. 'Oh, no, no, no. I'm not gonna give you my favourite novel for you to rip it to shreds and tell me everything you think is wrong with it.'

He puts his hands under his armpits and starts to flap his elbows. '*Bok . . . bok bok bok.*'

My mouth falls open. I shut it. Then open it again. 'Are you calling me a chicken?'

He shrugs one shoulder annoyingly. 'Are you?'

I thrust my finger at him – 'Stay there' – and then march into my bedroom to my keeper bookshelf. I like that these books are the last thing I see when I go to sleep and the first thing I see when I wake up. I contemplate only giving him one of my near-favourites, but I am not *chicken*, so I pluck *Faking It* by Jennifer Crusie off the shelf and take it back to him.

He reads the title, then turns it over to read the back. 'This looks old.'

I lift an eyebrow. 'The best romance novels all stand the test of time.'

'Okay, then.' He continues reading, then asks, 'Did you cover this in contact?'

'Yes. It's not a crime to protect your books,' I say defensively. 'And that one's very hard to get now, so you'd better look after it.'

He holds it close to his chest. 'I promise I will.'

I jump out of my skin as I open the door to find Fabio, his hand raised to knock. I'd almost forgotten he was coming.

He glares at Sully. 'What are you doing here?'

Sully holds up the novel. 'Just borrowing a book.'

Fabio eyes the cover and looks sceptical. And although it's the truth, I feel weirdly guilty about him finding me alone with Sully.

'Mikey was just leaving,' I say, all but shoving him out the door.

I hear him growl at the name as I shut it behind him, then I pull Fabio into a kiss. 'Good evening, gorgeous.'

'I thought you *deteste* that guy?'

'I do,' I lie as I grab his hand and drag him into the kitchen. 'Hate' is a strong word and not how I feel about Sully any more, but I don't want Fabio worrying about something he doesn't have to. 'Do you want some dinner? I might not be as good in the kitchen as you but—'

He pulls me against him, then lifts me up and dumps me on the kitchen bench, pushing my knees apart and stepping between them. 'I don't care how you are in the *cucina*. It's how you are in the bedroom that's important to me.'

My laugh is stolen by his mouth as his hands cup my butt, dragging me even closer to him.

His lips leave mine. 'Hey, what's this?' He's found my copy of *Fifteen Minute Italian*.

'Um . . . that's . . .' I blush, feeling weirdly stupid and embarrassed.

'You're learning Italian? For me?'

I nod. 'I know your English is really good, but I always wanted to learn a language and I figured it might be nice for you to be able to speak Italian sometimes with someone other than your sister. I've only just started, but I thought then maybe I could take an online class or something?'

'That's very sweet, bella.' He plants a kiss on my nose. 'But there really is no need. I'd love you even if you couldn't speak at all.'

My heart trips. *Oh oh oh oh oh!* Did he just say he loves me?

I don't want to make a big deal of it – he's Italian and I think they might throw the L-word around like confetti – and although I'm falling for him, I'm not quite ready to say it back yet, so I simply grab his lapels and press my mouth to his again.

Needless to say, I don't end up cooking dinner.

48

The G-Spot

After my usual coffee and walk on Saturday morning, I have brunch with Lola and Laura at Duck Duck Bruce. We sit inside because Lola feels the cold even more these days and she orders a dish called 'Orange is the New Stack' – a massive stack of pancakes with orange curd, toasted almonds, a poppyseed cheesecake whip and ginger-bread crumb – even though we all know she struggles to eat much these days. I order the same, because who wouldn't be sucked in by cheesecake whip, and Laura gets the 'Auber Jean is Not My Lover', which consists of crispy potato, spinach, almonds, eggplant, eggs, something coconut, chilli, roti and cumin raita. Whoever came up with these concoctions is an honest-to-God genius, and it's unsurprising that this cute little café is one of my favourite places to indulge.

The food arrives and Lola's eyes widen at the sight of it. 'I can't believe you used to be able to starve yourself.'

'Lola!' Laura scolds, then gives me an apologetic glance.

She shrugs. 'What?'

'Bee might not want to talk about this.'

'It's fine,' I say, before she tells her mother that she can say what-ever she wants because she has cancer. 'When I taste food like this,

I sometimes can't believe it either, but food felt like the enemy. My brain was messed up and thought that eating food would hurt me, when really it was the other way around.'

'Did something happen to you to make you think that? How did it start?' Lola asks.

'In hindsight, it was a combination of things.' I tell them a condensed version, that when I was little Mum was always on one diet or another, so I kind of just thought thin was what you aimed for. As a kid I was always skinny, but when I went to boarding school at thirteen and hit puberty, that changed. I missed home so much, I comfort ate.

It wasn't long before the weight piled on and I started getting teased by the boys at our brother school. I felt so fat and ugly, so I decided to try a diet like my mother did. I figured if I was thinner, people would like me. Only problem is, while it never worked that well for Mum, I was *really* good at it. I remember she'd aways cave after a few days, but not me. I had great willpower and after a few weeks, people – teachers and other girls – started telling me I was looking great, which spurred me on to lose more weight.

'And I guess it just became an obsession, to the point where I became afraid of food. I was terrified of getting fat again because I felt like people would only like me if I was thin.'

Lola and Laura listen intently as I tell them about fainting in class and being taken to a doctor who immediately recognised what was going on. From then on, the teachers watched me like a hawk and so did Mum when I went home for the holidays, but I learned to play those around me who I thought just didn't understand. I believed Mum was jealous that I could lose weight and she couldn't. If I was being watched, I'd eat things that had next to no calories, and if I was forced to eat something like bread or meat, I'd exercise late at night when everyone else was sleeping.

'Wow,' Lola says.

Laura frowns. 'Didn't someone notice you weren't getting better?'

'Anorexics can get very good at misleading loved ones, but one night when I was exercising, I fainted again and knocked my head on the side of my bed. I cried out in pain and the boarding supervisor heard me. Things got serious after that – I was in and out of hospital the next year or so as I got treatment, seemed to get better, then relapsed.'

'So how *did* you recover?' Lola looks worried for a moment as her gaze skims my body. 'You are recovered, aren't you?'

I nod. 'I'll always have a complex relationship with food. The feelings of self-loathing and guilt when I eat something "naughty" sometimes still happen, but I recognise the signs of disordered thinking now and work hard against them. As to how I recovered, it was a combination of things – the doctors were great, I had awesome therapists and . . . I actually read a book that shocked me into getting better.'

'Oh?' They both look intrigued.

'Yeah, a nurse saw how much I was reading, so she brought me a book her daughter had read when she was in high school. It was called *Even If It Kills Me* and it was about an anorexic in hospital like I was. She thought exactly like I did, that people didn't understand her and were overreacting, but then someone she'd met in the hospital – another anorexic more far gone than her – died. That shocked me. Although I'd been told how serious my condition could be, reading about someone in her teens dying was my turning point. I wanted to be thin, but I didn't want to die.'

'So you just started eating again?' Lola asks.

I shake my head. 'It wasn't as simple as that – it would have been dangerous for me to start eating normal amounts again straight away. It took time and therapy and lots of love and understanding from those around me.'

'Wow, but it was a book that saved you?' Lola grins. 'I guess that's why you're so keen to help with my project – you know how important books can be to sick people.'

I nod but feel the need to lighten the conversation. 'Speaking of books, what did you think of *Things You Save in a Fire,* Laura?'

Laura latches onto the change of subject like a cowboy grabbing a bull's horns. Lola and I had conned her into reading one of our favourite books by Katherine Center so we could start our own little book club over brunch on Saturdays. She didn't require much conning.

'Oh, I loved it,' she says. 'When I was young, I always wanted to marry a firefighter.'

'Doesn't everyone?' I laugh.

After saying goodbye to my new bookish friends, I head home and am anxious when JB isn't waiting to greet me. His bark from the back of the house both alleviates my worry – at least he's here and alive – and elevates it.

'What's wrong, baby dog?' I call as I hurry towards him.

Before I reach him, I hear the whir of Sully's lawnmower. Only this time, when I look out the window, I realise why JB is going even crazier than normal: Sully is in *my* backyard.

Mowing *my* well-overdue-for-a-trim lawn.

Dumping my bag on the kitchen bench, I open the door. Sully must sense movement as JB launches himself off the patio, because he kills the engine and lifts a hand to wave as if me finding him in my backyard mowing my lawn is an everyday occurrence.

'What are you doing?' I demand.

He frowns and reaches up to rub the back of his neck. 'Thought that was fairly obvious.'

'I didn't ask you to do this!' I don't know why but I feel peeved at him for not checking with me first.

JB is not peeved – he's jumping around Sully like a dog possessed.

'I know,' Sully says, chuckling as he dodges JB's slobbery kisses, 'but I was doing my lawn when I glanced over here and saw yours could do with a trim.'

That is a gross understatement – my lawn needs a full-blown bikini wax. Maybe that's why I feel annoyed, because him doing this puts me to shame. 'I've been busy.'

'That's why I thought I'd help. It's no problem. Just a few more minutes and I'll be done.'

I sigh. 'Well, thanks. And thanks for having the decency to wear clothes this time.'

Smirking, he starts up the lawnmower again as I head back into the house, thinking about that time all those months ago when I first saw him mowing. I can't help thinking it's a pity it's winter, because him half-naked was a sight for sore eyes.

Bridget, I silently scold. How would Fabio feel if he knew what I was thinking?

Despite the cool temperature outside, I down a glass of cold water in an attempt un-fluster myself. When it doesn't work, I shove my head in the fridge instead, making the most of the opportunity to rifle through the vegetable drawer to see what needs to be discarded.

'All done.'

I startle and bang my head on the roof of the fridge.

'Sorry!' Sully says from the back door. 'I thought you'd have heard me switch off the lawn mower.'

'You'd think,' I say, rubbing my head. That's what happens when you're having illicit thoughts about previously grumpy neighbours. I'm closing the fridge again when I spy the sixpack of beer I'd bought for Fabio.

'Want a beer?' I ask. It's past noon, so reasonable weekend drinking time, and this feels like the least I can do to say thank you.

Sully nods. 'Yeah, thanks. That'd be great.'

I grab two beers and pass one to him. We crack them open and then I lift mine in a toast. 'Thanks so much for mowing my lawn.'

Now the shock of seeing him out there has passed, I really do appreciate it. Gardening – especially mowing – is one of my least favourite things to do.

He clicks his bottle against mine – 'Not a problem' – takes a sip, then nods at the two gnomes still sitting on my kitchen bench. 'You know, it's safe to put them back outside now. Promise. I'll even help you if you want.'

'I kinda got used to them being in here.' As well as the two on the bench, I have gnomes on the table, gnomes on my bookshelves, gnomes in my bedroom, and even a couple in the bathroom. 'They're good company.'

'Okay then.' I can hear the amusement in his voice. 'How'd you start collecting them?'

'Wanna take these out the back and I'll tell you all about it?'

Sully nods and follows me outside, where we sit on the back step, JB settling at our feet.

'My collection began with two my grandma had out the front. I used to play with them like dolls whenever I visited, then one day I broke one and I was distraught. Granny and Pop took me to Bunnings and I got to choose one of my own. Only it had to live at their place to keep the other gnome company. It kinda became a thing after that. Whenever I came down, we'd go and buy a gnome. That's why I was so upset when you took some. They're sentimental.'

'I'm sorry,' he says, visibly cringing. 'Have you ever been to Gnomesville?'

'Oh, yes. My grandparents took me there when I was little, and I've been back many times since. It's like my favourite place in WA.'

'I took my ex-wife there when we were down south once.' He smiles and it still disarms me because I'm not used to the sight. 'Fun place.'

I'm desperate to ask about his wife but feel that might be rude. 'How you are going with *Faking It*?' If Jennifer Crusie can't win him over, then Fred's right – he's a lost cause.

He takes another sip of beer as if to buy time. 'About three quarters of the way through. It's not what I imagined.'

'Oh?'

'Well, it's cool that they're not perfect people on a clichéd journey to happy ever after, but—'

Of course, I roll my eyes. 'Such a typical thing for someone who has never read a romance before to say. There's nothing clichéd about romance novels!'

'You sound a little defensive.' He smirks as JB brings him over a soggy ball he's dug up from somewhere in the garden. 'I do wonder if there's too many characters and too much going on.'

'That sounds to me like a you problem, not a Jennifer Crusie problem. *Poor* Sully, can't keep up with what's happening. Maybe I should have recommended *Dick and Dora.*'

He hurls the ball towards the back fence and JB races after it. 'I didn't say I can't keep up. Gotta say the sex scene was interesting. I felt for the guy when Tilda faked her orgasm. And when she tells him her vibrator is better than him! Ouch.' He puts a hand to his chest as if personally scarred.

I take another sip of beer to stop from grinning too widely. 'Sounds to me like you're enjoying it?'

'It's helping me pass some time. The Dempsey character can be a bit of a dick, though.'

'Benefit of it being a romance is that he'll be redeemed by the end.'

He nods. 'That's the formula, right?'

I resist bonking him over the head with my bottle. 'There is nothing formulaic about a Jenny Crusie novel. I won't have you say a word against her!'

'So . . .' He kicks at a stray leaf. 'Is that a thing women really do?'

'What thing?'

'Fake orgasms.'

I laugh. 'Of course.' I can't believe I'm talking about sex with Sully. 'Haven't you seen *When Harry Met Sally*?'

'Yeah, but . . . I thought . . .' His voice trails off as he takes another gulp of beer, and I wonder if he's wondering how often his ex-wife was pretending. 'How often do *you* fake it?'

I blink. 'That's a bit of a personal question, Mr Sullivan.'

He blushes sightly. 'Sorry.'

'I'll answer it, *if* I can ask you one and you promise you'll give me an honest reply.'

He considers this for a moment, then nods.

'Okay, then, yes, I have faked orgasms. Surely you as a doctor know that most men struggle to find the female G-spot, and that pounding harder and harder in the hope of breaking through is not only awful but can also be pretty painful.'

'You do know the actual G-spot's a myth, right?'

'Sounds to me like something a guy who'd never managed to find it might say.'

He snorts. 'Or a doctor who actually knows what he's talking about. Bet you didn't know the supposed G-spot was named after a man.'

'What?' About to take a sip, my hand freezes with the bottle midair. 'No way.'

'Yep. A woman and her team of researchers in the eighties named it after a German researcher called Ernst Gräfenberg. They believed it to be a sensitive small bean, but there is no such part on the female body. Other researchers since have proclaimed it as all sorts of things – most commonly it's known as a highly erogenous mass of tissue but not every vagina is the same—'

I feel like a ten-year-old boy hearing him say the word 'vagina' and try to maintain my composure as he continues. I take another sip of beer in an effort to cool off. Again.

'No such spot has ever been proven, despite numerous studies done on cadavers.'

'I'm sorry.' I blink again and tip my bottle towards him. 'Did you just say cadavers? As in *dead* people?'

He grins. 'Yep.'

I grimace. 'Isn't that a little . . . I don't know, *off*? Poking around down there in a dead person?'

'They've all given permission before they died for the body to be used as research,' he says with a chuckle. 'What was the question you wanted to ask me?'

After this enlightening anatomy lesson, I'd almost forgotten our deal, but I'm not wasting this opportunity. 'Oh.' I swallow. 'You said you're not bitter about the end of your marriage, but I thought Daisy said your wife cheated on you? As someone who's been cheated on a few times, I'm just wondering how you can feel so ambivalent about it.'

'I'm not ambivalent, and I didn't say I wasn't bitter about how my marriage ended. I said I'm not bitter about love.'

I guess that makes sense and although I know we only agreed to one question, I can't help asking another. 'How long were you and your wife together?'

Sully starts picking at the label on the bottle. 'Her name's Kristen. And just on twenty years.'

'Wow, you must have started going out when you were babies.'

'Not quite, but close enough. We met in high school and got together at sixteen. She was my first love.'

'And how long have you been separated?'

A whole chunk of label on the bottle comes off as he tears it. 'Almost six months.'

And in that time, I've never seen another woman come in or out of his house. I can't help myself. 'Do you still love her?'

'I think you've asked more than your one question.' He downs the dregs of his beer and puts the empty bottle on my bench.

Guess that's my answer. I never thought I'd feel sorry for Sully but I do. *Poor guy.*

'Anyway,' he says, summoning a smile, 'I'd better be going before your boyfriend turns up and thinks I'm trying to cut *his* grass.'

I laugh again. 'I'm allowed to have friends.'

But Sully stands anyway. 'Thanks for the beer, Bridget.'

My bones vibrate at the way he says my name. 'You're welcome.'

He ruffles JB's hair as the dog follows him to the back gate.

As he reaches it, I call out, 'Are you liking *Faking It* better than *Boy Swallows Universe?*'

'I've laughed a lot more,' he replies, waving as he disappears through the gate.

That's a win, I think, as I take the empty bottles inside. The house is still in need of its weekend tidy-up, but after my big breakfast and the beer, I'm no longer in the mood and I figure the mess will still be here tomorrow. I decide to do a little language practice instead – dreaming of going to Italy with Fabio one day and being able to speak the language is much more fun – but I can't find my copy of *Fifteen Minute Italian*. It's not on the bench where he left it last night, and I can't find it anywhere else in the house either. The only possible solution is that Sully took it.

But he left empty handed, and why would he take such a thing anyway?

49

A Good-for-nothing Scamp

Considering how much I dreaded taking over the Bookstars, I really look forward to the meetings now. Beth and Barbara arrive first, followed by Edgar, who's holding yet another Jack Reacher novel and a copy of *The Talented Mr. Ripley*.

He waves the latter at me as he comes over to where I'm checking the urn. 'Now this I'm looking forward to discussing. That Tom fellow had some nerve. Imagine living the high life, fooling everybody about who you were, killing anyone who dared to get in your way.'

I smile as I open the packet of Arnott's. 'I'm glad you enjoyed it.'

Daisy comes in next, walking well without the stick and nicely dressed in what Mum would call navy slacks and a cream blouse.

'No Mikey today?' I ask.

She shakes her head. 'I'm back to driving now. He's taken enough time off already, and there are people who need him more than I do.'

Yeah, people who need to get from A to B, not people who need urgent medical care.

I wonder if Sully isn't telling Daisy about his PTSD not only to protect her, but because he feels ashamed. Part of me thinks she could help him if she knew, but I know it's not my place to tell her.

'So great that you're all recovered now.' I find myself slightly disappointed that Sully won't be making an appearance, but I don't have time to dwell on this realisation because Fabio and Kerry come in, ushering a sobbing Rose between them.

Fabio gives me a brief peck on the cheek as I rush over. 'What's the matter?'

'It's all gone,' Rose sobs, clutching the string of pearls around her neck.

I frown as the three of us lead Rose to a chair. 'What's all gone?'

'Her money,' Kerry says. 'Some good-for-nothing scamp has scammed it all out of her.'

The rest of us gasp.

'I'll get her a cup of tea,' Beth says, because they're all of the generation that believe tea fixes everything.

'Good idea. And maybe bring her a biscuit.' Isn't sugar supposed to help shock?

The other Bookstars gather around Rose, and I do the same. 'Do you know how this happened?'

She sniffs and pulls a tissue out of her bag. 'My kids think it's because I have the same password on everything and must have been hacked. They've been telling me for years I should use different and more complicated passwords, but I can barely remember the one I have.'

'What's going on?' Lorna asks as she comes in with Ronice and Sue.

Kerry explains again what has happened.

'Bloody passwords,' Sue says, shaking her head. 'I'm always swearing at the computer machine about them.'

Rose gives her a grateful smile. 'I wasn't going to come today, but I knew you'd all be far more sympathetic than my children.'

The Bookstars nod in solidarity as Beth returns with the tea and Rose takes it in her shaking hands.

'I'm so sorry this has happened to you,' I say, 'but have you spoken to the bank yet? Don't they have insurance for this kind of stuff?'

'They're looking into it, but there are no guarantees because I used a password with my date of birth in it and apparently they warn us against doing that in the fine print.'

Oh, God, poor Rose. I don't know anyone who reads the fine print, but maybe I should change some of my own passwords.

'This is terrifying,' Ronice exclaims, glancing at Sue beside her. 'If it could happen to you, it could happen to any of us.'

As Sue takes her hand, I say, 'Shouldn't the bank be able to track where the money was deposited to and find the culprit that way?'

This is the first time Fabio speaks since entering the room. 'That depends on how expert the *criminale* is. The bank will look into it, but if it was laundered well, it will have passed through many accounts by now and it might be *impossibile*.'

At this news, Rose lets out another guttural sob, but her tissue packet is empty.

Fabio pulls a clean white hanky from his pocket and passes it to her. I'm so glad he's here helping me comfort her.

'Sometimes I think we should all keep our savings under our mattresses like my grandparents used to do,' Edgar declares.

'That's where I keep most of mine,' Lorna says.

'Perhaps don't advertise that fact,' I warn, then, realising that Fabio must know a bit about this stuff, I look to him. 'Hey, apart from changing passwords, is there anything else we can all be doing to protect ourselves from scammers like this? Fabio studied cyber security,' I explain.

He nods. 'I'd be happy to offer a few simple suggestions after the book chat.'

I glance at the anxious expressions around me. 'I don't think anyone is in the mood for talking about *The Talented Mr. Ripley* right now, so maybe you could give us all some tips about how to best protect ourselves now instead?'

I hope I haven't put him on the spot, but I really think his advice will make everyone feel a little better, a little safer.

'Okay. Good idea.' He sits forward and rests his elbows on his knees. 'As Rose says, the first thing to do is to change all your passwords to make sure they aren't easy to guess. Don't write them down anywhere or store them on your mobile phones.'

As he continues, his advice gets more and more complicated. Many of the Bookstars pull notepads and pens out of their bags to start scribbling, but when he mentions downloading software to protect against hackers, he starts to lose them.

'I don't know how to download anything,' Beth complains, snapping her notebook closed.

'I'd be happy to do it for you,' Fabio offers with his gorgeous smile. 'Won't take more than half an hour or so.'

Beth's expression lightens and she accepts immediately. 'Thank you, that would be wonderful. Of course I'll pay you.'

He waves away her offer. '*Non*. Not necessary.'

'Then I shall make you dinner. Tonight?'

He nods. 'That sounds *perfetta*.'

It's unsurprising when many of the others declare they would like his help too, and soon Fabio has a full diary of lunches, afternoon teas and dinners in exchange for his cyber security skills. I probably won't see much of him the next few days, but if he helps the Bookstars protect themselves, it's worth it.

'Well, I think it's time for afternoon tea,' I say, when our hour is up. It won't be long before Ursula will be storming in to throw everyone out.

Rose dabs Fabio's hanky to her eyes. 'I'm sorry I've taken up all our book chat time talking about my woes.'

Kerry pats her hand. 'Don't be silly, dear. There'll be plenty of time to talk books, but we're your friends, and you're what matters to us.'

I nod in agreement. 'It's absolutely fine, but since we didn't discuss *The Talented Mr. Ripley* today, shall we do that one next time and postpone *The Switch* till after?'

'I'm no longer in the mood for *Ripley*.' Beth glares at the book in her lap as if it caused her friend's troubles. 'It feels wrong to be discussing such a book when poor Rose has actually been scammed.'

'Hear, hear,' Lorna says. 'I say we go straight for the romance. I've already started it, and I can tell it's going to be delicious.'

We take a quick vote – the romance wins – and then they all hurry over to the coconut chiffon cake with lime icing that Fabio brought this week, where they elbow each other in their efforts to get the biggest slice.

They might be friends – but when it comes to cake, it's every senior for themselves.

50

(Not) The Whole Truth

Saturday evening, I'm reading *How Not to Catch Feelings* in bed but the truth is, I'm struggling to get into it. There are so many secondary characters that I can't work out who's sleeping with who, only that everyone seems to be sleeping with everyone. I'm no prude, and I don't mind a bit of smut in my romance novels, but I also like it to be there for a reason. I like sex scenes to make me *feel* something, but all this is making me feel is like I want to do anything but read it.

When JB barks, announcing Fabio's arrival at my front door, I leap up, welcoming the interruption, and hurry down the hallway to let him in.

'Hello, stranger,' I say, before we kiss.

Tonight, he's been at Ronice and Sue's place, safeguarding their computers. He tastes deliciously spicy, and I guess – correctly – that they had Indian for dinner. I was invited too, but the truth is as much as I like my time with Fabio, I also like my alone time to read.

Still, my baked beans on toast seem very unsatisfying in comparison.

'Want a beer?' I ask when we let go of each other.

He drops his head and sighs. 'Kill for one. It's been a long day.'

'Go sit, I'll grab the drinks. Do you want anything to eat?'

'*Non*. After cucumber sandwiches for lunch at Barbara's' – he screws up his face – 'and dinner at Ronice and Sue's, I'm not sure I'll ever eat again.' This is a big claim coming from an Italian who values food more than anyone I've ever met.

I head to the fridge, grab a beer and pour myself a glass of wine, then shove JB out of the way so I can sit next to *my* boyfriend on *my* couch. My dog looks up at me like I've broken his little heart.

'Thanks. Old people are exhausting.' Fabio lifts the bottle to his mouth and takes a long sip.

I chuckle. 'I'm sure they appreciate your help, though. It's a good thing you're doing.'

'It's the least I can do. The Bookstars have become like my *familia*, and if I ever get my hands on the person that scammed poor Rose . . .'

'I know how you feel,' I say, squeezing his hand. 'What kind of lowlife steals from old women?'

He shakes his head as he lifts my hand to his mouth and kisses it. 'Do you need me to help you protect your laptop too? I can fit you in after work tomorrow before I go to Lorna's. Actually, *no*, I'm helping Olga then. I can do it now.'

'It's okay. I don't need help with my computer. I've already put protection on myself.'

'Okay, but *per favore* say you'll come with me to her place. She terrifies me. And then you can come to dinner at Lorna's too – she's making a roast.'

I laugh. 'Olga terrifies everyone. Okay, I'll tag along tomorrow.' At least this way I get to see him, and a home-cooked roast sounds much better than beans on toast.

'*Grazie.*' He downs half the beer and leans even further back into the couch. 'Anyway, what have you been up to tonight?'

I gesture to the manuscript on the coffee table. 'Reading Fred's story.'

'You don't sound happy about that.'

'It's terrible,' I groan. 'From what she'd told me, I thought it would be amazing writing and an original story, and maybe it gets better – I've only read a third – but so far the writing is so pedestrian and there's not much happening but sex.'

He raises his eyebrows and picks it up.

A few seconds later, he lets out a rip-snorting laugh. 'Holy *fanculo*! I see what you mean. That story should come with an X rating.'

I snatch the book from him, feeling guilty about letting him read it when Fred had been so reluctant to even let me. 'No publisher in their right mind is ever going to pick it up.' And if I'm a good friend, I won't let her self-publish it either. If it wasn't my best friend's baby, I'd have DNF'd it at page ten!

'At least she's got a day job,' he says.

'But what am I supposed to tell her?' I yell, then down almost half my wine in one gulp. I feel like crying.

'Do you have to say anything?'

'Yes. I've been going on for months about how much I wanted to read her work and, aside from a few people in her writing class, I'm her first reader. She wants me to give her honest feedback.'

He lifts an eyebrow. 'Does she really?'

'Good question. In theory, I think she wants the truth but . . . how can I tell her that I hate it?'

I never thought I'd find myself in this predicament or I wouldn't have offered to read it in the first place, but Fred is so witty and sassy, I assumed that would translate to the page.

Fabio pulls me into his side. 'Maybe just don't say anything,' he says, kissing my neck in an attempt to distract me.

I scoff – if only it were that simple. She's already wondering what's taking me so long. So far I've managed to put her off by telling her I've been too busy going back and forth to the hospital about Lola's Library and having sex with Fabio. She very much approves of the latter.

'Then just lie,' he says simply.

'What? You mean tell her it's good?'

'*Sì*. You could give her little feedback.' He makes a tiny symbol with his fingers. 'Find some spelling mistakes or something? Tell her those are the only problems you found. That you loved it. Especially the sexy bits.'

I laugh as he wriggles his eyebrows suggestively. 'But I can't lie to her. That would be wrong. And the sexy bits are cringeworthy.'

'Would telling her the truth hurt her?' he asks.

I nod.

'Might it, ah, upset your friendship?'

I nod again.

'And are you *ex*pert in this area?'

I frown. 'Well, I have read a lot of books and I do think I can tell what's good and what's not.'

'But you are not a writing teacher or editor, so . . .' He shrugs. 'Who's to say your opinion is the right one, anyway? No point risking a friendship over it.'

I bite my lip, considering this. While in theory I'm absolutely against lying – especially to those closest to me – aren't little white lies okay if they're told with good intent? 'Maybe you're right.'

He puts his now-empty bottle down on the coffee table and takes my wineglass. 'Bella.' He looks into my eyes as he slips his hand up into my hair. 'I'm always right. Now, how about you forget about Fred's book for a while and concentrate on me instead?'

'That,' I say, 'is an offer too good to refuse.'

51

Something Iffy

The library has barely opened on Monday morning when Barbara, dressed in her usual winter outfit of woollen skirt, twin-set and pearls, accosts me at the main desk. 'I need to talk to you, Bee,' she says in her Queen's English accent. 'In *private*.'

Ursula glares at her but Barbara glares right back and, miraculously, my boss nods her consent.

'The book club room's free,' I tell Barbara, gesturing for her to follow me.

The moment we step inside, she shuts the door behind us.

I frown at her grave expression. 'Are you okay?'

She fiddles with the crucifix necklace around her neck. 'How long have you and Fabio been seeing each other?'

I blink. 'Um . . . almost two months. Why?'

She sighs heavily. 'I'm not usually one to dip my nose in other people's business, but I like you, Bee. My years of teaching have made me a good judge of character and you seem like a good egg.'

'Why, thank you,' I say, unsure where she's going with this.

'The thing is . . .' She clears her throat. 'Right from the start,

I've not had a good feeling about Fabio. There's something iffy about that man and I don't want you to get hurt.'

Something iffy? I struggle not to laugh. 'What do you mean?'

'I didn't teach Italian or ever speak it fluently – my languages were French and German – but I know a little to get me by, and yesterday when he came over to help me load the protection software on my computer, it confirmed my suspicions.'

I frown. 'What suspicions?'

'He's not really Italian.'

'What!?' This time I can't help but laugh. 'Are you serious?'

'I've noticed before that some of the words he uses aren't quite right. He gets the masculine and feminine wrong sometimes, or uses a word in the wrong context. At first, I thought maybe it was my hearing' – she touches a finger to her hearing aid – 'or his accent, but when it was just the two of us, I could tell I was right.'

'I've met his sister and she's as Italian as they come,' I say, thinking of the way Francesca kissed me on both cheeks the first time we met. 'Besides, why would he pretend to be Italian?'

Her slow shrug angers me on Fabio's behalf.

'Maybe you *should* get your hearing checked again. But thank you for your concern.'

Barbara looks at me pityingly, then simply nods. 'Yes, you're probably right. Have a good day, Bee.'

She lets herself out of the room.

I stand there, my stomach twisting as I contemplate her absurd accusation. It is without a doubt the most ridiculous thing I've ever heard. Perhaps Barbara is a little bit senile.

The door flies open again, interrupting my thoughts.

'What was that all about?' Fred asks, beaded earrings that are longer than her hair swishing as she enters. 'Ursula is on the warpath. She . . .' Her expression changes from annoyed to concerned. 'Are you okay? You look like you've just heard Marian Keyes is retiring.'

I shake my head – 'I'm fine' – and march out of the room, straight over to the returns shelf where I grab a load of books and deposit them on a trolley. Usually our library assistants do the returns, but right now I need something to occupy my hands that isn't going to tax my brain too much.

As I shove novels back into the large-print section, Barbara's words replay in my head, and a prickle creeps over my skin as I remember the expression on Fabio's face when he found my copy of *Fifteen Minute Italian*. I'd been so blindsided by his confession of love that I hadn't thought about the oddness of his reaction, but wouldn't most people be happy their girlfriend was learning their native tongue?

Maybe he didn't sound *unhappy*, but he'd been quick to tell me not to bother and now the book was missing.

My heart starts to beat faster.

There are only two possible reasons for Fabio's response to discovering my desire to learn Italian. He doesn't want me to because he wants to be able to speak his language to other Italians – like his sister – without me understanding what they're saying, and if that's the case, what doesn't he want me to hear? Or he doesn't want me to because he only knows a scattering of Italian words himself and doesn't want me to realise this. This seems even more ridiculous, but now other slightly *iffy* things are flashing into my head.

The fact that he told me his mother was dead, then spoke as though she wasn't another time. The snooping at Janine's house. Lying about reading the book club books. Telling *me* to lie about Fred's book – he clearly doesn't have a problem with deception.

His middle name being Bruce! That name had rolled so easily off his tongue, but maybe it was because that part wasn't a lie. He'd looked almost as shocked as me when that name came out of his mouth.

Perhaps if you come up with a fake name, you don't bother with a middle one.

Also, now that I think about it, he's always more eager to talk about me than he is himself. He's heard all about my life growing up on the station and my family, whereas he's never actually named the small town he supposedly grew up in. He always changes the subject or distracts me when I ask.

And, *oh, God* – my stomach roils – he only started showing proper interest in me when I told him I'd taken over the library's senior book club.

No. I've got to be wrong. This is crazy.

'I'm not buying it,' Fred says, popping around the end of the shelf.

Already on edge, I startle and drop the two books I'd just picked up. 'You shouldn't creep up on people like that!'

'Sorry.' She bends to pick up the books and then looks me dead in the eye. 'But I know you, and something's wrong. What did Barbara tell you?'

I feel like an idiot confessing this to Fred, but hopefully she'll put my mind at rest. 'She said she doesn't think Fabio is really Italian.'

Fred laughs like this is the funniest thing she's ever heard. 'What the hell is she on? Have you ever met a non-Italian called Fabio?'

'No, but . . .' Her mirth should relieve me – I want to believe that Fabio is Italian more than anything – but doubt has dug its heels into my heart.

'You don't believe her, do you?' She dumps the books on the trolley and grabs my hand, which I realise is shaking.

I want to say no, of course I don't, but suddenly I'm not so sure.

When I don't reply, Fred speaks firmly. 'Bee! He's Italian. Why would he pretend to—'

'So he can scam old ladies out of all their money!' A bitter cold floods my body as I say my fears out loud.

'What are you talking about? Isn't he helping—' Fred slaps a hand over her mouth.

'Yes. Exactly.' I nod as her brain catches up to a place where I don't want mine to be. I read *Identity* by Nora Roberts – I know the lengths criminals go to in order to deceive and rob the vulnerable. 'What if he hasn't really been helping them protect their computers but is stealing private and important information?' I start to hyperventilate.

'Bee,' Fred says sharply, 'you need to calm down. This is all speculation. You're not going to write off almost two months with a guy you really like on the hunch of a little old lady. For all we know, Fabio *has* been helping them.'

I tell her about the Italian book, his sometimes-dead mother, his middle name and how I found him snooping at Janine's house, and her eyes widen, her eyebrows creeping up towards her hairline. I don't tell her about him suggesting I lie about her book.

'Okay,' she concedes, fiddling with her funky earring, 'that does sound a tad concerning, but there could be a perfectly reasonable explanation. Maybe you should just message him. Ask him outright if he's really Italian.'

But what if he is and I insult him? *Argh.*

Before I can work out a game plan, Ursula appears around the corner, towering above us like a giant ready to crush us in her bare hands.

'What are you two doing? It doesn't look like much work is happening, and Bridget' – she pinches her thumb and index finger together – 'you're *this* close to another warning.'

'I need to take a break,' I say, then push past her out the door before she can object.

I don't even grab my bag from the staff room as I run up the escalator and out the library towards the café. I have no idea what exactly I'm going to say to Fabio, but this is not the kind of question I can put in a text, and I can't handle a moment longer with Barbara's accusations and my suspicions whirling around my head.

52

Citizen's Arrest

I don't pause for breath until I reach the Grouchy Sailor, where I find a long line, almost out the door. It goes against everything I was taught to push past the waiting people into the café, but this is an emergency. I search for Fabio as I get to the front, but there's only Tony, the owner, looking frazzled as he works the coffee machine.

'Is Fabio here?' I ask, still panting from my short run.

Tony shakes his head, scowling. 'The bastard didn't show up this morning. I've been calling him but he's not answering. Totally left me in the lurch.'

My gut churns. Now I think about it, my morning coffee – collected by Xavier – didn't taste quite as good as usual. He didn't mention Fabio wasn't there but then again, we don't get to chat much in the library now with Mary Trunchbull watching us like a hawk.

'Don't suppose you know how to use a till?' Tony asks.

'Sorry,' I say, already yanking my phone out of my pocket.

Outside, I call Fabio, but I'm immediately informed that the number I am calling is disconnected or unavailable.

My head pulses with the beginning of a headache. This cannot be a coincidence.

Could he have cottoned on to the fact that Barbara was onto him?

'Shit.' Tears spring to my eyes as I kick the wall outside the café.

I should go back to the library – Ursula is probably typing up my written warning this very minute – but there's no way I'll be able to concentrate until I get to the bottom of this. I order an Uber, half-hoping it's Sully who arrives, half-hoping it isn't. He'll take one look at me and know something is wrong.

Someone called Husan pulls up on the corner of Adelaide Street and High Street Mall two minutes later and merely nods hello as I climb into the back seat of his white Camry. During the short drive, I try to convince myself that this is all a silly mistake.

Maybe Fabio's family came from southern Italy and the tiny bit of Italian Barbara knows is more northern? Or vice versa. Maybe JB somehow got a hold of *Fifteen Minute Italian* and has buried it in the backyard? I didn't really look *that* hard. Maybe Fabio's so sick he couldn't call Tony to let him know and that's why he didn't answer my call as well.

'Is this the place?' Husan jolts me from my thoughts. The front door of Fabio and Francesca's house is open and the car they share is also in the driveway, boot open.

It looks like someone is coming or going.

'Yes. Thanks.' The car's barely stopped but I'm already pushing open the door.

As Husan reverses back out of the driveway, Fabio emerges wearing a backpack and carrying two over-stuffed recycling bags.

'Bee?' He looks shocked to see me. 'Um, aren't you supposed to be at work?'

'Aren't *you*?' I retort. 'Where are you going?'

'Sorry, Bee, but Francesca and I have to move on.'

I arch my brow – shock and hurt warring inside me. 'And when were you planning on telling me?'

He gives me a conciliatory smile. 'The less you know, the better. I'm really sorry.'

This apology is delivered in one of the strongest Aussie accents I've ever heard. Far-north Queensland or something.

'Oh my God, Barbara's right. You're not Italian, are you?' I cover my mouth with my hands.

Fabio – if that really is his name – has the good grace to look sheepish as he shakes his head. 'Really sorry, Bee. I didn't mean to hurt you. It was really—'

Francesca storms out of the house and glares at us both. She'd been all smiles the other time I met her but today she looks like a different person. 'Don't say another word, Josh.'

'Josh?' I say, but neither of them acknowledges me.

'Come *on*,' Francesca urges. 'We need to get out of here before your old lady friend realises her dough's missing.'

'That's why I told you we should leave last night,' he grumbles in reply.

She heads to the car, slams the boot shut and then jumps into the driver's side.

I look up at Fabio, willing him to tell me this is a nightmare. That I'm asleep and having the worst dream of my life. 'Whose money is she talking about? I'm guessing you took Rose's. But who else? All of them?'

His eyes flash with something like apathy. 'It's only money. They've all got plenty of it and—'

I cut him off, not willing to hear his pathetic excuses. 'Did you ever even *like* me? Or was I always just a way to get to the old ladies?'

He has the audacity to reach out and brush my hair behind my ear as he's done numerous times in the past. 'At first, it was just an excuse to be there hanging out with them and for them to trust me because I was your boyfriend, but then, I really started to fall for you.'

I flick his hand away from my face. Didn't I know he was too good to be true? But fool for love that I am, I ignored my initial hesitation and led him right to his victims.

'You're a cool chick,' he adds, reaching out to touch my face, 'and hey, we had fun together, didn't we?'

I slap away his hand. 'Fun? Fun!' He totally wins the prize for the worst person I've ever dated. 'You're an absolute psychopath!'

He glances over at the car where Francesca is waiting with the engine running. 'Guess that means you don't want to run away with us?'

At his chuckle, rage consumes me. He not only played with my heart *and* used me as a means to an end, but he doesn't seem to have one iota of remorse.

'You bastard,' I say, lifting my leg and kicking him right where it hurts.

He staggers and doubles over, dropping the bags as he clutches at his groin. 'You bitch!'

'That was for me and—' This time I kick him hard in the shins. 'That's for Rose and all my other friends you cheated.'

He hollers in pain.

Francesca revs the engine. 'Get up, you idiot. We need to go!'

Still moaning and cursing under his breath, Fabio attempts to stand but I kick him right back to the ground as I jab triple-zero on my phone. Adrenalin is pumping through my body.

'Police, fire, or ambulance?' answers an operator almost immediately.

'Police.' I rattle off the address and try to explain what the hell is happening.

'Shut the fuck up, you bitch,' Josh shouts, still trying to scramble to his feet.

I move closer to the car so I can give the operator the number plate, all the while keeping an eye on him in case he succeeds in silencing me.

'Just leave her,' Francesca shouts. 'Or I'm going to bloody leave *you*.'

He takes one final look at me and then runs awkwardly to the car. My heart's pounding as I'm talking to the police, when I notice someone out of the corner of my eye. It's Olga and a vicious-looking chihuahua sitting in an attached basket on her motorised scooter, watching us like we're actors in a movie.

'A squad car's on its way,' the operator says as Fabio – Josh, or whatever he's called – climbs into the passenger seat of the car.

'They're getting away,' I yell into the phone, and that's when Olga spurs into action, pressing the accelerator button on her Gopher.

'I don't think so.' She zooms the scooter towards the car, stopping so close to the boot that the two vehicles are almost kissing. The picket fence on either side of the driveway means there's no way Francesca can reverse without killing Olga or damaging the fence.

My heart rockets into my throat.

Francesca jumps out of the car and looms over the old Russian woman. 'Move the fuck out of my way, you old hag, or the next funeral you go to will be your own.'

The tiny dog bares its teeth and growls at Francesca, who takes a step back and jams her hip into the corner of the letterbox. 'Youch!'

'I really hope those cops are close,' I say into the phone, 'because otherwise we might also need an ambulance.' I'm just not sure who for.

Fabio follows his sister to Olga, glowering at me as he passes. I notice he's still holding his groin.

'*Bella*, Olga,' he says, once again adopting a fake accent. 'Bee has lost the plot and attacked me, and my sister needs to take me to the hospital to be checked out. Could you please move out of our way?'

'Like hell I will,' she spits, her knuckles turning red as she tightens her grip on the handlebar.

Annoyed, Fabio attempts to take control of it, but the dog throws itself at him, attaching itself to the side of Fabio's thigh. Judging by the noise Fabio makes, his jeans provide little protection.

At the same time, Francesca, still wincing, steps towards them as if to intervene but I hold out my hand, warning her off. 'The police are coming. Don't try and escape or you'll end up on the ground like he did.'

I don't know where my bravado is coming from – for all I know one of them has a gun, whereas all I've got is an old lady and a small dog with a big attitude – but I'm not going to let them go anywhere without a fight.

Francesca glares at me, then at him. 'Next time bloody keep it in your pants, you fool. I'm out of here.'

Before I can stop her, she grabs a handbag from the car and flees on foot. 'Come on, Josh,' she hollers over her shoulder, and then disappears down the street.

He manages to get the dog off his leg, but as he starts to run, Olga shoots out her foot and trips him. He flies forward and we both wince at the sound of his head thunking against the pavement.

Seconds after Francesca disappears down the street, a police car shoots around the corner and skids to a stop outside the house. Two young cops who look like they can't be long out of school, never mind the academy, jump out of the car and rush over to us.

'Is he okay?' The shorter of the two, a blond, drops to his knees as Fabio looks up.

'I've been assaulted by both these women and this dog.'

The taller, darker-skinned cop raises an eyebrow as he glances from Olga to me; it's clear he doesn't think either of us could take down Fabio.

'I did kick him,' I admit, despite the fact my heart is racing. 'Because he's a fraud and he just confessed to scamming and stealing from the elderly.'

Josh tries to yell over the top of me. 'That's bullshit. She has no proof. She just came over here and started laying into me.'

'If it's not true, then why did your sister run away when she heard the police were coming?'

Ignoring me, he pleads to the cops, 'How about you take her down to the station and I'll follow to press charges?'

Is he for real? I look to the cops for evidence that they might actually be buying his lies, but the taller one shakes his head. 'You're not going anywhere. We may look young but we weren't born yesterday.' He pulls handcuffs out of his pocket. 'I'm calling for back-up. You're *all* coming down to the station.'

He steps back a little and lifts his phone to his ear, but he and the other cop never take their eyes off Josh/Fabio and me. Right now, it's my word against his, and these guys *do* have guns. If either of us makes the wrong move, they could use them.

I hear the tall cop mumble something about a domestic and ask for another car asap, then he turns back and introduces himself as 'Senior Constable Tohu, and this is Constable Swan.' He looks to me. 'What's your name?'

'Bridget Jones,' I say, and the cops look at each other as if I'm lying.

Tohu chuckles. 'My mum loves that movie. That seriously your name?'

'Yes, I swear.'

Josh/Fabio sniggers.

'And your name?'

When Josh refuses to give it, Tohu turns to Olga.

'Olga Smirnoff,' she tells him.

'Like the vodka?' Swan says, sounding impressed. 'And what's your relationship to these two?'

'Bee is my friend. I'm in her book club.'

I swallow, feeling oddly teary at her calling me a friend and because what I'm about to say sounds ridiculous. 'I've been seeing this man for a couple of months. I think he's called Josh, but he told me his name was Fabio. I was warned by a friend this morning that he might not be who he says he is.'

'What do you mean?' Swan asks.

'She realised he was fooling us all, pretending to be Italian.'

'That's insane,' Josh/Fabio cries. 'She's insane.'

The young cops exchange a look as if they're in well over their heads.

'So,' I continue, ignoring Josh's cries, 'I came over to confront him and found him and his sister with a packed car about to leave. He all but confessed to stealing money from an old lady I know from the library – that's where I work – and so I—'

'Your word against mine,' Josh says, glaring at me.

'So I kicked him and called you guys,' I finish. 'I'm sorry for assaulting him but I . . . I couldn't help myself.'

Before any of them reply, another police car arrives and two much older officers – one man, one woman – join us. They introduce themselves as Senior Sergeant Evans and Senior Constable Wang.

While Tahu and Swan stand guard over Josh and me, the other two consult. It's decided that Olga, her dog and I will go in the car with the younger cops and Josh will go with the older ones.

'I'll take the bags,' Wang says, stooping to pick up the backpack that fell off Fabio's back when he was rolling about on the ground in agony.

'Just leave them,' he tells her, his tone edgy. 'They're not important.'

Wang arches an eyebrow and then looks to her partner, who nods. She rifles through the recycling bags, one after the other. 'Just clothes.'

'See, told you it was nothing,' Josh says, but as she unzips the backpack, he curses and tries to make a run for it.

Swan and Tahu both lunge for him, their hands closing around an arm each as Wang holds up a wad of cash. 'Not important, hey? There must be fifty thousand in here. Cuff him.'

Swan twists Josh's hands behind his back and Tahu skilfully clicks the handcuffs onto him.

'Right, let's get you down to the station,' Evans says. 'You've got some explaining to do.'

Josh is ushered into the car while Swan holds the back door of the other car for me and Olga, nodding politely as I slip inside behind her.

'You must have some kick on you,' Tahu says as he closes the driver's side door behind him.

'Thanks,' I say proudly. 'I'm a kickboxer.'

53

A Fool for Love

As we drive towards the station on High Street, I keep my head down and shield my face with my hand, not wanting to be spotted by anyone I know.

'Thanks for your help back there,' I whisper to Olga.

She's clutching the dog on her lap but sneaks a hand out to squeeze mine. 'Don't mention it. I hate nothing more than men taking advantage of women. And I knew when I saw you and him arguing that he wasn't a good egg.'

I nod – 'No, it turns out he's not' – then reach out to stroke the top of the dog's head. It's hard to believe this cute little thing viciously attacked Josh, but I could kiss him for it. 'What's his name?'

'She is called Doroteya – it is Russian for "God's gift".'

'That's lovely.'

Before long, we are driving into the rear car park of the Fremantle Police Station. Although I've walked past it, I've never been inside. I've never actually been inside *any* police station. We wait in the patrol car while the senior officers take Josh inside and then are led to separate 'briefing rooms'. I'm given a glass of water and told to wait.

The moment the door closes and I'm alone, my heart starts pounding. Aside from a desk, two chairs and a mirror on the wall that I'm guessing is two-way like on TV, the room is empty. And cold. I shiver, seriously regretting not grabbing my jacket on the way out of the library.

I can't believe it – this morning when I woke up, I had a boyfriend I adored and now here I am, in a police station, about to make a statement against him. Actually, Fabio doesn't exist – I'm making a statement about some guy called Josh. This thought makes me dizzy and I grab the water and gulp it down.

The longer I'm in this room, the more I start to panic. Who the hell is Josh? Who is his sister? *Is* she even his sister? How dangerous are they? Could I be implicated in any way?

My phone rings, scaring the life out of me. It's Fred but I'm not sure if I'm allowed to answer. I glance at the mirror, then decide to risk it. 'Hey, Fred,' I whisper.

'Are you okay? Where the hell are you? Ursula said I'd get a written warning if I followed you.'

'Ursula is the least of my problems right now. I'm at the police station.'

'What?! What happened? I thought you were going to see Fabio.'

'I did. Look, I can't really talk, but I'm okay and I'll fill you in later.'

'Do you want me to come down for moral support?'

'No, but thanks. Can you just tell Ursula I'm sick or something and that I'll be back tomorrow?'

'No worries. Love you.'

After disconnecting with Fred, I tap my fingers on the desk. What if they've forgotten me? Should I go out and ask someone?

I'm regretting not requesting a cup of coffee – it would at least have warmed me a little – and wondering if I can sneak out to find a bathroom when the door opens.

I look up to see to see a man and a woman, both wearing jeans, shirts and blazers. The man is carrying an iPad but they look like they mean serious business.

As the woman offers her hand and introduces herself as Senior Detective Tess Radevski, I get a whiff of her perfume – something flowery, with hints of vanilla. She gestures to her colleague. 'This is Detective Heath Knight. And you're Bridget Jones, is that right?'

'Guilty,' I say as they both sit down opposite.

'Bridget Jones,' Radevski muses. 'I love that movie. The third one with the baby was my favourite.'

I'm about to tell her I'm named after the book character, not the film one, but then I remember why I'm here. 'Am I in trouble for kicking Fabio?' I shake that name from my head. 'I mean Josh?'

'In trouble?' Knight asks, his brow creasing.

The detectives look at each other and Radevksi finally smiles as well. 'Are you kidding? We don't usually encourage citizen's arrests, but if you hadn't wounded Joshua and called us, he could have slipped through the cracks again. We should be giving you a medal, or a job. Ever thought of becoming a cop?'

'*Again*?' I ask, ignoring her question. 'Do you know who they are?'

Knight shakes his head. 'We think they might have been involved in a number of scams. Perhaps you might be able to shed some light.'

'I honestly don't know anything. I wish I did.'

Knight swipes at the iPad and shows me a photo. 'Do you recognise this woman?'

I nod. 'I'm almost certain that's Francesca, the person Josh told me was his sister, but she's got darker hair now.' The woman in the photo has pale blue hair and a nose ring.

He swipes to the next photo. This one isn't immediately recognisable, but when I take another look, I do believe it's the same woman, only this time she's wearing glasses and has brown, much longer hair, in two thick plaits. 'I think that's her as well.'

Radevski and Knight exchange a look, then nod.

'And what about this man?' The next photos he shows me are of Josh, but different to the Fabio I know – one of them looks like a blond surfer dude, another a geek with a terrible crew cut, wearing a business suit – but I haven't worshipped his face for the past few months without being able to recognise his core features.

'Yep,' I say, prickling shame rising to the surface of my skin. 'That's Fabio or Josh, whoever the man was I dated.'

Radevski offers me a sympathetic smile, but I can't imagine she'd ever be made a fool for love. 'These images are from the federal police, who have been chasing this pair for a couple of years now. We believe they are linked to numerous cases of suspected identity fraud.'

Identity fraud? It's the first time in my life I wish I'd been wrong.

'If we're correct about who they are,' he continues, 'these people use different fake names in different cities, always pretending they're from a different European country. Having Josh in custody could lead us to several important arrests.'

'Wow.'

Radevski nods. 'And hopefully thanks to your and Ms Smirnoff's latest descriptions, we'll be able to track down Josh's accomplice very soon. And then we'll have a lot more questions for them both.'

'Do you know who she is? Josh' – it sounds odd calling Fabio by his real name – 'told me she was his sister.'

It's bad enough that I've slept with a criminal, but while I'd been sitting here waiting, I've had the horrible thought that maybe they were a couple.

'Not yet – he's not speaking until he has a lawyer present – but we'll find out, don't you worry,' Radevski says, folding her hands together. 'How did you two start going out?'

I tell them about him being a barista and how he started showing more interest in me when he learned I ran a book club for seniors at the library. 'We started going out and then he even started coming to book club, pretending he wanted to spend more time with me.'

'Can you tell us why you decided to confront him today?'

I take a quick breath, then explain about Barbara's suspicions and subsequent warning. 'It sounded so ridiculous at first, but then when I started to put two and two together . . .' My voice trails off as I suddenly realise who the money might belong to. 'I think that cash is Lorna's!'

'Who's Lorna?' Knight asks, leaning forward.

'She's another member of the book club. She told us all a while ago that she keeps most of her savings under her mattress. Josh was at Lorna's place last night. Hers was the last of the Bookstars' computers he was going to *protect*. She might not even know it's missing yet.'

'We'll contact her immediately,' Detective Knight says. 'If it is hers . . . today might just be her lucky day.'

'And hopefully this fright will teach her that banks are the best place to keep your money,' Radevski adds with a shake of her head.

They ask me whether I can think of any other details that might be important, and then I'm free to go.

'Is Olga still here?' I say.

'Yes, she insisted she wasn't leaving until she saw you were okay,' Knight replies with an amused smile. 'She and that ball of fluff are waiting for you in reception. Come on, I'll take you to her.'

I'm stunned when Olga stands and wraps me in her arms, Doroteya squished between us. 'Are you okay, *kúkolka*?'

'I will be. What about you two? That was quite full-on back at the house.'

She snorts. 'Very little scares us Russians. The police are giving me a lift back to my mobility scooter, do you want to come and we can go for a stiff drink?'

I'm heartened by her offer, but all I want to do is go home and crawl into my bed. 'Thanks, but maybe another time?'

She nods and pats me on the arm, before Detective Knight sees me out onto High Street.

He glances up at the sky, which is filled with dark clouds that look like they might burst at any moment. 'You sure you don't need a lift?'

'No, thanks.' The police have better things to be doing than driving me home and my mood matches the weather anyway.

He takes a card out of his pocket and hands it to me. 'Call me if you think of anything that might help with the case.'

'I will,' I promise, tucking the card into my pocket. 'And do you mind letting me know when you've caught Josh's accomplice? I'd like to know exactly who they are.'

He nods. 'We'll keep you informed.'

Another thought strikes, one perhaps even more worrying than the possibility that Fabio and Francesca are lovers. 'Should I be scared? You know . . . might they or someone they know come after me because I'm responsible for them getting caught?'

Will I have to move? Go into hiding? Are dogs allowed in witness protection?

'I honestly don't think you're in any danger at this stage,' Knight says, 'but call me any time if you're at all worried about anything.'

I should go back to the library, but Fred's already told Ursula I'm sick and I don't think I could face work anyway. I call Fred and she answers immediately.

'Oh my God, Bee,' she whispers. 'I've been worried sick. What's going on?'

'Can you grab my bag and jacket and meet me at the emergency exit?'

'Sure. I'll get Xavier to distract Mary Trunchbull for me.'

It's a short walk to the library, and luckily the weather stays dry. Fred is waiting when I arrive.

'Thanks.' I shove my arms into my jacket, shivering. 'Long story short, Barbara was right – Fabio is not really Italian, his real name is Josh, and he's been stealing people's identities all over the country.'

Fred's eyes widen as I tell her about Olga and I working together to stop him getting away. She lets out a low whistle. 'Holy shit. I can't believe you did all that.'

'All in a day's work,' I say, although it's starting to feel a bit like the dream I wish it was.

'I'm so sorry, Bee,' she says. 'I know you really liked him.'

'I'll be fine. This isn't my first heartbreak. I'm glad I found out the truth before I got any more attached.' I almost believe my words. 'Anyway, I'm going home.'

'Do you want me to come with you?'

I shake my head – I'm mortified by what has happened and just want to be alone with JB. He'll offer comfort without pity. 'No point both of us getting into Ursula's bad books.'

'Are you sure?'

I nod. 'But thank you.'

'I'll come straight over after work,' she promises.

I'm halfway home when the clouds burst and rain spews down on me. Could this day get any worse? I pick up my pace. At first, I think it's rain I'm swiping off my cheeks, but then I realise I'm crying. Tears are filling my eyes and spilling down my cheeks as the reality of what's just happened hits me. Finding out Fabio was a fraud had shocked me. And then there'd been rage as I tackled him, adrenalin pumping at his arrest, and the almost out-of-body experience of being interviewed by the police.

But now all that has worn off and I'm . . . bereft.

It takes everything I have not to crumple to the ground, curl into the foetal position and howl. What is wrong with me? Why am I always a magnet for cheating, lying scumbags? I wonder if anything Josh told me was true. Is his mother even dead?

I've always joked about being doomed in love because of my name, but after today I'm seriously beginning to wonder if there is something to the Bridget curse.

Then again, even Bridget got lucky eventually.

Somehow, I manage to put one foot in front of the other, and the sight of my front door has never been more welcome. My adorable, faithful dog is waiting on the other side, tail wagging madly, and once I've shut the door behind me, my legs finally give way as I slide down to the floor and wrap my arms around him. He immediately starts licking at my tears, but this only makes me bawl harder.

I can't believe Fabio – I mean Josh, *argh!* – will never be here again. I can't believe we're over, and I hate myself for feeling sad about someone who is clearly a baddie but, more than that, I hate myself for being so stupid.

I don't know how long I sit there, but when JB starts whining to go outside, I drag myself up, let him out and then go into the bathroom. After stripping off my wet clothes, I consider taking a shower to help me warm up but even the thought is too much effort, so I head into my bedroom instead, put on my oldest, most comfortable tracksuit, and climb into bed.

Almost the second I lie down, I jump right back out again. The sheets still smell of Fabio's cologne.

I pull them off like a crazy person, before throwing them into the washing machine and then snuggling on the couch with JB and a blanket instead. My mind is loud, the happenings of the day are on repeat in my head, and I would do anything to be able to switch it off. In lieu of this, I reach for the nearest book, which happens to be *None of This Is True* by Lisa Jewell – at least it's not a romance – in the hopes of losing myself between the pages. Miraculously, I do get lost in the London suburb of Queens Park, where the characters' problems are almost impossibly worse than my own. I feel myself relaxing, immersing myself in a fictional world and seeking comfort once again from a book.

54

Hole in One

I wake to a pounding on my front door and Lisa Jewell's book spread-eagled on my chest. When I grab my phone to check the time, I see not only a message from Fred saying she's on her way over but also that it is 5.15 pm.

'Bee,' she hollers. 'Let me in! I brought ice cream and wine.'

I groan. Unsurprisingly, comfort eating has never been my thing and the thought of eating ice cream makes me nauseous. Although the wine sounds appealing. However, if I let Fred and the alcohol inside, she'll want to talk about what's happened. She'll try to be sympathetic, but she won't understand because she doesn't want what I do – true love and someone to come home to during the good and bad times. Sure, she'll have lots of choice four-letter words to say about Josh, but talking and swearing won't change anything. I don't want to rehash my latest relationship disaster; I want to forget it.

I grab my phone and punch out a quick message: *Sorry, I forgot you were coming over and went to an extra kickboxing class. I'm fine and will see you tomorrow. xx*

'I know you're in there,' she shouts a few seconds after my text shows as 'read'. 'And you shouldn't be alone at a time like this.'

'*Please*, Fred,' I yell, 'I feel like such an idiot, and I really don't want to face anyone.'

'I'm not just anyone – I'm your *best* friend. And this is not on you. That motherfucking bastard fooled us all.'

But I'm the one who slept with him.

I'm the one who bought a bloody Italian book and thought I was falling in love with him.

I'm the one who introduced him to the Bookstars.

'I love you,' I say, 'and I know you mean well, but I really do just want to be alone tonight. *Please*.'

'Okay,' she replies, 'but if I don't hear from you in a few hours, I'm coming back, and I'll break your door down if I have to.'

Usually, I'd laugh at such a threat but tonight my lips don't even quirk. 'Thank you,' I call. 'Talk to you later.'

I hold my breath but the moment I hear the tell-tale thunk of my gate closing, tears start falling again. Dammit, I don't want to cry. There's no point spilling tears over someone who doesn't even exist.

At the sound of footsteps in the kitchen, I freeze. Did I leave the door open when I let JB out earlier? No wonder I've been struggling to get warm. I reach out to touch my dog, whose head is cocked to one side, also on high alert.

'It'll probably just be Fred again,' I tell him. But then another thought strikes. What if Detective Knight was wrong and some undesirable acquaintances of Josh's have come to deal with me? *Oh, God.* The hairs on the back of my neck are rigid. Is this how I die?

That's when Sully appears in the doorway of my lounge room and JB leaps off the couch, tail wagging furiously, as he rushes over to greet him.

I breathe a sigh of relief as my fear gives way to irritation. 'What the hell are you doing in my house?' I exclaim, horrified at how I must appear. My hair will be all frizzy from the rain and I'll bet my mascara has streaked all down my face. That'll teach me for not making the effort to shower.

In reply, Sully strides across the room and sits on the coffee table across from me. 'I didn't think you had a problem with unannounced guests. Besides' – he shrugs – 'the door was open.'

I'm not in the mood for his humour. 'Well,' I say, 'you can shut it on your way out.'

He looks around, then gets up again and strides out.

Wow, that was easier than I imagined.

But I don't hear the back door close and seconds later he returns with a toilet roll.

'Here.' He hands it to me and then plonks himself back down on the table. 'I'm not going anywhere. Gran would kill me if she heard I abandoned you when you're clearly upset.'

I snatch off a few pieces of toilet paper, making a mental note to buy tissues. That's if I ever leave the house again. 'I won't tell her.'

'So I take it you've had a bad day?' he asks as I wipe my face.

'That doesn't even begin to describe it.'

'Your friend sounded pretty worried about you.'

'Were you eavesdropping?'

He snorts. 'Sadly, I wasn't wearing my headphones, so I heard everything. Bad break-up? Don't tell me Fabio cheated on you?'

'So much worse than that.' I sniff.

'What's worse than cheating?'

'Lying about who he is and scamming old people out of their money,' I say, before remembering I don't want to talk about it.

Sully recoils as if I've hit him. 'What?'

I actually laugh at his shock, and then groan and drop my head into my hands. If only this was a laughing matter.

'Did your grandma ever invite him over to help her with anything? To protect her computer maybe?' I ask.

'She doesn't have a computer, and I help her with anything she needs done. But she told me what happened to Rose. Is Fabio the one who took her money?'

'Looks that way. And it's Josh, not Fabio. He's not even Italian.'

'Jesus.' He shakes his head. 'I always thought there was something dodgy about him.'

I throw the rest of the toilet paper at him. 'Geez, thanks for mentioning it.'

He quirks an eyebrow. 'Would you have listened?'

'Probably not,' I concede. 'Do you have any wine?'

'What for?'

I give him an exasperated look. 'I want to drown my sorrows.'

He thinks a moment, then stands. 'I've got a better idea. Do you have a jacket or something?'

'On a hook in the hallway,' I reply without thinking.

He leaves the room and returns with not only my jacket but also the sneakers I leave by the door. 'Put these on.'

I frown. 'Where are we going? I can't go to a pub or anything dressed like this. Can't you just go and buy wine? Anything will do.'

'We're only going to my place,' he says, and then stoops down and starts putting on my shoes like I'm a little kid.

I put my jacket over my ratty old clothes.

'Good girl. Now, come with me.' Sully offers me his hand and, despite the fact his 'good girl' is super condescending, I allow him to pull me up.

I grab my keys, then lock my door. Leaving the verandah light on, JB and I follow him down the steps into my now-semi-dark garden. Thankfully, it's not raining any more.

'You'd better not be taking me to hear your bagpipes,' I warn.

He chuckles as he holds my back gate open for me. I'm curious about going into his house – the other time I was there I didn't get a proper look – but sadly we don't go any further than the basketball ring. He picks up an orange ball that's on the ground, throws it to me and walks over to flick on a switch, flooding light over us.

'What's this for?' I ask.

'Shooting hoops does wonders for releasing tension.'

I toss the ball between my hands. 'Are you sure you don't have *any* alcohol?'

'Nope, and the last thing you need to do right now is drown your sorrows.'

'Is that your medical opinion, Dr Sullivan?'

I feel immediately bad for saying this considering his circumstances, but he nods. 'It is.'

I sigh – unconvinced that basketball is going to mend my broken heart or wounded pride – but throw the ball towards the hoop anyway. What have I got to lose? The ball bounces off the ring and JB rushes for it, trying and failing to pick it up between his teeth.

'Why don't you try this one, Beast?' Sully tosses him a tennis ball as I retrieve the basketball.

I shoot, again, and miss, again, cursing the fact that when many of the other girls from school were playing netball, I was either in hospital or too weak to play, so I never perfected my ball skills.

Sully dribbles the ball for a few seconds, then jumps up and expertly flicks it with his wrist. Of course, it lands perfectly. Right in the middle of the hoop.

'Show off,' I mutter.

He shrugs but grins. 'Practice,' he says, and then runs a hand through his hair, moving it off his face.

I grab the ball and try again and this time it actually goes in. 'Oh my God,' I shriek, rushing over to high-five him.

'See, third time lucky,' he says, smiling.

Maybe he's right. Maybe this will make me feel better.

We take turns throwing the ball – some go in, more of his than mine – while JB runs crazily round us, still trying to nab the basketball whenever we lose it.

'Hole in one,' I shriek excitedly when I get another one.

He laughs. 'It's actually a basket, or a two-pointer from where you were.'

'Whatever.' I laugh too and shoot another almost-perfect hoop.

'You're not actually that bad at this.' He catches the ball before it bounces, shoots and scores. 'Is it helping?'

I pick up the ball and hug it to my chest. 'Yeah, it actually is. Every time I hear the ball slam against the backboard thing, I imagine it's Fabio's – *Josh's* – head thunking against it. Aisha's right, this *is* good therapy.'

'Yeah . . . well, I'm not sure that's exactly what she had in mind when she said exercising would help but—'

'You know what would be better?' I interrupt. It's a rhetorical question. 'Bowling. I could imagine Fabio as the bowling pin.'

Sully visibly shudders. 'Remind me never to get on your bad side. Again,' he quickly corrects. 'But let's do it.'

'Do what?' I ask.

'Go bowling.'

'What? Now?' I'm not sure if he's joking. 'Don't you need to go to work or something?'

'Nope.' He grins. 'The brilliance of being an Uber driver is you choose your own hours. What do you say? Do you wanna go hit some pins?'

I don't even hesitate. 'Yeah, why not?' It's got to be better than going home and sitting around feeling sorry for myself. 'Just let me wash my face and throw on some clothes.'

'No worries. I'll book us a lane. How long do you think you'll be?'

I hold up both my hands. 'Give me ten minutes.'

55

Hot Dogs and Goofy Shoes

Although this isn't a date, I'm ashamed of the way Sully found me and want to replace that horrible image in his head with a better one. There's no time to wash and dry my hair, but I scrub my face clean of day-old, smudged make-up and dress in record time. I choose a clean pair of ripped, relaxed jeans and an oversized stripy pink jumper. Usually, my skincare and make-up takes at least half an hour, but I slap on some foundation, a little bit of blush and some lip gloss.

I can't remember the last time I went out without a full face, but I don't want to keep Sully waiting, so it's a choice between mascara or running a brush through my hair.

'I'll be home in a couple of hours,' I promise JB.

Sully is leaning against his SUV when I get to his place. There's a bowling alley only a few blocks away, but we decide to take his car due to the weather.

'Wow. That was impressive,' he says. 'Nine minutes and fifty-two seconds.'

'You *timed* me?'

He smirks as he opens the passenger door for me. 'Yeah, because I didn't believe you could do it. My ex-wife needed at least an hour's notice before we could leave the house, even if we were only going to the supermarket.'

'Well, she probably looked a lot better than I do every time she went out,' I reply as I climb into the car.

'You look absolutely fantastic,' he says, then slams the door behind me.

I bite down to stop from smiling at his compliment. I know he's probably just saying it to be nice, but after the day I've had, it's appreciated.

His car is still pristine clean and there's a vanilla-scented air-freshener hanging from the mirror, but so much has changed since the last time I was in here. That was the first day I slept with—

No. I shake my head – the rest of the night will be a Josh-free zone.

Except when I'm imagining his head as a bowling pin.

We don't talk much on the super-short drive and, when we get there, I discover Sully has already paid for our shoe hire and game online.

'I'll pay you back,' I promise, and he shrugs. 'Whatever.'

We collect our ugly, goofy shoes and find our allocated lane, right at the far end of the building. It's surprisingly busy for a Monday night, but I quickly realise this is because regulars have a competition going. There are different teams all wearing match-ing gaudy-coloured shirts. Eighties music is blaring, but not quite loudly enough to override the die-hard bowlers shouting at each other and their balls.

We put on our shoes, choose our balls, and get started.

I soon discover Sully is really good at bowling. After three strikes in a row, I ask, 'Is this something else you do on the regular because Aisha said it would be good to take your mind off things?'

'No. But how's it working for you?'

'Great,' I say, grabbing my ball as it appears back up the ball return. I clear my throat, get a good grip and then hurl the ball down the lane and yell, 'Take that, Fabio-slash-Josh.'

Half the pins tumble over, and on my second bowl, I get the rest.

Sully laughs as I do a dance, jiggling back to the seat.

As we bowl, we chat easily about inconsequential stuff – which AFL team we go for (I'm the Dockers, of course, and I'm appalled to hear he's Eagles), and which schools we went to – and debate important things, like whether Chinese takeaway is better than Thai, Coke is better than Pepsi, and which way is the proper way to hang a toilet roll. Thank God we agree that the paper is supposed to go over the roll.

Only a psychopath would hang it under.

Just as I'm about to roll another ball down the lane, my phone starts buzzing with the ringtone I set up specifically for Fred. 'Shit,' I say, the ball flying from my fingers and thudding straight into the gutter. I forgot to call her! Sully laughs loudly as I run back to my bag and answer quickly. 'I'm so sorry. I lost track of time.'

'Where the fuck are you?'

'I'm at the bowling alley.'

'You're *where*?' Fred would never be found in such a place – she wouldn't be seen dead in the shoes.

'I'm bowling. With Sully.'

'You're with the crazy *neighbour*?'

My insides tighten as I glance over at him. He's just executed a perfect bowl and he took his hoodie off two turns ago, so his long-sleeved tee is pushed up to his elbows, exposing his muscular forearms. I've always had a thing for guys' arms. And his butt looks really good in his jeans as he straightens.

'Bee,' Fred speaks sharply. 'Are you okay?'

I swallow. 'Yeah, sorry.'

'Have you been drinking?'

'No.' Although I can see why she might think that, considering where I am and who I'm with. 'I'm sorry I worried you, but I promise I'm fine. I'll tell you everything tomorrow, okay?'

She sighs. 'Okay. If you're absolutely sure you don't need me to come and rescue you?'

'A hundred per cent, but thanks.' I say goodbye and turn back to Sully. 'How many strikes is that now?'

He shrugs lazily, then runs his hand through his hair again. Why is that so sexy? 'Nine. Your go.'

And why am I thinking about Sully being sexy when I've just been betrayed in the worst possible way? Shouldn't I be pining after Fabio?

Fabio doesn't exist.

My subconscious is right – there's no point wasting any more tears on someone who doesn't even have a birth certificate.

As if sensing my thoughts, Sully says, 'You okay? You don't have to pretend with me, you know. Break-ups are the worst.'

I smile sadly. 'I think he was planning on ghosting me rather than actually breaking up. Maybe I'm still in shock or something, but weirdly, I think I'm angrier than upset.'

'You've every right to be. The bloke lied to you and used you.'

'Yeah, but I'm just as cross at myself for falling victim to him. My friend Fred would never be fooled that way.' Then again, her philosophy of never staying with someone longer than a few nights means that she wouldn't ever be in such a predicament. I sigh. 'Maybe there's something wrong with me; I can't seem to attract a good man.'

The moment the words leave my mouth I regret being so vulnerable in front of my neighbour, but Sully looks almost angry at my confession.

'There's nothing wrong with you,' he says forcefully, staring intently at me. 'Do you hear me? Don't ever think that.'

'Thanks,' I say, turning away from him to grab my next ball so he doesn't see the tears in my eyes, because no matter what he says, my romantic history speaks for itself.

Unsurprisingly, Sully wins – at least where points are concerned – but I'm feeling much better, so I'm calling this a win for me too.

'Have you eaten anything today?' he asks.

I shake my head. 'Not since breakfast.'

He gestures behind us towards the snack bar that only sells the kind of fried food I still usually steer clear of. 'Shall we get something before our next game?' He booked two, just to make sure I had ample opportunities to exorcise my emotions.

'Good idea.'

We head to the snack bar, our hired clown shoes slapping against the polished floor as we walk.

'Since you paid for the ticket, I'm paying for our meals,' I insist.

'Thanks, but I'm kinda hungry and I don't want to take advantage.'

'Just place your order, *Mikey*.'

He narrows his eyes at me – 'Fine' – but I can tell he's struggling not to smile.

Sully orders two hot dogs with fries and a full-sugar Coke – how he eats like that and keeps a body like *that*, I have no idea – and I get one hot dog without fries and a Diet Coke. We take our buzzer, grab a table and sip our drinks while waiting for our food.

'So how's the Uber driver going?' I ask. 'Met any crazies lately?'

'Not since I picked up you.'

I poke out my tongue at him. 'Ha-ha!'

'Actually,' he says, twirling his can in his big hands, 'I did a short shift back in A&E yesterday.'

I gasp, delighted. 'Really? That's wonderful. How'd it go?'

'I survived. I was on with a mate of mine who knows what's going on with me, and so I knew he was there to back me up if anything went wrong. Thankfully nothing did. I plastered a couple of breaks, stitched up a foot, fished a peanut out of a kid's nose, treated pneumonia in some oldies and diagnosed an appendicitis.'

'Do you think you'll be able to start flying again, then?'

'I'm not sure. I might just take it easy, stay on the ground for a while. I don't know if I can trust myself without a bigger team behind me.'

I nod. 'Fair enough, but this is a great step anyway.' I lift my can and hold it out to him. 'It deserves to be celebrated.'

'Thanks.' He grins and we clink our cans as the buzzer beeps. 'That was fast.'

He gets up and returns with our order on a red plastic tray, just as a bunch of the competition players fill the tables around us. They're talking loudly, more like a bunch of teenagers than a group of middle-aged men.

'Should we take this back to our lane?' I suggest.

Sully agrees and we retreat back to our quieter corner.

I'm famished and although I can be awkward about eating in front of other people – especially men – I hoover down my hot dog.

'Have some of my fries if you want,' he says.

I pluck one up – 'Thanks' – and pop it into my mouth. It's *really* good.

'How are things at the library?'

I groan and tell him how much we all miss Janine.

'She's the old boss, right? Gran really liked her too. That lady who took over seems a bit stern.'

'Stern?' I repeat. 'She's a freaking monster. She's so rigid about what she thinks our jobs are.'

'What do you mean?' he asks, starting on his second hot dog.

I take another chip while working out where to begin. I tell him about the banned/damaged books, her horrendous treatment of our homeless people, and the library Lola and I are trying to organise at the kids' hospital.

'We've got publishers on board and the hospital has found a room that might be suitable. Make-A-Wish is involved too, but Ursula won't let me send any emails or make any phone calls on the project during office hours, which means I'm not being as much help as I promised to be.'

'She sounds like a right cow, but that hospital library is a really great idea.'

'Even to someone who doesn't like fiction?'

He grins. 'I'm behind anything that makes sick kids' lives better.'

A lump forms in my throat. That's probably one of the sweetest things I've ever heard anyone say.

'Earth to Bridget,' he says, waving his hand in front of my face.

I blink as I realise I'm staring at him, not only thinking about his kindness but also his ruggedly gorgeous face. What is wrong with me? Have I learned *nothing* today?

I jump to my feet, almost slipping on the glossy wooden floor. 'Maybe we should play our second game before our time runs out.'

He nods and stands. 'Good idea.'

It's my turn first and I execute the worst bowl ever. It's so bad, it goes straight into the gutter, gets stuck halfway down, and we have to get one of the attendants to come and fix it.

'By the way, I finished *Faking It*,' he says as he hurls another ball lazily down the lane, knocking down all ten pins.

I pause as I pick up my next ball. 'Dare I ask?'

'Predictable ending,' he says.

I knock down eight pins, annoyingly leaving one on each side as my jaw stiffens. 'What do you mean?'

'Tilda and Davy fell in love and got engaged. It was clear from the moment they met that was going to happen.'

Honestly, if I was stronger, I'd throw my ball at him, but instead I scream, 'It's a *romance*,' loud enough that the team next to us look over. 'That's the promise of the genre. Would you rather they broke up at the end?'

'That might be more realistic.' He nods towards the lane. 'Are you going to finish your round?'

I bowl my ball half-heartedly. 'I thought you weren't bitter about love?'

'There's a difference between bitterness and realism.'

'I should have given you *A Series of Unfortunate Events*.'

'What's that?' he asks.

'A kids' series about these orphans who have horrendous things happen to them and there are no happy endings. You'd love it, I'm sure.'

Sully grins at me. 'Maybe I'll have to pop by the library tomorrow and check it out.' He grabs his ball and executes yet another perfect strike.

I cross my arms like a petulant child and sink onto the bench. 'You're no fun to play with.'

He chuckles, then comes over and sits beside me. *Really* close. 'Would you prefer I threw a few gutter balls and gave you a chance?'

'Ha-ha.' He's so warm and funny now, it's hard to believe he's the same guy I was in battle with not long ago. 'When we first met . . . why did you refuse to tell me your name?'

He hesitates, then says, 'I was in a very dark place and in no mood to be neighbourly. I'm sorry. You didn't deserve some of the things I said. You're singing isn't *that* terrible.'

I smile as the warmth of his thigh seeps into mine. It's not an entirely unpleasant feeling. 'Was it because of your PTSD?'

He nods. 'That and the fact I'd just found out my wife was cheating on me with my best friend.'

'Your *best friend*?' I can't keep the shock out of my voice. Daisy hadn't told me *that*!

'Yep. We all went to school together.'

Wow. A double betrayal. 'Did this happen before or after you stopped working?'

He blinks at the question and for a moment I think he'll change the subject, but then he says, 'After.'

'That's terrible,' I exclaim. What kind of wife – what kind of friend – kicks a man when he's already down?

'I don't blame them,' he says, as if reading my mind. 'I really disappeared into myself. I didn't wash, I barely ate, didn't exercise. I was like a zombie and at first, Kristen and Brad – that's my friend – tried to help me, but I didn't make it easy, and . . . eventually they sought comfort in each other. In some ways, finding out about the two of them was the wake-up call I needed.'

'What do you mean?'

Sully lets out a deep breath. 'I suddenly saw myself how they must have seen me. And I realised that just because I might never be able to practise medicine again, it didn't mean I wanted my life to be over. I offered to move out, as Kristen was still working and didn't need the disturbance, but it was hard spending all that time with only my own company. That's when I decided to take up Uber – to give myself something to do rather than sit around feeling sorry for myself. And I started seeing Aisha more regularly. I'm not sure I'd have done any of this if Kristen and Brad hadn't made me take a long hard look at myself.'

'Do you still see them?' I ask.

'No.' He snorts. 'I'm not that magnanimous. At least we hadn't had kids yet.'

I nod. 'You wanted them?'

'I did,' he says sadly, then clears his throat. 'Anyway, this evening has suddenly become rather solemn, and that's definitely not what I intended when I dragged you out of your house. Shall we finish our game, or would you rather go play some arcade games?'

Two minutes later, we've returned our shoes and bought ten gaming tokens each. We laugh and tease each other as we both lose on an old-fashioned pinball machine, then I whip Sully's arse in a game of air hockey.

'Finally, something you're not good at,' he teases, and I poke out my tongue at him.

I get out a little more Fabio anger by bopping rabbits as they pop out of holes, and then Sully uses his last token on one of those claw-grab games and wins a disgustingly ugly rainbow plushie.

'Is that a cat or a unicorn?' I ask, grimacing at it.

He thrusts it at me. 'I don't know but you can have it. It'll look perfect alongside your gnomes.'

I push it back at him. 'I'm not having that thing in my house. It'll give me nightmares.'

'I bet JB will love it,' he says. 'Come on, let's go home.'

Sully, the grotesque cat-unicorn and I head back to his car. He opens the door for me, and I look over at him as he climbs into the driver's seat. 'Thanks for breaking into my house and—'

'I didn't break in; the door was open.'

'Shhh,' I say, pressing my finger against his lips without thinking. They're soft and warm and something inside me squeezes as I wonder what they'd taste like. Sully's eyes go wide, and I snatch my hand back. 'I'm trying to say something important.'

'Sorry. Go ahead.'

I take a quick breath. 'Thank you for salvaging today a little bit. I wanted to kill you when you came into my lounge room, but tonight's been . . . really good. You've helped take my mind off my shitshow of a day.'

'My pleasure,' he says, smiling warmly at me, his green eyes glinting in the streetlight. 'I wouldn't want you thinking *all* men are wankers.'

'Hmm . . . Whether that's true or not, no offence, but I'm done with the lot of you.'

He starts the car. 'No offence taken. I'm done too.'

I raise an eyebrow. '*You're* done with men?'

'Yep.' Sully nods. 'And women. Relationships are way more trouble than they're worth. I'm never falling in love again.'

'Same,' I agree, leaning back into the seat, exhausted at the thought of them. 'Real-life romance is highly overrated. Besides, I can get my swoon-worthy moments between the pages of a book.'

He laughs.

'But sex can be pretty good,' I admit before I can think better of it.

Sully turns his head slowly to look at me and his eyes seem to darken as they meet mine. My stomach somersaults and my mouth goes dry.

'Yeah, that's true,' he says after a few beats, his voice gravelly.

I swallow and lick my lips. Am I imagining the heat between us? We stare at each other and I find my eyes drawn to his lips, to the three-day shadow on his jaw that is chiselled like the jaws of the heroes in my books.

'You know,' I say boldly, almost unable to believe the words coming out of my mouth, 'sex doesn't have to mean a relationship.'

Isn't Fred always telling me exactly this? It's the title of her bloody book!

I see Sully's Adam's apple move slowly up and down – *God*, I never found them sexy until this moment – and then he smiles, hitting me right in the solar plexus. 'Are you propositioning me, Bridget?'

For most of my life, I've hated my name, but when he says it, I can't remember why. 'Yes,' I whisper. 'I think I am.'

'You *think*?' Something akin to pain flashes across his face. 'I don't want to do this if it's just a reaction to the whole Fabio thing and you're gonna regret it as soon as we're done.'

At his words I take a moment to contemplate whether it's sensible to sleep with Sully – sleep with *anyone* – so soon after breaking up with Fabio, but I'm not feeling sensible at all. Right now, I'm so hot for him, I think I'll die if we don't do this. Besides, if today has shown me anything, it's that you can never truly know a person, and how can I ever be in a relationship with someone I don't know?

But just because I'm giving up on love doesn't mean I have to give up on sex.

'I *know*,' I say, leaning over and pressing my mouth against his.

Just as I suspected, he tastes delicious.

56

(Not) Faking It

'Are you *sure* you want to do this?' Sully asks again as he parks in his carport.

After kissing until we really needed oxygen, we'd not said a word the short drive home, but his hand hasn't left my knee and my lips haven't stopped tingling. I'm almost certain Sully is still in love with his ex, and I mean it when I say that, after Fabio, I'm done with dating. I've read plenty of romance novels about neighbours-with-benefits and although they all end with the requisite happily-ever-after, this is real life, and I have no expectations that this is any more than sex between two people who both have an itch to scratch.

I'm cool with that. 'I've never been more certain of anything in my life.'

'Then . . .' He switches off the engine. 'Your place or mine?'

'Mine. I've already left JB long enough.'

It's only when we get inside and Sully is giving my dog the hideous plushie – he's right, JB *does* love it – that I remember. 'My bed isn't made.' I shudder as I think about another man's scent on my sheets. 'Maybe we should have gone to your place.'

'Who needs a bed?' He takes a step closer and his eyes skim my body, leaving heat in their wake. 'We're not actually going to sleep, are we?'

My body hums in anticipation. 'True,' I say, grabbing his hand and dragging him into the lounge room.

Barely before Sully kicks the door shut behind us, we're at it again. Kissing the life out of each other, our bodies so close you couldn't get a ruler between us as he walks me back towards the couch and all but throws me onto it.

Cushions scatter everywhere.

'How many bloody throw cushions does one person need?' he asks, hurling another couple onto the floor.

I laugh. 'You can borrow some if you like.'

'Cushions are not what I want from you, Bridget.' His voice is so deep and raspy, I shiver.

'Oh?' I lick my lips. 'What exactly do you want?'

He lowers himself down on top of me, his deliciously hard body almost crushing mine. 'This.'

He briefly kisses me again before lifting himself enough that he can grab the bottom of my jumper. I help him tug it up and over my head, desperate to be naked with him. As my clothes land somewhere, Sully finds my breasts and I groan as he squeezes gently before trailing his thumbs across my nipples. They peak instantly beneath his touch.

'And these.' He clamps his mouth on one of them and sucks, making my bra wet.

Pleasure shoots from his lips right to my groin.

'Anything else?' I pant, running my hands through his hair, pulling him even closer while pushing myself against the hardness in his jeans.

'I'm only just getting started,' he says, reaching around to unclip my bra.

Suddenly I'm topless and, despite the cool temp and the fact I haven't turned the heater on yet, I'm not cold at all.

He pulls back to take a look and his gaze grows hot – 'You're absolutely gorgeous' – before he buries his head between my breasts. He kisses his way back up my cleavage, his tongue drawing tanta-lising circles on my neck before our mouths meet once again in a hot hungry kiss.

It isn't long before I'm yanking at the buckle on his jeans, curs-ing my fumbly fingers for not managing to undo it because I'm distracted by his hand slipping inside my pants and his discovery of how ready I already am for him.

'You like that?' he whispers, teasing me with his finger.

I don't have the wherewithal to reply.

Later, I'll wonder if he's so good at this due to his professional knowledge of the human body, but right now all I can do is . . .

Scream!

'Shh . . . You'll disturb the neighbours,' he teases, clamping his free hand over my mouth. 'You don't need another noise complaint on your record.'

If I wasn't lost in the throes of pleasure, I'd laugh but I'm simply not capable.

All I can do is focus on the magical sensations streaming through my body.

'Wow,' I say, when I come back down from the stratosphere. I'm physically wrung out, yet somehow I have the energy and des-peration for more. 'Why am I the only one half naked?'

In reply, he pulls his shirt over his head and stands to remove his jeans.

I gape a moment, wondering if Prince Harry is as ripped as him – if so, Meghan Markle is a lucky woman – before realising I'm supposed to be doing the same. Usually I'm hesitant the first time I get naked in front of a man, but because this is just sex, I don't care what Sully thinks about my body.

'Condom?' I sound like I'm begging as I strip off the rest of my clothes. I don't even care.

But Sully's already holding a little foil packet in his hands.

I raise an eyebrow. 'Prepared?'

'Hopeful,' he counters, handing it to me. 'I've fantasised about this moment since the night you stormed into my place and insulted my musical abilities while wearing those tiny shorts and no bra.'

'You've got much better in the months since,' I tell him, ripping the packet open with my teeth.

He sucks in a breath as his gaze skims once again down my body. He's looking at me like I'm a forbidden dessert and he wants to lick the bowl clean. I shiver.

'You *sure* you're okay with this?' Sully asks.

'Shut up and hurry up!' I demand.

This is all the go-ahead he needs. He picks me up and walks us over to the wall. The moment my back hits it, he thrusts hard and fast. My hands clinging to his shoulders, I crush my mouth against his as our bodies move in time, again and again and again.

'Wow,' I breathe, entirely spent, my head resting on his chest as I try to catch my breath. We're both slick with sweat and he's still holding me up against him as if I don't weigh a thing.

'So, tell me something,' Sully asks, his voice still rough.

I lift my head to look at him, hoping he isn't going to ruin this with some post-coital confession. 'What?'

'Did you fake that orgasm?'

I cough out a laugh. 'What do you think?' When he grins cockily, I add, 'Are you *sure* you don't believe in the G-spot?'

He shrugs and I laugh again.

No wonder he was so surprised by that scene in *Faking It*. If his performance just now is anything to go by, there's no way his wife ever had to put on an act!

57

Unadulterated, No-strings-attached, Neighbourly Bonking

I'm not sure how I'm even awake as I head into the staff room the following morning, but I'm delighted when Fred hands me my takeaway coffee cup.

'Where'd you get this?' I ask, taking a sip.

'Some new café round the corner. Is it any good?'

'As long as it has caffeine in it, it's perfect.' I pause, wanting to relish this moment. 'By the way, you were right.'

She smiles over the top of her green juice. 'About which particular thing this time?'

I check we're still on our own. I probably won't be able to resist telling Persephone and Xavier about this later, but I do not want Ursula overhearing. 'Sex without feelings.'

'What?' she shrieks, her eyes widening and her hand rushing to her chest. 'No way! You and psycho neighbour?'

I can't help beaming. 'Yep.' My muscles are still aching pleasurably from our late night – or rather *all* night – shenanigans. I only managed a couple of hours sleep after Sully went home just before 4 am.

'But . . .' Fred shakes her head slightly. 'Are you sure you weren't drunk? Did he take advantage of you? Put something in your drink at bowling? How did this even happen? I thought you didn't even like the guy.'

'I didn't. I mean, I don't. That's the best part about it. Absolutely no chance of me confusing lust for love, because when he's not touching me or looking at me like he wants to, I can barely stand him. And the feeling's mutual.'

She whistles. 'Wow. Tell me everything.'

And so I do. From the moment he walked uninvited into my house to when he kissed me goodbye. How I realised that just because I was giving up on a happily ever after didn't mean my libido couldn't have some fun.

Reliving it is almost as good as the actual act, or three.

'I've never dated a doctor before, but if this is what a decade of medical school gives a person, then I can highly recommend it,' I say. 'The man has positions I reckon even *you* don't know about.'

Fred frowns. 'But you're not dating him, are you?'

'No,' I scoff. 'You know what I mean. This is purely just unadulterated, no-strings-attached, neighbourly bonking. No catching feelings.'

She laughs. 'That's okay, then. Where was John Brown while all this debauchery was happening?'

'Hiding in the pantry,' I say sheepishly.

'Speaking of not catching feelings . . . Have you read any more of my manuscript?'

My stomach twists and my grip tightens on my cup. 'Um . . . not a lot. I'm loving what I've read so far, but the thing with Fabio and then . . . Sully, um, distracted me.'

'Right.' She nods. 'You chose hot sex with your grumpy neighbour rather than read my book. Nuff said.'

Although her tone is jokey, I feel terrible. 'No, of course not. It wasn't like that. I promise I'll read more tonight.'

'Hey, I don't blame you. As much as I love books, I'd choose good sex over reading any time.'

Until last night I'm not sure I'd have agreed.

'So did he stay the night?' she asks, just as Persephone waddles into the room.

'Did who stay the night?'

Xavier enters behind her, not smiling as he always used to. 'Don't tell me they let Fabio out on bail?'

Clearly, Fred has filled them in on what happened.

'I don't know, and I don't care.' Not entirely true – I hope they both get their retribution and I'd also like confirmation that they are indeed siblings, but in this moment, I just want to bask in the afterglow of last night.

'Then what's going on?' he asks as Fred hands him his coffee.

She beams as she blurts, 'Bee slept with her neighbour.'

I'm not even annoyed that she's stolen my glory. Multiple orgasms in one night make it very hard for a girl to be cranky.

'What?' the others exclaim.

Persephone presses a hand against her bump, and I hope the shock doesn't send her into premature labour. 'So *did* he stay the night?'

'No. Of course not.' Not technically; the sun hadn't quite come up when we finally said goodbye.

'So . . . what's next?' he'd asked on the way to the door.

My stomach had twisted at the question. Were things going to be awkward between us now? 'Um . . . well, I guess that depends if you want to do this again.'

He laughed. 'I definitely want to do this again – if you're willing – but I mean, what book are you making me read next?'

'Oh.' I half-laughed as I let out a relieved sigh, feeling like an idiot. 'Nope. No more. You're a lost cause.'

'How about this one?' Sully asked, plucking out *Lenny's Book of Everything* from the shelves in my hall.

'You'll need tissues if you read that,' I warned him. 'And if you don't cry, you mustn't be human.'

He snorted and tucked the book under his arm – 'Sounds like a challenge' – before stepping out into the early morning darkness.

'So are you going to do it again?' Xavier asks now.

I'm secretly hoping so – ASAP – but I manage a nonchalant, 'I dunno.'

'It sounds like *Josh* actually did you a favour,' Fred says. 'If he didn't turn out to be a nefarious arsehole, you might still be having perfectly *nice* sex with him.'

'Bridget!'

We all jump at the sharp voice of our boss. She must have over-heard some of our conversation but I can't bring myself to care. I'd like to see her give me that warning: *Bridget, the staffroom is no place to talk about hot sex or any other kind of sex for that matter.*

'Yes, Ursula?' I say, pasting a bright smile on my face.

'My office. Now. The rest of you, get to work. It's already one past nine.'

My colleagues slink past her as she stands by the door, her arms folded staunchly across her chest like a bouncer, and then I follow her into her office. She all but slams the door behind us – so much for her belief that libraries should be quiet places – and gestures for me to sit. You could never see the top of Janine's desk due to the many books, cards given to her by satisfied customers, photos of her kids and grandkids, and papers from the half a million projects she was always organising, but Ursula's is almost bare except for the computer, a black leather diary and a bottle of water.

She lowers herself into her swivel chair, then presses the heel of her hand to her forehead and winces.

'Are you okay?' I ask.

'I'm fine,' she barks. 'Or at least I would be if I didn't have staff like you bringing disrepute to my library.'

As I blink at her harsh words, she opens a drawer, pops two painkillers out of their packet and then downs them with the water.

'Right,' she says, glaring at me. She opens the diary, pulls out a piece of paper and shoves it across the desk at me.

'What's this?' I ask, my question answered as I glance down and see the words 'Written warning' in bold at the top of the page. 'Are you kidding me?'

Ursula peers down her nose at me. 'I would not joke about something so serious. I *knew* you weren't sick yesterday, and then when I heard Winifred talking to Persephone and Xavier, my suspicions were confirmed. And what I heard was unacceptable. Not only did you leave this library on false pretences, but because of *your* boyfriend, members of our senior book club have been violated.'

I want to retort that it's not *our* senior book club – it was Janine's and now it's mine – but isn't she saying what I already think? I'm not sure I'd use the word 'violated', but they have been badly taken advantage of and it's all my fault. If not for me, Fabio wouldn't have known about the Bookstars, never mind had access to them.

How am I going to face them all again?

'I made it my business to ring each of them and apologise for your actions,' Ursula continues, 'and as punishment for what has occurred, I'm putting you on cataloguing duty for the foreseeable future.'

'What?' Cataloguing is the most boring part of a librarian's job. Every item that comes into the library has to be logged into multiple categories so that when a borrower searches for a topic, any related books will also come up. We actually have a full-time cataloguer, but her job requires such little interaction with the rest of us that we sometimes forget she's here. 'What about Fiona?'

'Don't you worry about Fiona. What I do with my staff is no concern of yours.' She opens the drawer again and pulls out a pen, dropping it on the warning. 'Sign here and remember that a written warning is your *last* warning. Any further indiscretions and you're out of here.'

Blinking back tears, I pick up the pen. 'I understand.'

I deserve to be punished for what's happened. But just as I'm about to sign, I stop. I didn't become a librarian to sit behind a desk cataloguing books – I did so to spread the joy of reading and help people find the right book at the right time to change their lives, and I can't do that locked away in an office.

But can you still do it anyway?

The voice in my head reminds me of my failure to find a book to wow Sully. Maybe I don't deserve to be a librarian any more.

'What are you waiting for?' Ursula snaps, leaning across the desk and tapping the piece of paper.

I push the pen back to her.

'I'm tendering my resignation,' I say, 'and in light of current circumstances, I'd like to take my notice as holiday leave. I've got plenty saved up.'

I stand and leave the room before Ursula has the chance to object, then I head straight to the staff room to collect my things. Next stop is the customer service desk where Fred is chatting to Edgar, of all people. I take a deep breath and head over.

'Hi, Edgar. How are you?'

He pushes his glasses up his nose and grins at me. 'I'm great. I've just finished a wonderful book about a cannibal crime-fighter. It's by Jack someone.'

'Jack Heath?' I clarify.

Edgar snaps his fingers. 'That's the one.'

'I've heard he's a great writer,' I say, 'but listen, how are you? I guess you've heard about Fabio?'

'You mean Josh? Sadly, I did.' He huffs his disapproval. 'And you think you know someone.'

'He didn't take anything from you, did he?' Dread sits heavy in my stomach.

'Nope. Don't think so, although he did tinker with my computer, so there's a fella from the police station having a look over it just in case. And I've been told to change all my passwords and to keep an eye out for any unusual transactions.'

I shudder.

'Never mind about me, lassie. How are you? You were quite smitten with the boy.'

'I'm okay.' I force a smile. 'Anyway, I've got to go. Bye, Edgar. I'll see you later, Fred.'

She frowns and chases after me. 'Where are you going?'

'I just resigned,' I say, stepping onto the escalator.

'What?' Fred stumbles as she steps on behind me. 'Why?'

'Ursula gave me a written warning and I . . . I just can't deal with her any longer. Besides, I'm not doing a good job any more. It's better for everyone if I go.'

'It's better for no one! This is ridiculous.' Fred grabs my hand. 'What exactly was your written warning for?'

I shake her off. 'Please, it doesn't matter. Just leave it. I've made up my mind. Can you tell Persephone and Xavier I'm sorry I couldn't say goodbye, but I'll catch up with them later?'

She nods. 'Course. And you'll catch up with them after work. Meet us at Darling, Darling. If you've really quit, then you deserve a proper pirate send-off.'

'Okay,' I agree, because I know she won't let me go if I don't, and now that I won't have work in the morning, I don't need to worry about weekday hangovers.

I stroll home slowly, wondering what I'm going to do with myself for the rest of the day, for the rest of my life. Maybe I should try to write a book like Fred? I've met plenty of authors, and they all say the best way to learn how to write is to read, read and read some more, so perhaps I've got what it takes. Then again, Fred thinks *she's* got what it takes . . . and even if I do, books take time to write, and I'll need some kind of income in the meantime. Maybe I should go home to the station – there's always work there – but the idea of living in such isolation again doesn't fill me with joy.

Feeling lower than I can ever remember – and that's saying something – I decide to worry about all that later.

Right now, I'm too emotionally exhausted to do anything but sleep.

58

In Case of Emergency

I jolt awake to the sound of bagpipes and no sign of JB. My phone tells me it's 2 pm and I'm feeling surprisingly refreshed. JB's in the pantry, his paws over his ears as he tries to drown out Sully's bag-pipe practice.

'It's not *that* bad,' I say, but give him a treat to appease him a little.

I'm tempted to interrupt the musician myself, but I'm not sure our neighbours-with-benefits scenario gives me free rein to just drop by whenever I feel like it. I figure I have two choices: I can either work out what to do with my life or I can get my house in order. The latter seems the easier option, and my sheets are still in the washing machine from yesterday, so I start with those. I pop my earbuds in, hit play on my latest audiobook and begin tidying up.

As Julia Whelan – one of my favourite narrators – and another guy read *Shut Up and Kiss Me* by Lauren Blakely, I collect three condom wrappers from various places around my house. The memory of our sexy times last night do help to lift my mood a little. I also find a T-shirt that is not mine and too big to be Fabio's, so must have been forgotten by Sully when he left in the early hours of the morning.

Did he leave it on purpose? Everyone knows that old trick – I've used it a few times myself – or am I just looking for excuses to go next door? Either way . . . I really *should* return it. I lift it to my nose and inhale the delicious scent of him. Or I could pretend I never found it and wear it in bed!

As I'm pondering this dilemma, I receive a text message. It's Lola: *I just finished* The Invisible Life of Addie LaRue. *You were right, it's not bad for fantasy.*

Not bad? It's actually one of my favourite books and it's pretty light fantasy.

Okay, pretty damn good. Sad, though. Anyway, how come you're replying in the middle of the day? Did Mary Trunchbull quit?

No. I did.

What? No way. But why?

It's a long story. Are you busy now? Maybe I can come visit?

That would be cool, but I've got a doctor's appointment in half an hour. I've picked up this cough and Mum wants to see if they can give me something for it. You could come over tonight, though. We could watch a movie. Or just talk about your sex life.

I laugh and roll my eyes. I'll have to tell her about the Fabio fiasco, but I doubt I'll be telling her about how soon I invited someone else into my bed – I can barely believe it myself. *That sounds good.*

Want to come for dinner?

I can't do dinner cos I'm meeting my work besties, but I could come over after for a movie. Do you want to check with your mum?

Two minutes later, her reply arrives: *She said yes!!! Do you prefer M&Ms or popcorn? I reckon both!*

I'm typing my reply when another message lands – I thought I was fast on my phone, but Lola makes me feel like a grandma: *Mum also said she'll set the spare bedroom up for you if you want, since you don't drive, or if you don't wanna do that, she'll drive you.*

Or I could get an Uber. I smile, thinking of Sully. *Thanks. I'll bring my toothbrush.*

Yes!!!!!!!!!!!!!!! Gotta go to the docs. Wish me luck. xx

Luck. xx

Much to JB's disgust, I vacuum next, and the washing machine beeps just as I finish. It's unlikely the sheets will dry this late in the day, but the weather promises another sunny one tomorrow, so I take them outside to hang.

As I walk over to the washing line, of course I glance next door. The caterwauling stopped a while ago and I figure Sully might have gone out, so I'm delighted when I see him sitting on the porch, his legs up on the table, feet crossed at the ankles, glasses on – *hello* – and a book in his hand. From the cover I can tell it's *Lenny's Book of Everything.*

'Good book?' I call over the fence as I start hanging out my sheets.

He jumps, looks over, grins, then discards the book on the table and stands. 'What are you doing home?' he asks, wandering across to the fence.

I abandon the washing and join him. 'You wear glasses?'

He shoves them on top of his head. 'Only when I'm reading or on a screen.'

'They suit you,' I say, when what I really mean is, *I didn't think you could get any sexier but now that I've seen you wearing glasses, I'd happily be your sex slave for the rest of your life.*

What has come over me? It's like one night with Sully and Fred has taken up residence in my head.

I notice his eyes are red, his face a little puffy. 'Have you been crying?'

'What? No.' He swipes at them. 'Just hay fever or something?'

'At this time of the year? It's the book, isn't it? It got to you.' I feel victorious, but then again, does it count if he selected it himself?

'Don't be ridiculous,' he says. 'Anyway, why are you home so early? Skiving off?'

'I quit my job.'

'You what?'

'I got a written warning and then I resigned, so I guess now I'm a lady of leisure.'

'I'm coming over,' he says and then launches himself over the fence.

'We have gates, you know,' I say, laughing as JB rushes at Sully, thinking he must be playing some kind of game.

'This was quicker.' He ruffles JB's fur, then takes a soggy ball from his mouth and throws it. 'Are you okay?'

The concern in his voice and the way he gives my shoulder a gentle squeeze threatens to undo me. It's like when you're close to tears and someone hugs you. I swallow.

Am I okay?

'Bridget?' He puts his hand to my chin and tilts my face to look at him.

God, he's gorgeous. 'I don't know,' I tell him honestly. 'It's been a crazy few days.'

'Can I make you a cup of tea?'

I half-laugh, half-scoff. 'I think you've been spending too much time around Daisy.'

'How about a hot chocolate, then?'

My mouth waters at the thought. 'You have hot chocolate?'

He nods and takes my hand. 'Come on.'

Forsaking the fence, we walk around to his place and I'm excited that I'm finally going to get a good look around. *Lenny's* is sprawled out on a plastic table on the back verandah, and although I cringe at his mistreatment of the book spine, I notice he's more than half-way through it.

'For someone who doesn't like reading, you're pretty fast,' I say.

He doesn't comment as he opens the door. We step right into his kitchen-slash-dining area and I'm pleased to report that it feels less like a showroom than the last time I was here. There are a couple of dirty dishes in the sink, some medical journals on the bench, a half-done puzzle on the kitchen table and a few quirky signs hanging on the wall. I read one – *The dishes are looking at me dirty again* – and laugh.

'Sorry about the mess,' he says, gesturing around him. 'I wasn't expecting company.'

It's hardly mess. 'I didn't know you like doing puzzles.' The moment the words are out, I realise how stupid I sound – we barely know each other.

'Gran loves them and now I'm kind of addicted. Feel free to do a few pieces while you're here.'

As Sully puts the kettle on, I step over to the table and take a look. 'We always have one going at the library, but I've never thought to bring one home,' I say.

I don't register his response because I'm distracted as he reaches up to get two mugs from the cupboard, his hoodie lifting in the process and giving me a tiny glimpse of his bare back. Just that one flash of skin has my mind skipping back to last night.

I glance at his kitchen counter, remembering what exactly we got up to against mine. *Oh Lord.* My legs turn to jelly, and I pull out a chair, sink down onto it, then turn to the puzzle. I pick up a random piece.

'Marshmallows?' Sully asks.

'Uh . . . yeah, thanks,' I manage. 'Hang on, I thought you didn't have a sweet tooth? How come you have hot chocolate and marshmallows?'

He looks sheepish.

'Did you lie about that?' I exclaim.

'Okay, okay,' he says as he spoons powder into the mugs. 'Maybe, but it was just a little white lie. You were pissing me off that morning, and when I found out the cake was from you, I didn't want to admit it was delicious. I *did* share it with Gran, though.'

I laugh. 'Who did you think it was from?'

He frowns. 'One of my mates or their wives. When everyone found out Kristen and I broke up, lots of them started leaving casseroles and the occasional cake on my doorstep. For some reason, people think a single guy can't look after himself. Here.' He delivers two steaming mugs to the table and sits opposite me. 'So, what the hell happened at work?'

I wrap my fingers around the warm mug and tell him all about Ursula.

Like Fred, he objects that what she's done is unacceptable. But even without the horrors of the last twenty-four hours, I don't want to work in such a toxic environment anyway.

'Xavier's already looking for another job and Persephone will be off on maternity leave soon. Without Janine and them, the place just won't be the same.' I take a sip, the marshmallows all sweet and gooey in my mouth.

'What about your other friend? Fred, is it?'

'She's tougher than me. She won't let Ursula get to her,' I say, suddenly noticing where the puzzle piece goes.

'Good one,' he says.

We spend a few minutes in comfortable silence, sipping our drinks and doing the puzzle together, JB lazing under the table between our feet.

'What are you going to do now?' Sully asks after a while. 'Look for another library job?'

'I haven't really thought about it. Maybe I'll become an Uber driver. Is it hard to register and stuff?'

His brow furrows. 'Can you even drive?'

'Of course! I grew up on a station – I was driving from the moment I could reach the pedals. I just choose not to because I don't really need a car here.'

'Okay, then. You'd have to buy one, but after that it's a pretty simple process to get started . . .' He shakes his head. 'No, this is ridiculous. You should be fighting that written warning and taking back your resignation. None of this is your fault.'

It suddenly hits me – I've quit my job.

While I don't have a mortgage, I do have bills, not to mention my books and skincare addiction.

Holy shit. What am I going to do?

'Can we talk about something else?'

'Sure.' He cracks a smile. 'What do you want to talk about?'

But that smile makes my insides quiver and I realise I don't want to talk at all. Talking won't change or fix anything.

'Actually,' I say, cocking my head to the side, 'I'm not in a very chatty mood. Maybe we could do something else instead?'

His lips twist into a grin. 'What did you have in mind, Bridget?'

Damn, I love the way he says my name.

Boldly, I push back my chair and walk around the table. 'This,' I say as I straddle him.

His hands knot in my hair as he pulls my mouth to his in a bone-melting, breathtaking kiss. I slide my hands under Sully's T-shirt, desperate to feel his warm, soft skin again. We stop kissing long enough for me to lift the top over his head and for him to remove my jumper and bra.

I squeak and close my eyes in pure bliss as his hands cup my breasts again, but he almost immediately pulls back.

'Second thoughts?' I ask, my heart thudding at the thought.

'No,' he says, 'but the dog is freaking me out.'

I look down to see JB standing next to us, gawking like a proper pervert, and laugh.

Sully stands, taking me with him. 'Let's take this to my bed. John Brown, stay!'

Miraculously, JB does as he's told, and only hours later do I suddenly remember Darling, Darling and Lola. 'What time is it?' I ask, scrambling to sit up.

Sully looks at his watch. 'Just after five.'

'Shit. I'm supposed to be meeting my colleagues at five-fifteen. The nice ones. Sorry, I'm going to have to rush.'

'It's fine. It'll be good for you to debrief with them.'

I shove my Ugg boots back on and then he walks me to the back door.

'Can I have your phone number?' he asks as he opens it.

'What for?' I tease, fluttering my eyelashes at him. 'Planning on sending me sexy photos?'

He snorts. 'If you want to see me naked, all you have to do is come over and I'll give you a personal performance of *Magic Mike* any time you like. But I just thought since we're . . . neighbours, we should have each other's numbers. You know, in case of an emergency.'

I nod faux-seriously. 'That is a very sensible idea, Dr Sullivan. If I have an orgasm emergency in the middle of the night . . .'

He nods, equally serious. 'I'm your guy.'

I grin and hold out my hand. 'Gimme your phone.'

59

Badass

Turns out the days drag when you're a lady of leisure. Yesterday it was a novelty to have absolutely no commitments during the week, but today I wake up feeling antsy. I should read Fred's book, but I'm already glum enough as it is.

During a long morning walk along Bathers Beach, I call my mum to tell her everything that's happened.

'Oh my goodness,' she says after I've given her the full story. 'That's like something that would happen in a novel. I can't believe Fabio was a fraud. He sounded so lovely.'

'You and me both, Mum.'

'Dad and I are supposed to be heading up to Broome for Phil's seventieth birthday party this weekend, but maybe we should cancel and come down to you.'

'Definitely not.' Mum's been excited about this trip for months. She and Dad both deserve the break, and the last thing I need is her fussing around me, worrying that this hiccup is going to send me into another downward spiral. 'Please don't do that. You don't need to worry about me, I promise.'

'Hmph. I'm your mother. It's my job to worry about you,'

she says, then perks up. 'Hang on . . . if you're not working, why don't you come up to Broome with us? There'll be plenty of people your age, because Phil's kids will all be there. Dad and I can ask for a trundle bed in our room.'

I shudder at the thought. 'Thanks for the offer, but I don't want to leave JB.'

I finally manage to convince her that I'm not about to stop eating again and promise that if I don't find a job in the next couple of weeks, I'll hire a car and drive up with JB to spend some time with them. Then I head home and immediately start looking online for vacancies at local cafés, restaurants and shops. One day I might go back to work in a library, but right now I want a job where I'm less likely to stuff up people's lives.

I put in applications with ten places and am about to make myself a late breakfast of avocado on toast when my phone pings with a text from Sully.

My heart leaps when I see it's from Sully. It's the first text I've had from him since we exchanged phone numbers. I almost texted him in the evening to ask how his second shift at the hospital went, but doing so felt too much like the action of someone in a relationship.

You busy today? Gran wants you to come over for lunch to say thanks for everything you did after her op.

So busy. I was sitting here wondering whether to paint my toenails so I could watch them dry or put away my summer clothes to make more room in my wardrobe for my winter clothes.

Um . . . you do know summer ended a couple of months ago?

Better late than never.

He replies with a laughing emoji, followed by, *Excellent. I'll drive you.*

What should I bring? Dessert? A salad?

Just your sexy self.

I put my phone down and I wonder how Sully and I will manage to keep our hands off each other while lunching with his
grandmother. Will she notice something's different between us?

It's still early, which means I have ample time to buy a bunch of
flowers and spruce myself up. For *Daisy*. I feel nervous about seeing
her after the Fabio Fiasco, but if she's gone to the effort of inviting
me for lunch, the least I can do is shower and put on a pretty outfit. It'll be good to talk to her, to ask her how book club yesterday
was with Ursula leading the discussion and find out how the other
Bookstars are going.

Maybe I can ask her to pass on my apology to them.

Sully knocks on my back door at twelve on the dot and wolf-
whistles when I open it. 'Wow. You look fabulous.' He kisses me on
the cheek.

As we walk to the car, I ask him how yesterday was at the
hospital.

'Really good, actually. More breaks, a dislocated shoulder and
a couple of car accident patients with concussion. I had one wobble
with a baby who came in with signs of meningitis but I managed to get through it. That felt pretty good, and I think the kid's
going to be fine.'

'That's great.'

As we hop into the car, Sully asks, 'Were you really about to put
away your summer clothes? Do people actually do that?'

I chuckle. 'My mum does – not that we really have much of
a winter up in the Pilbara – but I've never got around to doing it
before. I'd always rather be reading.'

'Guess now you're a free agent, you can read even more.'

'Yeah, except I'm supposed to be reading my friend's novel, so I'll feel guilty if I read anything else.' And Fred's manuscript is taking me longer than anything I've ever read before.

'Your friend's an author?' he asks, reversing towards the street.

I shake my head. 'She's hoping to be. She's just finished writing her first novel and I'm reading it before she sends it out on submission.'

'That's cool.'

I groan. 'It would be if it wasn't the worst thing I've ever read.'

He grimaces. 'Oh, dear. And she wants feedback?'

'Yeah.' I sigh. 'But I don't want to hurt her feelings. She's put her heart and soul into this novel.'

'If it's really important to her, surely she'll want to hear your thoughts and any advice you might have on how to make it better. You could mention a couple of good things, which will soften your constructive criticism.'

I feel sick at the thought of offering *any* criticism. Fred comes across as all tough, but I know she's capable of hurt just like the rest of us. She just handles it differently.

'What's the book about?' Sully asks as he stops at a red light.

By the time we arrive at Daisy's place, I've explained all the characters and the gist of what's happened so far.

'It certainly sounds original,' he says as he turns into her driveway.

'That's one word for it.'

Sully doesn't knock when we get to the house, but uses his key to let us inside, gesturing for me to go ahead of him. 'Gran's probably in the living room.'

Daisy's place smells lovely, like the potpourri my mum used to have in the bathroom, and I'm thinking about this memory when

I turn into the living room and gasp to find it crowded with people.

I let go of the flowers, but Sully catches them before they hit the floor.

'What's going on?' I ask as Fred lifts a hand from where she's sitting next to Edgar on the couch.

'Hey, bestie!'

Behind her stands Xavier, and to his right, in a rocking chair from the front porch is Persephone, who looks tired and fed-up. All of the Bookstar regulars are here as well – Rose, Beth, Barbara, Olga, Kerry, Ronice, Sue and Lorna – and also a couple of our library assistants perched on chairs brought in from the dining room. There's barely even standing room left.

Daisy comes over to greet me and pulls me into a quick hug. 'So glad you could join us.'

I blink. 'Thanks. The tulips are for you.'

'Oh, thank you. They're lovely.' She nods to Sully. 'Go put them in a vase.'

Lorna points to Moose's armchair – but he's nowhere in sight. 'We saved you a seat.'

As Daisy ushers me over to the chair, I look to my colleagues. 'Shouldn't you be at work?'

'We're on strike,' Xavier announces proudly. 'We've told Ritik we're not going back unless Ursula leaves.'

I don't know whether to laugh or cry. 'Are you serious?'

As they nod solemnly, the latter wins out, and Fred pulls a tiny packet of tissues from her pocket as if she anticipated this moment and tosses it to me.

'It was ridiculous that you were given a written warning,' Persephone says, shifting in her seat as if she can't get comfortable.

'Everything that woman does is ridiculous. And we know you wouldn't have quit without it, so we're demanding it be revoked, that she leaves, and you come back.'

I rip out a tissue and dab it to my eyes. 'You guys are the actual best, but I don't want you to get into trouble as well. And what if we all end up jobless?'

'Meh.' Fred shrugs. 'Persephone's going on maternity leave in a couple of months anyway, Rory can take care of Xavier while he looks for another job and I'll soon be rolling in royalties. Besides, I've always wanted to go on strike! It's so *badass*.'

My stomach drops as I think of her book and force out a laugh.

Sue snaps her fingers at Sully as he returns with the tulips in a vase and puts them on a side table. 'Mikey, get the girl a drink so we can start the book chat.'

'What would you like?' Sully asks as everyone conjures their copy of *The Switch* from behind their backs.

'Wasn't book club yesterday?' I say, ignoring him.

Daisy nods as she gets comfy in her armchair. 'Yes, but when that awful woman turned up to run it instead of you, we—'

'Told her she could take a flying leap,' Rose finishes, 'because there was no way we were going to discuss your romance novel without *you*.'

Aw. I sniff and wipe my eyes again. I feel so loved and appreciated that even after a few short months together, the Bookstars stood by me.

'Then she told us that wasn't possible since you'd resigned because of what you did to us. But you did nothing to us,' Edgar exclaims heartily and the others all nod in agreement.

'I introduced you to Fabio – I mean Josh.'

Olga shakes her head. 'Pah. You didn't introduce him to any of us. The scumbag introduced himself. He pulled the wool over all our eyes.'

'And . . .' Persephone shifts in her seat again. 'When Olga told me the plan to take the book club off site, we organised the strike. We wanted to do something to show our support as well.'

Barbara raises her hand. 'I'd like it on record that I didn't fall for Josh's charms.'

I smile at her – 'Thank God for that' – and then look to Lorna. 'I'm so sorry he took your money.'

Detective Knight had called me yesterday, confirming that the money had belonged to her. Thankfully, he also confirmed that Josh and *Haylee* were really siblings and the police had managed to track her down on her way north. Apparently they'd grown up in a poor household but both of them had been quite smart and gone to fancy schools on scholarships. There, their sense of life being unfair – the rich students constantly looking down at them – grew stronger and they vowed that one day they'd have more money than all of them. Josh didn't start uni intending to use and abuse his degree, but when Haylee met some white-collar criminals who made a fortune stealing identities, she lured Josh into business with her.

They'd almost been caught last year in New South Wales but absconded just in time and once again changed their identities and lay low a while, waiting for another opportunity too good to refuse.

'And your money too,' I say to Rose. Just thinking about Josh and Haylee is making my blood boil all over again. 'I hope the bank can get it back for you.'

Her smile lines crinkle. 'I'm sure they will, dear. But in the end, it's only money. I'm sadder he hurt you.'

'I think we have wasted enough time talking about a non-fictional villain.' Olga taps her thick-heeled boots on the floor. 'Time to talk about this fabulous book.'

'You liked it?' I ask, surprised. I didn't think Olga had a romantic bone in her body.

'I loved it!'

'Hear, hear.' Sue looks at Ronice. 'We couldn't stop raving about it yesterday at Mallwalkers.'

'Okay, then.' I smile, filled with warmth from all these wonderful people, then I look to Sully. 'I'll have a cup of tea, thanks. Black, no—'

'Sugar.' He winks – 'I got ya' – and then disappears into the kitchen.

As usual, we start with a recap of the plot. The best thing about *The Switch* is that there are two romances for the price of one. The main characters – Leena, in her twenties, who lives in London, and her grandmother, Eileen, almost eighty, who lives in a village – are both navigating loss and grief at the beginning of the novel. When Leena is forced to take a sabbatical from her job, she suggests switching houses with Eileen, who jumps at the opportunity.

It's Eileen's shenanigans in the city that the majority of the Bookstars enjoyed most. They're delighted to see someone of their vintage getting page time and some action.

'So unusual for a romance novel – *any* novel – to represent the sex lives of seniors,' Daisy says, just as Sully returns to the room with my cup of tea.

His cheeks turn bright red, and I smirk at him as he hands me my cup.

Rose chuckles. 'Possibly because most of us don't have sex lives.'

'Speak for yourself,' Lorna exclaims with a gleam in her eye as

Sully retreats to a Superman beanbag on the floor. I wonder if it's a remnant from his childhood.

'Has anyone actually used any of those dating apps for seniors?' Edgar looks into his cup as he says this. 'Asking for a friend.'

Kerry shakes her head. 'No, but after reading *The Switch*, I'm thinking I might give it a go. I've been a widow long enough.'

'You know . . .' Edgar looks down at his pale, wrinkled hands. 'We could always go out for dinner.'

It's the first time I've seen Kerry truly smile. 'I'd like that, as long as you let me choose the venue.'

'It's a date,' he says. I might have given up on romance myself, but I can't help grinning.

Eventually we move on to other aspects of the book. We discuss the colourful cast of secondary characters – I don't tell them that the neighbourhood watch group reminded me of them – and the beautiful relationship between Eileen and Leena.

'I'm not usually a romance reader,' Barbara says. 'They're so predictable, but I have to admit this book had more depth than most of them.'

'How many romance books have you actually read?' I ask, trying not to show my irritation.

'As I said, not many.'

'Then maybe you shouldn't make such an assumption. That's one of the myths about romance novels. Everyone thinks that because they have a happy ending they mustn't have substance or the ability to explore serious issues. But that's rubbish.'

'Oh boy,' Fred says, chuckling, 'now you've got her started.'

'Romance novels tackle big issues, but just because they're predominantly written by women and commercially successful, people are quick to write them off. And as for predictability, are crime novels predictable because they always solve the murder? Are fantasies predictable because good always triumphs over evil?'

Barbara blinks and Sully looks at me with an expression of both awe and fear. I wonder if I've been too heavy-handed. Not many things rile me up, but the mockery or unfair judgement of my favourite genre is one of them.

'You're quite right,' she says with a nod. 'I am unqualified to comment, but if half the romance novels are as enjoyable as this one, then I'd like to read more of them.'

'Excellent,' I say, relaxing into my seat, 'because I have heaps to recommend.'

'Why don't we alternate between romance and general fiction?' Edgar suggests. 'The odd crime wouldn't go astray either.'

I'm gobsmacked – not only was he a non-reader months ago, but now he can appreciate the merits of romance novels. I can't wait to introduce the group to some other types of romance, although I don't quite think they're ready for reverse harem yet, and I'm definitely not ready to go there with them.

At the end of our discussion, we write up our thoughts in the book club bible and then Daisy announces we should all migrate to the dining room for lunch.

'There's really lunch as well?' I ask.

She nods. 'Of course, dear. Everyone brought a plate. Come on.'

As they all stand and make their way out of the room, I notice Persephone gripping her stomach, her face twisted as if she's in pain.

'Are you okay?' I ask, rushing over to her.

She holds up a hand as she takes a deep breath, then finally relaxes and nods. 'Sorry, it's just a Braxton Hicks. They've been giving me grief this morning.'

I frown and look at Xavier, Fred and Sully, who are also still in the room. 'Isn't it a little early for you to be having them?' I don't know much about pregnancy, but I thought the fake contractions started much closer to delivery.

'No. Apparently you have them as early as six weeks, but you don't always feel them. I'll be fine.' She holds out her hands. 'Help me up. I'm eating for two and I don't want those OEPs to gobble up all the food before I get to it.'

As Xavier and I each grab a hand and tug, Sully asks, 'How many weeks are you?'

'Twenty-four.'

Persephone is almost on her feet when she gasps and clutches her stomach again. 'Oh, God. This is a bad one.'

Sully reaches out to steady her while she winces through it. The rest of us look on in horror – if this is part of normal pregnancy, maybe I don't want to have kids after all.

After about thirty seconds of Sully rubbing her back and Persephone looking like a red balloon about to explode, he says, 'I think you should sit down again,' already ushering her to the couch. 'Do you mind if I feel your bump?'

'Um . . . yeah, okay.' She looks too exhausted to argue as she leans back into Daisy's crocheted cushions.

He palpates Persephone's stomach, his expression giving nothing away. 'Have you had any other discomfort this morning?'

'I felt a little nauseous after breakfast and my back hurts, but it's been like that for weeks.'

I notice a slight encroaching of Sully's brows and my stomach clenches.

'What are you all still doing dithering about in . . .' Daisy's question evaporates as she returns to the room and sees us gathered around Persephone. 'Oh, no, what's going on?'

Sully ignores his grandma, focusing on his patient. 'And how often have you been experiencing these . . . Braxton Hicks?'

'I think they started about ten, and were about fifteen, twenty minutes apart maybe, but while we've been sitting here, they've become more frequent.'

'I think we should get you to the hospital just to be on the safe side. I'm just going to call an ambulance.'

'An ambulance,' she shrieks, her eyes widening in horror. 'I can't actually be in labour! I'm only twenty-four weeks!'

'It's just a precaution.' His voice is calm, but I can only imagine how he must be feeling inside as he leaves the room. I hope he's being overly cautious because of what happened to him.

Daisy sits beside Persephone and takes her hand. 'You're in good hands, pet. Sully's a very experienced doctor. Now, take a deep breath and try to calm yourself.'

Persephone inhales long and hard.

'Is there anything we can do for you?' Fred asks, looking anxious. 'Get some water or something?'

'You can stop this baby coming,' Persephone shouts and then her face crumples as she starts to cry.

'Maybe we should call Nick?' I suggest. 'Tell him to head to the hospital.'

Xavier is already dragging his phone out of his pocket. 'I'm onto it.'

Leaving Persephone with them, I go into the hallway to check on Sully.

'Are you really concerned?' I ask as he ends his call. 'Could she really be in labour?'

He nods gravely.

'Wouldn't it be quicker if we drove her?'

'Quicker maybe, but if she does deliver, that baby is going to need resus equipment, which I don't have.'

Oh, God. This can't be happening. Then I think about how terrifying this must be for him as well. 'Are you okay?'

'Let's just concentrate on Persephone,' he says, stepping past me on his way back into the lounge room. 'The ambulance is on the way. Can someone wait outside for it?'

Fred almost knocks me over in her rush to get through the door. 'I will.'

Sully crouches in front of Persephone. 'How are you doing?'

Tears are now pouring down her face. 'This is probably my fault. I've been complaining so much about being pregnant again at forty-five; half the time I'm not even sure I want this baby, but if anything happens to him . . .'

'This is not your fault,' Sully says, his tone daring anyone to argue. 'And nothing's going to happen to your baby. Nothing's going to happen to either of you. We're going to get you to the hospital and you and your little one are both going to be okay.'

I'm not sure whether he's trying to convince Persephone or himself, but I desperately want to believe him.

60

A Twisted Sense of Fun

We all wave Persephone and Sully off in the ambulance and then I drive his car with Fred to the hospital as Xavier follows behind. We might not be able to see Persephone, but it feels right to be there in case Nick needs help with the girls or anything.

As we're killing time out in the waiting room – me pacing back and forth, Fred stress-eating Skittles, and Xavier sipping on inferior coffee – Xavier's phone rings.

We all assume it's Nick, but he shakes his head. 'It's the library.'

'Don't answer it,' Fred and I say together. It's probably Ursula inviting him to join her written warning club.

Although he declines the call, it starts buzzing again almost immediately. 'I'll turn it off,' he says, but frowns when he looks down at the screen. 'It's Fiona.'

'From cataloguing?' I ask.

'Yeah.' This time he clicks accept. 'Xavier Perez speaking.' He's quiet for a moment, then his face goes pale. 'That's awful. Is she okay?'

Fred's hand, full of Skittles, pauses midway to her mouth, and I whisper, 'What's going on?'

Xavier listens a little longer, then tells Fiona, 'I'll be back as soon as possible.' He disconnects and looks at us, his expression bamboozled. 'Ursula had some kind of seizure. She's been rushed to hospital as well.'

'Holy shit,' I say. 'Maybe Persephone's spell worked after all. Is she going to be okay?' Just because I loathe the woman doesn't mean I want her dead.

He rubs his hand over his face. 'I hope so. It's probably our fault, due to the stress we caused her today.'

'You don't know that,' Fred says. 'It's just as likely karma for being a *terrible* person.'

'Either way, I have to get back there,' he says. 'Someone needs to help Fiona hold the fort.'

Fred pushes to her feet, shoving the rest of the Skittles in her bag. 'I'll go with you. Bee, do you want to wait for Sully?'

I nod, hug them goodbye and promise to keep them posted. 'Tell me if you hear anything else about Ursula as well.'

It's almost an hour later and I'm wondering if perhaps Sully has forgotten me and made his own way home, when he finally appears.

I rush over to him. 'How is she? Did you make it in time?'

He nods and pulls me into his arms, letting out a deep sigh. 'She's as good as can be expected, considering she's in premature labour, but they've given her Nifedipine to try and stop it, and they've given the baby steroids for his lungs so that if she does deliver, he'll have a stronger chance of survival.'

'Do you think she will?' I ask, still pressed against his chest. I try to imagine how tiny a twenty-four-week-old baby would be.

'It's highly unlikely she'll go to full term. The next twenty-four hours are crucial, but they're in the best place here and the team will do everything they can to look after them both.'

'Thank God.' I echo his relief, then pull back and scrutinise his face. 'Are *you* okay? I imagine that was pretty triggering?'

'I'm . . .' He pauses a second, then nods. 'Yeah, I think I am.' He almost sounds surprised by this.

'Good,' I say. 'You were amazing. So calm. Thank goodness you were there. It was so early, none of us would ever have guessed she was actually in labour.'

Sully smiles. 'As I was leaving her room, Persephone told me that she's going to call the baby Sullivan.'

'Oh my goodness, really? That's so cute.'

'Well, I'm not sure her husband was so keen and she's not really in the right frame of mind to be making such big decisions, but it's a nice sentiment.'

I laugh. 'If Persephone wants to call their baby Sullivan, that *will* be his name, but hopefully we won't find out for a while yet. Oh, you'll never guess what happened while we were waiting. Ursula had some kind of episode. They've taken her to hospital.'

'Who's Ursula?'

I suddenly realise I've only referred to her as Mary Trunchbull or demon boss in his presence. 'She's the library manager. My ex-boss.'

'Geez.' His eyes widen.

Just then my phone rings: Xavier. I put him on speaker so Sully can hear.

'Any news on Persephone and the baby?'

I tell him exactly what Sully just told me. 'What about Ursula?'

'Nothing. We checked her next of kin and notified her wife though, and she promised to give us an update when she has one.'

'Her wife?' I exclaim. We didn't know Ursula was married. In fact, we don't know anything much about her.

'Yeah. Her name's Ali and she sounds lovely. She said Ursula has been having lots of mood swings and headaches lately and acting a bit out of character. Ali just thought it was a bad case of menopause, but with those symptoms and the seizure, the doctors are keeping her in to run tests.'

'Geez. I hope she's okay. Now Nick's here and Persephone's stable, we're going to leave. Do you need me to come back to the library and help?'

'No, we'll be fine this arvo,' Xavier says. 'I know you've quit – and to be honest, I'm hoping we can change your mind about that – but do you think you could come in tomorrow to cover Ursula?'

'Of course. See you then.'

I end the call and turn to Sully. 'Any ideas what might be wrong with her?'

'I wouldn't want to say anything definite . . . It could be a number of different things. Epilepsy, a silent migraine, some kind of tumour. Didn't you say that your old boss was surprised by Ursula's behaviour as well?'

I nod.

'In that case, it could be a frontal lobe tumour. They sometimes affect personality.'

'Really?' I'm sceptical. 'Are you saying maybe Ursula isn't the demon we have her pegged as?'

He shrugs. 'It's a possibility, but I'm just speculating until her test results are in. Anyway, wanna go home?'

'Yeah,' I say, not reading anything into his use of the word 'home'. After all, our houses do share a common wall and roof.

Both of us exhausted, we barely say a word as Sully drives back to Fremantle.

'Do you want to come in for a drink?' I ask when we get there. 'I think we both deserve a wine after the day we've had.'

He hesitates a moment, then says, 'Yeah. I'd like that.'

JB greets us and Sully takes him out for a pee while I pour us glasses of pinot grigio. When they return, I hand Sully his glass. 'You hungry?' Neither of us had got lunch in the end.

'A little,' he admits. 'Stress works up an appetite.'

Although I'm the opposite, I make us simple toasted cheese sandwiches and we head into the lounge room to eat them, flopping onto the couch as if we've run some kind of marathon.

'At least we now know one of us is still good at our jobs,' I say.

'What do you mean?'

'You've had two successful shifts and today you stayed cool and calm in the face of a medical emergency. I know that doesn't mean you're completely re—'

'You're *amazing* at your job,' he interrupts.

'I almost got a dozen or so of our patrons scammed out of their money.'

He shakes his head. 'That had nothing to do with your work. Didn't today show you anything? No one blames you for what happened. They all adore you and love talking about books with you. I've seen you in action – you've got a passion that shines through when you're leading book club and you care about your borrowers. If the Bookstars didn't prove that, what you're doing for Lola would.'

'But *you* prove that I've lost my touch,' I retort. 'I became a librarian because I had a gift for recommending books – something not all librarians have. Not necessarily books that I loved the most, but ones that I just knew would be perfect for the recipient. I've lost count of the number of people I've converted to reading, and then you came along and baffled me. How can I be a good librarian if I've lost the thing that made me want to do it in the first place?'

Sully's nostrils flare. 'You're not serious.'

I nod and twist my wineglass between my fingers. 'I know it probably sounds stupid, but being able to pick the right book for anyone was the first thing I ever really excelled at, aside from starving myself. I was average at school, not great at team sports, last in every race – running *and* swimming – average to look at and a little bit pudgy too, but this was something that I could do better than anyone else. It gave me purpose in a way nothing else ever had.'

'Fuck, Bridget.' Sully looks like I've told him the world is actually flat. He puts his glass down and grabs my hand, pulling me up. 'Come with me.'

'Where are we going?' I ask, my canine shadow following behind us. 'I'm not in the mood for shooting hoops.'

But Sully doesn't say a word until we get into his house. His lounge room is still almost as barren as the first night I was in here, but there's a small bookshelf on one wall. 'Look,' he says as he takes me over to it.

I frown as I look at the small collection of novels on it – there's *Boy Swallows Universe*, and Trent Dalton's other books, alongside copies of *Anxious People*, *A Man Called Ove*, the Beartown series, and a copy of *Bet Me* by Jennifer Crusie.

'I looked in Elizabeth's Bookshop for *Faking It*. They didn't have it, so I ordered it online, but they did have this one. It's good, have you read it?'

'I . . .' I shake my head and look back at him. 'Of course I have. I've read everything she's ever written, but . . . I don't understand. I thought you hated the books I recommended.'

'Not exactly. In fact, I liked them so much I went out and bought copies of my own and everything else I could find by the same authors.' He's beaming now. 'This is my Bridget shelf, and I reckon it proves your track record is still one hundred per cent.'

I take a step back and look at him like he's a complete stranger. 'But . . . why would you lie about this?'

He gives me a coy smile. 'You were so adamant you knew me well enough that you could choose a book for me, and when you seemed to be right, that irritated me a little, so I decided to pretend otherwise. Then, your reaction was so endearing that I couldn't resist keeping up the facade.'

'I never said I knew *you*; I said I knew *books*.'

Sully shrugs as if that's the same thing. 'And also, being around you made me feel good and I thought if you thought you'd suc-ceeded, you might stop recommending books.'

I can't believe what I'm hearing. Sounds like my neighbour is a psycho after all. Who does something like this? 'Or maybe we'd have had something to talk about!'

'Hey, I think we've found plenty to talk about,' he says, smiling flirtatiously at me.

But I'm immune to his charms right now. All I can do is scowl.

'I didn't know this was such a big deal to you,' he says, his smile fading. 'But you should know, reading helped me. The music, the basketball . . . Those things were good, but it wasn't until I was lost in the pages of a book that I really was able to relax. I even started sleeping better, and with that clear head, I decided to try a shift at the hospital. If not for you—'

'Oh, well, then,' I snap. 'That's okay. As long as *you're* feeling better, never mind what you put me through.'

'Bridge.' His voice cracks. 'I'm really sorry. I never meant to hurt you. It was just a bit of fun.'

Fun? I let out a half-laugh, half-sob. 'Your idea of fun is twisted.'

'Please,' he begs again, putting his hand on my arm, 'I said I'm sorry.'

I shrug him off. 'It doesn't change what you did.'

He looks hurt, but I don't care. I'm *aching*. I can't explain it, but his betrayal feels almost worse than Josh's.

'Please,' I urge, 'just go. I can't deal with this right now.'

And then I remember that we're in his house. *Dammit.*

Before he can point this out, I storm past him – 'Come on, JB' – desperately hoping the dog follows me and Sully does not. The moment I get back to my place, I call Fred.

I guess because Ursula's not at the library, she answers immediately.

'Can I come stay with you? I don't want to be alone tonight.'

'Sure,' she says, sounding slightly surprised. 'I'll come pick you and JB up when I knock off work in half an hour.'

61

All Men Are Liars

'Your guy was a bit of a hero today,' Fred says as JB, my overnight bag, the rest of the bottle of pinot grigio and I pile into her Mini.

'He's not my guy,' I snap, yanking the passenger door shut.

She screeches off down the road before I've even had a chance to put my seatbelt on. 'Sorry, I meant fuck buddy.'

I sigh long and loud, feeling as if the weight of the world is on my shoulders, rather than JB's cute fluffy head poking over from the tiny back seat.

'Oh, that sounds like a boy-trouble sigh. I thought everything was going well between you two.'

'He's just the same as every other man,' I tell her. 'A liar.'

She glances over at me as she turns a corner. 'Don't tell me he's still married? Or shagging his ex? I've been out with a couple of guys who said their last relationship was definitely over, but they were still scratching each other's itches every now and then. Not that that would have bothered me if they'd been up front about it.'

'How many guys have you dated long enough to learn that about them?'

'Oh, these weren't guys I dated. They were ones I had

arrangements with, like yours and Sully's,' she says as she pulls into the car park near our favourite Chinese restaurant.

'Are we getting Chinese?' I ask.

'Yes. I've eaten nothing but Skittles all day, but I can't be arsed to cook. I ordered those dumplings you like.'

Suits me. I only nibbled the toasted sandwich and if we're going to drink, I should have something more in my stomach.

While Fred goes in to collect our order, I stay in the car with JB, who barks excitedly at every passer-by. Then, when she hands me the warm bag, smelling of garlicky, gingery goodness, he goes absolutely crazy, trying to get into the front seat. It's a miracle we arrive at her place in one piece.

'Well, hello,' Waylen greets us as we head in the front door, screwing up his nose at the smell of the takeaway. He doesn't eat anything that he hasn't prepared himself.

'Hi,' I say, holding JB's leash tightly to stop him chasing after the food. 'Off for a run?' It's a stupid question considering he's wearing sneakers, running tights and a long-sleeved Nike T-shirt.

He nods. 'Do you want me to take John Brown with me so you two can eat in peace?'

I could literally kiss the man. Poor JB has been cooped up inside all day, but I'm not in the mood to go for a walk tonight, even if it might be good for my mental health. 'Thank you, that would be wonderful.' I hand him the end of the leash. 'It's such a shame you're gay. You really are the perfect man.'

He chuckles at my sentiment as he and JB head off.

I follow the aroma of the food into the lounge room where Fred has already got the plastic containers open on the coffee table and two glasses for the wine I brought. I pour us both a generous amount and then sit beside her. Fred barely inhales between mouthfuls of two plates of Kung Pao veggies and fried rice, while I enjoy my beef and vegetable dumplings at a more leisurely pace.

Then, she takes a long gulp of her wine and turns to me. 'Right, now that I'm no longer hangry, are you going to tell me what's upset you?'

I put down the rest of my dinner and tell her about Sully and the books.

She listens attentively, then asks, 'Do you think you're overreacting a little due to everything else that's happened the last few days? I don't really see what the big deal is. In fact, I think it's kinda cute.'

I glare at her. 'Winifred, you *know* how important books and honesty are to me. Especially after Josh.'

'Yeah, I guess.' She doesn't sound convinced.

'What's that supposed to mean?'

She shakes her head and reaches for one of my dumplings. 'Nothing.'

'What?' I demand.

After eating it, she licks her fingers clean. 'Well, if you didn't care about Sully, do you think this would feel like such a big deal?'

'I didn't say I didn't care about him.'

'Actually, you did. The morning in the library after you first slept with him.'

'Okay,' I concede. 'Things have changed a little. He sorta became a friend.' Or so I thought.

'With benefits,' she adds smugly. 'But . . . he's told you your superpower is intact, and usually you have a good sense of humour, so I'm wondering . . .' She peers at me over the top of her glass. 'Are you sure you haven't caught feelings for him?'

I scoff. 'You're not the only one who can have sex without falling in love. I meant it when I said I'm done with relationships.

I still want to have kids and stuff – although after seeing Perse-phone today, I'm not so sure – but maybe I'll use a donor.'

'Ooh,' Fred says, her eyes twinkling. 'Can I be the godmother?'

'I think you have to believe in God to be a godmother.'

She pouts. 'Okay, I'll be the cool aunty then, who teaches them all about sex.'

I groan and laugh – this is why I wanted to be with Fred tonight. She always has the ability to make things seem not quite so bad.

As she grabs the wine bottle and empties the dregs into each of our glasses, she poses another question. 'Are you sure Sully is happy with your *arrangement?*'

'Yeah.' I can't help smiling as I think about the glazed look in his eyes every time we're together. 'I'd say he's satisfied.'

She cackles. 'Of course, he's *satisfied* – but that's not what I mean. Today at Daisy's place, I kept catching him looking at you with this really sweet expression on his face. And yeah, he might have enjoyed the books you recommended, but would he really have named a bookshelf after you if he didn't have *other* feelings?'

I shake my head. 'I don't know what you saw today, but he's def-initely not on the market for love. He's still in love with his ex-wife and he's also dealing with some other issues.' I don't tell Fred about Sully's PTSD because that would feel like a betrayal of confidence. 'And neither am I.'

That's why our arrangement is safe. *Perfect.* Or rather it was.

'Then I think you should forgive him,' she says. 'If the sex is as good as you say it is, then you'd be a fool to throw it away.'

I sigh – too emotionally wrought to contemplate this right now.

Fred's phone beeps with a text message. 'Don't worry; it's just Andy.'

'Who's Andy?'

'He's from my writing class. You remember, I brought him to Janine's retirement party.'

'Oh, right . . . have you slept with him yet?'

'Not everything is about sex, you know, Bridget. We're just friends.'

I laugh – not just because of the prim look of disapproval she puts on but because this is a sentence I never imagined coming out of Fred's mouth.

She laughs as well, and I can tell she's *absolutely* slept with him. But the mention of her writing friend causes the dumplings to churn in my stomach. For the last half an hour I've been ranting on about the importance of honesty between friends, so maybe this is the moment to tell my best one the truth.

I only hope she'll still talk to me afterwards.

'Fred,' I confess, my insides twisting into a tight knot, 'I'm struggling to finish your manuscript.'

She waves away my confession. 'It's cool. I know life's been a little bit crazy since I gave it to you. No rush.'

I swallow. This is my out – maybe it's Fate telling me to keep mum, but I've already made up my mind. I'd be a hypocrite if I didn't tell her the truth, and waiting longer isn't going to make it any better.

'That's not what I meant,' I say and then rush the rest. 'I've read quite a lot and . . . I'm so sorry if this is going to sound hurtful, but I have to be honest with you and admit that . . . well, the thing is . . . I'm not really enjoying it.'

Fred looks down into her now-empty glass. 'I see.'

Silence rings between us and I would do anything to be able to shove the words right back into my big fat mouth. I should have at least finished reading it before saying anything – maybe the second half gives Shakespeare a run for his money. Not that I ever got the appeal of his work either.

'I'm think I'm going to get more wine.' She heads into the kitchen, and I drop my head into my hands, hoping I haven't just ruined the best friendship I've ever had.

'Okay.' At Fred's return, I glance up to see her with her faithful Aldi cask under her arm. She refills both our glasses, then leans back into the couch. 'Hit me with it. What exactly don't you like about it? And, please don't hold back. I've got tough skin.'

No matter what she says, I really don't want to hurt her, so I take another sip, biding my time as I try to find the right words. 'Well,' I say eventually, 'the characters are interesting' – one of them is a cannibal after all, and another an alien – 'but I can't say I like any of the men. I don't find them very relatable.' And I've read my fair share of alien romance – *Planet Barbarian* is one of my favourite series. 'None of them are given enough page space for us to get to know them, and Ana feels a little one-dimensional, so I'm not rooting for her happily ever after.'

'*What?* Ana's fantastic. She's loud and feisty, and anyway, it's not a romance, so she's not looking for a happily ever after.' She makes an *ew* expression – as if I needed reminding about her thoughts on my favourite genre.

'Is it erotic fantasy fiction then?' There are so many romance tropes within her manuscript that it's not my fault I'm a tad confused.

Fred throws her hands up. 'I've told you; it defies genre conventions. I guess it's more a literary exploration of a modern woman who isn't afraid to ask for what she wants. Why do we have to give everything labels?'

'What is it exactly that Ana wants?'

At this Fred grins. 'She wants to fuck the patriarchy and as many men as she can. For all of time, men who sleep around have been hailed as heroes, yet women who do the same are scorned as sluts. Ana is on a mission to change the world.'

It's easy to see where she gets her inspiration, but . . . 'To be honest, that's not really a message that's coming across, but I think my main issue is that it lacks emotion. Romance or not, we both know that every good book should make people feel something. Right now, it's lacking soul.'

My best friend winces. I should probably shut up – it's clear that Josh was right about one thing, she doesn't want my true thoughts – but I can't resist one final question. 'What do you want to achieve with this book?'

'You mean aside from fame and fortune?'

We both laugh, breaking the tension slightly, because we know that most authors barely make ends meet and many have to supplement their writing income with a day job.

'I'm sorry,' I say. 'Maybe I'm just not your reader. You know I'm a sucker for a happy ending, even if I don't believe in them any more. Didn't you say Andy loved it?'

'Yeah.' She rolls her eyes. 'But we both know he just wanted to get in my pants.'

And then she bursts into tears.

Oh Lord. In our decade-long friendship, I've only ever seen Fred cry twice: when her cat Aunty's predecessor died, and when her mother remarried for the fourth time to a man who reminded Fred exactly of her father. I scoot across the couch so I can hug her.

'I'm so sorry, I shouldn't have said anything.' Just because I had a crap day didn't mean I had to make hers bad too.

She stays in my arms sobbing for about two minutes, then pulls back, wipes her nose and downs her second glass of wine. 'No.' She shakes her head, then squeezes my knee. 'I'm glad you told me the truth, even if it hurts. You read more books in a year than most people do in a lifetime, and I'd be stupid not to take your advice on board.'

'Mine's only one opinion,' I remind her.

'And to me it's the most important.' She chuckles. 'Guess I won't be giving up the day job just yet.'

'But you are going to keep writing?'

'Of course. I'm not gonna give up on my dream just because I don't get it right the first time.'

I admire her so much – I'm not sure I'd have the patience and stamina to write a whole novel.

'Besides,' she says, 'how else am I going to get on the *New York Times* bestseller list and have Reese Witherspoon make the movie adaptation so we can both cameo in it?'

I let out a relieved laugh, glad I haven't made her turn her back on her dreams. Or me.

Fred pauses. 'Can I just ask you one question?'

My gut squeezes again. 'Yes.'

'Do you think I should ditch *How Not to Catch Feelings* and start something fresh? Is *any* of it salvageable?'

'Well . . . I like the title.'

Fred snorts out a laugh. 'Probably better to put it aside. Hardly any authors get their first books published anyway.'

'Didn't JK Rowling have something like twenty rejections?' I ask.

She nods. 'I've just gotta keep at it.'

'Can I make one more suggestion?' I don't wait for her reply. 'This wasn't the book I was expecting from you. What's the one piece of advice all the authors who speak in the library give?'

She frowns for a moment. 'That you should write the kind of book you want to read.'

'Exactly! And you're not someone who reads sad-girl literary fiction. You love getting lost in dystopian worlds and going on crazy adventures, so I can't help thinking that's the kind of book you should be writing. Or even non-fiction – you could write a modern guide to dating without falling in love.'

The sound of the door opening and then JB pounding down the hallway puts an abrupt end to our conversation, but I hope I've given her something to think about.

'He was great,' Waylen hollers, 'but he might need a bath, as we sort of went for a swim.'

'Who goes for a swim in winter?' Fred squeals as JB charges into the room and throws himself at us. He's drenched and now so are we. 'I'll go grab some towels,' Fred offers, leaping off the couch.

When she returns, she clears up the plates quickly and then helps me dry the dog.

'Thanks,' I say when we're done.

'No worries.' She ruffles us both on the head. 'That's what besties are for.'

Besties. The word makes my heart swell. 'So you're not angry with me?'

'Why would I be angry at you?'

'Because I didn't like your book.'

She shakes her head. 'It would take a lot more than that for me to ever have any bad feelings about you,' she says, pulling me into a rare hug. 'I appreciate you not bullshitting me like Andy obviously was.'

I shrug. 'Hey, what have I been saying? All men are liars.'

62

Molten Lava

I've only been away from the library a few days, but it feels much longer, and I'm stoked to be back. With Persephone and Ursula both out of action, we've got more work than usual to do, but keeping busy will hopefully keep my mind off all the other drama in my life. Persephone updated us all first thing this morning and the good news is they've managed to stop labour for now. The bad news is she'll have to be on bed rest for the rest of her pregnancy – however long that may be – and we haven't yet hired her maternity replacement. Personally, I wouldn't mind being banished to my bed to do nothing but read and watch Netflix for a few months, but Persephone is normally such an active person that to her this seems like torture. Not to mention her two little girls who don't understand why Mummy can't be at their beck and call all of a sudden.

We're so busy that Xavier and Fred don't take a lunch break and I only sneak fifteen minutes to rush home, let JB out and grab a banana, which I scoff on my way back to the library.

Mid-afternoon, Xavier is in a meeting with the librarians from the surrounding schools about trying to get a Kid-Lit Festival off the ground, Fred is at the bank doing our weekly deposit and I'm behind the desk updating our Facebook page, when a woman who looks a bit like my mum – average height, a chocolate-brown bob, clearly dyed to cover greys, and a warm smile – approaches me.

'Excuse me,' she says. 'My name's Ali. I'm Ursula's wife.'

I smile. 'Oh, hi. Nice to meet you.' Xavier was right about her being lovely – she's got this aura surrounding her that indicates she couldn't be anything but sweet. 'I'm Bee, one of the librarians. How is Ursula?'

Ali's smile fades a little. 'Well, her test results came back and . . .' Her voice catches. 'She's got a brain tumour.'

Even though Sully's predictions had prepared me for this, I gasp. 'I'm so sorry.'

'Thank you. They did some further tests this morning so we're waiting to find out the severity. Fingers crossed it's benign, or if it's not . . .'

'Is there anything we can do?' I ask when she can't seem to finish her sentence.

She shakes her head. 'No. Thank you. I've come to collect some things from her desk, and also to apologise for any inconvenience her absence is going to cause. I can't be sure at this stage how much time off she'll need.'

'Oh, don't worry about that,' I assure her – the truth is we're all *much* more relaxed without Ursula. 'We'll be fine. I'll just go grab her things for you.'

'Please tell Ursula not to worry about the library,' I say when I return with her personal items. 'We've got everything under control. She just needs to concentrate on getting better.'

Ali surprises me with a hug. 'Thank you so much.'

'Who was that?' Fred asks, returning from the bank as Ali is leaving.

'Ursula's wife. Ursula has a tumour.'

When Xavier is finished with the festival organisers, I explain what Sully told me about frontal lobe tumours and how they can alter someone's personality. Fred is sceptical, but Xavier and I convince her to give Ursula the benefit of the doubt and throw some money in to get flowers delivered to the hospital. We send some, along with a box of chocolates, to Persephone as well.

I'm about to text Sully to tell him his diagnosis was correct when I remember I'm not talking to him. *Dammit.* Maybe Fred was right, and I did overreact. It wasn't like he meant to hurt me. I'm staring at my phone contemplating an apology – well, another truce – when it rings. My heart leaps when I see it's my contact at the children's hospital.

'Hi, Vicky.'

'Hello, Bee. Hope you've had a good week.'

'Great,' I say, not about to go into the truth with a stranger.

'Excellent. Well, I hope I'm about to make it even better.' I hold my breath as she pauses for effect, then says, 'The hospital board have signed off on the room. I thought you might want to give Lola the good news yourself.'

'Oh, that's wonderful,' I shriek, causing a few borrowers to glance my way. 'When can we start setting everything up?'

'The room just needs to be properly cleaned, but that should be done by Wednesday.'

We talk a little more about logistics and I arrange to pick up the key after work on Wednesday before ending the call.

I'm so excited I dance a little jig around the library, telling Fred, then Xavier, then anyone else who is willing to listen the good news before finally calling Laura, because Lola will be at school, but I can't wait till she's home.

Laura answers the phone on the second ring. 'Hi, Bee, how are you?'

'I'm good and I have good news,' I say. 'We got the room for the library. We can start setting everything up this weekend.'

Laura gasps. 'Oh, thank you. Lola is going to be so happy.'

'How's she been going at school this week?'

'So far so good. She's tired every night, of course, and she came home early yesterday, but I haven't had a phone call from the school nurse yet, so I think she's made it through today.'

I can't help beaming. 'That's wonderful. Do you want to tell her about the room when she gets home, or shall I?'

'I think you should. It's all your hard work that made this happen.'

'Okay. And I thought I might go to Ikea tomorrow, work out what shelving we need and see if they can deliver. Would you and Lola like to come?' I ask.

'I'd love to, but Luke's away this weekend for work and I've got to drive Leo to Mandurah and back for soccer tomorrow. Lola's already dreading it, but I still don't want to leave her alone. Maybe we could go Sunday?'

'Or I could take Lola,' I suggest. 'That way you can focus on Leo and she won't have to be out all day. I'll get an Uber and I promise I'll take care of her.'

'Oh, Bee, you really are an angel. I know she'd much rather spend the day with you than go to her brother's game. I could pick you up and drop you both off before I head to Mandurah with Leo if you don't mind an early start.'

We make the date, agreeing that I'll break the good news to Lola in person, and disconnect. I've never been more excited about a trip to Ikea in my life and I'm still grinning when I walk home an hour later. I've already forgiven Sully and am planning to make amends once I've let JB out, but he's beaten me to it. At least, I'm pretty sure no one else is responsible for the new gnome sitting on my front doormat. On closer inspection, I see the cute little statue is holding a bunch of flowers and beneath its feet is a white envelope.

I chuckle as I stoop down to slide it out.

Dear Bridget
Please accept my sincere apologies for hurting you.
I hate that I did so.
Sully

Clutching the gnome to my chest, I rush next door and ring Sully's bell.

'Do you think *this* is going to make me forgive you?' I ask when he opens the door.

He tilts his head to one side in the same adorable way that JB does when he knows he's done something naughty. 'I was hoping it would be a start, but I'm willing to negotiate terms if you're willing to consider.'

In reply, I step forward and kiss him.

In reply, *he* attaches his hands to my hips, pulling me flush against him as he drags me inside.

The gnome is abandoned as we tear at each other's clothes. I've never felt such suffocating chemistry with another person before – he smells, tastes and feels so good, and I want to have every last inch of him, but then I remember my dog. I'm such a terrible pet owner.

I pull back. 'Can we take this back to my place? I need to let JB out.'

His Adam's apple moves slowly up and down as his hands move to his jeans to do them up again. 'Your bed is as good as mine.'

We hurry next door and while JB greets Sully with his usual fervour, I grab the biggest dog treat I can find and throw it and him out into the backyard.

'Come on, angel,' Sully says, taking my hand and pulling me towards my bedroom.

Seconds later we're both naked and I've got him exactly where I want him.

'I think we should have disagreements more often,' he whispers after he's thoroughly played every inch of my body and our hearts are pounding against each other in their efforts to come back down to earth.

'What do you mean?' I manage, still panting.

'That make-up sex was the best sex I've had in my life.'

'Me too,' I admit. Maybe sex without commitment is the key to an amazing sex life. Sex where neither of you is thinking about the future or whether your lives and values will align long-term.

We lie there, skin slick with sweat as we hold each other.

'How was your day?' Sully asks.

We talk about Ursula's tumour but I lighten the mood again when I tell him about Lola's Library.

He rewards me with another kiss. 'That's brilliant.'

'Actually, you know how you still owe me . . .' I smile and look up at him from my comfy position on my side, leaning my head against his chest.

'Uh huh . . .' He presses his mouth against my ear and whispers a suggestion for exactly how he can make amends.

My body turns to molten lava.

'Get your head out of the gutter,' I say, unable not to smile. Or blush. 'Tomorrow I'm taking Lola to Ikea. Her mum's dropping us off, but she can't pick us up, so if you're not busy, do you think you could?'

He agrees immediately. 'Of course. Why don't we save Laura the trip and I'll drive you both there too?'

'You sure? We could be a few hours.'

Sully nods. 'That's fine, as long as I don't have to go inside. The only good thing about that place is the Swedish meatballs.'

I laugh. 'That would be great, thanks. I'll call Laura and let her know.'

'Speaking of food . . .' he says.

'Were we?' I ask.

'The Swedish meatballs,' he confirms. 'Wanna go out for dinner or something?'

I shake my head in amusement. 'Do you ever think about anything apart from your stomach?'

His chuckle is rough. 'I think you know the answer to that.'

You won't believe it, but we're already at it again.

63

Fake Dates and Swedish Meatballs

'Bee!' Lola exclaims, throwing the door open before I can ring the bell on Saturday morning. She wraps her arms around me, giving me a big hug. She looks super cute in wide-leg jeans and a purple cropped jumper. 'Mum said you've got a surprise for me?'

Laura appears behind her, along with Leo, dressed in red shorts and a white sports shirt, juggling a soccer ball, scruffy footy boots hanging off his wrist. 'Hi, Bee.' She pecks me on the cheek. 'Great to see you. I'm sorry but we've got to rush. Are you sure you can stay with Lola until we get back?'

'Of course.'

Lola rolls her eyes. 'I'm fifteen, I don't need a babysitter.'

Ignoring her, Laura says, 'She's got her key. Help yourself to whatever you want in the fridge. Leo and I should be back around three.'

As Leo heads past us outside, Lola grabs my hand, yells, 'Bye, Mum,' and starts towards Sully, who is standing by his car in the driveway. 'Is that Fabio?' she hisses, loud enough that he hears.

He chuckles, opening the door as we approach.

'No. Actually, Fabio and I broke up. This is my neighbour Sully,' I say, before she can ask questions. 'Sully, this is my friend Lola.'

He offers her his hand. 'Hey, nice to meet you.'

She blushes and nods – 'You too' – then looks to me. 'So where are we actually going?'

'Vicky from the hospital called yesterday; we've got the room. We can set up next weekend, so we're off to Ikea to shop for bookshelves.'

'OMG! That's awesome about the room.' She dances in her seat. 'And I *love* Ikea.'

Sully groans and I laugh.

It's about half an hour's drive and Lola chatters the whole way, barely leaving a gap in conversation for me and Sully to say anything. She talks about her return to school, in particular, her blossoming romance with the infamous Mason.

'He's been so nice since I started back again. We've been hanging out every lunch time. Guess having cancer makes you stand out from the crowd.'

I can't help wincing. 'I'm sure that's not why he's talking to you; he probably just realised he missed you when you weren't there.'

She shrugs, still grinning – 'Whatever' – as Sully slows the car to drop us off near the entrance. 'Aren't you coming in?'

'No, thank you.' He shakes his head adamantly. 'Whenever I go there, I have nightmares for weeks afterwards about not being able to find my way out.'

'Aw, poor Sully,' Lola says, reaching over and patting him on the head, like he's a cute little puppy. 'We promise to look after you, don't we, Bee? Besides, if you don't come, who's going to carry all the heavy things we buy?'

I laugh as I reach for the door. 'For one, I can carry my own heavy things, thank you very much. Haven't you heard of feminism?

Two, Sully's probably got better things to do. And three, we're not buying anything today. We're just going to place an order.'

'That's what you think.' She holds up a credit card. 'I wasn't sure where we were going, but I conned Dad into giving me this just in case we needed money. Now, go park the car and meet us inside, Sully. There's a good boy.'

He growls as she pats him on the head again, but we've barely made it to the main entrance when he comes up behind us. 'You'd better buy me meatballs for this,' he whispers into my ear.

I smile, a shiver going through me at the heat of his breath against my skin. 'I think I can manage that.'

We start our jaunt through the pretend rooms. We're supposed to be looking at bookshelves and possible chairs, maybe a few cushions, but who can resist a proper browse when you're at Ikea? You just never know what you might find that you absolutely can no longer live without.

Lola has fun, opening cupboards, pulling out drawers, switching lamps on and off, before insisting we test the couches with her.

'What do you think about this one?' she asks, bouncing a little on the edge of a black leather three-seater. 'This would be awesome for the library.'

I agree. 'That would be good. Easy to clean and long-wearing. And we can get some colourful cushions to brighten it up.'

We make notes of the couch and a couple of chairs and then walk through the beds section. Lola lies on a few but Sully and I don't dare – we can't be trusted lying down next to each other.

'You surviving so far?' I ask him.

He nods and hits me with his hot gaze. 'Turns out Ikea is bearable when you're here with two beautiful women.'

'Smooth talker,' I say as Lola walks ahead of us into the storage and shelving area.

A few moments later, she scares the living daylights out of us when she jumps out of a wardrobe as we pass by.

'Holy shit.' I step back into Sully and his arms wrap around me, steadying me. It feels so damn good.

Reluctantly, I pull away, Sully still chuckling as Lola makes a beeline for the bookshelves. 'She's a firecracker, isn't she?'

'Yep.' I smile after her. 'It's so good to see her starting to look better and getting back to a normal teenage life.'

'She reminds me of my sister,' he admits.

I look back to him. 'Yeah?'

He nods sadly. Sully hasn't told me much about his family but now is probably not the place for such a conversation, so I squeeze his hand, then let go again as we catch up to Lola.

We measure the shelves, trying to work out how many we might need. Sully proves very useful because maths was never my forte. A lovely gentleman helps us place our order for the shelving, the couch and a couple of chairs to be delivered to the hospital and then Sully reminds me I owe him meatballs.

'Settle, petal. You'll get fed,' I say, reaching up to pat him on the head exactly like Lola did earlier.

He rewards me with one of his sexy scowls.

After a quick browse through the kids' section where both Lola and I ooh and ahh over all the plush toys, we finally head into the café and join the queue.

'They even treat you like sheep when you want something to eat,' Sully grumbles as we barely move an inch in the line. 'It's so you end up buying more than you planned to, you know?'

I feign shock. 'Really? I'd never have guessed.'

Lola giggles. 'You two are hilarious.'

Finally, we get our food and find a table. While we eat, we talk – surprise, surprise – about books. Lola still hasn't got back her full appetite, so she does most of the talking, telling Sully about her favourite book boyfriends and then waxing lyrical about *The Invisible Life of Addie LaRue*. She tells him he should read it; he asks me if I have a copy. I say I do and agree to give it to him later.

'I'm just going to the bathroom,' I say, not sure Lola and Sully even hear me as they're so engrossed in book chat.

When I return, he gets up to take our trays away and Lola looks to me.

'He's so hot.' She flaps her hands around her face. 'Steamy. Is he why you broke up with Fabio? Because you're into him?'

'No,' I object, perhaps a little too vehemently. I glance across to where Sully is helping an elderly woman with her tray. 'We're just friends.'

She quirks an eyebrow as if she doesn't believe me, then shrugs. 'Guess you won't mind then that while you went to the bathroom, I pretended we were on a date. Do you think I can con him into kissing me? Then at least I can tick first date and first kiss off my bucket list.'

'You don't need a bucket list!' I scold. 'Besides, what about Mason?'

She shrugs again. 'We're not official and definitely not exclusive.'

I laugh and shake my head. 'Lola, Sully's older than me. Do you want to send him to prison?'

'Who's going to prison?' he asks, looking between us as he returns.

'No one,' I say, glaring at her as she giggles. 'Come on, let's get you home.'

64

Meet the Parents

'Thanks again so much for taking Lola out today,' Laura says when Sully arrives to pick me up.

He's waiting in the car, and although it's only been a few hours since he dropped me and Lola back at her place, I'm itching to see him. All I can think about is what he tastes like and how it feels when his fingers are playing me like a musical instrument. Let's just say he's a lot more talented with the human body than he is with the Northumbrian bagpipes.

'No, thank *you*. She's such fun to be around, and I almost pulled a muscle laughing at her commentary during *10 Things I Hate About You*. Although I think we might have tired her out, because she fell asleep just before the prom. She's been asleep ever since and I wasn't sure if I should wake her.'

Laura bites her lip, then shakes her head. 'Don't worry, it's been a big week at school. I'll go get her up now.'

'Tell Lola I said bye and see you both next Saturday.' We're forgoing our weekly brunch book club to start setting up the library instead.

'Can't wait,' she says, giving me a hug.

Sully waits until I have my seatbelt on before reversing out of the driveway, and then when we're on the road, he puts his hand on my knee. 'How was your afternoon?'

I tell him about watching the movie and then reading while Lola slept, and his fingers rub tiny circles on my inner thigh as I talk. Despite my jeans, my skin shivers beneath his touch.

By the time we get home, I'm on fire.

He parks at his place but we head over to mine. Now that we've discovered how compatible we are between the sheets – so to speak – we can't seem to keep our hands off each other.

As JB slips out to amuse himself in the backyard, we migrate immediately to my bedroom. Sully pulls my face to his and as he kisses me like I'm his last meal, I'm already tugging at the button on his jeans. I'd thought that after having sex with him a few times the urge might diminish, but if anything, it's only getting worse.

And the sensations even better.

We know each other now. It feels as if he knows my body better than anyone else I've ever been with, and I know his. We each know what the other likes and we know just how to give it.

When we're done, he pulls me into his side, inhales deeply into my hair and holds me tight. I'm not sure snuggling is really part of the whole neighbours-with-benefits thing, but after the week I've had, I can't resist the comfort his lovely strong arms offer.

'Thanks so much for today. Lola really enjoyed getting to know you.'

'She's a cool kid,' he says. 'It's really sad she's sick.'

'Yeah. Thank God her prognosis is positive.' And then I recall his confession at Ikea. 'You said she reminds you of your sister? What was her name?'

'Helen. She was five years younger than me. She was always

talking.' He huffs out a chuckle. 'Even more than Lola. She had a sore jaw and wore a splint at night for it and we always used to joke it was because she talked too much. How I'd kill now to hear her speak again.'

I squeeze his hand. 'What did she talk about?'

'Everything and nothing. She was really into musical theatre and was in every school production.'

'More talented than you then,' I tease.

He smiles wistfully. 'Definitely. They were on their way to see *Wicked* when she . . . when they . . . had their accident. Mum and Dad asked if I wanted to go too, but I couldn't think of anything worse. Sometimes I think about how things might have been different if I'd agreed to go with them. I might have been driving, we might have left two minutes later or earlier or . . .' His voice drifts off and my heart breaks for him.

I don't know what to say. I want to tell him that it isn't his fault and also that I wish I'd known her, but that might sound like I think this is more than it is.

Instead, I ask him about his parents and what his relationship was like with them. He holds me close, my head resting against his chest, his fingers absentmindedly playing with my hair as he talks about how different his mum and dad were, but how perfect they were for each other. His mother was a school principal and his father a chef. She was an early riser, he a night owl. She loved sport, he didn't get the hype.

'But they just worked,' he says. 'Due to their jobs, they didn't get to spend a lot of time together, but Mum always said it was quality not quantity that mattered when it came to love.'

I think that's one of the most beautiful things I've ever heard and am about to say this when there's a loud knock on my front door. We glance at each other, frowning, and both speak at the same time.

'Expecting someone?'

'You didn't order Uber Eats, did you?'

He laughs as I groan.

'It's probably religious callers,' he says with a knowing wink. 'Just send them next door.'

The knock sounds again, louder this time.

I climb out of bed and grab my robe from the hanger on my bedroom door. 'Stay there. I'll be right back.'

Ready to tell whoever it is that I don't want whatever they're peddling, I peel open the door and almost die of shock. 'Mum?! What are you doing here? You're supposed to be in Broome!'

'Oh, Bee.' She pulls me into a hug. 'I've been so worried about you. Are you okay, my sweet girl?'

What she really means is, after my disastrous break-up with Fabio/Josh, am I still eating properly?

'I'm fine, Mum. How did you get here?'

'I flew.'

Rolling my eyes, I say, 'I meant from the airport.'

'I caught a taxi. Now, are you going to let me in or leave me standing out here in the cold on your doorstep like one of your gnomes?'

I think about Sully only a few metres away in my bedroom and consider doing just that.

She glances around. 'Where are they anyway? And where's John Brown?'

'He's ah, outside, or maybe in the pantry.'

She frowns – 'What on earth would he be doing in there?' – and then starts down the corridor towards the kitchen.

Oh Lord. I yank my bedroom door shut and I follow to find her bestowing love all over JB like he's one of her actual grandchildren.

'Mum,' I say, crossing to the kettle to start filling it up, 'Why don't you make yourself a cup of tea while I go get dressed?'

She gives me a thorough once-over, registering the fact I'm only wearing my robe. 'Were you in the shower? Is that why you took so long to answer the door?'

I nod, grasping at this excuse like a drowning woman who's just been thrown a lifebuoy. 'Yes. Back in a mo.' I hurry back into my bedroom, shutting the door behind me.

'I thought you'd forgotten me,' Sully says, still very naked in my bed.

'It's my mother,' I hiss, gathering his clothes from their various places all over the floor and throwing them at him.

He smirks in clear amusement. 'So I heard. Did you know she was coming?'

'Do you think I'd have been in here acting out the *Kama Sutra* with you if I did? I'd have been madly cleaning my house from top to bottom.'

'I think the option you chose was much more fun.'

I smother a giggle. 'You need to leave.'

He nods. Our arrangement does *not* include meeting the parents.

'She's in the kitchen making a cup of tea. I'm going to take her into the lounge room and, when it's safe, you're going to sneak out the back. Okay?'

Sully gives me two thumbs up. 'It's a plan.'

I return to the kitchen to find Mum madly spraying multi-purpose cleaner all over my stovetop, a cloth in her hand.

'Leave that,' I say. Cleaning is her love language, second only to cooking. 'Let's take the tea into the lounge room and catch up.

There'll be plenty of time for you to scrub later. I assume you're staying for a few days?'

'Yes. I've got a flight back Wednesday night as I've got a dentist appointment in Port Hedland on Thursday, so we have plenty of time to hang out and catch up.'

'I'm working, Mum. I've got Sunday – tomorrow – off, but we're short-staffed at the moment with Persephone and Ursula both on leave, so I won't be able to spend much time with you,' I say as I throw two English Breakfast teabags into mugs and pour the now-boiling water over them.

'Oh, it'll be fine. I can meet you for lunch and I'll have a nice dinner ready for you when you get home. Let me spoil you for a couple of days, darling. You shouldn't be alone after what you've been through. A girl needs her mum when she's heartbroken.'

'Thanks, Mum. It's lovely to see you.' Despite the shock, it *is* nice to see her.

I barely give the tea time to take before yanking the bags back out, adding a splash of milk to each and ushering her into the lounge room.

When we're both settled on the couch, I say, 'Is Dad going to be okay up there alone?'

'Your father's fine, honey. We got to Broome last night and we were both so worried about you, we couldn't relax and enjoy ourselves. I decided to fly down and see you. I won't be missed – Phil's Dad's friend anyway and not all the boys were taking partners.'

I love the way she calls my father's grey-haired or balding friends from boarding school 'boys', but didn't she tell me last week there'd be lots of families and people my age there?

'We can't believe about that horrible business with Fabio,' she continues. 'He's lucky the police have him locked up because if he was still on the loose, I'd hunt him down and chop off his balls.'

I splutter out the tea I've just swallowed. 'Mum!'

'It's true, honey.' Ignoring the tea, she shuffles closer on the couch and takes my hand. 'I don't want you to let Fabio—'

'His name's actually Joshua.'

'Joshua,' she says like it's a swear word. 'I don't want you to waste your time being upset about him. You're a beautiful person inside and out, and I know your special someone is just around the corner.'

'Actually, Mum . . .' I'm about to tell her that I'm giving up on romance and relationships, but she sucks in a breath and clutches my hand hard.

'Bee. Did you hear that?' she whispers loudly. 'I think there's someone in your house!'

'I'm sure it's just the wind,' I say, just as we hear another thud.

JB's head snaps up from where he was stretched out on the floor and I push my foot into him, telling him to stay put. What the heck is Sully doing? He'd make a terrible burglar.

'So do you want to go out for dinner, or shall we eat in?' I ask, trying to distract Mum with food.

She stands up, walks briskly to the door, yanks it open and then disappears through it.

Oh dear.

I leap up and hurry after her to find she and Sully facing each other in the hallway just outside my bedroom. He looks like a mouse cornered by a lion.

'Bridget. Call the police!' Mum holds a warning hand at him. 'Don't move a muscle or my daughter will karate chop you to pieces.'

'It's kickboxing, Mum,' I say, and then glare at Sully. 'You were supposed to leave.'

He shrugs sheepishly at me. 'I did, but I forgot my phone.' He holds it up and I realise that must have been what we heard drop.

I roll my eyes.

'So, you're not an intruder?' my mother asks.

Sully's looking at me for direction, clearly wondering what to say.

'He's my neighbour,' I tell her. 'Sully, this is my mother, Julie. She's come to stay for a few days.'

He smiles and offers his hand for a shake. 'Pleased to meet you, Julie. I'm Michael but everyone calls me Sully.'

'Michael is a lovely name. If Bridget was a boy, I was going to call her Michael, after Michael Scorsinni in *Hollywood Wives*.' She rubs her chin and stares at him. 'What were you doing in Bridget's bedroom?'

'Ah . . .' Sully looks as if he'd like aliens to arrive and beam him up into outer space. 'Would you look at the time,' he says, without looking at his watch. 'I've got to be off. Enjoy your night, Julie.'

As he escapes out the back, Mum narrows her eyes at me. 'Bridget, are you sleeping with that man? Is that why you were naked when I arrived?'

Oh Lord. Heat rushes to my cheeks. I'm an adult, closer to thirty than I am to twenty, so why do I feel embarrassed to be having this conversation with my mother? 'Um . . . maybe.'

She blinks. 'But what about Joshua?'

'What about him? He's a low-life criminal. I'm glad to be rid of him.'

'Yes, but . . . you only just broke up.' Her eyes widen. 'Is Michael some kind of rebound relationship? You know they can be danger-ous, darling. You need to give your heart time to heal.'

'No,' I assure her. 'Not a rebound relationship. Sully and I aren't in a relationship. We're just . . . He's fresh out of a long marriage and also dealing with some other issues. And, after my last few disastrous relationships, I'm taking a break from dating for a while.'

She frowns again. 'But you're sleeping with each other?'

'Yes,' I confirm.

'So you're friends with benefits?'

I nod, kind of surprised she knows this term, but then I remember she reads even more romance novels than I do. Before she can berate me, I add, 'I know you probably don't approve, but this is what I need right now. Life's different now to how it was when you were young. Sex doesn't have to mean serious.'

In fact, now I've experienced non-serious sex, I'm fairly sure it's better when it's not.

She tsks. 'You make it sound like I'm a dinosaur, darling. Your generation didn't invent casual sex, you know – you can sleep with whoever you like, as long as you're being safe, but . . . I just don't want you to get hurt.'

'Thanks, Mum.' I pull her into a hug. 'But that's why this is so perfect. My heart's not involved, so it can't get broken. Now, restaurant or takeaway?'

There's only so much sex talk I can stand with my mother.

We decide to go out and I manage to score a last-minute table at Emily Taylor's – named after a ship that was wrecked off the coast in the 1800s – which Mum thinks is super fancy with its modern décor, high ceilings and open kitchen.

'Tell me more about your neighbour,' she says, barely glancing at the menu our waiter has just given us as he heads off to fetch our drinks. 'He's very good-looking. What does he do for a living?'

I contemplate reminding her that it doesn't matter what Sully looks like *or* what he does for a crust because she'll probably never see him again, but instead I tell her, 'He's an Uber driver.'

If I say he's a doctor, she'll lose her mind. I'm her youngest, the surprise baby five years after three boys in quick succession, and she's of the generation that believes doctors make very good husbands for daughters.

'How fascinating,' she says, her eyes glimmering as if she's plotting mischief. 'If I need a lift anywhere while you're at work this week, I know who to ask.'

'That's not how Uber works.' I gesture to the menu. 'Now, are you ready to order?'

65

Happily-Ever-After with the Boy Next Door

As I walk home from the library on Monday night, I text Lola about a book I think she'll like and is available on BorrowBox, but don't get any response. I figure she's probably doing homework and will respond later but the moment I step inside my house, I'm distracted by the rich warm scent of tomato with a hint of beef and . . . marmalade?

Mum must have made my favourite, osso buco.

My mouth waters in anticipation but then I hear laughter – Mum's high-pitched giggle mingling with Sully's deep throaty chuckle. What the hell?!

I march into the kitchen to find them sitting at the counter drinking wine as if they've known each other for years. Mum's in her typical station-wife uniform of smart jeans and a long-sleeved chambray shirt, with an apron I never use over the top, and Sully is wearing old jeans and a blue flannelette shirt, the sleeves pushed up to his elbows. He looks like the hero on a rural romance cover. There's a large pot of what I assume are potatoes bubbling away on my spotlessly shiny stove and a casserole dish I didn't even know I owned in the oven.

They're so captivated with each other's witty conversation, neither my mother, my neighbour, nor even my dog notices my arrival.

I clear my throat. Loudly. 'Um, what's going on here?'

As Mum and Sully glance my way, JB wanders over and greets me with way less enthusiasm than usual. *Traitor.* I bet Mum's been spoiling him with offcuts of meat.

'Ooh, hello, honey.' She slides off the stool and pulls me into a quick hug. 'How was your afternoon? Can I get you a glass of wine?'

I glare over her shoulder at Sully but he just gives me an amused shrug.

Wine feels like a very good idea. 'Yes, please.'

While I give JB his dinner biscuits, Mum grabs another wine-glass and fills it for me.

'Julie's been regaling me with stories from your childhood,' Sully says. 'It's been very entertaining.'

I give her a dirty look. 'You'd better not have told him the knicker story!'

'Would that be the one about you wearing your brothers' jocks on your head and demanding everyone call you Queen of the Undieheads, or the fact that you preferred not to wear any under-wear at all whenever your parents took you out in public?'

I take a large gulp of my wine, then, 'Mother, could we have a word?'

'Michael, do you want to take the potatoes off and drain them? Bee and I will be back in a moment, and I'll mash them.'

Sully laughs – 'Sure' – offering one of his charming smiles as he crosses to the stove.

'What the hell is going on here?' I demand the moment I have my mother safely barricaded in my bedroom.

She bats her eyelashes innocently. 'What do you mean, darling? You're not angry about those stories, are you? They're just a bit of fun. Michael wanted to know what you were like as a child.'

'You didn't have to tell him the embarrassing bits! Why is he even here?'

When I'd left her at lunch time, she'd told me she was going to ride my bike to the butcher and then spend the afternoon reading on the couch.

'We got talking over the fence when I was hanging out your washing. I remembered you said he was an Uber driver, so I asked him if he'd mind taking me to the shops quickly. Seemed more efficient than riding.'

'I hope you paid him!'

She gives a sheepish shrug. 'I tried but he wasn't having any of it, so I invited him for dinner instead. Did you know his wife cheated on him? The poor man probably hasn't had a decent home-cooked meal in months.'

I roll my eyes. 'Sully knows how to cook, Mum. He doesn't need your pity.'

'He's such a kind man. And he didn't only take me to the shops but ended up driving me around the city showing me all the sights. We had a lovely coffee together in Kings Park.'

'Oh my God,' I groan.

'And he's a reader. He couldn't be more perfect.' She's practically swooning.

'Mum,' I warn. 'He's not perfect – trust me – and he's only just become a reader. Besides, do I need to remind you, you're married?'

She laughs as she swats me on the arm. 'I mean, he's perfect for *you*. And why didn't you tell me he's a doctor?'

'He told you that?' It took me months to get this information out of him.

'Yes. And about the awful business with the dead baby. I told him about Justin's accident and how grateful we are for the flying doctors. He's very easy to chat with. I think your brothers and father will adore him.'

I hold up my hand. 'Stop right there. Dad and the boys are *not* going to meet him. I told you, Sully and I are not an item and never will be.'

'I don't see why not.' She pouts. 'You're both single and there's clearly chemistry between you.'

'I told you why not.' I'm done with heartbreak. It's hard enough having to deal with my own pain when a relationship ends, the last thing I need is my mother's disappointment in the mix as well. 'Besides, I thought you were against me getting into a rebound relationship? You said yourself I need to give my heart time to heal.'

She exhales loudly. 'Yes, you're right. I'm sorry, honey. I guess I got a little carried away, but you can't blame me for wanting you to be happy.'

'Aw, Mum.' Some of my irritation dissipates. 'I am happy.' Surprisingly, it's the truth. 'You have to promise me you'll accept this and stop trying to write me a happily ever after with the boy next door, or I'm not having dinner with either of you.'

'I promise,' she says, squeezing my hand.

I can't help enjoying dinner – not just because my mother's osso buco is literally the best thing you'll ever taste, but because conversation flows between us effortlessly. We talk about everything, from life on the station, to Sully's work, my work, and more mortifying stories from my childhood.

'This isn't fair,' I say when Mum tells him how she couldn't read me *The Monster at the End of This Book* when I was little because I was too scared. 'We should have asked Daisy to join us so she could give us all the gossip from *your* childhood.'

He smiles over the top of his wineglass. 'Lucky for me, she has ballroom dancing on Monday nights.'

'Daisy's your grandmother, right?' Mum asks.

'That's right.'

I look between them – what *didn't* they talk about this afternoon?

'I'd love to meet her,' she says.

'I'm sure she'd love to meet you too – Daisy loves Bridget. If you like, I can see what she's up to tomorrow and take you round to visit?'

Mum beams. 'That would be lovely. Does she like scones? I'll make scones.'

I roll my eyes and kick Sully under the table, willing him to stop encouraging her. Despite my terse words earlier, I can see her falling more in love with him with each word that comes out of his mouth. If she meets Daisy, I have no doubt the two of them will be planning our wedding before they've devoured even one scone between them.

'Gran loves scones,' he tells my mother, then smirks at me and moves his feet out of my reach.

After dinner, Sully insists he and I do the dishes and Mum take a cup of tea into the lounge room to put her feet up.

The moment she disappears, he pulls me to him and presses his mouth to mine. After a scorching kiss, he whispers, 'I've been wanting to do that all night.'

'Really?' I ask. 'I thought you were so enamoured by my mother's company you barely noticed I was here.'

He cups his palm against my cheek. 'I was just being friendly. You're not jealous, are you?'

'Don't be ridiculous,' I say, a tad defensive. 'I just don't want her to get her hopes up that something might happen between us.'

Sully slides his hands up my back under my shirt. 'I think something is already happening between us, don't you?'

'You know what I mean,' I say, but my words get lost because he's kissing me again.

And, honestly, he could give Ted Talks <u>on</u> smooching technique. How can I stay angry at him when he makes me feel so damn good?

My phone rings from the hallway and I grudgingly pull away. 'I'd better get that. It might be Lola.'

'Anything to get out of the washing up,' Sully says, patting me playfully on the bum.

But it's not Lola. It's her mum. 'Hey, Laura,' I answer.

'Hi, Bee. I saw your message on Lola's phone. She's been asleep on and off all day and didn't have the energy to reply.'

'Is she . . . okay?'

'She's . . . um . . .' Laura is whispering but sounds close to tears. 'She's caught pneumonia, so no, she's not so great at the moment. We're in the hospital.'

Fear floods my body – pneumonia is a serious illness, but even more so for someone whose immune system is already compromised. 'That's awful. Did she pick up an infection when we took her to Ikea?'

'It's just as likely she caught something at school. Please don't feel guilty – she loved that trip with you and Sully,' Laura assures me.

'Can I see her? Or is that not a good idea? I don't want to risk bringing her more germs.'

'I think she'd love that,' Laura says, then gives me the hospital visiting hours.

When we disconnect, I stand there frozen, wishing it was me who was sick instead of Lola and silently praying for her quick recovery.

66

Making a Move

'Take your time,' Fred tells me as I head out of the library to meet Sully on Tuesday afternoon. 'And give Lola my love. Xavier and I have everything under control.'

Sully is waiting for me just down the road and gives me a quick kiss on the cheek as I climb into his car.

'Thanks so much for doing this,' I say, clicking my seatbelt into place.

'Of course.' He hands me a brown paper bag.

'What's this?'

'Lunch. I made you a cheese and ham toastie to eat in the car.'

I lift the bag to my nose and inhale the delicious aroma. 'Aw, thanks.'

'You're welcome.'

'How was your morning?' I ask as he pulls away from the kerb. 'Did Mum and Daisy hit it off?'

'That would be an understatement. They've not only exchanged recipes but also phone numbers, and Julie's invited Gran to go up and stay on the station for a couple of weeks. If I didn't have to take Julie back to walk JB, I reckon they'd still be yakking.'

My attempt at a laugh falls flat and we barely say a word for the rest of the journey. I'm too worried about Lola to make conversation.

Sully parks and we walk inside together. I'm glad he's here, and not just because it's easier than public transport. A nurse at the desk directs us to Lola's ward and I can feel my heart pounding as our footsteps echo on the polished concrete floor. She's only allowed one non-family visitor at a time, so when we get to her room, Sully waits in the corridor while I go in.

I knock tentatively on the open door and am shocked to see Lola's face looking even thinner than usual. The colour that had come back into her cheeks in recent weeks is gone and her eyes are lacking their usual sparkle. Not wanting her to see my distress, I school my facial features into a bright smile as I pump sanitiser onto my hands from the bottle on the wall. She and her parents – who are sitting on either side of her bed – look up.

'Bee!' Lola's face fills with her beautiful smile and I try to focus on that, rather than her pallid complexion or the oxygen tank beside her.

'Hi, girlfriend,' I say brightly, standing at the end of the bed as I rub my hands together.

'Thanks for coming, Bee,' Laura says. She doesn't kiss me on the cheek like she normally does and I know this is because she doesn't want to risk spreading germs.

Luke stands. 'Yeah, good to see you again. I'm heading off to find some proper coffee – do you want one?'

'No, thanks.' I smile as he leaves, then I lower myself into his vacant chair and reach for Lola's hand.

It's freezing, and I fear this time I don't hide my shock.

'Mum's been reading to me,' Lola says, nodding towards a copy of *The Midnight Library* on her wheely table. 'Have you read—' She wheezes and then launches into a cough.

Laura passes a tissue to her daughter, standing with her hand on Lola's back as she spits phlegm into it.

'Sorry,' Lola says, when she's recovered.

I shake my head to let her know she does not need to apologise. 'You were talking about *The Midnight Library*?'

'Yes.' She pulls her blanket up a little higher. 'It's not a romance but I really liked it.'

'Me too,' I say. 'I listened to the audio when it first came out.'

Laura sits quietly watching us as Lola and I talk about all the possible lives we could be living right now. I've thought about this numerous times before – I love the idea of parallel universes where another Bridget is living a totally different life to me, simply because she made a tiny different choice to one I've made. I've thought about where I might be if I'd never started to restrict my eating, or if I'd chosen to stay up north rather than move to the city. Would I be a librarian now? Would I be married? Would I be living overseas? Have kids?

And I hope somewhere there's a world where Lola doesn't get sick. Where she's living a normal teenage life, hanging with her friends, staying up too late scrolling social media and worrying about make-up and boys, rather than trying not to cough in the middle of a sentence.

Is Laura thinking the same thing? Wondering if there's a different choice *she* could have made in her past that would have stopped this from happening?

'I want you to make sure there's always a copy of this book in Lola's Library,' Lola says, jolting me from my thoughts.

I smile through the lump that rushes to my throat. It sounds like she doesn't think she'll be here to see it, and I will not allow her to entertain that thought. 'Speaking of . . .' I say perkily, 'I'm picking up the keys tomorrow. Since you're here, maybe after work, I can come collect you and we can go check it out?' I quickly look to Laura. 'That's if she's allowed out of the room?'

Laura nods. 'Yeah, that sounds great. We'll check with your doctors. Maybe we can get a wheelchair.'

'That would be totally lit.' Lola coughs a little again, but she's smiling now.

'Saturday is just around the corner,' I say firmly, 'so you better work hard to get better. I've roped Sully and some of my other friends into helping us set up. If you're still not feeling well enough, you can direct us where to put the shelves and how to order the books.'

'How is Sully?' she asks.

'He's great. He drove me here so . . .' I nod towards the door. 'He's just in the corridor, actually.'

Her eyes light up. 'Can I see him?'

'Um . . . sure.' I stand. 'I'll go swap with him. I'm sure he'd love to see you.'

Lola looks to Laura. 'Mum, no offence, but do you mind leaving as well? I've got some' – she coughs again – 'some things I want to discuss with Sully. Alone.'

Laura and I exchange a curious look, but of course she nods – no one is going to deny Lola anything right now.

'I'll be right outside,' she promises.

'Lola wants a private word with you,' I tell Sully.

He blinks and points to himself. 'Me?'

I nod and he heads in to see her.

'Do you know what this is about?' Laura whispers as we linger by the doorway, both of us surreptitiously trying to watch and eavesdrop on their conversation.

'No idea,' I say as Sully leans over and gives Lola a kiss on the cheek.

Her smile could give the sun a run for its money and my guess is she'll not want to wash her face ever again.

Sully sits where I had moments earlier, and Lola beckons for him to lean in close. It's clear she doesn't want me or her mum to hear what she's saying.

Even if I was a lipreader, I can't see her face but I can see Sully's. Is that a smirk? What on earth could they be talking about?

Finally, they nod and shake hands as if they've made some kind of a deal, then Sully returns to the corridor. 'Are you ready to head back to work?'

'Umm . . .' I'm so consumed with curiosity, I'd almost forgotten my job. 'I'll just quickly say goodbye to Lola first.'

As Laura and Sully make small talk, I go back into the room. 'That looked like a serious conversation?'

Although I phrase it like a question, Lola merely smiles smugly in reply.

I take her hand again. It still feels like ice. 'I'm sorry, I've got to go back to work, but I'll see you tomorrow afternoon, okay?'

She squeezes my hand. 'Bye, Bee. Thanks for everything.'

I can't help noticing her breathing sounds shallow.

'Tomorrow,' I say firmly, waving at Laura as Sully and I start off down the corridor towards the elevators.

'What did Lola have to say to you?' I ask him the moment we are out of earshot.

He chuckles, making me all the more curious.

'What? Tell me,' I demand, sounding like a whiny child.

'She told me that I should make a move on you.'

'What?!' I burst out laughing and then cover my mouth with my hand when a nurse glowers at me. 'What did you say?'

He slows to look down at me and then wriggles his eyebrows. 'That's between me and Lola,' he says, but he's grinning widely. 'She's such a great kid.'

'You do know if she was ten years older, she'd be making a move on *you*,' I say.

'Then you'd have competition,' he says as he pushes the down button.

I laugh half-heartedly. 'Do you think she's going to be okay?'

'I hope so,' he says, and I decide perhaps it's best not to pry further for his professional opinion.

Sully drives me back to the library and as I get out of his car, I ask in jest, 'Will you be joining Mum and me for dinner again?'

He shakes his head. 'I'm gonna do some driving tonight. I'll leave you to have your last dinner with Julie, but do you want me to sneak over later?'

As tempting as that sounds, there's no way I'm having sex under the same roof as my mother.

'No,' I tell him. 'I'll sneak over to your place instead.'

67

This Wasn't Supposed to Happen

I knock off work early on Wednesday afternoon so Sully and I can drop Mum off at the airport and then head to the hospital to pick up the key from Vicky. I can't wait to see the look on Lola's face when we first step into the space. Sometimes it has felt like this project would never come to fruition, but in hindsight, it's happened rather quickly and I'm so proud of what we've achieved together.

'You got worms or something?' Sully asks as he navigates the traffic from the airport to the city.

I laugh at him catching me bounce around in the seat. 'No, I'm just excited. And hoping Lola's doctor has given her permission to come see the room.'

The traffic is excruciating and as I watch the time tick over on Sully's dashboard, I hope we're not too late to catch Vicky. Thankfully she's still tapping away at her computer when we knock on her office door.

She smiles as she plucks a key off her desk and passes it to me. 'Here you are. I checked over the room this afternoon and it's spotless and ready for you.'

'Thanks so much.' I could kiss her, but I make do with kissing the key instead.

She and Sully laugh.

'You're welcome,' she says. 'I'm happy to have helped with such a wonderful project. Just let me know if there's anything else you need. I won't be here on Saturday, but you've got my phone number if anything crops up. Good luck. I can't wait for the grand opening.'

We leave her area and head to the elevators, which whisk us up to Lola's ward.

The moment we near her room, all the joy and excitement drain from my body.

Luke is standing outside. He's on the phone and the grave expression on his face, his hunched over body, tells me everything I don't want to know.

'No,' I breathe, stumbling. Sully steadies me as Luke looks up and sees us.

He says something to whoever he's speaking to, then disconnects and slides the phone into his pocket. 'We lost her an hour ago.'

'What? No!'

'After the chemo . . . her lungs . . .' Luke sniffs, clearly trying hard to hold himself together. 'They just weren't strong enough to handle pneumonia.'

Oh, God. My eyelids feel hot, every cell in my body heavy. I don't know what to say. What *do* you say to a father who has just lost his fifteen-year-old daughter? This wasn't supposed to happen. She was having treatment. It was supposed to fix her. She was supposed to live.

In the end, I realise, there's nothing I can say that will make it better, or worse.

'I'm so sorry.' I swallow hard, trying not to cry. The last thing
he needs is *my* tears. 'How's Laura? And Leo?'

'They're in there with her now, saying their . . .' His voice
catches. 'Their goodbyes.'

I nod. 'Please give them my love.'

It's hopeless; I'm helpless to stop the tears streaming down my
cheeks.

Luke draws me into a hug. 'Thank you. Lola adored you, and
you brought so much joy to her last couple of months. We'll forever
be grateful for that.'

I feel terrible – it should be *me* comforting *him*.

'Please let me know if there's anything I can do for you,' I say as
we let go.

The door opens and Laura and Leo appear. In some ways Leo
looks much younger than his thirteen years, yet he also looks like
the weight of the world is on his shoulders. Laura's face is blotchy
red, her eyelids soaked with tears that are still coming.

'Oh, Bee.' She rushes at me, her arms wide.

Neither of us says anything. We just stand there, clinging to each
other, my tears soaking into her shoulder and hers into mine. Laura's
become like a big sister to me in the last couple of months, but I would
give anything not to have met her. Because she probably would never
have come to the library if Lola hadn't got sick. And if Lola hadn't
been weak from the cancer, pneumonia wouldn't have taken her.

Eventually, we draw apart and Laura lets out a deep sigh, slowly
letting go of my hands. 'I'll let you know about the funeral.'

I nod, say goodbye and then Sully and I slowly walk back
towards the elevator. He slips his hand into mine without saying a
word. It's so warm, so full of life; completely opposite to how Lola's
felt yesterday. Part of me wants to let go but I can't.

The doors open and an elderly couple step out, not even seeming to notice our existence. They're clasping each other's hands, their expressions are sombre, and I just know they're here for Lola too.

My heart aches for them. Grandparents are supposed to die long before their grandchildren.

'I still want to see the room,' I tell Sully as the elevator begins its descent.

'Lola's Library?'

I nod.

'Okay.'

When we get to the ground level, we press the button to take us back up to a different level and he's still holding my hand as I lead him towards the room we've been allocated.

My hand is shaking too much to negotiate the lock, so Sully takes the key and opens the door. The room is as clean as Vicky said it would be, but it's not empty. The flat packs from Ikea are here already, and alongside one wall are the first boxes of books from a few of the publishers.

I look to Sully and he nods – we don't need to speak but we both know we're not going anywhere until we've unpacked and put together the shelves. He rolls up his sleeves, gets his keys out of his pocket to use as a knife to open the boxes and then we get stuck in.

We don't talk much as we work, but we get into a rhythm – Sully putting the base frame together and me slotting in the shelves. We're a good team, and within a couple of hours we've built every bookshelf and the room is starting to take shape. The couch and chairs haven't been delivered yet, but I can imagine what they'll look like. As we begin to put the books on the shelves, I smile sadly, thinking about how proud Lola would have been to see this come to fruition.

How unfair it is that she never will.

'I can't believe she's really gone,' I say, staring at a copy of *The American Roommate Experiment*. We'd disagreed over Elena Armas's first three books. Lola thought *The Spanish Love Deception* was the best, but *The Long Game* is my favourite. Elena has another book out later this year – one Lola had been desperately looking forward to reading. 'I hope they have books in the afterlife.'

'Aw, Bridget.' Sully pulls me into his arms and holds me close. 'I'm sure they do.'

When we're finished all we can do for now, he drives us home, his hand a comforting reassurance on my knee the whole way there. It's fully dark outside now and the almost deserted roads tell me it's way past rush hour.

'Do you want me to pick up some takeaway for dinner?' he asks.

I shake my head. I don't want to eat, but it's not because I need control or am worried about getting fat, I simply can't. I feel ill at the thought of anything going into my mouth when Lola will never eat anything again.

JB greets us when we walk into my house, but he must sense our sombre moods because instead of jumping all over us, he nudges his head into my hand and licks me tenderly. I fall to the ground and wrap my arms around him. Sully heads into the kitchen and I hear him put the kettle on. A few minutes later, he gently eases me off the ground and ushers me into my bedroom, where I see a mug, steam wafting from the top, on my bedside table, next to the book I'm halfway through reading.

'Let's get you out of these clothes,' he says, starting to remove my jacket.

Another time this might sound seductive, but all I can hear is tenderness and concern. Gently, he peels back the layers of my day and then, when I'm standing there in nothing but my bra and knickers, he goes to my dresser and finds a pair of flannelette pyjamas.

'Why am I not surprised to see these have books on them?'

'Janine gave them to me,' I say as I take them from him and put them on.

He smiles. 'She has good taste. Now, get into bed and have a cup of tea. I know it won't fix the pain, but I think you need it.'

I do as I'm told. Sully tucks the blankets around me like I'm a little kid and then hands me the mug. He sits on the edge of the bed and JB jumps up to snuggle next to me on the other side.

'Thanks,' I say, then take a sip. It's sweeter than I usually take it, and I guess this isn't because he's forgotten my preferences, but because I'm in shock and haven't eaten anything. He's taking care of me, and it feels good. 'Why did this happen to Lola? What did she do to deserve such a short life?'

His shoulders slump. 'Absolutely nothing. Sometimes life just sucks.'

I nod – truer words were never said – and drink the rest of my tea. With every mouthful, I feel my limbs getting heavier and my eyes fighting to stay open.

'Why don't you try to get some sleep?' Sully takes the empty mug from me. 'I'll take JB out and then lock the door on my way out.'

'Do you mind staying?' I blurt. I know *sleeping* together isn't part of our arrangement, but . . . 'I don't want to be alone tonight.' When he hesitates, I add, 'It's okay if you don't. I can call Fred.'

'I'll stay,' he says. 'I'll just take JB out, go brush my teeth next door and then I'll be back.'

'Thanks.' I should brush my teeth too, but as JB jumps off the bed and trundles after Sully, I snuggle down into my pillow instead.

68

Kicking Puppies

I wake on Thursday morning to Sully's arm tenderly across my side and JB nestled at the end of the bed between our feet.

Well, hello there. This is a first. And a very nice one at that.

And then I remember. Sully isn't here because he passed out after we ravaged each other into exhaustion, he's here because I begged him to stay after . . . after Lola died.

No. My whole body goes cold. *Please tell me that was a nightmare.*

Although I know deep down it's not, I don't want to accept this reality. I can't deal with the pain such knowledge brings, and the only thing I can think of right now that will bring me total oblivion is him.

I glance at the time on my phone – 6.30 am. Not too early to wake him, and I doubt he'll be grumpy when he realises why I've done so. I wiggle slightly, manoeuvring myself against him. He moans and his arms tighten around me, but I don't think he's awake yet. I smile at the thought he probably thinks he's having a really good dream.

I take his hand and slide it under my top, relishing the warmth as I put it to my breast.

'Morning, Bridget.' His whispered greeting is music to my ears.

'Morning, Sully,' I say, turning to face him, desperate to kiss him.

But as I press my lips to his, he jerks back, moving his face from mine and taking his hand with him.

Oh my God. I remember I didn't brush my teeth last night and cringe. I can't believe I was about to inflict my terrible morning breath on him. 'I'm sorry.' I laugh awkwardly. 'I'll go brush my teeth.'

Sully grabs my arm before I can climb out of bed. 'It's not your breath.'

I frown. 'Then what's wrong? Is it because of Lola?' Maybe he doesn't want to take advantage when I'm feeling sad. 'I'm okay and I need this. Please help me feel better.'

He shakes his head. 'I can't. I'm sorry. I just can't do this any more.'

My heart hitches. 'What do you mean "this"?'

'I can't have sex with you and pretend that's all it is.'

What? My head spins. 'But that's all this *is*. That's what we agreed on.' If I'm shouting, it's because I'm panicking. JB snaps his head up, suddenly awake, but I ignore him. 'I can't believe you're doing this to me now! Today of all days.'

He looks like he's just kicked a puppy. 'I know. It's shit timing, but . . . I can't help how I feel. I'm falling in love with you, and I can't pretend I'm not.'

My heart goes numb. No one has ever told me they're falling in love with me before. Even Tim, who I was with for six months, never felt ready to say anything close to that and Sully and I haven't even *known* each other that long.

'You're falling in *love* with me?' The words sound foreign on my tongue.

He nods solemnly, like he's confessing to some kind of terrible crime. Even worse than kicking puppies.

'But . . .' I struggle to find words. 'That night we went bowling . . . you told me you were done with relationships.'

'Women aren't the only ones who can change their minds, you know. It's not like I wanted this—'

'Oh. Nice,' I spit, clutching at anger. 'I'm sorry I'm such an inconvenience.'

He closes his eyes briefly and sighs. 'That's not what I meant. I mean I didn't plan on feeling this way. It just happened.'

'But . . . what about Kristen? I thought you were still in love with her.'

'What gave you that impression?'

I blink, thinking back. 'Um . . . the time I asked you outright if you still loved your ex-wife, you couldn't even answer me. You just left. And then when we were bowling, it was clear you blamed yourself, not Kristen, who did the cheating. Only someone who still has a lot of love in their heart could feel that way. And she left you. If she hadn't, wouldn't you still be together?'

'Maybe,' he concedes. 'And I guess I do still love her, but I don't know if I've been *in* love with her for a long time. How I feel about her doesn't even come close to the way I feel about you. We were really young when we got married – probably too young – and my PTSD just made the cracks in our relationship stronger. I'll always have a soft spot for her, but I don't think about her every minute of every day. She's not the last person I think about when I go to sleep, or the first person who lands in my head when I wake up. She's not the one I want to tell when I hear a funny joke or make a breakthrough with my PTSD. She's no longer the one I picture as the mother of my future kids.' He rests his hand against my cheek. 'That's you. All you.'

Oh, God. Did he have to mention children? My eyes prickle at his beautiful words. I thought I'd be all out of tears after yesterday's agony, but . . . apparently not!

As Sully wipes his thumb across my cheek to catch my tear, I think about the fact that he's fallen out of love with Kristen. Even if he is falling in love with me now, what's to say that in time something won't happen to make him fall right back out?

Why should our relationship be any different to the doomed ones that have come before?

Suddenly the whole shock and intensity of the last few weeks feels like it's going to crush me – Josh's betrayal, Persephone's pregnancy scare, Mum's surprise trip, and now on top of all that, *Lola*.

It's all just too much.

'You can't be falling in love with me,' I yell. 'You barely know me. We barely know each other.'

'I know you're kind and funny, and a little bit crazy. I know that you're passionate and loyal to those you care about. I know that you make me laugh, you make me feel like everything's going to be okay. You make me feel things I didn't know I was capable of any more.'

Sully sounds so vulnerable as he utters these words but all I can feel is panic.

'Why are you doing this?' I say. 'Why do you want to complicate things when everything was going so well?'

'Exactly. What we have is . . .' He shakes his head as if searching for the right word. 'It's precious. It's something that doesn't come along every day. Chemistry, yes, but also an amazing connection. I'm not complicating things. I'm being honest. Surely you feel it too?'

I blink back tears of shock. It doesn't matter how I feel. 'I'm sorry, Sully, but no, I don't want this. I just . . . I just can't.'

He rolls away from me, and we both stare up at the ceiling.

After a long moment of awkward silence, Sully says, 'Okay, that's fair.'

Despite trying to protect myself, something feels like it's cracking inside me. I hate that I'm hurting him, but the only other option is risking hurt myself. It was safe when I thought this was nothing but no-strings attached, neighbourly bonking, but I don't want my heart involved, because that's when things become dangerous.

'So where to from here?' I ask, struggling to speak past the lump in my throat. I'm furious at him for putting us in this position, yet the thought of losing him completely is too much. 'Can we still be friends?'

He sighs, but his gaze doesn't shift from above. 'We can try. I don't want to lose you.'

'Thank you,' I whisper, sliding my hand down to take hold of his. 'I don't want to lose you either.'

But deep down, I worry that maybe I already have.

69

Head over Heels

'I'm going to go home and have a shower,' Sully says, letting go of
my hand. 'Let me know if you need anything today. I've got a shift
at the hospital tonight, but . . .'

I nod as he climbs out of bed. 'Thanks. I've got work so—'

He pauses and looks back at me. 'You're still going? After Lola?'

'She's not a relative, so I'm not entitled to time off, and Xavier
and Fred need me there. It'll help keeping busy, but I'll make sure
I get time off for the funeral.'

He doesn't look convinced but doesn't say anything more.

I wait until I hear my front door close behind him before I get
out of bed and let JB out the back. While he's outside snuffling
around, I shower, crying again when I think about the times Sully
and I have had sex in here. My heart – every bone in my body –
aches at the thought that we'll never laugh together in here again.
There's no joy in my usual skincare routine, and after I'm done,
I throw on suitable work clothes, brush my hair and do the bare
minimum when it comes to make-up. I don't bother with mascara,
already suspecting I'm not going to get through the rest of the day
without more waterworks.

It begins almost as soon as I walk into work to find Xavier and Fred analysing his morning coffee. He hands me mine and I take a sip.

'Well, what do you think?' he asks.

I shrug. 'It's okay.'

'Okay?' he shrieks. 'I have a good mind to report the barista to our friend Mark at the shire. He shouldn't be allowed to call this drain water "coffee".'

'Lola died yesterday,' I say.

Their faces drop in unison.

'Oh my God.' Xavier presses his hand against his chest.

'Why didn't you call me?' Fred asks.

'I'm sorry, I wasn't thinking straight. It was such a shock, and then—' Here come the tears. 'And then Sully and I ended up making up all the shelves in her library. It was really late by the time we got home.'

'Aw, Bee. I'm so sorry.' Fred and Xavier wrap me up between them. 'At least Sully was there with you.'

'It would have been better if you were,' I sob.

'What do you mean?' She pulls back to look at me and her eyes narrow. 'Did he do something to hurt you?'

Xavier is also immediately on guard, as if they're both ready to march over to Sully's house and give him a piece of their minds.

'No,' I rush to assure them. 'At least, he didn't mean to, but the sex thing without feelings . . . It didn't work out.'

'Oh, Bridget Jones.' Fred sighs and rubs her forehead. 'I was worried that you wouldn't be able to handle it. Not everyone's got what it takes.'

I glare at her, putting my coffee on the table – on second taste, it's undrinkable. 'It's not me who can't handle it. It's Sully. He reckons he's falling in love with me.'

At this declaration, I feel my face crumble as more tears pummel their way down my cheeks.

Xavier and Fred exchange looks of helpless horror, then he says, 'This calls for Persephone and Janine on FaceTime.'

'No, it doesn't.' I wipe my eyes on my sleeve and sniff. 'I just want to forget about it, and anyway, we need to open the library.'

But his phone is already out of his pocket and I can hear the dial tone.

'What's up, Xaves?'

As Persephone answers, he angles the phone so Fred and I can see the screen. She's in her bedroom – Sabrina climbing all over her. Not exactly the bedrest the doctor ordered.

'Ooh, it's almost the whole gang.' She waves at us. 'Is this about Ursula?'

At that moment, Janine joins the call, Dave appearing beside her. 'We're in an underground café in Coober Pedy,' he tells us excitedly.

I'm impressed there's wi-fi down there.

'Shouldn't you lot be opening the library?' Janine says.

'That's what *I* said.'

Xavier shakes his head. 'We've got something important to discuss with you before we do.'

Fred, of course, is the one to deliver the punchline. 'Sully told Bee he's falling in love with her.'

Janine squeals excitedly and Dave gives us the thumbs up.

Persephone, pushing Sabrina off her bump, grins. 'That's wonderful. I'm so happy for you, Bee.'

'Happy for me?' I snap. 'This is terrible. He's ruined everything.'

'Nah, it's brilliant.' Xavier is grinning. 'Fred and I were just saying how perfect you are together. The way he looks at you—'

'The way you look at him.' Fred beams in a most un-Fred-like way. 'He's taken such good care of you since the whole Fabio-Joshua thing and was such a good sport with your mum. Not to mention Lola. He's exactly the man you've been waiting for.'

What has come over her? She should be shaking her head about the idiocy of men and telling me to return to Tinder.

'Did you put some whacky tobacky in your green juice this morning?' I ask. 'You're the one who's always telling me that relationships and love aren't worth the effort.'

She laughs. 'Yes, for me. But you're not me. You were *made* for love.'

Xavier and Persephone nod solemnly.

'Ever since we've known you,' Janine chimes in, 'you've been wanting to meet a man to settle down with and have a family. You love romance novels because you love *love*. And you deserve it. No one deserves a happy ever after more than you do.'

'She's right,' Xavier says. 'And I think Sully would make a pretty good book boyfriend. As Rory would say, hubba-hubba.'

Persephone chuckles as she snatches a hairbrush from Sabrina. 'I'd agree with that. And your meet-cute was worthy of a screen adaptation.'

'Hell, yeah.' Fred taps her index finger on her chin. 'Who do you think should play my character?'

I sniff again. Are they insane? But as they throw around the names of celebrities and talk about possible cameos, I start to wonder. Am I the crazy one turning my back on the possibility of what I've always dreamed of?

'Do you really think Sully could be my romance novel hero?' I shout over the top of them.

They go quiet and stare at me like that's the stupidest question anyone has ever asked.

Janine's the one to break the silence. 'That depends on how you feel about him. Do you think maybe you feel the same as he does?'

'Maybe,' I admit, 'but I can't . . . I can't bear the thought of being hurt again. After Kieran, and then Joshua, I don't know how much more pain I can take.'

Janine gives me a motherly smile. 'Life is full of pain, and joy – Dave and I have had plenty of ups and downs in our marriage.' He nods his agreement. 'You'll never know what's around the corner and you can't control what other people do, but you can decide to be the hero of your own story rather than the victim.'

'*Ooh*, I like that,' Fred says. 'I'm gonna put that in my next book.'

Janine continues, 'Ask yourself this – would you rather regret trying with Sully or *not* trying? I know you want to protect yourself from another betrayal, another heartbreak, but Bridget . . . there's every chance you won't have to.'

The others are all nodding, and I know they mean well.

Janine, Fred, Persephone and Xavier aren't only my colleagues, they're my best friends, my family. They love me. They know me probably even better than I know myself.

'Maybe all the other relationships didn't work out because they weren't with him,' Fred says.

'At least go and talk to him,' Xavier suggests.

Despite their stance, I'm still so uncertain, and look for an excuse to chicken out. 'But what about work? You're already so short-staffed.'

Fred shakes her head. 'You shouldn't be here today anyway. Not after Lola.'

At her mention of Lola, it's like a bubble of fog explodes in my head. Suddenly everything becomes clear. I think of what Lola would do in my situation. I think of her bravery and positivity throughout her fight with cancer and I think of her desperation to experience not only a first kiss, but love.

I think of what she told Sully – that he should make a move – and wonder what she'd say to me if I told her he had, and I'd rejected him.

She'd tell me I'm a fool. And she'd be right.

'Are you sure you can do without me?' I ask.

'Yes,' they all shout in unison.

'Okay, then.' I grin and then point at them all. 'If this doesn't work out, I'm blaming the lot of you, and you'll have to pick up the pieces.'

But I don't stay to hear their replies. I'm already running out of the staff room and out the closest emergency exit.

Whoops, I think, as alarms erupt behind me.

Thankfully, it's a beautiful winter's day as I rush through the streets of Fremantle back to our duplex, so although I'm panting from the exertion, I'm not looking like a drowned rat when I arrive at Sully's gate, only to find him standing on his doorstep with another woman. She's gorgeous and I can just tell from their body language that they have history together.

Kristen.

My heart leaps to my throat as burning jealousy rages through my body. What is she doing here? Did he call her after I rejected him? Or did she come here of her own accord? Has she realised the error of her ways and is here begging him to forgive her and take her back?

If this really was the novel my friends think it is, then these are the conclusions I would leap to. Now would be the time I'd turn and run, but having read a zillion romance novels in my life, I know that would be the wrong decision.

No one likes the miscommunication trope.

And, even if this *is* what it looks like, even if this woman is his ex-wife wanting to get back together, I'm not going to decide to risk my heart to love again only to give up at the first hurdle.

I'm going to fight for my man.

They turn at the sound of the gate creaking as I push it open.

'You really need to put some oil on this,' I say.

'Bridget? Are you okay?' Sully sounds half-wary, half-hopeful as I step towards them.

I nod and look to the other woman, waiting to be introduced.

He remembers his manners. 'Bridget, this is Kristen, my ex-wife. She just came to give me some old paperwork.'

Paperwork. *Thank God.*

'Hi,' I say, trying not to sound too hostile. This woman cheated on the guy who might just be the freaking love of my life.

'Hello.' She smiles warily at me. 'And you are . . .?'

Sully clears his throat and shakes his head. 'Sorry, this is Bridget, my uh . . . neigh—'

'His girlfriend,' I interrupt, grinning widely as I offer her my hand.

'Oh!' She seems delighted by this news, laughing as she clasps my hand, then looks to Sully. 'You dark horse. I just asked you if you were seeing anyone and you blatantly lied to me.'

I withhold a snort – like *she* can throw stones. 'It's just new . . .' I say, smiling at him. 'He probably didn't want to jinx things.'

'Really?' he whispers, hope in his eyes.

I nod. 'If you still want me.'

In reply, he pulls me into his arms, lifts me up, then presses his beautiful, delicious lips against mine.

'Well, congratulations to you both,' Kristen says. 'Nice to meet you, Bridget. You've got yourself a good man here.'

I hope she'll forgive me for not thanking her, but I have other priorities right now.

'Am I dreaming?' Sully asks, tearing his mouth from mine as we hear the gate shut behind his ex.

I cling to his hands. 'No. I'm sorry I freaked out this morning – I'm falling in love with you as well, and it scares the bejesus out of me. I'm so scared of getting hurt, of being taken advantage of again. Love terrifies me because I know it's something I can't control.'

'Ah, my sweet Bridget.' He cups my face in his hands and smiles down at me. 'I can't promise we're not going to have disappointments in our life together, but if you'll stand by me, I can promise that you'll never be alone through any of the dark times, and I will never betray you. Although I did lie when I said I was falling in love with you. The truth is, I'm already head over heels, and I don't say that lightly.'

Tears are once again streaming down my face, but this time they're happy ones. 'I love you too.'

A bark sounds from next door and we both look towards the sound.

Sully grins. 'Sounds like our boy is feeling a little left out. Shall we go tell him the good news?'

'Yes.' I nod as he pulls his door shut behind us – the same door I mistook for my own that night we met.

Thank God our first impressions were wrong.

Epilogue

Lola

Although I always liked the idea of ghosts, I didn't think I believed in them until I became one.

Being dead isn't as bad as you might think. I can still read, but a lot quicker than I ever managed to while alive. Also, you can walk through walls and people, but that's not as much fun as you might believe, and it really freaks the latter out. The first time I walked through Leo, he peed his pants. I don't think I ever felt so guilty in my whole life. The best part is being able to be somewhere unseen, which means you can eavesdrop on some delightful conversations.

And I'm not stuck in the hospital where I died either.

The day after my death, I found myself at home with Mum, Dad and Leo and I have worked out that I can go wherever they do. I think it's something to do with love and the fact you never completely leave the ones who own your heart. A couple of times, I've hitched along with Leo to school, but then left him and found my friends. They talk about me often – sharing funny memories, sometimes crying, and often saying to each other how much they wish I was still alive.

Of course, there are downsides too. I miss hugs, laughing with my family, gossiping with my friends and fighting with my brother. Ghosts don't need to eat either – it's actually physically impossible, so I can no longer enjoy my favourite foods – and sometimes you linger too long in a room and see something you'd rather you hadn't. Like your grieving parents, who you worried would grow apart when you died, in their bedroom late at night.

Ugh.

Yes, ghosts can shudder too.

Anyway, today it's the grand opening of Lola's Library and there is no way I'm going to miss that. Not only am I desperate to see my vision in all its colourful, bookish glory, but I know Bee will be there, and I haven't seen her since my funeral. The last time I was here at the hospital was that fateful day, but I refuse to dwell on that shocking plot twist, choosing instead to enjoy today's celebrations.

Bee, Sully, Vicky from the hospital and some lanky blond in his early twenties I don't recognise are already there when we arrive. I gasp at the sight of the room, lined with the shelves we ordered from Ikea and filled with books that, rather than alphabetical order, are grouped in colours, which looks so much cooler on the shelf. There are beanbags and oversized cushions, and it feels exactly like the cosy space I imagined.

Mum and Bee immediately close the distance between them and share a long, tight hug. I can't help feeling jealous of them both. You don't realise how therapeutic hugs are until you can no longer give or receive them.

'This library looks amazing. Thank you for doing this for Lola,' Mum says.

I notice Bee blinking as if trying not to cry. 'It's an honour. I just wish she was here to see it. How are you? Probably a stupid question.'

Mum half-sniffs, half-laughs. 'We're taking it day by day, hour by hour. It's silly, but sometimes I forget she's gone, because . . . it feels like she's always with me.'

Bee nods tenderly and I smile because it's true; I always am.

More people start to enter the room and they keep coming until I'm scared they won't all fit. There's a lot I don't recognise, but Bee seems to know most of them. As she introduces the strangers to my parents, I learn that the tall, skinny, dark-haired woman in pink overalls and silver Doc Marten boots is Fred, Bee's best friend and work colleague. She arrives with two men, who Bee tells Mum and Dad are Xavier, her boss, and his husband Rory. I'm surprised these extra librarians came but I guess as well as loving and wanting to support Bee, they love books.

'Janine told me she's sorry she can't be here, but to give you this,' Xavier says and then yanks Bee into a hug.

Bee laughs as she pulls out of his embrace. 'Thanks.'

They've barely let each other go when two little girls run into the room and rush at her. 'Aunty Bee!'

'We have a baby brother,' the slightly taller of the two shouts. 'He was born two days ago. He's tiny because he's not s'posed to be born for another nine weeks.'

Bee grins. 'I know. Congratulations. I can't wait to meet him.'

'He's called Sulli-man,' the other says.

'Sulli-*van*,' her older sister says, tsking. 'I told you this already.'

The adults laugh as a man, who I predict is the girls' father, kisses Bee on the cheek, then looks around. 'This place is amazing. It's bigger than Persephone made it sound.'

'Thanks. How are she and Sullivan doing?'

The man grins like he's just won the lottery. 'They're both perfect and doing well. Persephone should be out in about a week, but we probably won't be able to bring the little guy home until nearer his due date.'

'Let us know if we can do anything,' Bee says, glancing up at Sully, who I can't help notice hasn't left her side since I arrived.

He nods, then threads his fingers through hers, and the look of affection between them sends my heart soaring. *Yes!* It reminds me of all the swoon-worthy romances I read in the last few months of my life. I wonder if I had anything to do with them getting their act together by telling Sully he should go for it?

Either way I'm stoked for my friends, even if I won't ever have anything like they do.

No. I banish that thought, refusing to get all melancholic. Today is supposed to be a celebration.

Bee, Mum, Vicky and the lanky blond head to the front of the room and it's then I notice that what I thought was a stack of books on a small table is actually a cake. If I were alive, my mouth would water at the sight, but alas, my tastebuds are long departed, so I'll just hover and admire its beauty instead.

'Excuse me, everyone,' Bee shouts. 'Can I have your attention?'

As the chatter in the room stops, I hear footsteps at the door and look to see my three best friends and two guys, also from our school, sneaking in just as Bee welcomes everyone and thanks them for coming today. I really should be listening to what she's saying, but you can't blame me for being distracted, because you'll never guess who is here.

Mason!

And he looks hot as hell in black jeans and his football hoodie, his lush black mop of messy hair as perfect as ever. The fact he's come here for me is almost worth having died for, and I have to restrain myself from going over and walking through him!

It turns out the lanky blond is a representative from Make-A-Wish. After Bee and Mum speak glowing but embarrassing words about how selfless I was to choose this rather than a fancy holiday, he says a few words about the charity. Then they cut a ribbon across one of the bookshelves – it's a proper launch, like you see on TV, and I don't think I could be prouder if it *was* on TV.

After the speeches end, Leo and Dad hand out cake, and Mason walks over to Bee. I'm already right beside him so I overhear every word of their conversation.

'Hi, I'm Mason. A friend of Lola's. She told me about you, and I just wanted to say . . .' He swallows as if trying not to cry. 'Thank you. For doing this for her. She was pretty special.'

Aw. I bite down on a smile, wishing I could tell him how special I think he is as well.

'Yes, she was,' Bee says, her lower lip wobbling. She managed to hold herself together through the speeches, but I think this – talking to the boy I have a crush on, the boy I dream of kissing but will never get to – is going to be her undoing.

I watch as a tear slides down her cheek. *Oh, Bee.* If only I could tell her I'm here and offer some kind of comfort, but it turns out, I don't have to.

Because Sully is beside her again.

As she gives in to a sob, he wraps his arm around her shoulder and draws her into his side.

'Sully,' she manages, 'this is Mason, Lola's friend. And this is Sully, my boyfriend.'

'Nice to meet you,' Sully says, offering Mason his free hand.

'You too, sir.'

I'm not sure Sully's ever been called 'sir' before and I smother a smirk at his raised eyebrows.

'Are you a reader like Lola?' Sully asks.

Mason looks a little sheepish. 'I wasn't, but . . . just before she died, she recommended I try the *Fourth Wing* series, and now I'm addicted.'

'Ah, yeah.' Sully nods approvingly. 'Bee got me onto that one too.'

Mason shoves his hands in his pockets. 'Well, I think my friends are going now, so . . .' His voice drifts off.

Bee nods and summons a smile. 'Thank you so much for coming. It means a lot.'

And then, as Mason leaves, she turns into Sully and presses her now-wet eyes into his chest.

'You okay?' he whispers into her shiny hair.

I don't hear her answer because somebody else speaks.

'What's going on in here?'

It takes a moment for me to realise this whispery-type voice is talking to me. This is a surprise because since I took that final breath, I've been waiting for someone to see or sense me, but so far I've been invisible to the eyes of the living.

I blink at the body of a sandy-haired boy who looks to be about my age, with piercing blue eyes. 'Are you dead too?' I ask.

'Nah.' He shakes his head and winks. 'I see dead people.'

It takes me a second to realise he's joking and then I burst out laughing. 'So what did you die of?'

'I was born with a heart condition. Was a miracle I lived to fifteen. You?'

'Pneumonia.'

He screws up his face as if personally offended for me. 'That sucks.'

'No more than dying of a heart condition,' I retort.

'Touché.'

'Why did you come in here?' I ask.

He shrugs his surprisingly broad shoulders. 'Heard a lot of laughing. Mostly this place is pretty bleak, so I thought I'd come see what all the fuss was about. What's going on?'

I quickly explain about the library and that this whole beautiful space was my brainchild.

'Wow. That's cool.'

'Thanks.' I grin at him. My first after-life friend. 'Do you know any other dead people?'

'There are a couple of kids floating around here and an old bloke who's a real grump. You?'

I shake my head. 'You're my first.'

This makes him smile – the kind of smile that reaches eyes and shows teeth. 'It's an honour. By the way, my name's Jake. What's yours?'

OMG. 'That's the name of my favourite book boyfriend,' I tell him. 'I'm Lola.'

He laughs. 'Well, that's the name of this annoying kid from this picture book series my parents used to read me when I was little, but you seem a lot cooler than she was.'

I learn one more thing it's possible to do as a ghost – blush. Or at least it feels like that's what I'm doing.

'I know we've only just met, and this is perhaps presumptuous of me,' Jake says, 'but do you want to get out of here?'

I look to my family – to Mum, Dad, Leo, my grandparents, cousins, and Bee, who became like family in my last few weeks. If I go with Jake, they might not be here when I get back. Without them, I might not be able to find my way home, but suddenly I realise that's a risk I'm willing to take.

I don't know what the future holds, no one does, but right now, I'd like to get to know Jake a little better.

Acknowledgements

My name may be on the cover of this novel, but the following people all played a massive part in bringing it to fruition, and I'd like to take a moment to raise a toast to them all:

To Ali Watts, Publisher Extraordinaire – I feel so very grateful to be working with you on this book and hopefully heaps more. For many years I heard others waxing lyrical about what a joy you were to publish with, but nothing could have prepared me for the truth. Thank you for welcoming me into your nest and for offering your wisdom and knowledge as we worked together on *The Other Bridget*. No wonder you're so well-loved in the industry.

I am hugely grateful to the wonderful team at Penguin Random House Australia – Holly Toohey, Amanda Martin, Jo Baker, Bek Chereshsky, Bella Arnott-Hoare, Michael Windle, Janine Brown and Veronica Eze, to name but a few. Oh, and to Will Bennett for putting up with my terrible dancing!

To Nikki Townsend, the creative genius behind the beautiful cover design – I've wasted many hours simply staring at it.

To my agent, Helen Breitwieser – I'm glad I made you cry all those years ago. Thanks for everything you do.

To my friend and fellow author Rebecca Heath, who accidentally gave me the idea for *The Other Bridget* in an email exchange about her son and a mixed-up hospital appointment. And for our daily writing sprints, which help get words on the page, and for being one of the best friends and writing buddies a girl could ask for.

To my work wife, travel buddy, partner in bad TikTok dances and co-host of the Rachael Johns' Online Book Club, author Anthea Hodgson – you da best! Big thanks also to our mutual friend Sarah Pexton for introducing us.

To my cousin Lizzy Dent – it's such a joy to be able to brainstorm ideas and celebrate and commiserate the highs and lows of this crazy writing life together. I hope we can do it again in person soon.

To the authors I love and admire who kindly read an early copy of *The Other Bridget* and gave it endorsements – Katherine Center, Kathy Lette, Maisey Yates and Paige Toon – you are all my heroes! Thank you.

And to my other wonderful writing friends who I wouldn't be without – Tess Woods (if this writing gig fails, we should definitely become private investigators), Emily Madden (when are we going overseas again?), Amanda Knight, Scarlet Wilson, Fiona Palmer, Kelly Golland, Lisa Ireland, Clare Connelly, Fiona Lowe, Alissa Callen, Amy Andrews, Tricia Stringer, Anita Heiss, Penelope Janu and Jane Tara, to name but a few.

To Janine Kimberly for being one of my favourite librarians and for answering all my library questions. I hope you like your namesake!

To Brooke Testa from 1Girl2ManyBooks for reading early versions of Bridget, encouraging me to keep going, and for all our chats on books and life over the years. Book friends are the best friends.

But speaking of best friends . . . to two of my BFFs, Kristen Francis and Leigh-Anne Randall – thank you for answering my tricky medical questions and reading a couple of the crucial scenes in the book. And to my cousin Mike Denton for also doing the same. I'm so lucky I have such clever friends and family.

To Coca-Cola – thank you for keeping me caffeinated with Diet Coke through the writing of all my books. PLEASE don't replace DC with Coke No Sugar – it's NOT the same!

To Craig, Mum and my sons, Hamish and Archie (not Lachlan as he told me not to put him in these) – thank you for listening to me ramble on when I'm excited about a new idea and for putting up with me when the words aren't flowing and I'm a real grump to live with. Love you all so much.

Thank you to my loyal readers for not only buying my books but spreading the word to your friends. I'm so very grateful for each and every one of you.

To the booksellers, librarians, book reviewers, bloggers, Bookstagrammers and BookTokkers – you all rock.

And finally to Helen Fielding for writing one of my favourite books ever, which in turn provided not only inspiration for this book but for my whole writing career.

Book Club Notes

1. Bridget believes that, due to her name, she has been placed under a romance 'curse'. Do you think her view is justified?

2. 'Love happens when you're least expecting it.' Discuss.

3. Are dating apps a blessing or a curse for singles?

4. What's the best meet-cute you have ever heard of, or experienced yourself?

5. Do you think the romance genre gets a bad rap?

6. Who was your favourite Bookstar member and why?

7. Do you agree with Bridget that books have the power to change lives? Is there a book that has changed yours?

8. What do you think is the greatest romance novel of all time?

9. Have you ever seen a film adaptation that's better than the book?

10. Discuss the importance of friendship in the novel. Which friendship was your favourite?

11. Are little white lies ever okay if they're told with good intent?

12. What do you think Janine means when she says, 'You can decide to be the hero of your own story rather than the victim'?

13. Do you agree with Bridget's friends when they tell her 'No one deserves a happy ever after more than you do'?

14. Have you read any other Rachael Johns novels? Which is your preferred genre of hers, and why?